The Big Reap

"The breakneck pace of the narrative, and the world Holm creates, [illegible]e for a thrillingly brutal ride."

[illegible]

"A strong urban fantasy that will cement Holm's reputation in the field. 8/10"

SciFi Bulletin

"Holm's touch is deft and his language surefooted, a rare feat in the realm of dark fantasy. The best books combine the smart with the careening, and Holm does that so well."

Sophie Littlefield, award-winning author of Aftertime

"Exactly what the urban fantasy genre needs. It's an action-packed thrill ride that blends elements of the best urban fantasy, pulp crime, and adventure novels have to offer ... Highest possible recommendation."

The Debut Review

"The fight between heaven and hell takes a turn for the hardboiled in Chris F. Holm's fantastic debut novel, *Dead Harvest,* where he's created a character as pulpy and tough as anything Chandler or Hammett dreamed up in his doomed Soul Collector. Holm's writing is sharp, powerful, and packs a wallop."

Stephen Blackmoore, author of City of the Lost

"Fans of the Harry Dresden series and those who like their modern-day fantasy with a twist of hardboiled detective story will love this."

Ed Fortun[illegible]

Also by Chris F. Holm

Dead Harvest
The Wrong Goodbye

CHRIS F. HOLM

The Big Reap

The Collector Book Three

ANGRY
ROBOT

ANGRY ROBOT
A member of the Osprey Group

Lace Market House,
54-56 High Pavement,
Nottingham NG1 1HW
UK

www.angryrobotbooks.com
Popped in, souled out

An Angry Robot paperback original 2013
1

A catalogue record for this book is available
from the British Library.

ISBN 978 0 85766 341 2
Ebook ISBN 978 0 85766 343 6

Set in Meridien and Helvetica Neue by EpubServices

Printed and bound by CPI Group (UK) Ltd, Croydon, CR0 4YY

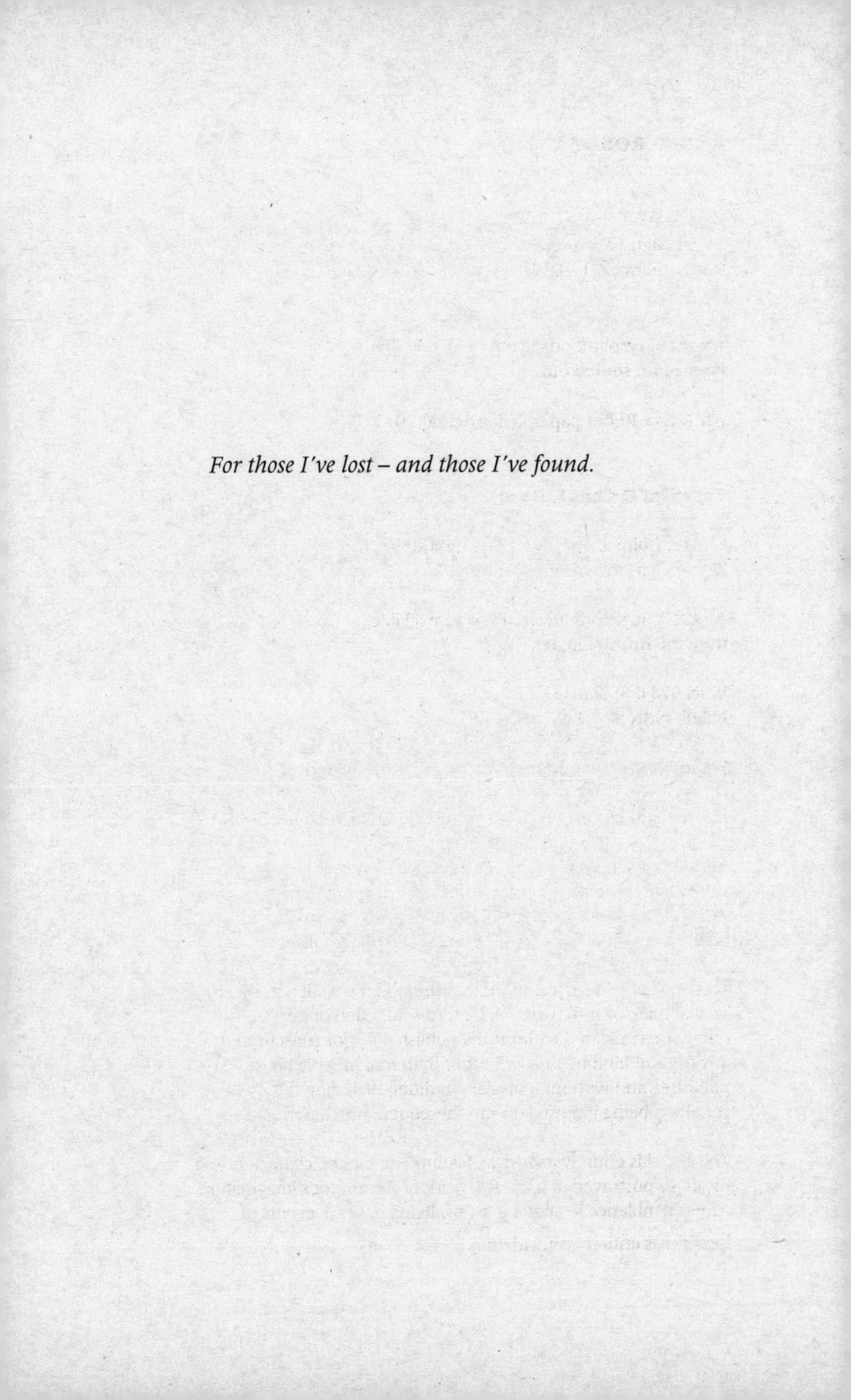

For those I've lost – and those I've found.

"The past is never dead. It's not even past."

William Faulkner

Then

The last thing I remembered was dying.

Autumn, 1944. A bitter cold October day. A bustling Manhattan street. Me invisible among the throng, one of the many homeless and bedraggled whose presence is willfully undetected by those more fortunate than they, as if the condition were contagious and acknowledgment the mode of transmission. I'd spent my last few weeks among the living camped outside my beloved Elizabeth's new abode, desperate for even a glimpse of her – for she refused to see me, too, though her reasons were far better than those of the passers-by. I'd spent my nights inside a bottle, hoping whatever rotgut I could lay my hands on would soothe my soul and dull the aching chill that leeched upward through the park benches and concrete stoops upon which I lay my head.

But there was nothing I could do to soothe my soul. Because that soul was no longer mine to soothe. I'd bargained it away to a demon named Dumas in a desperate attempt to save my dying wife. It worked, for what it's worth. But I was unprepared for what it wound up costing.

She'd been sick – tuberculosis. Latent for years, and then it wasn't. Liz tried to put on a brave face, but it was no use. I could see her wasting away before me, her pallor growing gray. She tried to hide her red-flecked handkerchiefs from me so I wouldn't worry. I worried plenty. Back then, full-blown tuberculosis was a death sentence, and when you're as dirt-poor as we were, that death was bound to be anything but pretty. I tried to fix that, to make some scratch so we could afford to take her to a decent doctor, but work was hard to come by for a gimp like me. See, a few years back, in San Francisco, me and my union at the foundry walked the picket line for safer work conditions and better wages. At least until our boss sent in some strike-breakers who took their job too literally and busted up my knee but good. That picket line's the last I ever walked without a limp.

Elizabeth was getting sicker by the day, and I was out of options, so I reached out to a local Staten Island hustler by the name of Johnnie Morhaim, who hooked me up with a gig as an errand-boy for union-guy-slash-mobster Walter Dumas. Dumas assured me he could help us, that he could get Elizabeth well. All I had to do was say the word.

Problem was, Dumas, aside from running rallies and rackets from Riverdale to Rockaway Beach, also happened to be a demon – not that I realized it at the time – and my half of our handshake deal was my immortal soul.

Dumas got Elizabeth into an experimental drug trial – some newfangled antibiotic called streptomycin – and I wound up Dumas' errand boy. Which is to say, I had my fingers in a lot of rotten pies – political payoffs, drug smuggling, a brass-knuckled lesson here and there. All justifiable in my mind, because I was helping get Elizabeth well. All anathema to Elizabeth, who slipped away from me with every act of corruption I committed.

I realized that too late. Mistook Dumas for the problem, blamed him for Elizabeth's cold distance – when really, it was me. *I'd* chosen this path. *I'd* allowed myself to be corrupted. But I didn't see that then. All I kept coming back to was: end Dumas, and all my problems go away.

I had no idea how wrong I was.

I ain't the most educated guy you'll ever meet. Never been much for reading fancy literature; dimestore potboilers are more my speed which is to say, I never had the finest grasp on the concept of irony. Until Dumas gave me a master-class, that is. See, I shot Dumas dead, or so I thought – only it didn't take, since he's not of this mortal coil. But when I did it, I was certain I was taking a human life. I'd crossed a line you can't uncross, and the blood I spilled – though fruitless, since the son of a bitch was no worse off for it – served to seal my devil's bargain, condemning me to eternal damnation.

If that ain't irony, I don't know what is.

Of course, that evil bastard let me think him dead long enough to confess to my Elizabeth that I had killed him. After that, she couldn't so much as look at me. Couldn't stomach what I'd done, what I'd become. She threw me out, and who could blame her? I was no longer the man she married. As far as we both knew, I was a murderer.

Eventually, she got well, moved on. Shacked up with some doctor from her drug trial. I told myself it was more for comfort and security than love, as if it mattered, as if it eased the pain a whit. Whatever it was that drove her into his arms, hell let me kick around long enough to watch it happen from afar before finally cashing in its chit on that cold October city street.

It was early evening. The sidewalk was packed. Liz was carrying a bag of groceries as she walked briskly down the street toward the apartment she and Chet – for in my mind, that's what I'd dubbed the toothsome oaf – shared. I'd been living on the streets some time by then – drunk, sickly, and feverish – and though I spent my every waking moment trying to catch a glimpse of her, I must have drifted off a while, because I hadn't seen her leave.

We hadn't spoken since the night of my confession. There was nothing left for me to say – Elizabeth had made that excruciatingly clear. But on that day – the day of my death – her face was downcast, her brow furrowed in worry, and in that moment I wondered if she was thinking of me.

As she passed, I called to her.

When she heard my voice, Liz spun around, her grocery bag falling forgotten to the sidewalk. I watched her peer into the crowd, searching for my face, but with my ratty hair and my twisted scraggle of a beard, she didn't see me looking back at her.

But *I* saw. I saw too much. I saw the weight she carried in her cheeks, rounding out her face and glowing pink in the chill autumn air. I saw the round swell of her belly, protruding from beneath her woolen jacket. And in that moment, I understood. Why she had pushed me away. Why she'd been forced to let me go.

She'd been protecting her child. Protecting *our* child.

Protecting it from the killer I'd become.

It was then, as I stood staring at the woman that I loved and the unborn child I'd never know, that hell's minion struck.

Hunched inside his woolen overcoat beneath a low-slung pageboy cap, he looked just like any other man on that busy city street, with two exceptions. One: where the others' eyes slid right off of me, his locked on and never deviated. And two: where most folks' hands were glove-clad or thrust deep into their pockets to protect against the cold, his were bare and exposed.

When he reached me, I found out why.

At first, I thought nothing of him running headlong into me. My focus was on Elizabeth, and he seemed nothing more than a rude New York pedestrian, not watching where he was going. Then he plunged his hand into my chest, a mad cackle escaping his lips.

His fingers clawed at my soul. The pain was excruciating, and I shrieked in sudden agony, though the many passers-by seemed not to notice. Then they and the world around me disappeared, replaced by a swirling gray-black – he and I at the center, locked in a morbid, blasphemous embrace.

And as he gouged my soul free from my chest, my body collapsing lifeless to the sidewalk, I could swear I heard Elizabeth call out, one heartbreaking syllable, her voice tremulous and full of hope: "Sam?"

But she was too late.

I was gone.

Dead.

And for a time, there was nothing.

Blissful. Horrible. Absolute.

Then I woke to the sound of rolling thunder.

Its bass-drum boom shook the walls and ceiling of the dingy tenement apartment in which I found myself, loosing patters of plaster-droppings from the patches of bare wooden laths that dotted the cracked and broken ceiling above like exposed ribs. Its vibrations rattled upward through the cool porcelain beneath me. A bathtub, I realized, freestanding in the corner of the room beside the tiny kitchen, with a curling lip of smooth white all around and a dirt-roughened basin the color of tea. Empty of water, thankfully, since I huddled in it fully clothed, knees to chest, olive drab from head to toe.

My stomach seized. I doubled over, acid scratching at my throat as I spewed yellow-green toward the hair-caked tub drain. For five minutes I sat there puking before my nausea subsided. Then I climbed sweat-slick and trembling from the tub, on limbs sleep-numbed and clumsy. My legs wouldn't support my weight. I assumed – mistakenly as it turns out – that they were merely asleep due to the position in which I found myself when I awoke. I slumped to the floor, leaning heavily against the lip of the tub as I waited for my circulation to return. But the smell of vomit was overpowering, and my stomach once more threatened mutiny. I twisted the bulbous cold-water X to rinse away the sick; the knob squeaked, but nothing happened. So instead, I pushed away from the tub in an awkward, leg-dragging crawl and looked around, trying to suss out where the hell I was, and how I'd wound up here.

The room was gloomy, cold, unlit. Empty, but for me. An unmade bed. A rickety dining room table and four chairs, one upturned. A face-down bookshelf beside a yellowed basin sink. Crumbling, nicotine-stained walls barren of art, of photos, of cheer. Age-dulled wooden floors more gray than brown, and coarse beneath my stocking feet. Scarcely three hundred square feet of space – small even by New York standards – and every inch of it depressing. The size suggested I was still on the island of Manhattan – tenements in the other boroughs had a hair more breathing room; that's why me and Liz wound up on Staten Island. The run-down condition suggested I was someplace dodgy; Alphabet City or the Village. But I'd expect the latter to be funkier than this, what with all the artist-types about, and the former should be awash with city sounds. All I heard was continuous thunder, though no lightning flashes accompanied it, and, from somewhere distant – through the wall, perhaps – a radio nattering on in angry, animated German. Of course, as near as I could tell, *all* German sounded angry. The latest of Hitler's polemics, no doubt. Couldn't wait for our boys to finally take that asshole out.

The sky outside the apartment's gap-toothed window frames was overcast. Morning, afternoon, or evening, I couldn't tell. Another rumble – this one closer – and I was dusted with fine powder from above. It pricked like pepper at my sinuses, daring me to sneeze. A jagged triangle of glass that had clung stubbornly for God knows how long to the right angle of its frame when the rest of the pane shattered finally surrendered, tinkling to the floor with a champagne-toast *clink*. Or, at least, what I *imagined* a champagne toast to sound like. Me and Elizabeth, we never had the dough to pay for bubbly, let alone the fancy stemware in which to put it. Our idea of splurging was a wicker-basketed Chianti and a thin-crust pie in one of the Italian joints that lined the streets of Rosebank, Staten Island, a short hike from our apartment.

Of course, it wasn't *our* apartment anymore. And she was no longer my Elizabeth. But maybe, just maybe, I could change that. Make things right. Maybe that's why I was here.

Maybe God had given me a second chance.

"Oh, good," came a voice from behind me, bourbon layered over honey. "You're up."

I wheeled toward the voice, or tried. My equilibrium was out of whack; I wound up dizzy, disoriented, and staring, cheek pressed to rough wood floor, at a sideways woman in a slip dress of black trimmed in red that seemed designed to highlight her bare legs, feet, and shoulders. She was standing between me and the tub, not three feet from where I lay, in a spot I was certain had been empty, having recently vacated it myself. My passing had disturbed the plaster fines that dusted the wooden floor like powdered sugar on a cake, mirror-image handprints on either side of the wide swath left by my dragging legs. And my every movement elicited a squeal of protest from the creaky floorboards. But the dust around this woman remained undisturbed, and I hadn't heard so much as a mouse-squeak from them to mark her passage before she spoke.

Foolish as it sounded, it was as if she appeared from thin air.

I propped myself up on one arm and sat agape as, upright, her full beauty became evident. She was, it shames me to say so soon after selling my soul to save the love of my life, the most stunning woman I'd ever seen. And apparently, I wasn't the only one to find her so – even the radio in the other room had fallen silent upon her arrival. Her eyes glinted emerald and onyx, somehow suggesting throaty laughs and whispered secrets and traded glances from across a crowded room that led wordlessly to clothes discarded and limbs tangled in passion. Her cheeks and shoulders were dusted with freckles, and the sultry scent of sun-warmed skin clung to her, as if she'd wandered through a summer orchard on her way to these bleak environs. Her hair tumbled lustrous red across her shoulders in undulating waves and curls, the last of which on either side curved to frame her perfect breasts, which seemed to ever-so-slightly strain the mere molecules of silk that attempted to contain them. And her lips, painted the color of fresh blood, were so sensuous – so transfixing – I couldn't help but wonder what foolhardy acts men had perpetrated with the hopes of kissing them, of tasting her breath, of simply seeing them smile.

They weren't smiling now.

Her gaze traveled from my prostrate form to the vomit-specked tub and her face crinkled with distaste. Then she strode past me so close the silken hem of her dress dragged cool across my cheek – clean-shaven, I was surprised to discover, as last I recalled I wore the ratty, unkempt beard of an indigent – and righted the upturned kitchen chair. She dropped into it with an easy grace and crossed her legs. Her toenails, I saw, were painted blood red to match her lips. No footprints marked her trip across the room.

"Who–" I said, but then I stopped. The word felt foreign and awkward on my tongue – my lips contorting as if unsure how to wrap themselves around it – and sounded so, as well. I wondered then if I'd suffered a stroke. Perhaps the stress and scavenged food and rotgut booze had finally caught up with me, and my memory of dying was nothing more than a hallucination brought on by a blood clot lodging itself somewhere in my brain and starving it of oxygen.

Hell, maybe the clot had been building for a while, and was responsible for ginning up the whole Dumas-is-a-demon-to-whom-I-sold-my-soul madness I'd been clinging two these past few months. I had to admit, it seemed the likelier option. And if it were true, maybe it was modern medicine and not God who'd granted me my second chance. Either way, I swore then and there, to myself and to Elizabeth, I wouldn't squander it.

If I only knew then how hard a promise that would be to keep.

"Don't worry," said the woman, noting my puzzled reaction to my own halting utterance, "speech is tricky at first, particularly in a foreign vessel such as yours, it requires close marriage of thought and fine motor skills, and his are calibrated to another tongue, but I've no doubt you'll get the hang of it."

I swallowed hard and tried again to speak, this time with exaggerated care. "W-who *are* you?" It came out with a few more syllables than I intended, and my voice sounded unfamiliar to my own ears, but I think it got the point across. Herr Grumpypants on the radio in the other room seemed to disagree. His nattering started up again, far louder now, with a barked *Nein, nein, nein!* It was an ice pick to the temples. I could barely hear myself think.

"*Who* I am is not as important at this moment as *what* I am. Just as *who* you are is no longer as important as *what* you are. My name is Lilith. I'm to be your handler. And you, Collector, are to be my little undead pet."

"M-my h-h-handler?"

"That's right," she said.

"I d-d-don't understand."

She heaved an exaggerated sigh, as if she were a schoolmarm and I a particularly obstinate student. "You wouldn't, would you? Your kind never seem to. It's been forever since my last babysitting assignment – I would have thought you lot would be savvier by now. Too much for me to hope for, I suppose. So allow me to explain to you how your afterlife's to work. It's quite simple, really. Your job, for all eternity, is to collect the souls of the damned. My job is to communicate to you your assignments, and to ensure you do not step out of line. Do as I say, and you and I shall get along just fine. Disobey me, and I'll be forced to take action to ensure you won't again. Are we clear?"

None of this was making sense. I said as much. Lilith rolled her eyes like *I* was the crazy one.

"Look," I said, my words coming easier now, requiring less concentration, though the din of the radio made it hard for me to hear them as I spoke. "I don't know who you are, or what you're playing at. But you're going to have to play at it by yourself. I need to go find my Elizabeth."

"Elizabeth?" she asked, the faintest hint of a smile dancing across her perfect lips. "Ah, yes, your star-crossed wife. I assure you, she's quite well. After all, those were the terms of your bargain as I understand them. But I'm afraid seeing her is out of the question."

"Like hell it is."

"Finally, Collector, you're catching on."

"Why do you keep calling me that? My name is Sam."

"*Was*," she replied.

"I don't follow."

"Your name in life was Sam. In death, I may call you anything I wish. And I prefer Collector. It suggests an air of professionalism, don't you think?"

"I think this whole conversation suggests an air of flat-out crazy," I replied, "and I've had about all of it I can take. Now you're either going to help me up or not, but either way, I'm getting out of here – even if it means I have to crawl. I've got a wife to apologize to."

"No, you don't," she said, not unkindly. "You have a widow. One you're forbidden from seeing – unless, of course, you wish to nullify your deal and send the poor girl into an unfortunate state of relapse." At that, I blanched, and swallowed hard. Lilith took note, nodding once to indicate her satisfaction that her message had been received, and then continued. "And I suspect by now your legs will work just fine. It always takes a while for a Collector's vessel to acquiesce to its commands. Of course, unless this vessel's a world-class swimmer, those legs won't get you where you wish to go, working or no."

"You're telling me this ain't Manhattan? So where, then? Brooklyn? Queens?"

"I think you misunderstand the nature of our relationship," Lilith replied. "I am to be your master, not your tour guide. And this is your first lesson as a Collector, not some meet-and-greet. Now how about you do as I've suggested and test those legs of yours?"

Two-thirds of everything this chick said made no goddamn sense, but she was right about my legs at least. I flexed each of them in turn, wincing reflexively in anticipation of the broken-glass crunch of bone on bone in my bum knee, only to be surprised when it extended smoothly and pain-free. "But how could I… what did you *do* to me?"

"Tell me, Collector, what's the last thing you remember?"

"I was outside Elizabeth's new apartment, waiting to catch a glimpse of her. She and I… we'd parted ways, but I hoped maybe I had a shot to change her mind. I saw her through the crowd, and called to her. Someone bumped into me, and the world went gray. At the time, I thought he reached into my chest and ripped out my goddamn soul. But that's nuts, right? I mean, it was probably a stroke or something. A blood clot traveling from my heart to my brain, and making me think all kinds of crazy shit. Whatever it was, it hurt like hell. And then I woke up here. Next thing I know, I'm in that bathtub," I say, nodding, "and now you're here, talking some world-class crazy. You're what – some kind of nurse? And all this nonsense is, like, one of them newfangled psychological treatments, meant to poke and prod me to see if my brain's wired right?" After all I'd seen and done, it was a stretch – a fantasy – I knew. But I wanted desperately to believe it. It sounded better than *I'd never see Elizabeth again*.

"Would that it were, Collector. I'm afraid the truth's somewhat harder to explain, and harder still to swallow. Perhaps it would be better if I showed you?"

Lilith extended a hand, delicate as a flower. I took it, and she lifted me off the floor as a parent would a child, damn near wrenching my shoulder from its socket in the process. She looked around a moment, and then – spotting what she was looking for – walked to the far end of the room and righted the toppled bookshelf. She kicked aside its former contents – a single dented pot, some bent utensils, a man's shaving kit, the broken remains of several dinner plates – unearthing a small, face-down, paper-backed picture frame. A braided metal wire ran the width of it, frayed to splitting at the center. Above the sink was a square of darker plaster that matched the frame's dimensions. At the center of it was a nail.

Lilith handed the frame to me. I turned it over, and found not a picture staring back at me, but a strange man's visage, a starburst crack distorting his fresh-faced Aryan features.

I blinked in confusion. The stranger blinked as well. As one, our eyes widened in sudden realization. The constant patter of radio-German rose to a fever pitch, drowning out all rational thought.

The mirror fell from my hand, and shattered into a million pieces on the floor.

"How?" I asked her.

"Possession," she replied. "Samuel Thornton's corpse is, by now, no more than hair and bone – one of a thousand John Does interred last year in New York's Potter's Field. And it's a good thing, too – we can't very well have you slinking about for all eternity in a decaying sack of meat and bone, frightening the villagers. So, freed by death from the confines of your human body, you now require a living vessel. Well, that or newly dead, though I'd recommend against the latter. They *are* quieter, I understand, but after a time, they do begin to stink.

And think of what would happen if you were to bump into any of their relatives? Believe me, it's happened occasionally throughout the whole of human history, and it's never been pretty. Half the time, your kind declares it a miracle, and the other half, they burn the poor undead bastard at the stake. Either way, it's more attention than we care to attract."

"Wait– Did you say that I was buried *last year*?"

"That's right," she said. "You died this October past. It's now April 1945."

"But only moments passed for me."

"Consider yourself lucky, then. Your time was spent in the vast, formless Nothing of the In-Between, while your fate was being debated. If you remembered it, you'd wish you didn't."

"Debated?"

"Yes. It seems someone on high – or perhaps on low – has taken quite a shine to you. There was much discussion as to your ultimate fate. Perhaps that's why you were assigned to me, rather than simply to a demon, as are most Collectors. I confess I was surprised. My last foray into supervising your kind was not the smoothest of endeavors. Truth be told, I'm not sure if our pairing is intended to punish you or me or both."

"A demon," I echoed, disbelieving. "Like Dumas?"

"That's right. Though understand, his human appearance was a projection, nothing more. He chose it to better pass among your kind. Most like him make no attempt to mask their true natures – and though they often walk unseen among the living, the dead such as yourself do not have the luxury of such blindness. The monsters at the edge of the map are, in fact, quite real. The sooner you come to grips with that, the better."

"You're not a demon, though," I said. "You're human, like me?"

"I fear my ontological status is somewhat more complicated than that, but I was once human, yes. Though it was so long ago, I remember little of my life."

"How did you wind up here? Did you make a deal, like me?"

"Would that I were given such a choice. No, I was cast out of Paradise for sins that, until I committed them, were as yet undefined, by a Maker as petty and mercurial as a poorly socialized toddler."

"I'm sorry," I said.

"Not nearly so sorry as you will be when you reach my age," she replied.

Her age. Funny, she didn't look a day over thirty. And that body hardly conjured images of shuffleboard and bingo. Stunning as she was, I found it hard not to ogle her.

She caught the meaning behind my lusty stare and raised an eyebrow. I blushed and looked away. "So," I said, "this is what I'm going to look like from now on?"

She laughed then. Sweet Lord in heaven, did Lilith have a laugh. It curled toes, straightened other things, prickled my new flesh with goose pimples. I felt the color rising in my cheeks. "Don't be ridiculous, Collector. You'll be here long after this vessel's dead and gone. His grandchildren, too, should he survive long enough to have them. No, you're just borrowing his body for as long as it suits your purposes. By assignment's end, you'll learn to take another at will, and to tamp down the thoughts of the individual inside."

Realization dawned. "This goddamn radio I'm hearing – it's no radio at all."

"No," she said. "The city's been without power for at least a week. There's not a radio to be heard for miles. Those are your vessel's thoughts."

"You're telling me I hijacked a Kraut?"

"*Jawohl,*" she said. "A rising member of the Hitler Youth, in fact."

"His chatter's pretty goddamn annoying."

"I would expect so. I imagine he's not pleased with your sudden occupation of his body. The irony is delicious."

"And your body," I said, "is it borrowed too?"

"No," she said. "Like Dumas, I look this way because I choose to. I've no need to drape myself in meat. Unless, of course, I find that meat desirable enough, and even then, I prefer to be on top."

I'd never heard a woman make so frank an innuendo. And I'd never seen a woman as beautiful as Lilith in my life – not even on the silver screen. The combination was enough to take my breath away. Lilith seemed to delight in that.

Thunder struck once more, shaking the building so hard, my teeth rattled.

"We should move," she said, crossing the room to the empty window frame and peering skyward. "They're getting closer."

"Who?" I asked, following.

She didn't answer. She didn't have to. As I approached the window, I saw outside a ravaged city – streets cratered, buildings crumbling, tattered Nazi banners fluttering red and white and black from every flagpole and cockeyed lamppost – and above it, the slate sky was dotted here and there with fighter planes. Each wore a single star on its tail, and another on its fuselage. I recognized them from the newsreels that ran back home as Soviet Hunchbacks. As I watched, the nearest of them opened its belly and loosed a payload of bombs that once more shook the earth beneath my feet. Smoke billowed from where they landed some blocks away, and once the sound of their impact died down, I heard a woman's anguished cry.

"Welcome to Berlin," Lilith said.

Berlin. The thought – not to mention Lilith's sudden closeness as we stood, touching, by the window – was exhilarating. Sam Thornton, bounced from recruitment station after recruitment station thanks to a bum knee and a lunger wife, dropped behind enemy lines on a mission to collect damned souls. I felt like a soldier. Like a superhero.

Maybe this undead thing wouldn't be so bad after all.

"So," I said, smiling for the first time since I awoke from the sleep of death, "you said something about an assignment?"

"I did, at that," Lilith replied, skipping gaily toward the door. "Now follow me."

"Where are we going?"

"Fear not, Collector, I suspect you'll find the task to your liking."

"C'mon, spill it. What's the job?"

Lilith beamed, all dimples and pearly whites.

"You and I are off to kill the Führer."

1.

Even before the Welshman drew down on me, I was pretty sure I was in trouble.

I'd spent the morning minding my own business, paying my respects to a dead friend. A friend I thought I'd long since lost – over a girl, because that's too often how these things go. We had the kind of falling-out that feels like it'll last forever, and in the case of folks like me and Danny, I suppose it could have. Only it didn't last forever. We patched things up just in time for me to lose the boy for good.

Least he didn't die for nothing. Hell, technically, he didn't *die* at all, or at least, not recently. The sack of meat and bone that was Danny's mortal vessel was three decades in the ground before I ever met the guy. Danny, like me, is a Collector. *Was*, I should say, since he ain't much of anything anymore.

That girl I mentioned? She – another Collector by the name of Ana – took Danny for one hell of a ride, which culminated in the destruction of his immortal soul. Sucks, huh? Only Danny got the last laugh. If her batshit scheme had gone to plan, she would have broken her bonds of servitude to hell, but at vulgar cost. Last time any of my kind pulled that sort of juju, it triggered the Deluge – you know, Noah and a big-ass boat – and damn near wiped humankind off the map. This time woulda done the same, had Danny not stepped in. So I guess you could say the poor bastard died, or whatever the hell you call it when the dying guy's already dead, saving the world. If that ain't worth a few moments of quiet graveside reflection, I don't know what is.

So that's precisely what I did. Went to Danny's mortal grave – a humble, weather-beaten headstone already draped with moss in a quiet, half-forgotten corner of a quiet, half-forgotten cemetery deep in the Kent countryside this fallen hero's only monument – and said my piece. I didn't figure the universe would begrudge me a few minutes' mourning.

I didn't figure, but I should have.

You wanna know what really irks me about being damned? It's not the big stuff – the guilt, the torment, the recriminations; those I figure I've got coming. It's the little things that get me. Drop a hundred slices of toast, and none of 'em will land butter-up. Flip a hundred coins, and not once are you gonna call it right. Take a bad beat from the cosmos, lose a friend, and need one goddamn morning to yourself to get your head straight? Well too bad, because that's precisely when the Welshman in the Bentley's gonna show.

I'm not talking metaphorically or anything. I mean I was standing in the cemetery, the chill November mist beading up on my meat-suit's pea coat, when this dove-gray Bentley – mid-Sixties, if her curves were any indication, and in fresh-off-the-floor condition – splashes up the rutted drive, and out steps this big bruiser of a guy with arms like trees, no neck, a crooked nose, and a suit he probably coulda bartered for a second, lesser car. Black worsted-wool and well tailored, it somehow only served to accentuate his massive frame, his cauliflower ears, and his meaty boxer's face. A pewter cravat hung around what passed for his neck – how it looped around *and* tied, I'll never know – and a matching scarf was draped across his shoulders. Black leather gloves stretched tight as he flexed his ham-hock hands. He eyed me a moment in my borrowed meat-suit, a rail-thin teenaged boy who'd been struck down by an aneurism just last night. Then, in a heavy Welsh accent – all odd angles and hairpin turns – he said, "Sam Thornton?"

"Never heard of him," I replied, in my best attempt at cockney.

"Your accent is bloody rubbish," he said. "And anyway, you are him."

"Okay, I'm him." I was aiming for nonchalant, although inside, I was reeling. When you make your way through the world in stolen bodies, hidden behind borrowed faces, you come to expect and even value a certain level of anonymity. Collectors ain't the type to get bumped into by old classmates at the grocery store. "And *you* are?"

"Just the hired help. The boss would like to meet you."

"Who, exactly, is the boss?"

"That's really for the boss to say, isn't it?"

"So I'm to come with you right now?"

"That's right."

"What happens if I don't?"

The big man shrugged. His gloved hands tightened into fists. "Find out," he said.

I thought about it. Decided not to.

"No," I said. "I'll come."

And so I did.

We drove for just over an hour, first on country roads, puddles gathering in the hollows of the tire-buckled tarmac and reflecting back a dotted line of cold gray sky, and then on roads with proper lines, and pale brick homes on either side. Eventually, we hit the motorway and headed north-west toward London. The whole time, my driver never said a word. My only company was the clatter of the tires against the pavement, and the swoosh of the wipers clearing the constant drizzle from the windshield. For a time, I tried to question him as to who his employer was and where, exactly, he was taking me, but the big mook just smiled at me, gap-toothed and crooked, in the rearview. So eventually, once his choice of roads tipped London as our likely destination, I gave up, settling into my leather seat back as warm and supple as first love and sleeping fitfully. It's rare I find myself in such refined environs, and wherever he was taking me, there was no point in being exhausted when we got there.

When the Bentley rocked to a halt, I woke with a start, unsure at first what continent I was on, or what meat-suit I'd dozed off wearing. But the swank interior of the Bentley's cabin and the pale gleaming pate of my taciturn companion brought me back to the here and now right quick. If only I had a better handle on where here was, or what was gonna happen next. This steroided-out hunk of lab-grown meat didn't seem too likely to fill me in on either.

"We're here," he said. "Get out."

I got out. Looked around. Saw nothing familiar, not that that surprised me any. London wasn't really my beat. In all my years as a Collector, I've never been able to suss out any geographic rhyme or reason to the assignments on which I've been sent, but for whatever reason, I've never snatched a soul in London proper. Oxford, sure. Manchester once or twice. Snagged a couple dozen sinners in Ireland in my day, a Scot or two – and one very surly Welshman. But never London. So unless this suited ape had dropped me on the banks of the Thames within spitting distance of Big Ben, it may as well have been Sheboygan for all I knew.

But what I did see suggested Sheboygan might've proven a step up.

The driver and I stood on a narrow strip of weed-split sidewalk hemmed in on one side by the low-slung curves of his boss' vintage Bentley, and on the other by a crooked, handbill-plastered plywood construction barrier whose panels zigged and zagged as though tacked up by a cadre of impatient drunkards, none of whom had any facility with a hammer. The building beyond was gargantuan – occupying an entire city block, as near as I could tell – but its shape and purpose were lost to me behind layers of sheet plastic and scaffolding and yet more plywood, which was tacked over what few windows faced the street. Truth be told, it was a hard place to pin down; it seemed to resist being looked at. And when I tried to force myself to do so, I got the disquieting impression those blank plywood eyes were looking back at me.

Spooked, I diverted my gaze. The feeling passed. I tried to play it off like I was taking in the neighborhood at large, but from the smug grin on the driver's face, I'm pretty sure he wasn't buying it.

Across the street from us sat an ugly yellow brick building stained gray by exhaust and tagged here and there by artless vandals. Its tired façade and the makeshift curtains that showed in its windows – a tapestry here, a beach towel there – suggested low-income housing. Despite the chill and the escalating rain, several of the building's windows were open, and from them poured an olfactory cacophony of discordant yet not altogether unpleasant spices representing at minimum three continents' cuisine, and the song and conversation to match.

To my right, across a narrow side street, was a shuttered convenience store, its dented stainless steel overhead doors down despite the fact it was scarcely midday. The cars that lined the street's low curb were old and cheap and not worth stealing. The Bentley aside, of course, since it was parked along the curb as well – its driver had somehow managed to not only find a space that accommodated this beautiful behemoth of an automobile with scant inches to spare, but to parallel-park said behemoth without disturbing my beauty sleep until the deed was done. An impressive feat, to be sure, but not half as impressive as simply having the balls to leave such a stunning work of automotive art parked in a dodgy neighborhood without so much as locking its doors.

I stretched, then, working the sleep and tension from my limbs, and turned to ask the driver, "What now?" But the words never passed my lips.

Because that's when I noticed the gun in his hand.

For such a big guy, it was a dainty, slender little thing. A Ruger Mark Two, unless I was much mistaken – and believe me, I've been on the barrel-end of enough firearms in my time, I know most of 'em on sight. A good half the bastards who pointed 'em at me even pulled the trigger, which is how I knew the dinky little .22s that baby was packing were unlikely to put me down on the quick. But unless my buddy here'd shot off a few rounds on his way to picking me up, he had ten rounds in the mag and one in the chamber, and, dinky or not, that was plenty to put this meat-suit in the ground once and for all. So I showed the guy my palms, and sent out my best we're-all-friends-here vibes. Of course, I spend my days killing people at hell's behest, so I confess, the happiest vibes I've got at my disposal are pretty fucking far from cheery. But if it means not getting my ass shot, I'm willing to, you know, fake it.

"C'mon, man, is that thing necessary? I came here willingly, if you recall."

But he just tossed me a key ring and gestured with a twitch of his gun barrel. "Unlock that and head inside. Do it."

The *that* in question was a fist-sized padlock looped through the lock-hole of a two-dollar gate latch – what it cost in Pounds Sterling, I couldn't say – which was in turn affixed via four Phillips-head screws to the sole hinged plywood panel in the row. Why people bother putting decent locks on shitty doors and latches I'll never know. Sure, the padlock could take a bullet – at least if the old Super Bowl commercials were to be believed – but who needs a key when a Phillips-head screwdriver could get you in just as quick?

The door was marked as such by the laminated pressboard sign affixed to it that read:

ANOTHER URBAN RENEWAL PROJECT
COURTESY OF MAGNUSSON INDUSTRIES
Magnusson: Making Life Better

Though by the look of the project's perimeter – a buckling plywood security wall discolored with age and papered with layer after layer of handbills – it didn't look like much renewing had been going on for quite some time.

I unlocked the lock. Handed it to the mook. He gestured with his barrel yet again.

I took the hint, and pushed open the plywood door – or tried. The moment I touched it, my body was suffused with sudden, crawling dread. It slid down my arm and coiled around my heart, my lungs, my stomach. Like a litter of pythons, freshly hatched and hungry – tightening, choking, crushing my will as they contracted. And, though I'm certain now it was only in my mind, I felt as much as heard a low, raspy whisper in my ear accompanied by hot swamp breath that reeked like rotting flesh, uttering perhaps the most compelling command I've ever received: *"Leave."*

The driver's Ruger jabbed into my back, a cold hard finger between my shoulder blades. I shoved the door open and staggered through. He followed close behind, careful not to touch the door along the way. The rusty spring affixed to the hinge protested as the plywood door swung closed and the city outside disappeared.

2.

"The fuck was *that*?" I asked, crossing my arms and rubbing at my borrowed shoulders in a vain attempt to dispel the dread that had settled upon me as I'd forced open the door.

"Security," he said. His gun was still drawn but no longer trained on me, instead hanging relaxed at his side in one gloved hand. "The whole fence is like that. Protects the would-be squatters and nosey bloody parkers."

"Don't you mean protects you *from* the would-be squatters and nosey bloody parkers?"

"No. Although in the Bentley's case, that's true enough. Its bodywork is hexed to match. Even with the gloves on, I don't like touching it."

"It's a cute trick," I said. "You'll have to teach me."

He shook his head. "Not mine to teach."

"The boss?" I hazarded.

"The boss."

Inside the perimeter of the site the air was somehow darker, closer. It took me a moment to realize why. The sky above was a formless gray far deeper than it had been a moment before, and oddly distorted, as if seen through dirty leaded windows. And though outside the gate the rain continued unabated, I neither saw nor felt any trace of it in here, and the sidewalk beneath my feet was dry. I smelled not moisture, nor exhaust, nor simmering spice, just a still alkaline nothing, like the air inside a fallout bunker. Here, as outside, the sidewalk buckled under countless weeds' persistence, but while outside they were thriving, the weeds inside were withered, black, and dead. And inside the plywood perimeter, it was dead silent as well. I heard no city sounds, no song, not so much as the quiet patter of the rain. Just me and this mook breathing in the silence. It set my teeth on edge.

"Well then," I said. "What say we two go meet him?"

Muffled footfalls against concrete. Massive front steps looming. Now that we were inside the barrier, the building no longer resisted being seen. It was an imposing structure in the Edwardian style with hard lines and thick columns, faced in weather-beaten limestone that gathered in heavy geometric pediments above every window. As we approached the outsized arch of the entryway, I noted the lettering carved into the rectangular cartouche atop the keystone, which read, *Pemberton Baths*.

"We going for a swim?" I asked.

"Something like that," he replied.

We scaled the broad stone stairs. My gaze lighted on something on the topmost step that seemed incongruous with our surroundings, a brush-stroke of stark white against the gray. I crouched over it, and found to my surprise it was a good-sized bird, or what was left of one. I'd never seen one like it, or so I thought. When I said as much to my fair foreign companion, he snorted and said, "You never see a crow before?"

With a start, I realized he was right. It *was* a crow. Emphasis on the *was*.

The crow lay on its side, wings splayed as if felled in mid-flight, though it showed no signs of trauma from whatever felled it or from the fall itself. And every inch of it, from beak to wing to three-pronged feet, was as pale as sun-bleached bone. Save for its eyes, I realized. The one that I could see was a blackened crater with a corona of charcoal all around. It looked as if it had been burned out of the poor creature's head.

Suddenly, the driver's comment about protecting would-be squatters and looky-loos made a whole lot more sense.

I reached down to turn the bird over, to try to understand what sort of magic it had fallen victim to, but when I touched it, it crumbled to ash.

"Your boss has quite the bag of tricks."

"He does, at that."

"And he doesn't seem too fond of visitors."

He shrugged. "He's a very private man, isn't he?"

"So how come you and me could pass?"

He looked at me like I was dense. "We were *invited.*"

"That didn't seem to stop the fence. Or the mojo on the Bentley."

At that, the big man hesitated, a pained look on his face as if worried what came next might be perceived by his employer as speaking out of turn. "We weren't harmed because the boss wishes us no harm. If I had to guess, I'd say he's *less* concerned whether he hurts our feelings. And if I were you, I'd get a move on. He's not a man who takes kindly to being kept waiting."

The front door was unlocked. We stepped inside. Our footfalls echoed through the broad expanse of the room. The interior of the building was dark, lit only by the faint light that trickled through the dirt-crusted panes of the skylight that stretched the length of the ceiling, and the soft glow of two gas lamps at the far end of the room. All the windows save for the skylight were boarded up.

Situated beneath the skylight was a vast, white-tiled swimming pool. Circling it was a narrow walkway no doubt once dotted with low-slung lounge chairs, but now piled here and there with detritus – nail-studded boards; hunks of masonry run through with metal rebar; a pile of public restroom sinks. The pool itself was free of such detritus. A set of stairs in either corner nearest us – one crumbling, one intact – invited would-be swimmers into the shallow end a scant three feet below the walkway, and from there the pool's bottom sloped gradually downward toward the far end.

The driver gestured toward the undamaged stairs, so I took them, he trailing just behind. Together we descended toward the gas-lit glow of the deep end. Though the pool had long been drained, I couldn't help but feel as my sightline passed below the walkway that surrounded it that I was in over my head.

The deep end featured on its right-hand side a cluttered office. A gas lamp turned down to barely burning rested on an elegant mahogany desk, but afforded too little light to make out anything but black shapes surrounding it. The deep-end's left-hand side was taken up by a makeshift room framed in two-by-fours and shielded from view by hanging sheets of plastic of the type I'd seen outside. Another lamp burned inside the makeshift room, this one brighter, projecting shadows of the activity therein against the walls like some nightmare paper lantern. I saw a table's distorted shadow, its flat plane broken by a sleeping body – or a cadaver. The vague shape of a man's head and shoulders were visible hunching over it, his hands an impossible blur of activity. He was humming, I realized – a Wagner opera. And, though the table's supports were stick-skinny, light showing underneath, the man appeared to have no legs.

Beside me, the Welshman stiffened for a moment as though receiving an electric shock, and then he nodded. "The boss is just finishing up," he said, dress shoes clattering against the tile as he crossed into the office and adjusted the gas lamp. It flared white-hot a moment as the first rush of air hit the wick, and then settled into a pleasant, amber glow. "He said to make yourself at home."

I squinted in the sudden light, the wick's green afterimage a dancing ghost at the center of my vision, and then forgot myself once my eyes adjusted.

The back wall of the office was lined with waist-high wooden, glass-doored shelves of the kind one might find at an old-time pharmacy. The shelves were chock-a-block with jars containing peculiar liquids that seemed to amplify the lamplight and reflect back strange, entrancing hues of their own. As I looked at them in turn – dusky purple, vibrant green, soft pink – my mouth was filled with the taste of plum, of sage, of rose petals.

Atop the shelving was a collection of taxidermy the likes of which the world had never seen: a three-headed owl; a piglet's head with hooked, reddish beaks where its eyes ought to've been; a cheetah with the face of a baboon.

The right-hand wall was largely given over to an array of medical equipment – a heart monitor, a respirator, an IV stand ornamented with two bags of fluids – surrounding a luxurious four-post bed done up with a half-dozen thick down pillows and sheets of gleaming silk. The pillows were fluffed up and arranged so the bed's occupant might comfortably sit; the sheets were turned down in anticipation of said occupant.

I strolled across the mildewed tile toward the desk at the center of the space. My driver watched idly, arms crossed, apparently unconcerned by my curiosity. The desk was piled high with books, papers, and odd artifacts: A glass bell, under which sat a sliver of blood-flecked wood; the broken corner of a stone slab, inscribed with words I could not read; a life-sized bronze bust, its face contorted in pain.

Two high-backed leather club chairs faced the desk on one side. The side the blotter faced contained no chair. The blotter itself was leather as well but paler than the club chairs, and less burnished. I ran a finger along it, wondering idly at its strange matte finish, only to recoil when I realized the seal at its center was not a seal at all, but in fact a Royal Navy man's tattoo.

An anemometer sat on one corner of the desk, a device like a propeller with four hemispherical cups attached, intended to measure wind-speed. As I approached, it began to rotate slowly. But there was no wind in here, save for that which the instrument itself generated as it spun, and anyways, the cups were arranged such that it should have spun *clockwise*, not counterclockwise.

It picked up speed, spinning so fast it shook. Papers flew off the desk, scattering across the floor. Something about the device pricked at a distant memory, and unnerved me in a way I could not define. Almost without volition, I raised a hand to stop it.

"I wouldn't," said a thin, wizened, aristocratic voice, its vaguely continental singsong accent lending a quiet air of condescension to its words.

"Excuse me?" I said, tearing my attention from the anemometer, and turning it instead to its owner. Who, as it happens, was the ugliest man I'd ever had the displeasure of laying eyes on.

He was a skeletal little wisp of a thing, gliding toward me in a motorized wheelchair that hummed quietly as it cleared the plastic sheeting and rolled into the ersatz office. Twin ribbons of herringboned red trailed behind it, one from each tire, patterned like a printmaker's stamp, ever fainter as he approached. He wore a silk smoking jacket – bold blue paisley trimmed in brown velvet – and a loose-woven brown lap blanket over his legs. One ashen, liver-spotted hand, its knuckles gnarled as tree roots, gripped the chair's joystick. His other hand, oddly brown and muscular, rested lightly on his lap.

His face looked like a patchwork quilt assembled by a mad cannibal – an age-creased pale white nose, narrow and aquiline; a left cheek and jaw as soft and unlined as a young woman's; a patch of skin around his right eye blood-crusted at its borders as if it were a new addition, whose tone and epicanthic folds indicated it was Asian in origin. His right eye was pale green and rheumy. His left eye was vibrant blue, and clear as cloudless day, but it bulged inside its socket as if it didn't quite fit. The skin on the right side of his face was as thin and brittle as old parchment; it cracked and peeled in the hollow of his cheek.

"It detects your kind, among other things," he said. "Consider it a warning system. You touching it will only make it spin faster. You're liable to lose a hand."

"Why's it spinning backward?" I asked.

"Because you, Sam Thornton, are no angel."

He raised the hand in his lap and gestured. The anemometer's spinning ceased.

"And just who or what are *you*?" I asked.

The patchwork man laughed, a steel brush on concrete. "Isn't *that* the question," he replied.

"I'll settle for a name," I said. "After all, you apparently know who *I* am."

"Ah, but what's in a name? Particularly for one such as myself, who's had so many. In Sebaste, they knew me as Atomus. In Samaria, I was Simon Magus. In Cologne, Albertus. In the verdant isles of this fledgling kingdom, they sang my praises as Merlin. And this century past, I was best known for my groundbreaking if misunderstood research, conducted under the name of Doktor Men–"

But then he broke off – mid-name, it seemed – as if deciding he'd already shared too much. "My apologies," he said. "You care not to hear an old man's ramblings; you simply wish to know how to address me. At present, my name is Simon Magnusson. I'm sorry to have kept you waiting, my last procedure proved more difficult than anticipated."

I glanced back over the Magnusson's shoulder at the plastic-sheeted room, and wondered if I even wanted to ask.

I asked. "What kind of a procedure?"

"The unsuccessful kind, I fear. My patient lacked the fortitude necessary to survive the harvest. Now she's just so much wasted flesh. And as you can see," he said, tilting his crumpled parchment cheek toward the light for me to see, "I've little time to find another suitable donor."

"I hope that's not why you brought me here."

"No," said Magnusson. "We've other business altogether. Could I tempt you with a cup of tea? I suspect your trip to the cemetery has left you chilled." I shook my head. "A sherry, perhaps?" Again I declined. "Well, then, I hope you don't begrudge me some myself. Gareth," he said, addressing the driver, "would you be a dear and fetch me some Amontillado? Then kindly clean up the surgical suite. I fear I left it quite a mess."

The Welshman nodded once and disappeared up the deep-end's sole ladder, his footfalls receding into the darkness. Seconds later he returned, expertly navigating the ladder with a sherry glass in one hand. I found myself wondering how he would have managed it with two drinks.

He set the sherry on the desk atop the blotter, and then ducked behind the plastic sheeting, three-thousand-dollar suit and all. Soon, I heard the sound of a hose running, and pink water sluiced across the tiles from beneath the sheeting, headed toward the floor drain at the center of the deep end.

"Please," he said, gesturing at the leather club chairs opposite the desk. "Sit down. We've much to talk about."

I did as he requested, eyeing awkwardly the desk's contents while the patchwork man maneuvered his electric wheelchair into place. The breeze generated by the anemometer had shifted the mountain of paper atop the desk, and unearthed treasures that had heretofore been hidden to me. Two in particular caught my eye.

The first was a Maneki Neko figurine – you know, the sort of chintzy ceramic cats that grace the counter of every noodle house and pachinko parlor from here to Hokkaido. They're meant to bring good fortune to whosoever owns them; I had reason to believe this one did that one better. See, a year or so back, I wound up in a tussle with a demon, a demon I killed with a talisman identical to this one. Far as I knew at the time, that talisman was unique. Now, I suspected, I was looking at another.

The other item that caught my eye, mounted as it was on two narrow arms such that it ran parallel to the far edge of the desk, was an ornate, filigreed skim blade, its beveled cutting edge gleaming in the lamplight. The base on which it was displayed read:

To my beloved brother, Simon.
Until the stars burn out,
Grigori

A skim blade is demon-forged, and as hard and sharp as the fury of the Adversary himself, but it is no weapon. It's used in the manufacture of skim, a demon drug of sorts made by shaving fragments of life experience from souls recently collected.

But skim blades have another function, too. They can be used to cleave a human soul entirely, a sacrifice so great and terrible it's only used to fuel the most violent and desperate of magical rituals. A skim blade is what Ana used when she destroyed Danny's soul as part of her rite to escape hell's bonds. A rite she learned of through decades of painstaking research into what I'd thought to be an old wives' tale – of a group of Collectors some three thousand years ago who called themselves the Brethren, and who, through a ritual in which they tore a soul asunder and brought forth the Great Flood, broke free of hell's orbit forever.

I was pretty sure I was now in the presence of one of them.

"Quite the collection you've got here," I said, plucking up the Maneki Neko all casual-like, as if I were inspecting it, rather than weighing the odds of bashing it into this dude's skull if our little tête-à-tête went sideways.

He smiled. "I understand you're something of a Collector yourself."

"Cute."

"It won't do you any good, you know."

"What's that?"

"The lucky cat. I assume that's why you're holding it, no? In case this meeting comes to blows. And I'm telling you, it's no use against the likes of me."

"You sure about that?" I asked, remembering the havoc the last one wreaked on beings doubtless more powerful than this poor wretch.

"Of *course* I'm sure," he snapped. "I *made* it. Originally, I enchanted a case of twelve, dimestore trinkets bought wholesale from a manufacturer in Taiwan. Stashed them wherever I thought they might prove useful. But objects of such power have a way of walking off. Much as my brazen head once did, when that bastard Pope Sylvester decided he had to have it, and stole it from me."

I eyed the bust he indicated – bronze, tarnished, and unremarkable. "The fuck's it do?" I asked.

"It's an oracle of sorts. It's said that it can answer any question truthfully, provided that question is phrased such that it may answer yes or no."

"Does it work?" I asked.

"Yes," replied the head, damn near causing me to jump out of my chair.

"No," replied Magnusson.

"B-but it just said–"

"Oh, I didn't say it couldn't *speak*. Just that it no more knows the secrets of the universe than you or I. Well, more *you* than I. I assure you, the human mind that I encased inside it was quite infirm to begin with, and has only grown madder as the centuries have passed. The only thing keeping it from gibbering like an idiot all day long is it's mystically forbidden from saying anything but 'yes' or 'no'."

The old man gave me the stare-down for a moment, and then, more serious now, continued. "Tell me," he said, "do you know why you are here?"

"I'm starting to get an inkling," I replied. "You're Brethren, aren't you?"

"Aren't *you* the clever one," he said. "For over three thousand years we Nine lived unmolested, protected by the same Great Truce that stemmed the tide of war between the heavens and the realms below. And then you and your idiot friends ginned up delusions of grandeur, and decided to recreate our ritual to free yourselves from servitude as we once did."

"That ain't exactly how it all went down," I said, but Magnusson raised his good hand to silence me.

"Spare me your frayed yarns and tired excuses," he said. "I assure you, I'm interested in neither. Do you know why we Nine were successful in our endeavor?"

"I have a feeling you're about to enlighten me."

"Oh, I doubt very much your capacity for enlightenment, though I shall try. We succeeded because we had vision. Creativity. We escaped the bonds of slavery because not a being in the universe but us believed that it could work. You and your friends had no such advantage, which is why you were doomed to fail, and fools to even attempt it."

"And here I figured you got by on your rakish good looks."

His face twisted momentarily into a gruesome mask of fury, quickly mastered. "You mock what you cannot understand. When you look upon me, you see something to be reviled, yes? Pitied, perhaps?"

"I wouldn't expect much of a line at your kissing booth, if that's what you mean," I replied.

"Again with the juvenile humor. A pointless act of childish rebellion. But your words hurt me not a bit. You see, when I look upon my own reflection, I see not a monstrous visage worthy of your scorn. I see the culmination of fifty lifetimes spent in the service of science and magic both; the great triumph of human ingenuity – *my* ingenuity – in besting death. For you see, the eternal life my siblings and I fought so hard for is not without its drawbacks. Unlike you, we cannot simply flit from vessel to vessel. Our flesh and soul are fused. We can scarcely stretch our consciousness enough to control those most dimwitted of humans who happen through our sphere of influence," he said, eyes swiveling toward the plastic-sheeted surgical suite, where Gareth – still hosing down the effluvia left behind by Magnusson's procedure – suddenly began to whistle the selfsame Wagner opera Magnusson was whistling upon our entry. A few notes in, he fell silent once more.

"And even then," Magnusson continued, looking drained, "only temporarily. Since we are condemned to our fleshly prisons for all eternity, we require constant replenishment to push back against the ravages of time. In our early days, we bathed in the blood of innocents – stoking the flames of war and of distrust, even drumming up an Inquisition or two if need be – to ensure our cups ever runneth over. A few of my kind still do, in fact, so entrenched are they in the old ways they refuse to acknowledge the world has moved on without them. Others found the unpleasant necessities of our lifestyle so distasteful, they broke from the pack to form another, taking refuge on a wooded continent as far from civilization as they could manage, so as to not be tempted to feast on the life-sustaining flesh and blood of the living. Their efforts proved shortsighted, as that vast, sparsely populated continent they chose to make their home was discovered not long after by our standards. Turns out the poor, misled bastards starved themselves just long enough, subsisting for centuries on the scant life-force of wild game, to drive themselves quite mad. Now they're nothing more than feral beasts, feasting on the very species they sought to spare. Through rigorous application of the scientific method to the so-called arcane art of magic, I alone have happened upon our true path, our true future; one to which I hope my dear siblings will one day come around. Thanks to the great strides I've made in my own nascent field of molecumancy, muscles, bones, and organs – and yes, even skin – may be replaced as they each in turn fail. Vitality may be replenished through regular transfusions. Immune responses can be managed mystically to avoid rejection, and ensure a perfect join between old and new, regardless of the source. Which means our bodies can even be augmented, transformed into something greater than human; what Nietzsche called the *Übermensch*. A true self-made man."

"Christ," I said. "You give that speech to every mother whose baby starts wailing when it catches a glimpse of you? You're no fucking superman, you're a decrepit mess with delusions of grandeur, and you look like the goddamned Crypt Keeper. I fail to see how that makes you better than the people you prey upon."

Magnusson waved a hand dismissively in my direction. "Your choice of words, though no doubt borne of carelessness, is apt. You do, indeed, fail to see. My outward appearance I manage by employing a simple glamour – one which projects an image of a kindly old man to anyone who looks my way. I can even, for short stretches in controlled environments, force that glamour to imprint itself onto film – a discovery that proved a revelation to one so long relegated to the shadows. Now I'm known the world over as a great pillar of the international business community, one whose holdings in the fields of technology and biosciences have improved humankind's understanding of themselves and quality of life in ways none but me had the vision to imagine. My false face graces billboards, and speaks to thousands of Magnusson Industries employees every year via my very own dedicated satellite network. But I refuse to wear it here. Here, I am my truest self."

"Here, where you slaughter innocents, you mean. Your methods may differ from those of your fellow Brethren, but it seems to me you pillage the living just the same."

"For now, yes, but only by necessity. I derive no pleasure from it. One day soon, I shall possess the means to cultivate my own replacement parts, at which point I'll no longer have any need to pester the living. And I assure you, those from whom I borrow are hardly innocent. I own a number of institutions both penal and mental from which I draw as needed – once the potential donor has met my rigorous screening requirements, of course. Borrow portions of an undiagnosed schizophrenic's frontal lobe just once, and you too will become a stickler for prescreening, although the dreams, I confess, were quite engaging. I removed it a week later to stop the voices, opening my skull with hammer and chisel by my reflection in the washroom mirror and scooping it out with a soup spoon in my desperation. But sometimes, they taunt me still."

"Least you're never lonely," I replied. "Speaking of, maybe you and they could finish this conversation without me. I mean, thanks for having me and all, and really," I said, looking around the dank, echoey space of the abandoned public bath, "it's a lovely home you've got here, but I've had about as much hospitality as I can stand for one day. So, if you don't mind..."

The old man laughed once more. "My home? You think this is my *home*? Oh, no, dear boy. I've a penthouse not far from here on Piccadilly, a country estate some hours north, a small island in the Caribbean, the top five floors of a high-rise in Hong Kong that bears my name. This place is merely a refuge of sorts, where I can carry out my more... esoteric experiments away from the prying eyes of those who might wish to put a stop to them."

I pictured a bleached white crow, its eyes burned out of its head. And a man made of crows three stories high; an old god named Charon, whose dominion was the vast nothing separating life and death known as the In-Between, and the Collectors who routinely passed through it as they traveled from vessel to vessel. It was he who absorbed the energy released by Danny's riven soul during Ana's recreation of the Brethren escape-ritual, thereby sparing the living world a horrid fate. I had it on good authority he was none too fond of the Brethren. He didn't cotton much to folks who took advantage of his beneficence.

"You're hiding from Charon," I said.

"Amongst others," said the old man. "Unaffiliated deities such as he can prove as volatile as they are unpredictable, and he's no great fan of me or mine. But there's value in staying off heaven and hell's respective radars as well, particularly as they descend once more toward all-out war. Ours are dangerous times, Mr. Thornton – for the living and the dead both. For the first time in three thousand years, I wonder just how long any of us on this spinning rock have left. And speaking of hell's radar, where does your handler think you are right now?"

"Lilith found me at the cemetery, same as you, so she knows that I'm in Jolly Old, but I didn't exactly have time to file a flight plan with her before your goon – excuse me, *driver* – absconded with me."

At the mention of Lilith's name Magnusson started, but whatever emotion just passed through him, his hodgepodge features were inscrutable. "That is reassuring to hear," he said. "For it would not do to have her waiting at the gates, once I take my leave of you this night. It's shame enough I had to sacrifice my sanctuary just to neutralize the threat you pose, the last thing I need is to tussle with the likes of *her*."

At the implied threat behind his words, I tensed. Fear, cold and slithering, coiled itself around my stomach. "You must know I can't be killed," I told him. "If I were, I'd be reseeded somewhere else."

"Fear not, Collector, I've no intention of killing you. I simply chose to remove you from the field of play."

That's when it occurred to me. "The bed…" I said.

"…is yours, of course. And I do hope you find it to your liking. You'll be sleeping in it for centuries to come."

"The hell I will."

"Oh, I fear you haven't any choice. And Samuel?"

"Yeah?"

"You really should have accepted my offer of tea."

And that is when the patchwork man attacked.

3.

Look, I'm no idiot. This gig of mine, as awful as it is, comes with its share of downtime, much of it passed surfing cable in fleabag motels, or thumbing through whatever tacky airport thriller happens to grace my meat-suit's nightstand. So sure, I'm well aware when a creepy-ass mad scientist transports you to his secret lair unblindfolded and then lays in on the mustache-twirling monologue, you oughta figure your day's about to take a turn for the shark-mounted death-ray. But what I *didn't* expect from this decrepit sack of patchwork skin and bone was that he'd try to take me on himself. Nor did I have the faintest inkling the freaky son of a bitch would be more than equal to the task.

When Magnusson first began to rise from his wheelchair, my brain couldn't make a lick of sense of it. Then his lap-blanket fell away, and my confusion and mounting fear were replaced by revulsion. What I'd taken for spindly old-man legs beneath the woven blanket were in fact the front-most two of four ropy, mismatched arms, which angled elbows-up away from his withered trunk in such a way the knot of mottled scar tissue at their join where his junk should've been was visible as his robe slipped open. The two rear arms, which had been hidden under his robe, folded beneath him, and then pressed palm-down on the wheelchair's seat, lifting him upward. As I watched, they first one and then the other moved from the leather seat to the wheelchair's armrests like a gymnast gripping pommels. I had just long enough to think that suddenly the flurry of activity I'd half-glimpsed through the plastic sheeting on my way in made a lot more sense, when this monster rendered in stolen flesh and bone launched himself at me.

The wheelchair shot backward, slammed into a set of shelves, glass shattering and noxious smells. Magnusson vaulted over the desk, his two proper arms extended toward me as if to throttle me, the palms of his two front leg-hands slapping the mahogany to maintain his momentum, and spilling the desk's contents across the pool tiles. His silk smoking jacket trailed behind him like a paisley cape, its belt tie flailing open on either side. The gas lantern hit the tiles with a wind-chime crash, its fuel igniting as it splashed across the floor and scattered papers and casting long, flickering shadows through the vast, empty space – a storybook hell made real.

I had no time to react. The club chair tipped over backward as he slammed into me – his one dark, beefy proper hand on my throat, pinning me in place; the two hands on his forelegs gripping white-knuckled the leather of the chair wings; his two hind-leg hands digging into my knees. The naked join of his four lower limbs was scant inches above me, scarred and filthy and reeking like an open sewer. With his one withered hand, he reached into an interior pocket of the smoking jacket and withdrew an old, glass syringe filled with a sickly amber liquid, cloudy and flocculent. Attached to the syringe was a heavy-gauge needle three inches long.

I clawed and scratched at the old man's face. Skin sloughed off in patches beneath my fingers, revealing yellow adipose tissue like fresh-plucked chicken and glistening cords of blood-red muscle streaked with purple. Its scent hit my nostrils, earthy and animal and tinged faintly with rot, and the loosed scraps fluttered black and withered to the ground, aging decades in the seconds after they were set free from this monster's horrid form. But the bastard just laughed, and removed the protective sheath from the needle with his crooked, gray-black teeth. Vision growing spotty, I couldn't help but note how long and sharp those teeth were, now that his cracked, parchment-colored lips were pulled back to display them in all their glory. Like an animal's I realized – or maybe several animals'.

A mouth full of stolen canines.

"Do you see now how little chance you stand against me? You who cling to your petty human worldview, your myopic human sense of what is possible?"

But I didn't see. My eyes were clenched tight in concentration. My consciousness probing. Seeking. Reaching for another meat-suit.

I brushed against Magnusson's own consciousness, but recoiled as soon as I made contact. It was too foreign, too alien, too goddamn corrupted for me to work with. I'd barely grazed him, and I hope to God he didn't notice, but God ain't one to listen to me, I guess, because Magnusson roared in sudden rage and backhanded me twice in rapid succession.

Made sense. He had backhands to spare.

I reached my mind toward Gareth's next. When I touched him, I realized the Welshman was frightened. I found him huddled, shaking in the far corner of the plastic-sheeted room, a toppled tray of bloodied surgical equipment scattered all around. The stainless steel mortuary slab was thankfully above his eye level, and harsh white light from the surgical light above cast a corona all around it, so my hazy, impressionistic remote-view afforded me blissfully little detail of its viscera-draped surface. But I saw one bare leg, female, dangling off the nearest edge. The dead woman's toes were painted a glossy coral pink, and her calf was tanned and shapely. Well, the bit of it that was still whole. There was a scalpel-slice below her knee the circumference of her leg, and a perpendicular cut proceeding halfway down her shin. The skin below her knee was folded down over itself like an unzipped leather boot. Fluids dripped from the corners created by the vertical slice onto the floor, the tap-tap-tap echoing dully in the emptiness.

I extended my consciousness toward him, the seconds stretching as I myself stretched across the hollow Nothingness between my waning vessel and the promise of a new one. Mere seconds passed as I thrashed beneath the patchwork madman's grasp, but the flood of images that struck me painted a picture of a lifetime. A simple man, his mind laid bare before me on account of countless violations on the part of his sadistic employer, his whole world shattered by all that he had seen and felt and, yes, been forced to do, as if the front door to his mind had been ripped off its hinges, the path to it worn shiny from constant use – from heavy things both dragged in and removed.

You know what's funny? We all have thoughts, even the stupidest of us. Reams of them, all day long, from sunup to sundown. And yet most folks have no idea how those thoughts are structured, or what makes them tick. They're not some kind of mental home movie, a series of vignettes that traipse from A to B to C with a handy-dandy voiceover narration making sense of the whole thing. They're more like water droplets scattered across a spider web after a spring rain; little pockets of experience, caught at random it seems, each a lens through which distorted images of the world *as we see it* can be viewed, but never, *ever* as it truly is. Those moments that aren't captured by memory's web speak to character every bit as much as are the ones that stick, and the way they're organized is dictated by the many-eyed wooly beast that guards the keep – our basest survival instinct, our truest and most horrible self. Each mind's a pattern, a thousand strands of silk joined in one purpose. Some read as easy as the funny pages.

Others read like Joyce – constellations within constellations, thoughts within thoughts within thoughts. And others still are like trying to read a Braille transcript of a bad translation of a foreign lunatic's street-corner rants with your stockinged feet.

Lucky for me, this guy was of the funny-page persuasion, the thread of his life easily unwound. Unfortunately for the both of us, that's where his relationship with funny ended.

I caught a fleeting glimpse of a shoddy housing estate in Cardiff; a single mother – pretty once – wasting away to nothing, as her omnipresent cigarettes were replaced in Gareth's memories by a chipped, green-painted oxygen tank, the narrow tubes too small and delicate in his mind to entrust with so vital a task as conveying her life's breath; a sparsely attended funeral, his heart cold and gray beneath a sky of brilliant blue; a youth spent in and out of juvenile detention centers, his anger both uncontrollable and preferable to his crushing sadness; a boxing gym heavy with the scent of liniment and sweat socks, a heart once more full of hope; the doctor's hand atop his shoulder as he explained how the random squiggles on the CT meant he'd never fight again; and a kindly old man behind the wheel of a stunning '65 Bentley, asking the weeping giant sitting on the chill stone curb if he might be interested in an exciting employment opportunity. And then horrors, half-glimpsed by me before Gareth pushed them aside. Never did he think the old man's offer would come to this, to a young woman, so beautiful and so vibrant – her verbena-scented auburn curls so much like his mother's own – lying dead and mangled on a slab beside him, just another workday mess to be carried to the curb.

The meat-suit I wished to leave was losing consciousness. Copper on my tongue, spots in my eyes, a tinny sound like a corded phone left off its hook in an adjacent room echoing in my ears. Magnusson's needle plunged into my neck. I heaved with all I had toward Gareth.

Magnusson sensed what I was doing – sensed, or guessed. He stretched his mind toward the Welshman's shattered one as well. He was faster than I, and managed Gareth's meager psychic locks with the ease of one maneuvering one's own living room with the lights off. All while I fumbled and struggled to gain hold. But I felt first one arm twitch, and then another, and felt the bile rise in Gareth's throat as his body tried to cast me out. It happens every time my kind possesses a new vessel – more or less the only thing *The Exorcist* managed to get right. The body's way of trying to expel that which does not belong, not that it ever does a lick of good. I thought that meant that I stood a chance, that I might yet best Magnusson as we struggled for control.

I was wrong. I never stood a chance.

Because Magnusson didn't need complete control. Couldn't even use it if he did manage to get it. As he himself had told me, "We can scarcely stretch our consciousness enough to control those most dimwitted of humans who happen through our sphere of influence – and even then, only temporarily."

But what he could do, I discovered, was plant a seed.

A kernel.

A single, irresistible suggestion.

I felt it bubble up from the depths of the Welshman's psyche as if the thought were his own. But the malice behind the thought was unmistakable.

Through Gareth's mind's eye, I saw a gun – his gun. Not as a threat, or a defensive weapon, but as a choice, a cure, a salve to soothe his aching soul.

I saw it through his mind's eye as salvation.

And from the sudden giddy hope that surged in Gareth's breast, it was clear he saw it that way too.

I pulled back in time, but only barely. In time to hear the bullet-blast tear through the cavernous room, rather than feel it blow off the Welshman's skull. I clenched back tears, at the senseless loss of life, at the lingering notion implanted by Magnusson (but no less achingly authentic-feeling for it) that it was the only answer, the truest answer. A righteous fuck-you ending to so piteous a life.

That's when I decided I was going to make this motherfucker pay.

Magnusson's dead weight sagged atop me, the needle still buried in my neck. Limbs on top of limbs on top of limbs. I heard him grunt with exertion, felt his fingers scrabble ineffectually at the syringe plunger like a drunk too far gone to operate his keys. Saw by the flicker of the firelight that his lids were heavy, his mismatched eyes all whites. Turns out his powers of persuasion didn't come without a price.

I heaved him off of me. He caught himself before his face met tile, one hand a weak protest against gravity, propping him up. He shook his head, and forced himself onto his hands and knees – although in his case, it was hands and elbows. I heard a snarl build in his throat, saw him eye me with a blinding fury as he gathered to pounce at me once more, his eyes twin suns, radiating malevolence so palpable it stung my cheeks. They blistered and peeled beneath his gaze, and my eyes burn-itched like I'd just peeked at an eclipse, which is when I realized it wasn't anger but juju his baleful glare was sending my way. He was channeling the power of the building flames around us.

Figured I ought to stop him. Thought a mirror would make for some quality playground comeuppance of the rubber-and-glue variety. But I didn't see any goddamn mirror, and I was running out of time. My meat-suit's clothes were smoking, and starting to singe at the edges.

Then I remembered I had a needle chock full of noxious who-the-fuck-knows-what still sticking out of my neck.

Which I rectified, forcibly, by removing it and driving it as hard as I could into Mr. Angry Eyes' shoulder, depressing the plunger with my thumb as the needle breeched his leathery flesh.

Magnusson roared then, and smacked me so hard I sailed clear across the pool, shattering a display case containing a fetal cow with two front-ends on my way to cheek-firsting into the tiles. A tinkle of glass and a water-balloon splash accompanied the skin on ceramic *slap* of my landing, and the bonfire air grew heavy with the dizzy, gag-inducing scent of formaldehyde. The poor dead calf-times-two spun on its side like a top until it skittered to a stop above the floor drain, plugging it and preventing the formaldehyde from draining. Then an ember from the growing fire drifted into the noxious puddle, and, with a sudden, breath-sucking *whoosh*, fire and fumes were one.

Magnusson and I were separated by a wall of flame, he eyeing me, me eyeing him. My borrowed heart soared as I realized the fire had encircled him, cutting off any hope of egress as it transformed itself from minor emergency to full-blown conflagration. Then the spidery bastard, after crouching low a moment like a snake coiling in preparation to strike, hurled himself straight upward into the air, all six hands and no small amount of magic working in perfect synchronicity to launch him far higher than Newtonian physics could possibly have justified. There, he clung with his hand-feet to the rafters, hanging like a bat and glaring down at me in anger and in challenge.

His freakish hand-feet alternated one over the other down the rafter until he was directly overhead. I moved. He followed suit. I ducked through a growing wall of flame – my sleeve over my face in a vain attempt to avoid the bitter sting of the burning formaldehyde fumes in my throat, my nasal passages, my eyes, trying to escape the rigid line of the rafter to which he was confined. But I underestimated the agility of his monstrous, many-limbed form. He swung on two arm-legs first once, then twice, then thrice, and with the agility of a gymnast , leapt from one rafter to the next, catching it such that he once more hung upside-down above me. Grinning. Taunting.

"Do you really think you can escape me, child? I assure you, you cannot. I am in every way your better, and you're trapped beneath me in your lake of fire, with no hope of escape, no options left to you except to surrender, or to succumb. I can wait you out all day if need be, but I suspect the flames will take you far sooner than all that. And when they do, I'll pounce. Perhaps by then this place will be halfway to cinders, and I'll be forced to find another sanctuary in which to house you during your great slumber. Perhaps this place can yet be saved. Either way, you've accomplished nothing but to forestall the inevitable. Well, that, and to force me to take the life of a loyal servant."

"You sure about that?" I shouted, my voice hoarse and weak from the fumes. I fell to my knees amidst the flames. By choice, I told myself, since the air down low was cooler, clearer, and seared the tender tissues of my eyes, my throat, my lungs less. But, the fact is, the air was so thick I couldn't keep my feet.

"Excuse me?" he asked, as if he hadn't heard my words.

I stayed low, belly-crawling across the tile in an attempt to change my position relative to his under the cover of the thick, black roiling smoke. My elbow bumped something and bled warm and wet onto the tile. That something skittered off into the darkness. I pressed a palm to the wound, and cast about for whatever it was that just sliced through clothes and skin like so much nothing, spotted it glinting polished gold some feet away. Like hope; like the beginning of a plan.

I picked up the skim blade. The dull throb in my elbow, so subtle and deep a slice it scarcely even hurt, told me the ancient blade was still diamond-sharp, and as my fingers wrapped around it, searing it to my skin like chicken to a grill, I learned all too well it was still blister-hot from its time spent in the flames. But as it bonded to me, and weapon and flesh became one, I did not cry out, so unwilling was I to display weakness to the monster above.

I called to him again, the blade in my hand lending steel to my voice. "I asked you, are you sure?"

"Am I sure of what?"

"That my delaying is nothing more than forestalling the inevitable?"

"I'm afraid I don't take your meaning," he said. His tone carried a note of condescension, like an adult indulging a small child in its silly, pointless ramblings.

I figured it shouldn't be too hard to push said condescension into anger, and said anger into a rash, ill-conceived response.

"Then let me be clearer, you ugly son of a bitch. Whatever the hell that chunky nastiness was you were gonna stick into me to send me off to my big sleep is now coursing through your system. And as creepy as you look, the parts you're made of are still human. So my guess is, it'll work on you as surely as it'd work on me. So yeah, I'm stuck down here, but the upside is, there ain't no further left for me to fall. So the question you've got to ask yourself is, how's that grip-strength of yours doing? Is the scary hand-monster getting sleepy?"

By the time I finished my taunting little soliloquy, the air was so heavy with roiling, thick black smoke, I couldn't see Magnusson any longer, so I didn't know whether my words had riled him. But then I heard him roar once more, followed by the slap of six hands meeting tile, and I knew he'd decided to come after me, rather than waiting in the rafters for the sandman to whisk him off to sleep.

The smoke pressed in around me. The pool had become a gas chamber, a killing floor – thick dark poison all around. The world was roaring now, and the billows of smoke tinged at their edges in sunset orange as the fire climbed ceilingward, engulfing everything combustible along the way. I couldn't hear Magnusson, couldn't see him. Could barely feel my extremities, I was so dizzy.

Magnusson, despite the dope and smoke, did not seem similarly afflicted. Which is to say, I never even saw him coming.

When he hit me from behind, I went down hard. He made sure of it – two hands on the back of my head, driving it into the tiles as I fell. I felt a snap, and my left eye went dark, my meat-suit's orbital socket cracked and jutting. The sensation of vitreous fluid sticky against my cheek made me gag.

His lower limbs he used to pin my arms and legs, while he slammed my head into the tiles again and again and again. My nose gouted. My lips split. I was dazed, disoriented, and fading fast – losing blood, losing consciousness, losing hope. Two thoughts, slippery and hard to hold onto, were all that kept me going.

One was that Magnusson was too smart, too scientifically and mystically adept, to let me die. And yeah, even predeceased meat-suits can kick the bucket; possession's like the magical equivalent of a defibrillator, capable of shocking the newly dead and relatively undamaged back to life. But if that meat-suit sustains enough damage – as this one was on its way to – it'll give up the ghost all over again. Meaning *me*. When that happens, the invading consciousness is expelled. If we're talking demonic possession, their consciousness simply returns to their physical form, possession for them is more projection than anything. But Collectors have no bodies of our own, so what winds up happening in instances of death is we're reseeded someplace else at random, stuffed forcibly into someone half a world away. These days, the odds were one in six I'd wind up in China. Though I confess, however reseeding works, it never seems to track with expectations. Twice now, for example, I've ended up in Guam. The reseeding process sucks, because death for a Collector, while not final, is painful as all get-out, but it'd be a ticket out of here at least, and Magnusson knew it. Since he'd gone to all the trouble to bring me here, he wasn't about to let me off so easy. He'd bash my meat-suit's head in until it had barely enough juice left for me to slump drooling on a chair, let alone body-hop away, and then he'd hook me up to all manner of life-saving machines, leaving me trapped and sedated for an eternity, or near enough.

The other thought was that I could feel his grip-strength weakening. And if his drugs were taking hold, they might provide me with the opening I needed.

When he slammed me once more into the tiles, I shuddered and went slack. I knew he'd have to stop playing Gallagher to this meat-suit's melon long enough to make sure he hadn't taken things too far, and I was right. He nudged me. I didn't move. He rolled me over. I flopped wet-noodle against the oven-warm tile, my one good eye half-lidded despite the scorching, toxic air. He recoiled, startled, when he saw the skim blade in my hand, but then he nudged it with a knuckle on one of his lower limbs, laughing when he realized it was attached.

He stepped back a bit, his form hazy from smoke, and suddenly out of my reach. I wondered if something tipped him to my possum act. But then he rose on four of his six hands, and uttered something rapid-fire and guttural in a language I could not understand. I heard an ungodly shriek in the darkness, but in reverse, the kind of noise you might make by sucking in, not blowing out. And then a mighty wind kicked up, the flames that engulfed the baths began to gutter, and the smoke around us to clear.

As I lay there, trying my damndest to see what was going on without moving anything but my eyeball lest I tip my hand, I was puzzled – puzzled and amazed. Amazed because this man was without a doubt the most powerful mage I'd ever come across, and puzzled because all magic, from the smallest of location spells to breaking the bonds of servitude to hell, requires a sacrifice. The former, blood. The latter, a tainted human soul. The through-line between the two being life.

Then, as the smoke cleared as surely as via a fume hood, I saw where it was going, and what that wretched noise was, and I realized what Magnusson had done.

Gareth's corpse thrashed atop the pool tiles, his limbs contorting and his ruined, gunshot head thrown back as his thick boxer lips parted wide and drew in an impossible, endless breath of soot and flame and swirling smoke. His body – sacrifice and containment vessel both – bloated and rippled as it struggled to contain the conflagration. His clothes rent. His eyes ruptured. His naked flesh, veined black, stretched to the breaking point and beyond, splitting like an overripe tomato, and glistening wet black like campfire coals after a rain. By the time the fire was contained, he was a massive whale of a man, gray-black and oozing, left to slowly deflate as the firestorm inside him subsided.

The fire contained, this self-made monster, Dr. Frankenstein and his unholy progeny both, grabbed a fistful of my shirt and hoisted me upward. He swayed a bit as he did, staggering as he regained his balance, his strength sapped by the drugs and magic. He said to me, short of breath and slurring: "I confess, Mr. Thornton, you had more fight in you than I suspected. If you can hear me in there, I commend you. But as you can see, your efforts, as in Los Angeles, have proven futile. But fear not; you shall slumber soon enough. Perhaps you'll even come to understand that for the kindness that it is. After all, is an eternity of dream not preferable to one spent in slavery to hell?"

It was a fair point. An angle I'd not considered. So I thought about it for a good half-second before I decided to roll the dice and stick with hell.

Then I stabbed him in the chest.

He released me when I came to life in his hands, but too late to deflect my blow. The skim blade pierced the desiccated flesh of his chest like scissors going through paper, and I felt his sternum beneath it shatter.

And that's when things got *really* weird.

Once the blade passed through Magnusson's chest, it began to thrum in my hand, as if coursing with an electric current. Magnusson's eyes went wide, and then clenched shut as the blade burst out of his back, shattering his spinal column to dust. At the blade's end was the shriveled little walnut that passed as Magnusson's soul – no light left in it, no experiences washing over me as it separated from his body. Removed from its earthly vessel, said vessel began to crumble like a mummy exposed to the humidity of the open air after centuries spent entombed.

We fell to the ground, his flagging strength no longer capable of supporting my weight. As we landed, he slid down the blade, and then my arm. My hand was clean through his chest, blade still extended, the dead husk of his soul impaled upon it.

Brown faded to ash. Firm became fragile became so much dust. Soon, I was lying broken and bloodied but alone in the charred remains of the dead man's office, a tumorous nodule skewered like morbid fondue-fodder at the edge of my blade, and a bloated, blackened Gareth beside me.

I lowered the blade, raised my free hand to Magnusson's soul. It crumbled like chalk between my fingers.

My vision dimmed. My meat-suit failing.

I slipped away.

Exquisite. Excruciating. As if some sadistic needle-fingered creature was tearing every nerve out of my meat-suit's body one by one like a gardener yanking up a particularly pernicious root, and running them across a bed of lemon-juice-soaked sandpaper before lighting them on fire.

It took moments.

It took forever.

And then, next thing I knew, I was in Guam.

4.

"Good evening, Collector. You're looking well."

She was lying, I was pretty sure; I must've looked like shit. My leg-wound seeping lymph through its bandages, my thick dark hair on end, my meat-suit's early-twenties baby-face dusted here and there with patchwork stubble. Of course, the fact that Lilith was lying to me was no surprise.

That she was *complimenting* me, on the other hand, was a major cause for concern. It set off big red lights and klaxons in my borrowed brain. Then again, that could have been the booze. Cause I'm not going to lie, by the time she tracked me down, I was pretty fucking drunk.

I opened my eyes and lifted my head up off my threadbare beach towel, propping myself up on one elbow, which dug into the powder-fine sand through the thin layer of tropical-fish-printed fabric. The sun was setting over the Philippine Sea, a disc of lava that bled orange across the horizon on either side where it touched. As the green afterimage of the brilliant sunset faded, I saw that Lilith was standing some ten feet down the beach from me, her creamy white skin untouched by sun despite our tropical environs. And my, how much skin she showed.

She wore a string bikini of royal blue, stunning against her pale white skin, three scant triangles covering her naughty bits, intended, it seemed, more to heighten anticipation than out of any sense of the demure. A gauzy white sarong was tied about her waist and fluttered in the southern breeze, as did her thick mane of lustrous red. Her feet were bare. Nails painted crimson, hands and feet. My footprints cratered the white sand in a meandering dotted line from trail head to where I lay just above the high tide line, churning the beach in a rough circle around my chosen spot, but Lilith stood among a field of pristine white.

The beach was empty but for the two of us. Faifa'i Beach is secluded even by Guam's standards, a jounce along a pitted gravel road into the jungle and a hike up the narrow cliff-walk trail past the rusted anti-aircraft gun leftover from World War II, and across a narrow wooden footbridge over roiling surf. Most of its visitors don't relish the thought of making the sun-drunk trek back to their four-wheel-drives in darkness, which means they clear out early. Me, I don't give a shit. If I fall and break my neck on the walk back, smart money says I wind up right back in Guam anyway.

Besides, I wasn't planning on walking back. My plan consisted of polishing off this-here bottle of rum which, I was surprised to discover, I was well on my way to doing, and passing out till morning. Far as I was concerned, the universe owed me a drunken night beneath the stars in a balmy tropical paradise after the cosmic bitch-slap that was reseeding. When my last meat-suit kicked, I found myself eyes-open on the floor, puking blood and grand-mal seizing in the middle of some cheesy island bar. Patrons huddled over me, eyes wide as those of the lacquered fish that graced the walls, while a short, lined Japanese woman dressed all casual and fanny-packed like she was on vacation held my shoulders down and wailed. By the time the ambulance arrived, my trembling ceased. I stopped puking before we pulled into the hospital. But despite my best efforts, I couldn't convince the docs to let me go, nor the poor, distraught woman who – language barrier aside – I was pretty sure was my new meat-suit's wife to let me out of her sight. So after a night spent tossing and turning under her watchful, worried eye, I gave up on my new ride – a salt-and-pepper Japanese man of maybe fifty – and hopped a ride in the fresh-faced, indigenous Chamorro kid with whom I shared a room. He was maybe twenty-two or -three, and from what I could gather, came in sometime yesterday thanks to a sea-urchin-stick in his left leg while cliff-diving with his friends. I waited till my meat-suit's missus ducked out to use the bathroom, and then body-hopped on over, puking in the trashcan beside his bed and pulling his privacy curtain before walking, flip-flopped and board-shorts-clad, right out of the hospital. I lifted a wallet out of some dumb-ass tourist's beach bag, and then spent twenty minutes trying to track down a toothbrush and some toothpaste to get the taste of vomit out of my mouth, finally hitting paydirt at a strip-mall drugstore with signs in English, Mandarin, and Japanese. Woulda bought a pack of cigarettes there, too, but I feel shitty smoking in a meat-suit that's gonna keep on breathing once I vamoose. Better to save the death-sticks for the already dead. Once I was minty fresh, I rounded out my shopping spree with a bag of fast-food burgers and a bottle of rum, and set out to find a nice, quiet patch of sand where I could drink away the memory of dying yet again.

I shoulda known Lilith would come along all pretty-like and ruin my fun.

"Evenin' yourself, Lily," I said. "Pull up some beach and stay awhile."

She hates it when I call her Lily. It's kinda why I call her Lily. But this time, instead of correcting me, she just plopped down on the beach beside me. We sat awhile in silence, our eyes trained on the horizon, watching as the sun was slowly extinguished by the sea. As darkness descended, she plucked the rum bottle from its resting place between my knees, and took a long, slow pull. Then she offered it to me. I drank as well. Her lips tasted of peaches.

"Lily, are you all right?"

She took so long in responding, I began to wonder if she would. "The Truce is broken," she finally said. "The peace has failed. The heavens are at war."

I digested her words a moment, took another swig of rum. "Funny – you don't sound too happy about that. There was a time you looked to spark that selfsame war."

She looked at me. Her eyes were pained. "There was, indeed. For centuries, it's all I thought about. And if given the chance, I'll regret that fact for centuries to come. It was a foolish act of rebellion against an absent father whose crass withholding I should have long ago accepted. It's mortifying, really, the lengths to which I was willing to go for just a moment of His attentions – even if those attentions were in the service of punishing me. Now, I realize the cost is simply too high – and the payoff far too meager."

I was taken aback by her words, so blunt and so unguarded. Not once since New York, when she conspired to jump-start the End Times by framing an innocent girl for a vicious crime and attempting to condemn her soul to hell, had she ever admitted what she'd done. Not once had she expressed remorse. I was beginning to think she was incapable.

And yet…

If there's one thing I should have learned in all my years with Lilith, it's that she has a limitless capacity to surprise.

"If heaven and hell are at war, what's to happen to the human world?"

"It's difficult to say. This is but one of many realms, one of many potential battlefields. And this war has little to do with humankind, so as yet they remain untargeted. But of course, no realm is safe, and none of them will remain untouched. Already, many demons of the lower orders have taken the declaration of war as tacit permission to act on their more base desires without fear of reproach from their superiors. Surely you've heard the reports of mass rape and roving death squads out of central Africa, where resource-scarcity, ethnic divides, and political uncertainty leave some among the local populace ripe for plucking, and all too eager to succumb to demonic influence. Greed and envy have reached the boiling point throughout the whole of the Western world, where corporations who recognize no borders seem intent on choking the life from the very people they used to rely upon as customers. False prophets abound in the Middle East, preaching doctrines of violent intolerance. And all the while the gluttonous masses try to pack the gaping wound of their aching souls with yet more useless shit because they too can sense the shift – some paying heed to the hateful whispers of those demons who reside in dreams when that fails, and taking up arms against their fellow sufferers. In the absence of the constant ministrations of the Maker's many servants, your world has been abandoned to the base corruption that lies beneath. It's a veritable feast of sin – perpetrated not as part of any grand design, but instead by lone operators for sport – and it threatens to consume your kind just as surely as any overt offensive."

"So what are you and I supposed to do? Business as usual? Hunker down and wait it out?"

Lilith smiled, but there was no mirth in it. She looked sad. Tired. Broken. In spite of all we'd been through – or perhaps because of it – I actually felt bad for her. "I wish I could tell you it was either, because the truth is, your current assignment is far from usual, and farther still from safe. I understand you had some fun in London since last we spoke."

I misread, got defensive. "Lily, listen, what happened in London wasn't my fault. That crazy motherfucker came looking for *me*. I swear to God, I had no intention of killing him, let alone the faintest inkling I even *could*."

Lilith raised her hands, a placating gesture. "Relax, Collector. You're welcome to swear upon your Maker all you like, but no one's accusing you of any wrongdoing, and anyway, in my experience, it's far more satisfying to swear *at* Him than *upon* Him. I only bring up your recent unpleasantness because it has a direct bearing on today's business. I trust you know who and what your victim was?"

"He went by the name of Magnusson," I replied, though thinking back, I couldn't help but fixate on Gareth the Welshman's thrashing, bloated corpse and wonder if I'd left one victim in my wake that day or two. I took another glug of rum and wiped the excess from my lips with the back of one sand-gritted hand. My guilt receded, but only a bit. "And I hear tell he was Brethren."

"Magnusson is but one of many names he has assumed throughout the millennia," she replied. "But yes, he was Brethren. And until yesterday, we were unaware his kind could be killed at all, let alone by the lowly likes of you. That, and the Truce by which we until recently abided, were all that prevented the Nine from being hunted down and slaughtered. Their very existence flies in the face of the natural order, and represents a slight to the Maker and the Adversary both. Have you any notion how you did it?"

I thought it over a sec. "Wasn't me. He had a skim blade lying around. In the scuffle, I managed to get my hands on it and put it through his chest. My guess is, whatever wacky demon mojo those things carry did him in."

But Lilith shook her head. "You guess wrong. That skim blade was, in fact, no such thing. It was a replica; sharp, beautiful, and expertly forged, but by human hands. The original upon which it was based was rendered so much slag by the ritual that freed the Nine. What's left of it was chiseled free from the stone altar onto which it fused, and interred alongside the Ark of the Covenant at... Ah, but that's a story for another time.

The point is, the blade you wielded was not the instrument of Magnusson's demise – *you* were."

"But the blade… it, I don't know, *hummed* or something."

"So I understand. The working theory is that what you experienced is simple conductance, nothing more."

My eyes narrowed. Suspicious. "What do you mean, *So I understand*? How could you, when you weren't even there?"

"Whatever protection spell Magnusson had erected around his lair collapsed when you… when he expired. Since then, our chronomancers have had their run of the place, casting their minds' eyes backward to generate as complete an account of the scene as they can manage. As you well know, their discipline is inexact at best. They truck mostly in impressions, sensations, and static images, but in this case, you and Magnusson, and his manservant in particular, threw off enough trauma-echoes to afford them a fairly detailed picture. That's why you're being lauded rather than strung up, by the way. And it's what makes you so valuable now. You've accomplished what few can. What even fewer still would dare, particularly now."

"What do you mean?"

"The Great Truce may have rendered the Brethren off-limits, but that doesn't mean we've been ignoring them entirely. We've kept tabs on them throughout history, to ensure they do not exert undue influence on the course of human events, or through their actions pose a material threat to hell's dominion. Over the course of our surveillance, a number of them have… reverted, shall we say, to scarcely more than feral beasts, and as such, we've left them to wander as their instincts and hunger led them. But others have grown stronger as they've weathered the storm of ages, amassing fortunes, building empires, befriending the great movers of the world, abetting some of humankind's greatest atrocities. They, we've kept a close eye on indeed."

"Like Magnusson."

Lilith nodded. "Magnusson is one of four kept under watchful eye," she said. "Though you needn't concern yourselves with the others – yet."

My stomach dropped. I was beginning to see where this was going. "Yet?"

"Last night," she said, "once word of your little adventure in London Town spread throughout the Depths, the powers decided – after no small amount of debating, I'm assured – that Magnusson's move against you constituted a significant enough breach of the terms of the Truce, and his death a significant enough demonstration of vulnerability, that the remainder of the Brethren were to be eliminated."

"And?"

"And apparently Magnusson's not the only member of his kind to have taken precautions. The other three members of the Brethren whose whereabouts were known were moved on twelve hours ago by a small cadre of foot-soldiers. None survived."

"That's good, right? That means we got 'em."

"You misunderstand, Collector. None of the foot-soldiers survived. There were forty-two in total, all lost."

I puffed my cheeks, and blew out slow. Wished I had a goddamn cigarette. A year and change back, I killed two demons half by accident, and it earned me one hell of a rep in the Depths. The Brethren took out forty-two. "How many of the Brethren were killed?"

"None, and not for lack of trying. Seems your blade-through-the-heart routine only works if you're, well, *you*."

"Come again?"

Lilith flushed then, closer to flustered than I'd ever seen her. "Not you *specifically*, you understand, your *kind*. Collectors. You see, whatever the Brethren are now, they're human at their core, and their souls – such as they are – will only present themselves to one with the ability to collect them."

"You're fucking kidding me."

"I assure you, I am not. In all your years, you must have wondered why hell would employ lowly monkey middlemen to do their dirty work when every demon in creation is chomping at the bit to get their cloven hooves on a real, live human soul. The fact is, they physically cannot access a living soul. If they could, it would be a bloodbath, which is why Collectors are employed. Your kind are mediators of sorts – final arbiters, so to speak. Or at least that's how the role was envisioned to be. Ever since the last Great War, and the shaky Truce that's followed, the autonomy of Collectors has been on the wane. Hence you having me."

"So you're saying only a Collector can kill a member of the Brethren."

"That's right."

"And what? We're gonna mount up a Collector army and march on the remaining three?"

"Something like that," she said, "with only two corrections."

"What's that?"

"Correction the first: there is no army. It's been decided the assignment falls to you and you alone."

"Are you out of your goddamn mind? I barely killed *one* of these crazy fuckers, and in case you failed to notice, I managed to get myself evicted from a perfectly good skin-suit doing it. How the hell am I supposed to take on *three*?"

"Actually, that brings me to correction the second," Lilith said, pursing her perfect lips a moment before continuing. "I'm afraid in light of recent events, we're no longer merely targeting those three."

"Come again?"

"What I'm saying, Collector, is it's been decreed that you're to kill all nine."

5.

When I kicked open the flimsy screen door that marked the entrance to the dingy, nameless bar, the doorframe parallelogrammed a moment, its joints squealing in protest. My shadow projected against a field of sunset-orange as I stepped across the threshold. Then the rusted hinge caught and slammed it shut behind me with a nail-on-chalkboard creak.

A bracket hung above the door, the kind you'd hang a bell off of to announce the arrival of new customers. But all that hung from it was a frayed piece of twine, knotted at both ends. The topmost knot was a frizzy-haired bun jutting through the bracket. The twine was kinked above the bottom knot – thanks, I'd imagine, to the erstwhile bell – so that it hung off to one side, the idle strands poking through the bunny-hole to form the knot and feathering down to nothing just below. It put me in mind of a strung-up voodoo doll. I wondered if somewhere in the world there was a full-sized hanged man to match.

The absence of a bell didn't matter much. The door itself announced me fine. But even if it hadn't, the three men inside the bar – for they were all men, and all burly, stress-jumpy, and armed, shooting pool beneath a ceiling fan that shook, palsied, as it spun – would no doubt have noticed me. This was their bar, after all, or, at least, their employer's, and to own the truth, it wasn't even a real bar. A careful observer would note that no one ever came or went from the property but for they and their cohorts, and the neon *Open* sign might well have been dead when they purchased it, for all the use it got. The bar itself sat empty and unused – no old-timers thousand-yarding the bottoms of their glasses, no dolled-up women preened and plucked and perched atop the barstools in front of it, eyeing their lipstick in the soot-streaked, dirt-specked Sauza mirror mounted crooked on the wall. The men here were not interested in the women or the drink that any bar worth frequenting promised, or at least heartily suggested. What they were interested in was underneath. A system of tunnels, leading deep into the desert in four directions from this squat adobe structure plopped smack in the middle of hot dry nowhere, each popping out a mile or two past the sad, desperate mud-caked trickle that is the Rio Grande. See, this glorified tent of mud and rough-hewn beams sat smack in the middle of a small, landlocked peninsula of Mexico that jutted northward into Texas thanks to the meandering line of the river that marked their border, which meant that the United States lay just north *and* east *and* west from where I stood. The men inside the bar were here to see the tunnels leading there were well-protected – and the local officials who stopped by well-bribed – so they'd stay open to serve as pipeline for the parade of drugs, guns, and strung-out little girls the Xolotl Cartel provided to the fat wallets and bottomless appetites of their American neighbors.

Come to think of it, it might have made more sense to possess one of the aforementioned local officials. Then maybe they wouldn't be looking at me so bug-eyed for showing up unannounced. Eyes wide in purple-gray hollows. Sallow skin, sickly-hued and grease-shiny from lack of sleep, pulled taut across their cheeks and their wifebeater-bared shoulders. Muscle-corded arms rigid at their sides, fingers splayed and twitching as each in turn calculated the odds of getting to their piece before I could put them down.

Oh, did I not mention I was carrying an assault rifle? Well, I was. Which might explain these fellas' wiggins.

It was a Mexican-Army-issue FX-05 Xiuhcoatl carbine, which made sense, on account of my new meat-suit being Mexican Army, though he and I were in civilian clothes at the moment on account of I'm not *completely* stupid. He was a dark-skinned, wiry thirty-something man with hard eyes, a black bottle-brush mustache, and a jagged scar that traced his cheekbone from right eye to age-lined dimple. Given all he'd seen in his years at the front lines of the drug war, it's hard to believe that dimple came from smiling. His gun was a boxy, industrial, matte-black carbon-fiber motherfucker with thirty rounds in its magazine, and though it was capable of going fully automatic, at present it was set to three-round bursts. If it weren't, and I were forced to pull the trigger, the magazine would likely be empty before the first shell casing hit the ground, and these lovely gentlemen would wind up a fine paste. Since I needed them alive, three rounds a pop was as much stopping power as I was willing to risk, and even still, I was aiming for their knees.

These men were not Brethren. But I had reason to believe they might know where I could find one. And that reason's name was Lilith.

"Take a look at this," she said to me back on that beach in Guam, producing a paper from God-knows-where. It's disconcerting, I'll tell you, spending one's days with beings whose physical form is simply a projection of how they wish to look. From where I'm sitting, Lilith doesn't look a day over thirty, her flawless porcelain skin on ravishing display thanks to a bikini so small that if it were made of postage stamps, it wouldn't get a four-page letter around the block. And yet she's been around since the dawn of time, since Paradise was a for-serious place and not a pitch to sell time-shares, and somewhere on her person, she'd secreted an entire fucking newspaper. Best to not ask where, says I. Point is, out it came just after she said I'd have to make with all the Brethren-killing as if she'd been just waiting for the moment, and when she saw me squinting by the pale light of the rising moon as I tried to read it, she snapped her fingers and conjured a steady orange flame. It gave off no heat, and despite the ocean breeze it never flickered, so my guess was, it wasn't a magic trick so much as showing off. A flame appeared because Lilith elected to project one, not because she'd conjured fire.

Come to think of it, that's a way cooler magic trick than if she'd simply conjured fire.

The paper was a copy of the Houston Chronicle, dated three days prior. The top story was about yet another bloody border-town body dump, courtesy of the Mexican drug war. You know the kind; we've all read about them. Heads and hands removed. Bodies left someplace public, in this case, the busy north-south route of US Highway 83, where it jags eastward along the border, to send a message. No witnesses. No IDs on the vics. Gruesome, senseless, and unfortunately these days, a dime a dozen.

I scanned past it, looking for whatever it was Lilith wanted me to find. But when I made to flip the page, she shook her head. "No, that's the one," she said.

I skimmed. Missed the point. Four columns on the front page – complete with lurid shots of tarp-draped bodies and pavement stained red-brown – and another eight or so pic-free buried in the middle of the "A" section. I combed through a second time, Lilith watching lips pursed. Then I folded it over in frustration and said, "This thing's five thousand words long, Lily, how about you just give me the bullets? Starting with why the hell I should give a shit about a bunch of rival dirt-bag drug-runners slaughtering each other?"

"Well, for one," she said, clearly annoyed I hadn't deduced what she wanted me to, "those victims weren't gun-thugs or drug-runners. Their clothes were tattered, filthy. They weren't armed. And what little's left of them suggests malnourishment and poor health-care, likely stretching back to birth. They were illegal immigrants, who'd probably paid a pretty penny for the privilege of being smuggled safely across the border, likely utilizing the same pipeline as the cartels, sure, but that alone is not enough to make them a target to a rival cartel. For two, you'll note the bodies were discovered on the US side of the border. Any cartel smart enough to stay in business is too smart to drag the US military into their fight with so brazen and foolhardy a move as that; to a one, their high-profile body dumps have all taken place south of the Rio Grande. And for three, those heads and hands? They weren't sawed off to prevent identification, though I'm sure that's what the perpetrator wanted anyone who happened by them to think. They were gnawed off. Eaten, perhaps. As, my friends among the Fallen tell me, were their hearts, though *that* fact didn't make the paper. Purposefully withheld, I'm sure, by authorities too foolish to realize the perpetrator or perpetrators of this horrific act are beyond the reach of their justice system, not to mention beyond their ken."

I fell silent a moment, listening to the waves roll in, while I digested what she told me. When I finally spoke, it was to say, "Whatever did this ate their fucking *heads*?"

"Maybe," she said. "But I doubt it. The flesh and bone would provide little by way of sustenance for a creature subsisting on the life-force of living beings, though I will admit that cheek meat, well-braised, is quite delicious. Brain, heart, and blood are all far better. Eyes, too. Spinal column will do in a pinch. So my guess is, the hearts were consumed fresh, and the heads removed so that the brains might be eaten at the perpetrator's leisure. Though skulls are difficult to break open, they are quite well-suited as storage vessels for the gray matter inside, and cellared properly, they *will* keep."

"Jesus," I said, more to myself than to her. Her utter lack of revulsion at the topic of eating human heads and hearts chilled me as thoroughly as the gruesome acts themselves. Yet another reminder that, despite her appearances, Lilith was pretty fucking far from human.

"Mind your tongue, Collector." As if *I'm* the one whose utterances offended.

"I'm just saying. There's gotta be someone else who can do this."

Lilith sighed. "There's a war on, Collector. Each of us is being asked to do our part. I would have thought ridding humankind of these creatures who've been feeding off the living for centuries would appeal to that pesky conscience of yours. You'll be eliminating untold evil, preventing no shortage of human suffering. I won't deny the assignment is high-risk, but even if I could convince the powers that be to reconsider, what are the chances your next task would prove so palatable? This is your chance to make a difference in the world, to fight the good fight for a change. See it as the gift it is, would you? For once, just be a good little soldier, and do what you're told."

She was right. I knew she was. But that didn't mean I had to like it.

"So this thing," I asked hesitantly, wanting yet not wanting to know the answer, "is it one of the members of the Brethren the Fallen moved against?"

"You mean does it know you're coming? No. Its very existence is, at present, my own conjecture, pieced together based upon the evidence at hand. And I've only the vaguest of notions where you might find it. But I am certain that I'm right. And if I am, this is one of several that dropped off hell's radar centuries ago; gone mad and feral, we'd assumed, since until recently we had no idea they could die. It seemed to me you might have better luck in hunting a quarry unsuspecting of your approach. The first time out, at least."

"Okay, then, how do I find this as yet hypothetical quarry?"

Lilith nodded toward the newspaper once more. "There's another story in that issue I've reason to believe is connected to the bodies found on 83."

"What's that?"

"Check the police blotter."

This one was easier to spot. Seems at three AM the morning prior to the paper's release, a known lieutenant of the Xolotl Cartel by the name of Javier Guerrera who currently sat at seventh on Mexico's Most Wanted List wandered blood-soaked and panicked into a police station in McAllen, Texas, babbling nonsense and insisting he be locked up. Local PD kindly obliged. Guerrera now awaited extradition, said the piece, at the Willacy Detention Center in Raymondville, Texas – the largest detention center in the country for illegal immigrants, which also functions as a high-security prison for the most dangerous and recidivistic of border-breaching offenders.

Beside the blurb ran two pictures, one taken from his Wanted profile, and the other a mug shot taken upon his arrest. In the former, his hair was black as Texas crude. In the latter, it was white from root to tip, though the man beneath the shock of white couldn't have been more than twenty-seven.

It made me wonder what he'd seen, and where exactly he'd seen it.

So to Raymondville I went.

The mission was a delicate one. They don't let people wander willy-nilly into a maximum-security prison, so my preferred method of possessing a recently dead meat-suit wasn't gonna cut it. Guerrera was in isolation on account of his position in the Xolotl Cartel – both to ensure his safety prior to extradition, and to guard against those who might wish to break him out. So to get to him I needed access. I needed credentials. I needed a ride no one would dare question if he asked to speak to Guerrera.

I figured the warden would do just fine.

Distance isn't a factor when body-hopping. To leap from one vessel to another, my kind must travel through the Nothingness of the In-Between, which is both infinite and membrane thin. So to us, the trip's the same whether it's five feet or five thousand miles.

What we *do* need is a target, a person in mind. Something to stretch our consciousness toward, and latch onto once we find it. And I'm not talking, like, conjure an image of George Clooney in your head and blammo – you're there. You need a location to fix on as well, or no dice.

Which is why, once the sun came up over Guam and I stumbled, stomach churning and head throbbing, from the beach, my board shorts grit-sticky from booze-sweat and sand, I popped five damn dollars into a payphone and gave ol' Willacy a ring, and asked to speak to the man in charge.

They don't call him the warden, as it turns out, because to their mind, Willacy isn't a prison. It's a "privately managed detention facility," and he's the goddamned CEO. I wonder if the inmates – or "detainees," or "involuntary guests," or whatever the hell they call them – would agree. Maybe they could register their nomenclature-based complaints on their comment cards once their stay was finished.

We never call things what we mean anymore. The obtuse language somehow makes the sharp edges and harsh angles of life easier to swallow. A candy-coated shard of jagged glass that's sweet on the public's tongue before it tears apart their insides. A pat on the back with one hand while the other steals our wallets or our souls. And people are all too willing to let it happen, because any insulation from the big and scary that surrounds them is welcome, no matter how obvious a lie it proves to be.

Whatever they call the guy, they were understandably reluctant to patch me through to him, at least until I mentioned I had information on a planned break-out for one of their inmates. The corporate shill manning the phone – who called himself a "public liaison" when he answered – didn't sound like he believed me. Maybe if I called it an "unplanned departure," he would have. Instead I offered up a name – Javier Guerrera. And a time – midnight local.

Amazing what name-dropping a Xolotl Cartel lieutenant will do. Because if there's one thing a big, soulless corporation recognizes, it's another big, soulless corporation. And make no mistake, the only thing keeping the Xolotl Cartel off the Fortune 500 is the nature of the products they peddle.

The warden answered without so much as identifying himself, instead barking a gruff, "Who is this? Where are you calling from?" And I'm pretty sure, given the lag time before I was connected, there were a dozen or so people listening in on the call, some no doubt intent on tracing its source.

Let 'em, I thought. Ain't a security camera around with a sight-line on this payphone, and in the unlikely event they manage to track down the kid whose body I'm tooling around in, all the way in little old Guam, anything he tells 'em is gonna make him sound all cuckoo crazypants.

Instead of answering him, I bleated: "Oh, God – they're here!" and dropped the receiver. And then, mentally fixing on the voice I'd just heard on the other end of the receiver, in some bland office in some bland facility in a broad, flat patch of brown and gray just off Route 77 in Texas, I threw myself at him with all I had.

For a moment, there was a tinny, echoing nothing – like dropping off from anesthesia – and next thing I knew, I was in a tipped-over faux-leather office chair, tasseled loafers aimed soles-to-ceiling, and the back of my head smarting something fierce from where it smacked against the institutional vinyl tile floor. Been happening more and more of late – the body-hopping was getting easier, the force previously required now enough to knock folks back. Even the subsequent meat-suit nausea hasn't been so bad, I think. But as soon as the thought arced across my mind, Mr. CEO here's stomach revolted, and I barely made it to the dented metal trash bin beside his desk before his lunch of enchiladas came up.

It was just past 7am in Guam when I dropped my quarters into the payphone. That made it 4pm or so Texas-time. Sunlight slanted oven-hot through vinyl-blinded windows. Beyond them, ten enormous pill-shaped Kevlar tents studded the three football-fields of fence-looped gray dirt in two rows of five, with paved paths bleached pale gray linking them together like a circuit board. At the outside end of every oblong structure, nearest the perimeter fence, was a small paved yard – some empty, some milling with brown-skinned men. If there were women, they weren't housed within sight of my new meat-suit's office, which appeared to be housed in a low-slung building of more quotidian design than the tents outside – less funky marshmallow prison, more dull-as-dirt industrial park.

I couldn't help but notice it was surrounded by razor-wire just the same.

Ortiz. Larry Ortiz, so said the nameplate on his desk, at any rate. If I had to guess, I'd say the *Ortiz* was to appease the critics of the facility, who claimed its very existence was racially motivated – and the *Larry* was to appease the white-faced white-hairs who kept on funding it and didn't want anybody "too ethnic," in their parlance, to be in charge. A portly man in a too-tight dress shirt, unbuttoned at the collar, and iron-creased jeans. The lone picture on his desk showed two smiling kids, a smiling wife, and a round, graying, florid man in a Stetson and cowboy boots, a chambray shirt and jeans.

Me, I figured.

I considered paging Ortiz's admin or secretary or whatever, but I didn't know if he had one. Plus, his office phone was so damned complicated, I couldn't figure out how. So instead, I marched straight out of his office, and declared to the perfume-drenched pile of teased-up Texas hair and tits behind the desk outside, "I need to see Guerrera. *Now.*"

I half-expected her – or the guards she summoned to escort me – to ask me why. To tell me we had three Guerreras in custody, and they didn't know which one I meant. To flat-out refuse to take me to him. But they didn't.

Sometimes, it pays to be the boss.

Nor did they take me to his cell. They brought Guerrera to me. Or rather, had him waiting in an interrogation room when I arrived – handcuffed to a table, an empty chair opposite for me. There was no cop-show two-way mirror. Just a table, two chairs, a corner-mounted video camera, and one very frightened man. And then me.

The two guards who'd escorted me made to enter the room, but I waved them off without a word. They took up posts in the hall, on either side of the door, which I promptly shut.

Guerrera did not look well. His skin was pale and sheathed in sweat. His exposed flesh had the look of having been picked at, his forearms furrowed with fingernail scratches, a constellation of tiny half-moons on his cheeks a scabrous red. His hair was a mangy shock of white, as if he'd been pulling it out in clumps. His eyes darted around the room – vigilant, paranoid. His fingers drummed a rat-a-tat atop the metal table. Sitting still – being chained – was torture for him, it was clear. His finger-tapping soon spread to his feet, and as I fixed my gaze upon him, he began to rock back and forth, his breath coming so quickly through gritted teeth I actually worried for his health.

Then I remembered he was human garbage, responsible for no shortage of deaths, dismemberments, and drug-dependencies in his tenure with the Xolotl Cartel.

It helped, a little.

I approached the table. He watched – nervous, rapt – as I dragged the cheap metal chair over to the corner of the room, its legs squealing against the painted concrete floor. I said nothing to him, nor he to me. Then I climbed atop the chair and, after a moment's fiddling, yanked the wire out of the security camera. His eyes went wide with fear of a different sort. Immediate, explainable. Human in origin. In his mind, I was a bad man, here to do bad things to him. Guerrera understood that all too well. Though usually, he was on the other side of the table. Or the ax. Or the flamethrower.

The man had quite the colorful file. Made whatever scared the piss and pigment out of him twice as oogly-boogly in my mind as I might have thought it otherwise.

When I returned from the corner, leaving the chair behind and circling the table toward him, he spat and said, "I tell you *nothing.*"

"That's all right," I said. "You don't have to."

My hand found his chest and reached inside. As my fingers wrapped around his corrupted soul, his eyes widened yet further – his face a mask of pain and disbelief.

The interrogation room fell away, replaced by a swirling black morass and a lifetime of experiences. A village, slaughtered. Countless women, raped and killed. Enough coke to fell an army, blown off the naked skin of men and women both. A young boy who looked like him, into whose bed he snuck a time or two while his wife slept. And countless nights of Gulf breezes and swanky parties, on yachts, in palaces, on island beaches. As if this bastard hadn't a care. As if his conscience weren't touched by all he'd done, his heart full in those moments of laughter and light.

Again and again, though, one memory bubbled unbidden to the surface of his mind. Of a tunnel – dirt and darkness. Of men and women screaming. A low growl. Teeth gnashing in the black. The popcorn pop of gunfire. The metallic tang of discharged firearms and blood. Cool, clean air as the dirt above gave way to starry night, but still, the creature followed. And then the wet, sticky sound of flesh ripping from bone.

And then running. And then here.

One phrase over and over, a sturdy stitch that held the tattered scraps of memory together: *El Chupacabra*.

I released his soul from my grasp. He collapsed, gasping, to the table, tears streaming down his cheeks. Tears streamed down mine as well, and my borrowed flesh trembled with the fresh hell of its doubly borrowed memories. Like Guerrera, I couldn't stop the tears. My strength comes from knowing not to even bother trying.

The two of us sobbing, I slammed him backward in his chair once more. His eyes were so full of fear – all the more so for seeing the echo of it on my borrowed cheeks. Cheeks built for smiling, not for this. It was clear to me he didn't understand. Why I was crying. What it was we shared.

I didn't need him to.

What I needed was a location.

Memories aren't like a road map. They're messy. Partial. Untrustworthy. I needed him to unpack them for me. To make sense of them. So I reached my hand back into his chest and squeezed until he wailed like an injured child. Then I let go and asked him questions. He answered – mostly lies. I squeezed again. And asked again. He changed his tune. Screamed so hard I bet he tasted blood.

It took longer than I expected. An hour, maybe more. But eventually, his answer stayed the same, no matter how hard I pushed. So I stopped.

Then I remembered that little boy, and I pushed a little harder, just for kicks.

It was Guerrera who gave up this rathole bar, and Telemundo who led me to my current meat-suit. A sergeant in the Mexican Army. Once I was through with Guerrera, I spent some time live-streaming the network's coverage of the body-dump on I-83, trolling for a decent bag of bones to tool around in. Ortiz was far too soft for what I had in store. When this guy – Solares, according to the sewn-on patch on his uniform, since my fifty words of halting Spanish couldn't keep up with what the well-quaffed talking heads back in the studio – stepped up to the mic, all sinew and barely concealed rage, I knew I'd found my man. Because I didn't need to know what his words meant to know from his grave expression, his unwavering glare into the camera, that he was promising the perpetrators of this horrible act would be brought to justice.

What he didn't know was that to make good on his promise, he'd need my help.

I waited until he finished his statement and left the makeshift podium, and then I left Ortiz behind. Solares flinched as if struck as I took him, but he didn't fall – and though his mouth flooded with saliva as it prepared to purge me, he didn't vomit. He was too disciplined – his mind too orderly. Like entering a strange kitchen, only to find it arranged exactly as you would have done. I opened a drawer, and boom bam – there was the button for his nausea response. Anyone who saw me/him mop the flopsweat from our brow probably assumed it was simply a case of delayed stage fright kicking in.

Of course, it's possible Solares was not as disciplined as I'm giving him credit for. That the reason the transition was so easy was me. See, historically, I've preferred the quiet of the newly dead to the cacophony of a living meat-suit. Only these past few days, I've found myself hitching rides with the living more and more, and what's worse, I've not minded it. Partly because the living have access to all manner of creature comforts in which the newly dead cannot indulge. Their credit cards have not been canceled. Their homes are not off-limits to the likes of me. Their IDs and access badges afford entry to all manner of hard-to-reach places, from prison cells to border crossings, and one never has to worry one's meat-suit will be recognized by some poor sap who'll subsequently piss himself and run screaming to the nearest tinfoil-hat blogger about how their uncle Merle is Patient Zero in the pending zombie apocalypse.

Like I said, partly for that reason. But partly not.

See, the dead – even the newly dead, so fresh and unspoiled by autolysis and/or putrefaction you'd have to check their pulse to tell – drive like that car you had in high school with a busted muffler and no third gear. They're all tricky. Goofy. Hard to get the hang of.

But the living – they're Ferraris, built for speed. for handling. They ride like a dream. Only catch is, you've got to subjugate their owner's will before they'll relent to your commands. Used to be, I didn't like that much.

These past few days, though, I've begun to develop a taste for it. Found I kinda sorta enjoy it, like playing a game of psychological Whac-a-Mole. Only the mole I'm whacking is the thinking, feeling, human owner of the body I've gone and hijacked. And the fact I'm having fun is terrifying.

This gig of mine is a punishment for a life misspent. And as punishments go, it's a doozy. When I collect a mark, there's this beautiful, horrible moment in which I experience every decision that's brought them to the front door of damnation, just as surely as if I made those choices myself. And likewise, every time I abandon one meat-suit in favor of another, I leave a little bit of what makes me *me* behind. The sum total of those two events is that every job, my humanity is slowly eroded, until one day – ten days from now, or ten minutes, or ten thousand fucking years for all I know – I'll be as cold and vicious as the demons who pull my strings. I used to think that I could stave it off, that I could avoid my fate.

Now, as I admire the handling of my military-tuned meat-suit – its owner howling bloody murder from the makeshift cell I fashioned for him in the back corner of his own mind – I think it's gonna be closer to ten minutes than ten thousand years.

In fact, I was beginning to wonder if I've already lost too much of me to well and truly care.

All this emo-bullshit inner turmoil meant nothing to the men in this nameless, rathole bar, though. All they saw was my fully automatic rifle aimed right at them, since I'd stopped off at the address on Solares' ID long enough to swap my olive-drab fatigues and sergeant's bars for some jeans, a T-shirt, and a gun. These were not Mensa cardholders – they were men of action, men of violence. Given half a chance to consider their predicament, one of three was bound to roll the dice and come up shooting. And while I doubted the world at large would miss any one of them, these men weren't mine to kill. So best to head off any such ideas at the pass.

"Any of you fellas speak English?" I asked. None of them responded. though the one nearest me flinched when first I spoke, as if surprised to hear uninflected English come from so clearly Mexican a face.

I locked my eyes on him as I continued. "I spoke to Javier," I said. "I know what happened. I'm not here to harm you."

The two on the other side of the pool table looked twitchier than ever, my words clearly so much nonsense to them. But before either of them could do anything rash, the one nearest me raised his hands and patted the air on either side of him in a cool-out gesture.

"Then... why?" he asked in heavily accented English. "Why do you come here?"

I took a gamble. Lowered my weapon. Held my hands out to my sides, clutching the assault rifle by its stock rather than its trigger. If these men wanted, they could have pumped me full of bullets before I could bring it around to bear again.

The fuck did I care? I'd probably just end up back in Guam.

"I need your help," I replied, hands held up as if in surrender. "I need you to give me access to your tunnels."

At that, the men shared a look. Apparently *tunnel* is close enough to Spanish for them to get the gist. "Even if I know what you mean," said the lone English speaker, "why would I help you?"

"Because I know what's down there," I told him. "And because I aim to kill it."

6.

The tunnels were nothing short of astonishing.

I'd seen other smuggling tunnels before, of course. Flipping channels past news specials during downtime in fleabag motel rooms. Killing time in waiting rooms reading magazines before killing time. Once or twice in person on a job. But most of those were rudimentary, unfinished – straight shots of a hundred yards or less that, had the cops not busted them before completion, would have been as likely to bury alive those using them as they were to successfully convey black market goods across the border.

These were something else entirely.

Seven miles of interconnected tunnels cut into the sandy soil, all bare-bulb lit and beam-reinforced, shored up here and there with rebar and chicken wire to hold the pressing desert earth at bay. They fanned outward from the bar in four spokes – east, northeast, northwest, and west – each bisected here and there by smaller tunnels at various points. Some of those tunnels led from one spoke to another, yet others to food or weapons caches. A few were designed to confuse would-be pursuers, with camouflaged trapdoors leading to hidden chambers deeper in the earth, or booby traps that could be triggered once past that would collapse the passage behind.

They'd been carved out of the desert over a period of years – men working in secret, under the cover of darkness, carting out tons of rock and dirt hidden in containers made from jury-rigged beer kegs, lest anyone should see. First one main branch, and then another, and then another – the interstitial passageways added over time to allow cartel spotters Stateside to call audibles should there be too much heat surrounding any one outlet point. Eventually, when all the spokes were connected, the system served not only as a conduit for narcotics to cross the border, but also as a safe-house of sorts for cartel agents operating within the US. They could duck into one of the access points and lay low, leaving either from the same place they entered or somewhere two miles away. The freedom to move both across the border or laterally along the US side was key to the cartel's business plan.

How long the creature had inhabited them, these men had no idea.

It began, as all things do, with stories. Hardened men, chests puffed with false bluster, recounting tall tales over shots of tequila: low growls half-swallowed by earthen walls, the dragging rasp of claws along dirt floors, a plume of hot breath against their cheeks as they navigated the wells of darkness that lapped at the edges of the dim, swinging lamplight of the dangling bulbs. By the light of day, such tales were no more than seasoning, intended to add zest to their self-perpetuated reps. But beneath the ground, in the choking dark of the tunnel system the cartel's foot-soldiers referred to as Mictlan – after the underworld of Aztec myth – those stories metastasized into something far more sinister in the minds of the men who carried them. Those stories made them quake, though to a one they blamed that on the chill damp earth, so far removed from the sunbaked desert surface. Those stories made them cautious.

Those stories likely kept them all alive.

The first person to disappear was an illegal immigrant-to-be, who'd paid for the privilege of using the cartel's tunnels with his life-savings before ultimately paying with his life. He was part of a small group – the first such group to be granted access to the tunnels. Sneaking migrant workers across the border wasn't part of the cartel's business plan; in fact, it was expressly forbidden. The tunnels were for human trafficking and narcotics, and funneling countless civilians through them – any one of whom might be rounded up by US authorities, only to use the knowledge of the tunnels' existence as leverage – was a sure way of shutting the lucrative pipeline down. But the men manning the tunnels thought that they could keep their sideline business quiet enough their superiors would never catch wind of it, and make a goodly chunk of change while they were at it.

They were wrong.

The man who disappeared was traveling alone. He gave no name, and scarcely spoke to anyone during his brief, ill-fated journey. In truth, that was not uncommon – most of these would-be illegals were migrant workers, family men looking to send back cash enough to their loved ones to make up for the upfront investment of buying their way across the border. They had no interest in placing said family on the cartel's radar, for although they were glad to take advantage of these men's assistance, they were not fools enough to think they could be trusted with the information as to when and where to find women and children left unprotected. Pretty wives and daughters – and, on occasion, sons as well – had a habit of disappearing when the cartel came to town. So when this man vanished from the small group of huddled, terrified border-crossers on his way through the tunnel system, there was no one to complain, to worry, to insist he be tracked down. The tunnel's minders assumed he must have simply wandered off, and either died down there or found himself another exit. Either way, it didn't trouble them at all.

At least until they found his headless, eviscerated remains hanging from a cross-beam in one of the lesser-used side-tunnels, nails driven through his splayed hands as though he'd been crucified and left to drain. But the dirt beneath was not bloodied, instead it was marred with the signs of something that had rested there and been dragged off. A tarpaulin, it turned out, which when found was still blood-sticky and looked for all the world like something had done its best to lick it clean. That something left tracks – two by two like a human's, but dotted here and there with claw marks on either side as if the beast occasionally used all fours – that led deeper into the tunnels, toward a section where it seemed the power to the lights had been disrupted.

Not disrupted, the men discovered, but bulbs broken one by one.

They sent a party of four men armed with lanterns, blades, and rifles in to find out who or what was responsible for stringing up the nameless man. That party never returned. So the remaining men decided to wait out whatever lurked in the darkness. They set guards at the tunnel mouth to ensure whatever it was could not escape, and to kill it if it tried. The guards were found slaughtered as the nameless man had been. Their heads, like his, were never found.

And that's when Guerrera, rising star within the cartel and the lieutenant entrusted with the day-to-day operation of the Mictlan tunnel system, caught wind of his men's ill-fated side-business, and decided to step in. Step in he did, killing anyone who'd participated in the unsanctioned border-crossing scheme, and placing charges at the mouth of the creature's chosen lair – the fetid air that emanated from it now heavy with the sickly stench of rotting flesh, of corruption, of violent, messy death – sealing it off forever. Every corner, every chamber, every blind alley and secret hidey-hole of the sprawling tunnel system was then inspected, and no further sign of the creature or its horrid appetites was seen.

For seven months, there was quiet, and – as the war between the cartels and the Mexican government reached a fever pitch – Guerrera came to realize that ensuring safe passage across the US border could be more than simply a profitable, if risky, sideline, it could be a public relations coup. A service the cartel was in a position to provide that the government could not. A way to influence public opinion that slowly turned the populace so thoroughly against them that even fear could not be expected to keep them all in line.

His higher-ups reluctantly agreed, so long as he oversaw the operation himself.

The bodies found on I-83 represented his first shipment.

What the authorities did not realize is that one of the four main spokes to the system let out a mere hundred yards from where the bodies had been dumped, into a storm drain which ran perpendicular to the highway just below. It was as Guerrera and his charges were exiting that the creature struck. And once it took the heads and hearts it came for, it was into that storm drain, and back into the depths of Mictlan, a shattered Guerrera watched the beast return.

Which meant if I was going to kill it, I'd have to go in after it.

When I told these men – Castillo, Alvarez, and Mendoza, as it turns out, the latter being the only English speaker in the group, and therefore my de facto translator – what I needed from them, they balked. I mean, they were happy enough to sketch out a rough map of the tunnels, for no paper map existed, thus ensuring only those familiar with them could successfully navigate their winding, booby-trapped passageways, marking the location of the collapsed side-tunnel and the storm-drain outlet for me as best they could. And they seemed content to part with grenades and additional ammunition as well. In part because I'd presented myself as an American cartel operative embedded as an immigration officer, and in part because they were so scared shitless of what was down there – and of their post directly above it – that they would have clung to any method for eliminating said threat as if it were a life preserver. And you couldn't blame them. The tunnel system had only five entrances: one here, and four on the Texas side of the border. Which meant these poor bastards stood a one-in-five chance of being this thing's next meal once it's stomach started rumblin' and it caught on they wouldn't be sending down any more deliveries.

But when I told them they were coming with me, they weren't too keen.

Guess the way they figured it, that bumped their odds from one-in-five to sure-fucking-thing.

What they didn't get was I wasn't asking.

"I do not understand why we cannot simply blow the tunnels," said Mendoza, "and bury this beast for good."

"Yes you do. You know damn well it didn't work before. What makes you think you'd kill it this time?"

"But you cannot expect us to come with you. It is too dangerous."

"Funny, you seemed just fine with me going down there all by my lonesome."

Mendoza shrugged. "Whether you live or die is of less consequence to me."

"And what of the people who will die if this thing gets loose?"

"So long as I am not among them, it is not any of my concern. I would prefer to take my chances on the surface."

We were sitting around the wooden cable spool that served as the bar's sole table, drinking tequila from filthy shot glasses as we spoke. Castillo and Alvarez watched the conversation as if it were a tennis match, occasionally interjecting with rapid-fire Spanish that Mendoza would then translate, or requesting that he do the same of my comments for them. Outside, shadows grew long as the fire of day was extinguished, the sun snuffed out like a spent cigarette by the desert sands. Between the tequila and the thought of the job to come, I was hankering for a smoke something fierce, a jones not helped any by the fact these three puffed away like goddamn steam engines. Which, upon reflection, may have had as much to do with inspiring my little demonstration as did their obvious reluctance.

"Look, I don't think you get it. Guerrera's orders–"

"–were heard by you and you alone, and that is not enough to convince us to risk our lives."

"Is that right? Then maybe I can find other means of convincing you." I pushed back from the table, toppling the rusty folding chair on which I was perched. Mendoza did the same, drawing a 9mm from the small of his back as he did. Castillo and Alvarez were a half-second behind. Three guns trained on me, and my own weapon a good ten feet away atop the bar.

I raised my hands, all casual-like, and smiled. Mendoza smiled back, predatory and triumphant. We were separated by a good six feet of plank floor, and a table far too bulky to be easily tossed aside. They were armed. I was not. The situation didn't look too good for me.

Which meant I had them exactly where I wanted them.

"Perhaps next time you choose to make a move, you will first consider where your weapon is," Mendoza said, cigarette bobbing in his mouth as he spoke.

"Perhaps," I echoed. "But I figured instead I'd just use yours."

Mendoza eyed me quizzically. His cohorts looked first to me, and then to him, trying to suss out their next play. Their trigger-fingers were getting itchier by the second, their faces ever more worry-lined.

I drew the moment out as long as I could stand, letting the situation simmer. And then I hurled my meat-suit to the floor. And then I struck.

My consciousness hit Mendoza so fast, I scarcely felt the last meat-suit drop away before I was inside. So fast, the Solares body was still falling when I took control. Solares wailed in fright as consciousness returned to him, and covered his head with his hands, waiting for the shots he was certain were to come.

But they didn't come. I made sure of it.

Mendoza's stomach clenched. Bile and tequila splashed his boots. His buddies turned toward him instinctually, and I took full advantage. Castillo was to my right. I twisted toward him, and pressed the barrel of Mendoza's piece to his temple. His gun clattered to the floor. Alvarez stepped in to stop me, and I buried my hand inside his chest. I grasped tight his soul, gave it a little tug. He squealed like a stuck pig, and then collapsed, eyes showing white, fell so fast I almost failed to release his soul in time.

Woulda sucked if I'd held onto it. The boy wasn't mine to collect. Though the life he led, my guess is he'll be somebody's to someday.

Alverez was out. Castillo stood frozen, eyes clenched in anticipation of my bullet. I was puke-streaked and gasping from the sudden exertion, Mendoza's smoker-lungs struggling to keep up with the demands I made on them. Which reminded me. I looked around, saw his butt lying in a puddle of sick, more tequila than stomach acid. I ground it out with the toe of his boot. Wouldn't do to have the place go up in flames. That'd attract all manner of attention I'd just as soon avoid. But it did bum me out to have to waste the smoke.

"Siddown," I said to Alvarez. "I'm not gonna kill you."

His eyes widened when I spoke to him in unaccented English, but he didn't listen. He didn't listen because he didn't speak a lick of English, but it took me a minute – and a prompt from my former meat-suit – to catch on.

"You know he can't understand you," said Solares, eyeing me cautiously from the floor. His English was less stilted and less accented than was Mendoza's. His face was no less hard. As I watched, his gaze flitted from me to Alvarez's piece, which skittered to a spot on the floor maybe four feet from where he lay once I kicked it aside.

"I wouldn't," I told him. "You'll make me do something we'll both regret." His attention returned instantly to me. "Now, tell this one to take a seat. Tell him I'm not going to hurt him."

Solares did as I asked. Alvarez relaxed a tad. Righted a chair, dropped heavily into it, and downed two huge gulps of tequila before burying his face in his hands and crying like a child. I gestured with Mendoza's gun and Solares took a seat as well. Castillo, still unconscious, moaned and twitched as if his dreams were far from pleasant. Can't say I was surprised. Can't say I cared much, either.

"What *are* you?" asked Solares.

"That's complicated," I replied. "And I've neither the time nor inclination to explain it to you. What's important is you, and they, have gotten a taste of what I can do."

Solares smiled humorlessly. "I suppose we have, at that. What now?"

"I assume you heard what I came here to do."

He nodded. "You came here to kill the beast below."

"That hasn't changed."

"I would not expect it had," he said. "And how, precisely, do I fit into this plan?"

I heaved a sigh. "Look, you're a soldier. You know how this shit works. You must realize I can't let you leave this place until the job is done. It wouldn't do to have the Mexican Army showing up and making a hash of things."

"I've no intention of leaving," said Solares. "Those were my people this creature slaughtered. The very people I am sworn to protect. I would like to help you kill it if I can."

"I can't ask you to do that. It's too risky."

"Unless I'm mistaken, you were going to bring me along without my consent, were you not? And anyways, you've asked these men."

"These men are drug runners. Human traffickers. Murderers. I've no problem risking their lives."

"I'm a soldier. It's no different."

"It's very fucking different. You're an innocent. And if I'm not in your driver's seat, I can't protect you."

Solares frowned then, and nodded, as if he'd just come to an unpleasant decision. Which, as it turns out, he had. "Then, as you say, drive," he said.

Jesus. A willing vessel. As fucking awful as possession was for the possessed, I had to admire this dude's stones.

"You sure?"

"If it helps you kill this beast, I'm sure."

"All right then. It's settled. But not just yet," I said, patting at Mendoza's pockets. "Because I could really use a fucking cigarette."

7.

Truth be told, body-hopping back into Solares took a little longer than a cigarette.

First, I sent him out in search of supplies. Watched Castillo tend to Alvarez, his ministrations oddly sweet, while the latter slowly came around. Kept Mendoza's gun beside me on the table the whole time, but they didn't give me cause to use it. The fight had gone out of them. They were now victims, not aggressors, and my presence was to be weathered, not contested.

I smoked half Mendoza's pack before Solares returned with a heavy padlock and a good eight feet of chain, the thickest he could manage. And he managed pretty thick; each clanking link was the size of a woman's fist, the whole tangle heaped to overflowing in his ropy arms as he wrangled it through the door. He sounded like Marley's ghost shuffling across the dusty floor while trying his damndest not to drop it. Every time the chain shifted and a portion hit the floor, he winced. I didn't have to ask him why. Though realistically we all knew the creature could be hiding anywhere, not a one of us could shake the notion it was just below the floorboards, waiting.

Past the screen door, the night had reached full dark. This far out into the desert, there was no blue, just black; stars like chipped diamonds against the velvet of the sky. The air was cold and crisp and thin, the wild swing from the stultifying day enough to make my borrowed heartbeat quicken, lizard-brain instincts kicking in and telling me the atmosphere was thinner and more fragile a protection from the ice-sharp sting of space than by day I might've thought. To which I told my lizard-brain instincts chill the fuck out – you'll be in a tidy little underground hidey-hole soon enough, the perfect burrow in which to weather the chill ache of desert night.

"So," said Solares. "What now?"

"Now," I told him, "we go hunting."

I asked Alvarez if he was up to coming with us. Knew after what he'd been through, he'd be too scared of me to say no. He proved me right, nodding sweat-slick and wan, and eyeing me the whole time like if I didn't find his answer enthusiastic enough, I might plunge my hand into his chest a second time. Instead, I handed him the remains of the tequila, which he killed in three quick glugs.

On my instructions, Solares gathered up as many guns as he could carry. I scooped up all but one of the rest with my left hand, taking the final one in my right and training it on Castillo and Alvarez. I told them to grab the lanterns and walkie-talkies that I'd found stashed behind the bar. And then it was time to head into the tunnels.

The entrance was behind a low cinderblock fireplace, which looked to be affixed to the far wall. It wasn't. A switch flipped, a little elbow-grease from Castillo and Alvarez both, and the fireplace slid forward, some kind of runner system keeping it just off the floor so it wouldn't scrape.

Behind it was a sad little smuggler's notch, inside which was a rusted cash box and a couple pounds of low-grade ditch weed apportioned into eighths and quarters. I eyed the two of them like, are you kidding me? But the smuggler's notch proved nothing more than a clever ruse, a rodeo clown to disguise the true reason for the sliding fireplace. Because Castillo dropped to one knee and looped a finger into a gaping knothole in the wooden floor, and next thing I knew, a three-by-three section of it hinged upward. A ladder descended from it into still, quiet darkness. Solares dropped in his pile of guns. I did the same. The clatter of their landing was swallowed almost immediately by the insulating earth. That done, Solares clanked down the ladder rungs. Once he reached the bottom, he called up to me, and then covered Castillo and Alvarez with one of their own weapons while they climbed down the ladder. Soon the tunnel entrance glowed like pirate treasure as they fired up their lamps.

I entered the tunnel last, yanking closed the hatch by the rusted iron loop bolted into its underside. Then I chained that loop to the ladder such that the hatch could not be opened, and set the lock. Below me, Alvarez said something in rapid-fire Spanish. I asked Solares what he was going on about.

"He says you do not need to do that. They are brave, and will not run."

I shook my head. "He only says that cause right this sec, he's more afraid of me than he is of what's down here. I can't take the chance that once I'm out of sight he'll change his mind. So we lock the hatch, and the question's settled."

Solares translated what I'd said. Alvarez replied.

"He asks, 'What now?'" said Solares.

"There are four main tunnels out of here," I said, "and four of us. Tell him all he's got to do is follow one of 'em right out of here. He can take whatever guns he wants – there's no point shooting me and doubling back, since I left the padlock key topside. The only way out is through. We'll each take a different tunnel, and a radio as well. If anybody sees anything, they're to call me, and I'll be there in an instant, like with Mendoza in the bar. I promise I can protect you all, so long as you give me half a chance. And I promise I can kill this thing.

We do this right, and no one but the creature has to die down here tonight, okay?"

Solares translated once more. Castillo and Alvarez looked doubtful, but still, they nodded their assent. Then Solares turned to me.

"Is it time?" he asked.

"Yeah," I said. "I'm afraid it is."

He handled it like a champ. When I took over, his mind was quiet. He didn't protest, didn't scream. And once again, he didn't puke, though once again, it was a near thing. When I was well and truly back in control of him, I turned my attention to a dazed and fuming Mendoza.

"You get all that?" I asked him.

"I understood your plan," he spat. "What I do not understand is why you left my cigarettes back in the bar."

"I need you sharp," I told him. "That means your eyesight can't be compromised by lighter-flicks. That means your nostrils need to pick up more than smoky full-flavored goodness."

"When this is through," he told me, "I will kill you for what you've done to me and my men."

"You're welcome to try," I told him. "But you'll have to take a number and get in line."

We split up then. Each of us with a small camp lantern, doused for now on account of the dangling light bulbs trailing off in all directions, as well as a radio, an automatic rifle (two, in Castillo's case), and a handgun. Castillo brandished his rifles one in each hand like some kind of gangster as he sauntered out of sight down the eastward spoke. All I could think was if he tried to fire the fucking things holding them like that, he was gonna break his thumbs with the recoil and spray bullets wide to either side. Mendoza, the most senior of the men, walked calmly but with purpose down the western one, battle-weary but determined, and he held his rifle like he meant to use it. Alvarez, clearly frightened, hugged his tight to his body to hide his trembling as he trundled reluctantly into the northeast tunnel. He was also the only one of us to fire up his lantern straight away, despite the burning bulbs. Its aperture was open as far as it would go, letting enough air in the wick glowed pure white, and he held its wire-thin handle with the same white-knuckled hand that clutched his gunstock. I worried his mind would give out long before he reached the other side of the tunnel. I – in the tight, responsive Solares once more – took the northwest tunnel, from which I was told the creature's collapsed lair once stretched, and through which the slaughtered group had passed on their way to their brief, doomed taste of so-called freedom. I wore my automatic slung across my back, and my handgun at the ready. Seemed to me the quarters were close enough, I was likelier to get off a shot if I had a shorter barrel to bring around, and anyways, when it came to killing this thing, I had less faith in these glorified pea-shooters than I did in my own bare hands. The unlit lantern I affixed by its lanyard to my belt to keep one of the aforementioned bare hands free.

Ten paces down the tunnel, and I could no longer hear my companions. Twenty paces, and I felt alone as I had ever been, my fellow travelers a distant memory. Earth pressed in all around me. Dry dirt like cake crumbles left in an empty pan crunched beneath my feet. My tunnel smelled like a fresh grave. The air was stale and close and hard to breathe. A twinge of claustrophobia I didn't realize I suffered from until just this moment wound its way up my spine like a millipede with needle-legs. I wondered idly if I could blame Solares for the sensation, some phobias are strong enough for sense-memory to trigger physiological reactions even in the absence of the consciousness that created them. I've possessed dead meat-suits that still got woozy at the sight of blood, or skin-crawly at the sight of bugs. But Solares wasn't dead, and in an experience that proved a first for me I got the distinct impression he was laughing at me for trying to pass the buck at what apparently was my fear and mine alone.

I've had meat-suits wail and scream and cry and beg, but he's the first I've ever had one get cheeky.

I pressed onward. The quiet between footfalls was so very, I began to jump at nothing. The subtle shift of my gun strap against my shoulder. The brittle crunch of gravel beneath my feet. The burst of static from the radio as my reluctant scouts checked in – every ten light bulbs, just like we agreed. I made that distance out to be no more than fifty yards, though the twisting of the narrow wood-ribbed tunnels ensured you could never see more than two or three bulbs ahead at a time. They sounded off with just their names, two Alvarezes for every one Mendoza or Castillo. Kid was trying to get through and into open air as fast as he could manage, and I couldn't blame him. But his fear did more than make him quick. It made him sloppy, inattentive, which is to say I wasn't terribly surprised when he failed to check in.

At first, I confess, I thought nothing of it. I figured maybe he'd just slowed. But then Castillo checked in twice, and then Mendoza, but still no Alvarez. So I closed my eyes, stretched my consciousness, and felt nothing where he should have been.

So, okay: dead, you're thinking. And you damn sure aren't wrong. But that's only the half of it. I spend most of my time inhabiting the recent dead. Collector juju's strong enough to restart halted hearts, and to shake the meat of mortis, rigor and livor both. So when I say I reached out and felt nothing, that meant more than Alvarez just being dead.

That means something took him apart so thoroughly, he no longer registered as viable. And that something managed to do so in a span of minutes. Not to mention it was on him quick enough that, jumpy though he was, he never managed to so much as trigger a burst of static from his radio. I hadn't heard any gunfire, either, but I had no idea if down here the sound would carry.

Two minutes later I got my answer. It sounded like distant fireworks. The grand finale, seemed like, when they launch all the stuff they've got left at once. I figured that for Castillo – he of the two autos locked and loaded – a guess that was confirmed when Mendoza took to the radio, calling out to him in rapid-fire Spanish. Solares filled me in on the gist, which I could have guessed – Mendoza was demanding to know Castillo's position. Mendoza spoke with the breathlessness of a smoker suddenly exerting himself. I knew at once he was headed toward the artery Castillo had chosen as his own, either by backtracking, or through one of the secondary tunnels.

Lucky for me, I wasn't limited to such earthbound modes of transportation. Not when I had a meat-suit to lock onto, and an approximate location in which to look.

I closed Solares' eyes and probed the darkness for the spark of life that was Castillo. It took longer than if I'd had a better fix on his location. I hoped it hadn't taken too. I hurled my consciousness at him with all I had, and when my eyes next opened, they were no longer Solares's, but Castillo's.

The sharp reek of kerosene. My lantern, shattered beneath me, glass biting skin. I was on the ground, face pressed to dirt. A hard metal rod beneath my cheek, searing hot. Castillo's recently fired gun barrel, blistering a brand into his cheek that will last him until his dying day. Which may well be upon him, come to think.

I vomited – possession reflex. Then I rolled over, and blinked against the dark. It was near me. I could hear it breathing, low and wet and oh so patient. But as I cast about in search of my quarry – my prey turned predator – I could not see it. There was a faint glow behind me to the west, toward the bar, toward Mexico. Nothing but pure black headed east.

Something shuffled in the eastern darkness. I patted the ground around me, trying to arm myself. Castillo's handgun was nowhere to be found, nor was his second rifle. One borrowed shoulder was wet and burning, the corres-ponding arm cold and numb, my mind dull and slow to focus.

I grabbed the gun beneath me – the one that had seared Castillo's cheek – and checked it for ammo, or tried. Couldn't make my numb arm do anything I told it to. Pop the magazine, I said. Work the slide to check the chamber. But it wouldn't.

Spacey as I was, it took me a sec to realize why.

Working the slide was hard to do from twenty feet away.

Castillo's other arm lay in the faint half-light to the west. Palm down, and trailing gore at the shoulder, all wormy blood vessels and gleaming flat, white tendons. Still twitching, it seemed to me, but that could have been my vision jumping with every mutinous heartbeat, every pump hastening this meat-suit's death.

That's why the creature wasn't striking. It didn't have to. It could just wait out the clock and feast on food that wouldn't fight back.

"Coward," I called into the darkness.

The darkness hissed. I heard a rustle, and caught a flash of movement, too fast to track. When I glanced once more back toward Castillo's severed arm, I discovered it was gone. Slurping noises filled the manmade cavern, like a hobo eating soup.

"I know what you are," I said.

Another hiss, a voice like rusted hinges. "You know nothing."

"I know you were once a Collector, just like me. I know you're an abomination who feasts on blood and brain and God knows what else to fuel your bastard half-existence. And most importantly, I know you can be killed."

"You lie." A nauseating pop as Castillo's elbow-joint separated, and then a sucking noise like a baby with a bottle. But this thing was no one's baby, and it sure as hell wasn't drinking mother's milk.

"I don't."

"If I could be killed, I assure you my beloved mountain cousins would have found a way. They begrudge me my appetites, as if their method of procuring sustenance is any more humane. As if the very word humane applies to such misbegotten souls as we. They cast me out as they cast out poor Ricou so many centuries ago. Ever since, I've been forced to contend with the crushing loneliness of exile – and an endless diet of Mexican."

"Yeah, I bet it's hell on the digestive system," I said, gritting my teeth against the ice-cream-on-exposed-nerve ache that built with every heartbeat in my shoulder. "And anyway, I never said that *they* could kill you, but *I* sure as hell can. You could ask your brother Simon if you don't believe me, but you might find him a little hard to get a hold of at this point, seeing as he's dead and all."

At the mention of Magnusson, the creature in the dark went silent, and its breathing quickened. I couldn't tell if it was fear, or merely anticipation of a meal. Woozy as I felt, this creature wasn't gonna have to wait long to run out the clock. Castillo was fading fast. But when I stretched my flickering consciousness back toward Solares, he wasn't where I left him, and weak as I was, I didn't have the mental energy to scan the tunnels for my next meat-suit.

Then I saw a golden wobble in the darkness, and just this once, thanked God for my good luck. Because that wobble was Mendoza emerging, lantern-lit, from one of the side-tunnels just east of there and, even as weak as I was, if I could see him, I could *be* him.

This time, my approach was less freight-train and more newborn kitten, all shaky and timid, which means Mendoza felt me coming. As I stumbled, clumsy, into his mind and fumbled for the controls, I heard him mutter, "*¡No otra vez!*" and clutch his stomach in anticipating of the coming barf-fest.

But hey, at least he didn't fight me. Weak as I was, if he had, I would have wound up bounced back into rapidly cooling Castillo, which would have likely meant a one-way ticket back to Guam.

The creature misinterpreted Castillo's subsequent collapse as he and I both lapsing into unconsciousness, when in fact I had escaped mere seconds before. It descended on him in a fury of wet tearing sounds and low grunts of effort and animal desire, eager to feast before this new light – this new snack – was upon it.

Luckily, Mendoza's stomach was still empty, and my sudden peristaltic seizure did little more than spray the tunnel floor with spittle. He'd shouldered his rifle at some point, likely deciding he could travel faster with it on his back than in his hands, leaving him with the lit lantern in one hand, and his pistol, an outsized Magnum-knockoff, in the other. The lantern swung wildly on its hinged handle as together he and I closed the gap between us and poor, doomed Castillo, the world swaying like a boat in choppy seas by the arcing lamplight. And as its sphere of illumination blazed like sunrise up Castillo's legs, I got my first true glimpse at the creature I'd been sent to kill.

It was a lean, spindly thing, once human in form, no doubt, but warped somehow by its environment, by its predilections, by the dark mojo that created it and demanded constant sacrifice to sustain the very blasphemy of its existence, into something… less. Something terrifying. It was naked, sickly gray-brown, and emaciated, which, its vaguely humanoid form aside, gave it the appearance of a stick-insect. The creature crouched over Castillo's gaping chest – his ribcage split open at the middle like a clamshell – its hands buried deep inside the dead man's viscera, its ropy forearms purple with gore. Disproportionately long legs angled out on either side, famine-skinny and liver-spotted. Flesh stretched paper-thin across its ribs, and its stomach was bloated and swollen. Its head seemed outsized for the neck on which it sat, perhaps rendered so wide to accommodate the manic grin of needle-sharp teeth that gleamed, blood-streaked yellow, back at me. Gore dripped black off its pointed chin. Its skull had warped itself around two massive, bulbous eyes – the better to see you with, my dear – which swam a liquid red in the lamplight like twin IV bags of blood, no whites or pupils to be seen. Twin slits sliced two short lines between those eyes in a hasty suggestion of a nose. As the light hit the beast, it recoiled, its leathery lids clenching shut. Then it threw its arms wide in challenge, gnarled, clawed hands stretching from one wall of the tunnel to the other and flinging offal everywhere, and roared, its mouth hinging impossibly wide.

The sound shook the very ground around us, and loosed a flurry of dust and pebbles. The stench of rot and death was carried on its breath. Some fragile, child-me portion of my psyche wanted to crawl beneath the nearest set of bed sheets and hide. Adult-me damn near pissed himself at the sight, the sound, at the perfect, wordless threat. Mendoza, hardened drug-runner that he was, huddled penitent in the back of his own mind, and rattled off over and over a mantra in hushed Spanish that even I recognized as the Lord's Prayer.

Sure, now His name be hallowed, I thought at him. But how many times have you and your cohorts played the part of the evil from which innocent folks are begging to be delivered?

But Mendoza wasn't taking questions from the peanut gallery at the moment. And since I was pretty sure the Big Guy wasn't about to take his call, I figured it was up to me to take care of Captain Ugly here. It had a good three feet of reach on me, so my odds of getting past those claws to gain access to the withered lump of God-knows-what that passed as its soul weren't great. So, as it gathered on its haunches and launched itself at me, I did what any red-blooded American who wants to keep said red blood on the inside woulda done in my shoes: I shot that fucker in the face.

Well, the eye, to be precise. And had I not been terrified at the thought of imminent violent pointy-sharp death hurling toward me, I might have curled fetal at the world of gross doing so unleashed. Hot wet chunks of mottled tissue and vitreous eye-goo sprayed the cave like the devil's own ambrosia salad, but still the creature kept on coming. It hit me like two hundred pounds of razor-tipped clothes hangers, all knees and elbows and teeth and claws. We tumbled to the ground as one, my gun-hand aimed harmlessly away thanks to the creature's iron grip around my wrist, my lantern dropped as I kept the creature's snapping jaws away from the tender flesh of Mendoza's face with a palm to its misshapen forehead.

A *whoosh* of hot kerosene breath, too close for comfort, Mendoza's lantern setting the spilled fuel from Castillo's broken one alight as the former shattered against the hard-packed earth. Our world went briefly campfire-orange and choking hot. The creature's one good eye slammed shut against the bright, its jaw still snapping all the while. I held it away from my borrowed face as best I could, but my/Mendoza's best wasn't gonna cut it for long. Our smoker lungs seared, our vision went dim. Our elbow was on the verge of giving out.

Guam, here I come, I thought.

Then Solares – that beautiful, brave, stupid son of a bitch – came barreling around the corner, popping five shots into the beast quick as a drum machine. Chunks of flesh tore free of the creature, gouting green-black blood, and it howled in pain and animal fury. Then all the sudden, the goddamn thing was off of me. I watched in horror as it sailed through the air toward Solares with all the deadly grace of a jungle cat. He popped off three more shots before it tackled him. All three shots landed center-mass, but they didn't slow the monster down a bit. He and it bounced off the rusted honeycomb of chicken wire holding back the loose dirt of the tunnel wall, and wound up a tangle of limbs amidst the mess that was Castillo. When teeth and claw found flesh, Solares didn't even scream.

Then it ripped his throat out, and he couldn't if he tried.

I wanted to mourn him, to apologize for dragging him into this. But there wasn't time. Not while this thing was still breathing.

The spilled kerosene on the tunnel floor burned off, and the fire extinguished itself, leaving the tunnel full of thick black smoke and precious little oxygen.

My eyes stung. My lungs burned for cool, clean air. I crooked my elbow and breathed through Mendoza's shirtsleeve, blinking back tears as I cast about for a weapon.

Guns were useless against this thing, they didn't do shit. And there was no skim blade in this private hell of mine, replica or otherwise.

There was, however, rebar.

The men who'd constructed the tunnel had used it to anchor the chicken wire. It jutted from the dirt floor and walls as well. Not everywhere, just here and there. Took a good thirty seconds of fumbling in the smoky dimness to find some. It poked out cold as nighttime desert from a nearby wall, and came out reluctantly. I can't say how long I yanked at it before I finally freed it from the wall. Long enough for the beast to disappear into the deeper dark of the eastward tunnel, I suppose, because when I looked back toward Solares, where I'd last seen it, it was gone.

It didn't stay gone long.

I heard its ragged breathing, back and to my left. I spun, but saw nothing.

A sudden pop like a gunshot, only quieter. Then another, then another. All to the west, from whence I came, which was now as dark as was the eastern passage.

The creature had broken the nearest three light bulbs.

A rustle of scale-dry skin. A flash of slightly paler dark amidst the black. And then needles in my shoulder. Teeth or claws, I didn't know.

I swung blindly at the creature's point of contact with the rebar, and hit the fucker so damn hard, I heard something crack. If its reflexes had been better, that crack would have been my meat-suit's collarbone. Instead, given the muffled yowl the beast let out, I'm guessing I took out its jaw. No telling how long that jaw would take to mend. Minutes, maybe less. This thing had been feasting, after all. Its powers were no doubt at their peak.

It retreated some, and let me stew in the black a bit. I didn't much enjoy it. Played Babe Ruth and swung for the cheap seats once or twice with my rebar, succeeded only in tiring myself out. So little air left in this still, dark tomb of a tunnel.

I fell to my knees, then onto my back. Felt consciousness bleeding away, the choking air a pillow against my face. My eyes fluttered shut. And then it struck.

Just as I'd been hoping.

I knew I hadn't much time left, so I figured playing possum was my best bet. A bluff's all the more believable when it's half true. And I'd seen this fucker's game once or twice already. I knew it liked to cover ground all lickety-split with a well-timed pounce.

Unfortunately for it, I was ready. Got the rebar up in time. Felt the thrum of electricity through the iron as it broke through the creature's chest, traveling from my meat-suit's hand up the bar like Lilith had suggested was the case. I pray the Lord its soul to take. Its one intact eye gleamed wet and wide in the near-dark. Its body slackened as the rebar broke through the ancient flesh of its back. Atop the rebar, stuck like iron filings to a magnet, was the gnarled, lifeless hunk that was this creature's soul. I could feel the vibration of it through the three feet of rebar. Weak, but still alive, though the body I'd removed it from was nothing more than empty flesh.

I lay a moment, pinned beneath the impaled creature. Then I heaved it to one side and climbed out from underneath. "You know what?" I asked its corpse as I wrapped my hand around its soul and crushed it to dust like so much chalk. "That one *was* kinda personal."

The ground rumbled all around me, swinging light bulbs on their naked cords and loosing dust from the ceiling, while the creature's lifeless figure crumbled to bone and dust. My memory cast back unbidden to the collapsing Pemberton Baths, and I feared for a moment the tunnel was going to come down around me. But whatever mystical juice Magnusson had tapped into in the length of his unnatural existence proved weaker tea in this subhuman, feral beast, because almost as soon as it began, the rumbling quieted, and the swaying lights stilled. The cave still stood. And eventually, creakily, so did I.

Then, my task completed, I left the cave of cooling dead behind, and stumbled out into the half-lit predawn of the slowly waking desert alone.

Then

To call the place a bunker was misleading.

For one, Hitler's *Führerbunker* was a massive, elaborate complex comprising two levels and some forty rooms. For two, it was buried eight meters below the courtyard of the Reich Chancellery, the Third Reich's formal seat of power, whose ornate buildings and landscaped grounds stretched from the thoroughfare of Hermann-Göring-Straße at its western edge to Wilhelmstraße at its east, and rivaled all the architectural pomp and circumstance that London, DC, or Moscow had to offer. Of course, both Hermann-Göring-Straße and Wilhelmstraße were sandbagged and razorwired for blocks around the complex, and closed to any non-military traffic, as was Voßstraße to the complex's south, and the Ministry Gardens to the north. But the Hitler Youth that I was wearing must have looked every bit the good little Aryan to the guards manning the makeshift barricades at every major intersection that he did to me, because, decked out as I was in his drab military fatigues, I was waved through every checkpoint with the same tense, jaw-clenched, thin-lipped smile. A silent acknowledgment of these trying times, of a war now all but lost, to a fellow comrade-in-arms, to another true believer.

Not a soul besides myself – and, I suppose, the beautiful and mysterious creature who'd introduced herself as Lilith and set me on this mission – suspected that I was there, Teutonic and tow-headed, to hasten their precious Reich's demise.

Speaking of Lilith, it was on my way to the Reich Chancellery that I discovered she was far more than simply the beautiful and inscrutable woman she appeared to be. As I stumbled, new-body-clumsy and foreigner-hesitant, through the gray apocalyptic landscape of this war-torn nation – pummeled to crumbling mortar and scorched concrete by Russian forces desperate to claim the glory of a killing blow, the city's windows blacked out and streetlights shattered by her own citizens bent on avoiding the same – the stunning vision that was Lilith flitted into and out of being at will. First, she was at the foot of the stairwell of the tenement building in which I woke, still barefoot and black-dressed, cooing up to me to follow while I looked dumbly over my shoulder, wondering just how in the hell she got around me and down the stairs so fast, only to vanish into thin air as I heeded her command, tugged onward by the thrill of her attentions. Then, she waved and smiled like a wife greeting her husband on the docks at the end of his deployment from atop a pile of steel and stone that was once no doubt a good-sized building, several blocks from the tenement's front door. She was, it seemed, now inexplicably wearing what looked to be a set of drab fatigues to match my own, and her hair was twisted up and hidden beneath a military cap. But given the way the fatigues clung to her comely figure – the way the watery sunlight through the clouds seemed amplified as it glinted off her gleaming teeth framed by blood-colored lips as sultry as sin itself – her quick-change outfit was more a mockery of a disguise than a legitimate attempt to mask her gender; which of course in the moment was secondary to the fact that I had no idea how anyone could move as quickly as she. But I was determined to suss out the trick behind it, locking eyes on her as I trotted, shoulders hunched against the subtle threat implied by the diesel roar of Soviet bombers' distant prop-engines.

The ducking, of course, was as preposterous as it was unnecessary – the planes were nowhere close, and even if they were, keeping my head down made about as much sense warding off their deadly payload as did an umbrella. And given that – blond-and-blue-eyed person-outfit aside – I'd be made as a Yankee by any Kraut within earshot the second I opened my mouth, I shoulda been a damn sight more worried about the Nazis on the ground than the Russian comrades in the sky. But the fog of war being what it is, I kept on ducking anyway, my borrowed face twisted into a perma-cringe as if anticipating an attack that only grew all the more inevitable the longer fate forestalled it.

From somewhere behind me came a *pop* that, to my stressed mind, suggested gunfire, and a rush like rustling fabric and footfalls, like a mob fast approaching. My only thought, which raced through my brain as my limbs prickled with adrenaline, was: I've been discovered. Instinct kicked in, and I dove into the dry, cracked remains of a fountain – absent water and spare change, now just a broken, empty vessel. I prayed that I'd been quick enough, that no one's gaze had followed me to my hiding place.

I waited. Listened. But there was nothing much to hear.

Then I heard another pop, this one quieter, and another flutter, once more trailing off to nothing. When I peeked my head back out over the stone lip to see what had caused the noise, I found myself staring at a matronly German woman, all furtive glances and worried eyes, hanging half out her second story window with a small throw rug in her hands. As I watched, she gave it a good snap, loosing a plume of dust into the air and startling a flock of pigeons into flight. I let out a breath I hadn't realized I'd been holding, and relaxed my death grip on the fountain's edge.

It was only then that I realized whatever the hell this life was I'd fallen into – be it madness or dream or death-rattle hallucination – I was more frightened than I'd ever been before. Lilith told me back at this vessel's apartment that I was already dead, and yet I couldn't help but fear for my own improbable existence anyway. I'd been given a second chance, it seemed to me, and I was stricken at the thought of letting it slip away too soon.

It was survival instinct, nothing more. Vestigial echoes of the mortal existence I'd left behind. Easy for me to say now, but it would take me some years as a Collector to come to that realization. Unfortunately for me, not all my fledgling-Collector notions were so difficult to disabuse me of. I'd soon learn that I was no goddamn superhero, and that there are far worse things to experience than death.

Once I climbed, red-faced and chagrinned, out of the fountain, I discovered Lilith had disappeared once more. I cast about for her – lost, confused, a stranger in a strange and hostile land – only to catch a wisp of sunny summer dress disappearing around the corner of a building, a glimpse of bare sole unsullied by city grime before it vanished down the cross-street out of sight. I set out after her, determined to end this ridiculous game of tag and to ask her if that quick-change wardrobe trick was something she could teach me; these fatigues were cheap, coarse, and itchy. Maybe *Übermensch* aren't bothered by such things, but this here undead American was crawling out of his stolen skin.

I hadn't seen the entrance to the compound coming. I rounded the building's corner at a trot, expecting to find Lilith. What I found instead was a large, fenced-in military installation at the center of what was once no doubt a beautiful courtyard, brimming with activity. The Reich Chancellery building was beautiful, but black-windowed, and unadorned by flags, no doubt in an attempt to make it less of a target. Wheeled heavy cannons sat at the square's four cardinal points, and rooftops for blocks around glinted with rifle scopes from the snipers that had set up on all sides. Makeshift battlements of concrete rubble and sandbags dotted the courtyard, behind which huddled men armed to the teeth and – if later reports were to be believed – dosed to the gills on *Panzerschokolade*, an ingenious concoction of chocolate laced with methamphetamine, which was slipped into the rations of tank crews and infantry alike and consumed happily by those too eager for a little chemical pick-me-up to realize their Führer had turned them into strung-out murder-zombies. There were some who said Hitler himself was hooked on the stuff, too, though his came via regular injections from his physician, Werner Haase. Explained his manic, spit-flying rhetorical style, I suppose.

Point is, I was closer to the black, beating heart of the Nazi empire than anyone in Uncle Sam's employ had ever been, and I felt as though I'd been miniaturized, given a flashlight, and deposited smack in the middle of a hive of killer bees. I was so freaked out just standing at the edge of the compound it took me a sec to realize someone was yelling at me.

He was a lantern-jawed Nazi stooge straight out of central casting, standing beside the weighted turnstile gate that marked the entrance to the compound. Six-five if he was an inch, with shoulders broad enough you coulda set places for a dinner for four atop them and still had room for a lovely centerpiece. His hands were the size of tennis rackets, and in one he held a Luger pistol, aimed down for now but ready nonetheless. And if his bugged-out, bloodshot eyes and the throbbing vein on his flushed-red forehead were any indication, I'd say this big boy'd been pushing down the lesser Nazis in the mess hall and stealing their goof-juiced chocolate for himself.

By the time I'd tuned in to his angry, guttural nonsense, the chiseled hunk of mean had worked himself into a literal lather, little blobs of spittle-froth collecting in the corners of his mouth. And when my backseat driver caught wind we were being addressed, he responded in kind, banging on the metaphorical bars of his cell and shouting his fool head off so loud it was a physical effort to keep my lips, lungs, and tongue from making the words he was thinking a reality.

"Solda!" he shouted – "soldier" – the only word of his crazed ranting I could understand. *"Ich fordere eine Identifizierung zu sehen!"*

I blinked stupidly at him. He jabbed me in the breastbone with one battering-ram finger. *"Ihren Ausweis, jetzt!"*

Then, from nowhere it seemed, Lilith's voice whispered toe-curlingly into my ear. "He wants to see your identification."

I wheeled, looked around. She was nowhere to be seen. And this big blond ape gave no indication he'd seen her at all. He just looked at me, eyes narrowing, as I spun madly in front of him, like he was weighing the odds I was perhaps some kind of mental patient who'd escaped the hospital through a mortar hole and wandered dazed into his camp.

I wanted to shout at that beautiful, elusive whatever-she-was I didn't *have* any damn ID. But the second I did, the jig would be up. Soon as I started talking all American, these bastards would ventilate me but good. So instead I glared into the middle distance and heaved a theatrical shrug, hoping wherever Lilith was, she got the gist.

She seemed to, because mere seconds later, I heard a whisper in my other ear. "Tell him *'Es gibt keine Zeit! Ich muss mit Ihrem Kommandanten sprechen!'"*

This time, I managed not to twirl around like a little girl in a field of daisies, instead just casting a sidelong glance toward the nothing from whence Lilith's voice had sprung.

The big oaf grabbed a handful of my uniform shirt and pulled me close. Lilith repeated herself into my ear. Between the two of them, they shook me out of my paralysis, if not the fear and confusion that caused it. And as the man began to raise the pistol in his other hand, I stammered, *"Kine zight! Itch muss mit eerim Commandant sprecken!"*

Predictably, it didn't help. He didn't shoot me, at least, but the second those few mangled syllables of idiot German spilled out of my mouth, his features changed from expressing anger to amused derision. I was a simpleton, he thought; shell-shocked, or else some kind of retard. And if that wasn't bad enough, I had Lilith's throaty laugh to contend with, ringing in my ear for me and me alone to hear.

"Mein Kommandant," he muttered, shaking his head and laughing as he gave me a none-too-gentle shove in the chest that sent me staggering several paces back from the compound's entrance. He waved his gun at me in half-hearted threat and shouted, *"Geh weg, du Idiot. Jetzt*!" And though Lilith didn't bother to translate, I got the gist, staggering defeated away from the compound gate, and plopping down despondently atop a nearby stoop, just out of sight of the glowering mass of hopped-up flesh who'd rebuffed my attempts to enter. My head was throbbing as the adrenaline-haze cleared, my stomach was roiling from the nerves. I patted the front pocket of my fatigues unconsciously, looking for the pack of cigarettes I should have damn well known wasn't there, for these weren't my clothes, and this wasn't my body. Both were now several months and a continent away, the former tossed out or donated, and the latter rotting six feet beneath a perfunctory John Doe plaque.

I buried my head in my hands. Tried to hold back tears. I wasn't sure where they were coming from, exactly, some noxious cocktail of exhaustion and frustration, of loss and heartache and regret. Of input, both intellectual and sensory, so insane, so beyond anything my prior existence had prepared me for, that I simply couldn't square it without feeling the insistent tug of insanity's dark depths.

I was broken.

Alone.

Or so I thought.

"That went well," came Lilith's voice from a good six inches to my left. Conversational, this time, not whispered. I flinched despite myself. This woman had a knack for scaring the ever-loving shit out of me.

"Kiss my ass," I snapped without so much as looking up at her. "The last thing I need right now is your sarcasm. You left me to twist out there. I had no idea what the hell I was even doing. I'm lucky I wasn't killed."

"Lucky," she replied. "Right." Then she sighed and put an arm around me. "But I assure you, Collector, I was not being sarcastic. I was actually quite impressed."

"Come again?"

"As you said, you could have easily been killed. In fact, I was rather counting on it. Most Collectors are on their first job. They don't understand their own abilities; they haven't learned to use the tools at their disposal. And yet, by poise and wits alone, you managed not to let that overgrown monkey end you. Consider your first lesson passed, and who knows? You may survive this collection yet."

I looked her over, to see if she was putting me on. Then I saw the taupe silk nothing she was wearing, and despite myself, half-wished she would. But, my own lame double-entendres aside, I saw no evidence she was anything other than sincere.

"So we're not sunk, then?"

She laughed. Teenaged boys the world over looked toward the sky and thought the very same impure thought I did. As, I suspect, did a goodly slice of teenaged girls. "No, Collector, I assure you we are far from sunk."

"Okay, then, what do you know that I don't?"

"A vast universe of things, many of which I'd give a great deal not to," she said. "But the most, ah, *germane* of them is one that I alluded to back at your vessel's flat: namely, the fact that you're not anchored to the body in which you presently find yourself. You may possess another at will."

"How?"

"It's a simple matter, really, of first finding one that's suitable and then projecting your consciousness out of your current one, across the void, and into your new one."

"Simple," I said. "Sure. But how will I know a vessel's suitable?"

"Any living human will do," she said, "as, in a pinch, would the newly dead, though I'd recommend against the latter; they're considered by my kind somewhat uncouth."

"Uncouth," I echoed.

She nodded sagely. "Uncouth. Not to mention ripe."

"Okay, Teach," I said, "avoid the dead. What else?"

"You want your vessel – living or dead – to be in decent physical condition. For one, you never know what you might end up demanding of them, and for two, because possessing your next requires your last to expend a decent amount of energy sending you on your way. If you were to end up in an infant or an invalid, for example, you might find it difficult – if not impossible – to leave."

"That sounds… unpleasant."

"It is," Lilith replied. "Pray you never have the displeasure."

"So do I, like, go touch them or whatever?"

"No. Distance is not an issue. You'll be projecting yourself transdimensionally," she said and then, when she saw the look of utter confusion on my face, clarified. "Outside the realm of the physical world."

"I see," I said. I didn't.

As if she read my mind, she replied, "No, you don't. How could you? But you will, soon enough."

"That sounds vaguely ominous."

"Then let's instead just say there's no time like the present." She clapped me on the back and stood. "Come on, Collector, let's go shopping!"

••••

When the great ape saw me wandering back and forth outside the compound gate once more, he couldn't help but taunt me, nudging a friend or two and getting them into the act as well. Lucky for me, their jeers were in German, so I couldn't make heads or tails of them.

Honestly, he might've been a raging asshole, but it's not like I could fault him for making fun. After all I was – as far as he could tell, at least – talking to myself. Lilith had pulled her stealth-mode trick again, and was whispering like Jiminy Cricket's sultry evil twin in my ear, as together we picked out my next ride.

"What about the loudmouth jackass at the gate?" I muttered. "He's big and strong, and clearly trusted by his higher-ups. Plus, he's kind of a dick."

"No good," she replied. "We want in the compound, and he's stuck manning the gate. Someone's bound to notice if he leaves his post."

"Okay, then, what about his wiry friend?"

"His uniform's infantry," she said. "Not a chance in hell he's allowed into the bunker."

I stood and watched a moment, and then I spotted him. I don't know how I knew he was the one, but I just did. Like a kitten seeing a bird outside the window for the first time and recognizing it as prey, I didn't need to be told; instincts I didn't even know I had had already told me.

"That's the one," I said, my eyes locked on my new vessel, my next suit of meat.

"Which one?" she whispered. "Don't point."

"The gaunt, skeleton-looking guy in the overcoat, hunching his way across the square. You see him?"

"You mean the fellow with the slicked back hair?" Though I couldn't see her, I thought I detected the hint of a smile in her tone.

"That's the one."

"Then yes I do. Why him?"

Her question wasn't hostile or challenging, I realized, but leading. A teacher, guiding her pupil. "Because he's wearing a suit and woolen coat – civilian clothes, not a military uniform – and yet he's the only person visible who's walking unaccompanied. Plus, did you see how those four soldiers gave him a wide berth? They're afraid of him. Taken together, that means he's someone powerful, someone who could get us into Hitler's bunker."

"You're not wrong," she said to me. "That's Dr. Joseph Goebbels, Hitler's Minister of Propaganda. He and his family have been living in the outer bunker adjacent to Hitler's own for weeks. So what're you waiting for, sport? Have at him!"

"How?"

This time, her whisper took on a darker aspect. "Figure it out," she told me, and then she fell silent, no longer responding to my pleas for some measure of instruction.

As the gatekeepers hurled jeers at me rendered incomprehensible by the language-barrier between us like surreal nonsense-talking schoolyard bullies, I closed my eyes and stilled my mind. And reached. And stretched. And found.

When my mind first skipped off the surface of the thin man's, we both recoiled as if struck. I now know it's rare for the soon-to-be-possessed to sense a Collector's approach, but in the case of Goebbels, it wasn't because the man was mystically sensitive in any way, it's just that I'm supposed to be as lithe and quick as a pickpocket, but he being my first, my approach was more like a drunk caroming into him at the *Biergarten* come closing time. But while he, visibly spooked, looked left and right in a vain attempt to determine what it was that had just rocked him back, I was emboldened by the fact that I had found him in the darkness once, and so I marshaled all the strength I could and willed my consciousness across the gap once more, no longer tentative, but committed, determined.

I didn't expect the man to fight.

When I next opened my eyes, I was looking out from within the compound through the fence at the body I'd until recently inhabited. I doubled over, puked all over my black leather shoes. My eyes slammed shut once more – this time, not my doing. I forced them open, and was once more outside the gate, looking in at an ill and plainly terrified Goebbels.

He pointed toward me, barked in German at the guards. The only word I caught was *Amerikaner*, though his meaning was pretty clear nonetheless. The guards' jeers ceased, their faces all the sudden stony-serious. Their rifles suddenly ready.

I raised my hands. Closed my eyes. Dropped to my knees and prayed.

And then I threw myself at Goebbels once more.

Gunshots. Dozens of them – hundreds – some single rifle pops, others an automatic *rat-a-tat-tat*. From the guards, the tower battlements, white flashes from the rooftops all around.

Once more in Goebbels, I teetered back on limbs both unfamiliar and uncooperative, and wound up on my bony ass. Again bile rose in my throat, and I expelled it onto the trampled grass on which I sat in a series of choking, acid coughs.

Through the fence I watched the poor, sad sap in which I'd ridden here be torn to shreds, hunks of meat and brain flying off him left and right amidst vast gouts of blood, each round that connected another spasm in his *Danse Macabre*. He was no innocent, I thought, for he'd aligned himself either knowingly or out of some twisted sense of patriotism with the most evil fighting force the world had ever known. And yet as that selfsame force reduced him to so much wurst, I couldn't help but feel a pang of guilt. The man was dead because of me, and anyways, I knew a thing or two about being roped into serving a less-than-savory master.

His flailing corpse tipped forward in slow motion, already dead but not yet still. The shooting petered out like popcorn nearly finished, and then stopped altogether, but not before one final round exploded his head like an overripe pumpkin dropped from a height, his lower jaw a toothsome horseshoe end-over-ending to the surface of the blood-spattered roadway. Then he was down, and it was over. Soon, rough hands gripped my narrow elbows, and lifted me up.

My first thought was, I'm caught. But the hands, though rough, took care to set me right and dust me off, and the words, inscrutable to me though they were, were worried, questioning. I nodded tersely at the men who'd helped me up, which proved an adequate response to their inquiries, because they – reluctantly – let me be, returning to their respective posts while other soldiers trotted past the barricades with shovels, bags, and jugs of water to rid the roadway of the traitorous slop now smeared across it.

Alone and in control at last – Goebbels mewling in frustration from the makeshift cell I'd envisioned for him in the back of his own mind – I raised my borrowed hands to touch my unfamiliar face, pausing a moment midway to look at them. They were skeletal and gray-complected, with faint yellow stains of nicotine between the first and second finger of the right. Oh, thank God, I thought, this guy might actually have a pack of cigarettes. I probed my face with said new fingers. Cheeks hollow, and shaved smooth; high cheekbones and deep-set eyes; lips thin, and raw from chill of spring. Eyebrows thick and bristly against my delicate, uncalloused fingers. Coarse hair oiled down to greasy excess. Joints creaking all the while as I test-flexed them each in turn.

Then, at once, I felt self-conscious as my circumstances came back to me. I'd (somewhat improbably) managed to penetrate the seat of Nazi power's defenses, but the quality of my present disguise was predicated upon my never being questioned, since the second I opened my mouth, the jig was up. If I wanted to take out their precious Führer, I was going to have to blend in. Play the part. Keep the lowest profile possible. And that meant, in part, not staring at my own hands and feeling up my face in the middle of the courtyard like some hophead in the park.

So, cognizant of the fact I may well have attracted an audience, I made a show of brushing myself off , trying to play off my prior behavior as nothing more than a post-tumble injury-check. Then I patted my jacket until I found Goebbel's cigarettes – hand-rolled inside a pewter case emblazoned with the oak-wreath, eagle, and swastika insignia of the Nazi Party – in a pocket alongside a box of matches. I stuck one between my lips and struck a match, cupping hands against the breeze as I puffed the cigarette alight. A sudden rush of calm and clarity fell over me as the nicotine hit. I smoked the cigarette halfway down in three quick drags, and then I turned my attentions to the small, cone-roofed tower that marked the entrance to the bunker proper. Two guards flanked the closed iron door, while beside them – somehow unnoticed despite her stunning beauty and her ridiculously out-of-place outfit, a scant black nightie and feathered kitten heel slippers to match – reclined Lilith, lounging invisible, it seemed, against the cold, boot-marred ground as if it were a plush chaise longue. I couldn't help but think her outfit was chosen more to shock than titillate, but it accomplished both in spades. When she caught me staring, she flashed a dazzling smile my way and wiggled her fingers at me in a mock-coquettish wave.

As I marched toward the bunker entrance, a warm wind kicked up from the south, and Lilith disappeared. I set my jaw and held my tongue, relying upon my familiar visage to gain me entry. The soldiers manning the door did not disappoint in that regard. Two sharp knocks against the door, and it swung open without a word.

I nodded at them each in turn, silent commendation from their superior for doing so superlative a job.

Then I descended the concrete steps into the bunker, determined to put their Führer in the ground.

8.

"Nicky! Nicky, are you effing *seeing* this?"

As a point of fact, Nicky *wasn't* effing seeing this, because Nicky wasn't home right now. He hadn't been for a while. When he and his cohorts stopped to film their live webcast Q&A in Boulder two days back, I took the opportunity to hitch a ride in ol' Nicky, stuffing that poor, befuddled neo-hippie burnout into a metaphorical steamer trunk in the back of his mind next to some half-remembered Rusted Root lyrics, the abandoned mental blueprints for his pot-themed amusement park, and that awkward memory of seeing his not-yet-stepmom naked that one time by accident only really on purpose.

Not that Topher (pronounced Tow-fer, like we didn't know his name was really Chris) or Zadie'd noticed. Firstly, because Nicky – the cameraman, equipment tech, weed supplier, and webmaster behind their all-the-sudden way-more popular web series *Monster Mavens* – who oh, by the way, really hated being called Nicky it's Nicholas or at least just Nick you guys c'mon – was the quiet type, usually too baked and too absorbed in tinkering with his many gadgets to offer up more than a crooked half-smile or a grunt to register his happiness or displeasure (excepting those rare instances in which he felt he'd been Nicky-ed to excess). And secondly, they were too busy basking in the their newfound fame.

Until two weeks back, Monster Mavens was a modest internet success, with their blog generating a couple hundred unique hits per post, and their YouTube channel clocking in at somewhere around twenty-five hundred subscribers, half of whom were smartass college kids at least as baked as Nicholas-not-Nicky, who only tuned in to mock Topher and Zadie's stubborn, moronic credulity in the face of no evidence whatsoever.

See, Topher and Zadie hunted monsters.

Badly.

Of course, they called them cryptids, and played them off as animals as-yet undiscovered. You know, Bigfoot and Nessie and the like, only they talked about them like they were a hair's breadth away from coelacanths, those fish everybody thought were extinct until some fisherman netted a live one off the coast of South Africa. But if you ask me, finding a seven-foot ape in the Pacific Northwest or a dinosaur in a goddamn loch is a frick-ton less likely than a new fish in the sea. As anyone'll tell you, there are plenty of them. Plus, these two patchouli-stinking, constantly bickering Deadheads (their shirts all said "Phish" or "Moe" or "Dave Matthews Band" on them, but I've been around a while, and I know the type) didn't strike me as the scientific-method type – all the jargon-laced talk of fossil records and investigative methods in the world couldn't convince me this gig of theirs was anything other than the two of them successfully forestalling their entrance into the real world, in favor of nights spent swigging jug wine around the campfire and boinking in tents while – and unfortunately, I know this part for absolute, if unscientific, fact – don't-call-me-Nicky here surreptitiously recorded audio for his own, uh, personal use.

Then came Ada Swanson.

And then came fame and fortune.

And then came me.

You've heard of Ada Swanson. Hell, anyone who walked past a TV set in the summer of '09 couldn't have missed her. Those blond locks all twisted up in perfect ringlets, the tweezed eyebrows and bleached baby teeth that somehow so grotesquely aged her. Cheeks rouged rounder than round. Lips sculpted by cosmetics until their childlike fullness more resembled a grown woman's. Every picture perfectly staged, her twirling a baton in the front yard of her family's modest raised ranch in their quiet Colorado Springs suburb; playing piano at the local senior center; volunteering at a Denver soup kitchen. Always in sequins and a smile. And all of America wondering what kind of sick fucks did that to a six-year-old. Dolled her up. Pranced her about in front of crowds and cameras. Toured the pageant circuit like she was some kind of prize poodle: sit up, roll over, beg.

It was only a matter of time, the eager sad-faced viewing public told themselves, before someone went and took her. After all, that's what happens in these twisted cycles of exploitation. They escalate, become self-feeding. Pageant-kids become targets for predators. And twenty-four-hour news networks make stars of murderers in their endless quest for new sets of bones to gnaw on.

The lack of irony with which we exploit the exploited to feed our endless need for misery-based entertainment is astonishing.

She was three days shy of her seventh birthday when she was taken. Straight out her bedroom window sometime between midnight and 6am, if her parents were to be believed. Not that anybody thought they were. They were creepshows, said America, and on that, at least, America probably wasn't wrong. Mom was a pill-popping, big-haired, crispy-banged former cheerleader who ran the front desk at a local Chevy dealership and occasionally, after hours, lay atop it with the owner/manager. Theirs was a symbiotic relationship: his bad back kept her in Oxy, and the jungle-gym sex she treated him to in return kept him in a bad back. Dad was a general contractor with big hands and a big mouth who'd been between jobs for going on six years, which didn't stop him from racking up a four-figure tab at the local watering hole, and low fives at the track. Then there was his best buddy, a local ski bum by the name of Dick Hartwell – five feet six of pure douchey smarm, always photographed in the same fleece vest and wraparound Oakleys, like he'd just stepped off the slopes. His picture was splashed across every news outlet the nation over for weeks when kiddie-porn was found on his computer. Never mind that it turned out to be a bunch of images downloaded from the sort of "barely legal" site where the chicks are all twenty-something behind their lip gloss, knee socks, and pigtails, by the time they cut him loose, his rep was ruined. Which was fine, I guess, since it turns out ol' Dick Hartwell of Colorado Springs was once Richard Hartwell of Jackson Hole, Wyoming, who just so happened to be thirty-two months in arrears on his child support payments for the three children by two women he'd left behind.

No one believed their story. Not even me. I mean, who pries open a second-story window in a quiet, closely packed development with no trees or hedges to speak of and absconds with a freakin' six-year-old girl and her trusty stuffed rabbit without raising enough ruckus to wake the whole damn block? The way I saw it, the parents had to know more than they were letting on. They seemed all lovey-dovey on the surface, sure. But once the media spotlight blistered off the thin veneer of normalcy they'd overlaid onto their life, the rot beneath only served to make them look even guiltier than the hard-to-swallow lack of evidence.

No wonder Ada's pop decided to eat a gun six months into the investigation.

Anyways, given the lack of evidence, the leads dried up pretty quick, and once every speck of dirt in the Swanson family's life had been well and truly inspected by the tutting masses, folks lost interest. Then some nutjob psychiatrist in Fort Hood went on a rampage that left thirteen soldiers and civilians dead, and America moved on. The grand pageant of misery had found another head on which to rest the crown. Funny to think the well-coiffed anchors said the shooter-shrink's name a thousand times, but the victims in that case were nothing but a hashmark on his tally. At least when a kid went missing, they were given the dignity of being exploited by name.

So what's any of that got to do with Topher and Zadie and Nicholas-you-guys-not-Nicky? That's easy. See, two weeks ago, the three of them were trudging through the chill Colorado wilderness, hot on the trail of some nothing-at-all they were convinced had to be Sasquatch (a local hiker snapped a blurry photo of something brown and maybe moving, which didn't seem that remarkable to me, since damn near *everything* in Colorado that isn't snow is brown, and half of it is moving) when they, uh, found her. Or she found them. Or not, depending who you ask.

You wouldn't think the event would be so contentious, so up for debate. I mean, Nicholas-not-Nicky caught the big moment on camera, and once word spread, the footage was picked up by the mainstream media, first local, then national. The handheld camera jittering in time with the sound of trundling footfalls, crunching over dead leaves and crusted, desiccated snow as dry and noisy as breakfast cereal. Topher's breath pluming as he whispered his narration – all mixed metaphors, malapropisms, and "majesty of nature" monologuing. Zadie with her emphatic "Nicky! Nicky, are you hearing this?" as their bull-in-a-china-shop parade through the stunned silence of the old growth forest was joined by a fourth set of footsteps – crazed, ragged, and coming ever closer. Topher, Nicholas-not-Nicky, and Zadie crouched for a moment, silent, behind a thicket of brambles, beyond which that fourth set of footfalls shuffled out a confused solo while it tried to figure out where its accompaniment went. Topher prattled on in a reverent whisper about how they were going to change the course of modern science when they revealed the gentle giant behind these bushes – this missing link between man and beast – to the world.

The big moment: Nicholas-not-Nicky's hand reaching out past the lens to push aside the branches. Zadie gasping. Topher shouting, "What the fuck?"

And then the three of them gang-tackled by a gaunt, hunched, and apparently stark-raving-mad woman – ninety years old if she was a day – with wild eyes, tattered pajamas, and matted hair that looked like strands of iron and steel against her blue-tinged hypothermic skin, which was speckled white with frostbite. She smashed head-first into the camera, mashing a cheap pink plastic barrette into the lens. The four of them went ass-over-teakettle – the five of them if you count the old lady's stuffed bunny – and slid down a small embankment to a creek. The whole while the three monster hunters are screaming, and the woman's prattling on the same nonsense five-syllable phrase over and over again. "Ahwahmahmommee!" stacked end-on-end, without so much as a pause for breath. She mouthed the words with every inhalation as well, sounding like a cross between a bullfrog and a set of soot-choked bellows. When they finally came to a rest at the bottom of the embankment, snow-dusted and sprinkled with pine needles, Topher and Zadie tag-teamed trying to calm her down, one soothing while the other asked Nicholas-not-Nicky if he was getting this. It didn't take, so Topher – fed up, I guess, or else he spent too much time in college watching soaps – slapped her. America didn't like that much, as it turns out, and he later admitted on the Today show he shoulda maybe had Zadie do it. But still, it did the trick; the old lady stopped talking.

"Now," he said to her, eyes glancing all can-you-believe-this at the camera the whole time, "nice and slow, how bout you tell us your name, and what it is you're trying to say, okay?"

The old woman swallowed hard and licked her cracked, bleeding lips, calming by degrees. Then she looked directly into the camera lens, and said, with all the attitude of a pissed-off tween diva, "My *name* is Ada Swanson, and I want my mommy."

Once the video hit the web, the response was full-on nuts – as, most assumed, was the old lady herself. But the obvious falsehood (in most folks' eyes, at least) of her claim aside, the fact remained that she was found in pajamas consistent with those Ada'd been wearing the night of her abduction, and she'd been carrying Ada's stuffed rabbit, Admiral Fuzzybutt, when she'd been found by these yahoos. Not a similar one, mind you, but the real effing deal, as identified some hours later by her mother. Seems the Admiral had himself a craft-project mishap one day when Ada was three – by which I mean his left ear was lopped off with a pair of scissors – and Ada's mother was forced to reattach the ear with the only thread she had on-hand, a royal blue. She did so inexpertly, though not without a certain flair. Anyways, her choice of thread and lack of skill were distinctive enough to convince Mom and cops both. They took the woman into custody and interrogated her for hours in an attempt to find out who she was and where she got the bunny.

But if the news was to be believed, her answers made no damned sense. She stuck with her story of being Ada Swanson, taken from her bed by dark of night. By whom? She didn't know, exactly. Seems she could only see them when the moon was full, whatever that means. Taken where? A cabin nestled in the woods as hard to look at as her captors or maybe not, she claimed, seeming confused and unsure because she also spoke of spending her nights beneath the stars, of bare dry earth beneath her feet (even on those rare instances in which it rained), and of the watchful eyes of animals in the darkness. When pressed on the question of where this maybe-cabin was, she couldn't say.

And how had she happened upon the Monster Mavens? Why, she'd escaped, of course, or maybe been let go, only to wander for days through the frigid Colorado wilderness, parched and starved and hypothermic, before finally running into the first people besides her elusive captors she'd seen since she'd been taken. Which was how long, exactly? Days, she thought sometimes, or maybe months, or maybe decades. Her story was vague and unhinged, full of nightmares of bloodletting and half-glimpsed half-human creatures who brushed her hair and cooed over her and plumped her up inside their imaginary cabin with stolen sweets and wild root vegetables and the spit-roasted meats of countless tiny woodland creatures even as they slowly drained her dry – but word for word, unnamed sources told the papers, it matched the big bucket of crazy she'd unloaded with scarcely a pause for breath straight into Nicholas-not-Nicky's camera as they'd trudged back to the Monster Mavens van with her in tow.

Word was, her fingerprints came back inconclusive. Which is what I woulda told the press, too, if I'd run 'em and they came back matching a missing six-year-old girl's. DNA results were pending, said the news – but the state was backlogged, their lab drowning under the rising tide of pending cases, so it could be weeks before they had anything to report. In the meantime, no one came forward to identify the woman, which made sense, because Lilith was pretty damn sure she was Ada. She told me as much a few days back, after popping in on me from out of nowhere and damn near scaring me right out of my borrowed skin.

••••

"Like the duds," she said. "Very… ironic. I hear the kids are into that these days."

The duds in question were a paunchy, lugubrious sixty-something Italian man with deep-set eyes, a gentle voice, and delicate, uncalloused hands, upon the third finger of the left of which he wore a clunky gold ring, absent jewels but stamped with the image of the crucifixion. A cardinal's ring, which made sense, on account of he was a cardinal. A cardinal Lilith damn near killed by sheer force of startlement, if his race-horse heartbeat and resulting dizziness were any indication.

I tugged free my meat-suit's Roman collar, setting it on the scarred wooden desk of the study carrel at which I sat, and gulped air in an attempt to calm him. He was a pious man, well-intentioned yet ill-equipped for the recent turn his life had taken, meaning me. The carrel was piled high with books, half of them older than the European conquest of the Americas, plucked from the shelves of the Vatican's Secret Archives in which I sat. The place was deserted; all the Vatican was abuzz with Easter preparations, leaving few with time for study or quiet reflection. It was five months or so since I'd vanquished Magnusson, four since the nameless creature in the desert, and I'd spent the ensuing days doing my damndest to locate any mention of the remaining feral Brethren, to no avail. Lilith figured it was best to take them out first, before tackling the ones who'd been tipped to hell's hate-on for them and would therefore see me coming. Problem was, they were the very definition of off-the-grid. Even the Pope's own private library didn't have shit-all on them, though I *did* find some peculiar references to Christ's own purported bloodline (which, apart from the fact that it shouldn't exist since scripture never mentions him fathering a child, seems to include two heads of state, four saints, and all three Bee Gees) and a centuries-old reference to a near-apocalypse ushered forth in a great city by the sea as a consequence of the damnation of an innocent girl – only to be foiled by one of the devil's own.

But I didn't put much stock in prophecies.

"Nothing ironic about it," I told her. "I needed access. This guy had it. End of story. Besides, you're behind the times. I hear irony is dead."

"Yes, well, so are you," she said. "Although I can't help but notice this meat-suit of yours is not. That makes what – eleven live ones in the past five months alone? Dare I hope you've lost your taste for piloting the dead?"

"Dare all you like, but it won't make it any truer," I told her. "Like I said, I needed access, and this guy had it. Dead cardinals are hard to come by, and anyways, even if I could find one, it wouldn't do me any good. He'd raise a few eyebrows if he was seen walking around."

"And here I thought his sort was big on resurrections."

"*Resurrection*," I corrected, "as in singular. Now, what're you doing here, Lily?" I confess, that last was testier than I intended, but truth be told, her teasing hit a little close to home. I *had* been taking a lot of living vessels lately. I kept telling myself it was on account of access or some other necessity, but the fact is, the Sam of old would have found another way. When it comes right down to it, taking living vessels was… easier than it used to be. Less hand-wringy. Maybe my heart was growing harder. Maybe something inside me had given up. Or maybe being so close to the dark energy released by Ana's failed ritual in LA – the one that resulted in Danny's death – had tarnished me in ways I'd yet to understand. Whatever the reason, it troubled me, but not enough to stop. That alone was enough to make me wonder if I'd lost something fundamental to what made me *me*.

"I have a lead," she told me. "A little girl who disappeared four years ago from her Colorado home just reappeared. Only she's not so little anymore."

"Look, Lily, I don't mean to criticize, but that sounds kind of flimsy. I know you haven't been among the living for a while now, but kids grow up. It's hardly news, let alone evidence of Brethren involvement."

Lilith gave me a look that could have shattered glass. "I don't mean to say that she got taller, you fucking dolt, I'm telling you she wandered out of the woods an old woman."

I sat up a little straighter in my chair. "She what?"

"You heard me."

"You sure she's not a nut?"

"That's what the authorities believe, of course," she said, "but they're wrong."

"And you think there's Brethren mojo behind her aging act?"

"Do you recall what Jain said to you?"

I narrowed my eyes at her in puzzlement. "Jain?"

Lilith shook her head subtly – more to herself than to me – and clarified. "The one you killed in Mexico."

I thought back. "If I could be killed," I quoted as best as I could remember, "my mountain cousins would have found a way. They begrudge me my appetites, as if their method of procuring sustenance is any more humane." Realization dawned. "You think the mountains are the Rockies, and the humane methods are sucking her life-force dry bit by bit but leaving her alive?"

"I do indeed."

I looked around. Slammed closed the book that I'd been poring over. A plume of dust that smelled like dried vanilla poofed out of it and pricked at my sinuses, daring me to sneeze. "Then fuck this place," I said. "Let's find me a new meat-suit and head to Colorado!"

"Excellent," said Lilith. "As it happens, I have just the candidate."

The police combed the woods, of course, aided by countless volunteers from as far afield as Fort Collins and Durango, sweeping through the brush in dotted lines of men and women with only ten feet in between. But despite the fact the area surrounding Colorado Springs was too dry for any significant snowfall to accumulate the terrain was steep, uneven, and tough to navigate, and there was just too much of it to cover with any degree of confidence. After a week spent trudging back and forth along a grid two square miles centered on the spot the woman had been found, the police called off the search.

Lucky for me, the Monster Mavens hadn't, and who could blame them? Their fifteen minutes of fame had brought them endorsements, late-night talk appearances, even the promise of a book deal. They were gonna milk it for all that it was worth, and with a YouTube audience now numbering in the hundred-thousands, that meant trying to find the mysterious cabin of which the old woman spoke. And, of course, the strange, subhuman creatures within.

Did they believe the woman to be Ada? Hard to say. Nicholas, based on what little I could glean from the not pot-dulled bits of memory I'd been able to access, didn't, but Topher and Zadie seemed earnest enough. Lord knows they played it up whether they believed it or not. And the internet gobbled it up like so many McNuggets. The old woman had her own Wikipedia entry, and the comments section of the Monster Mavens' blog was chock-a-block with speculation. SCULLY58008 was betting, against all odds, on some sort of hillbilly brainwashing cult, while LilMsGlinda was leaning toward a coven of witches looking to fatten up the old lady Hansel-and-Gretel style so they could eat her. VanH3llsing, predictably, guessed vampires. And Area69 said dollars to donuts it was aliens, or a government cover-up of same.

If they only knew how much weirder the truth really was.

It was six days in to the Monster Mavens' search – *our* search, I should say – that we'd found the cabin.

We'd been hiking in a haphazard zigzag – something Topher (never *Christopher*, a rule even Nicholas-not-Nicky obeyed, though neither Topher nor Zadie extended him such courtesy) cooked up between sips of Early Times straight from the bottle as he hunched over our maps beside the fire at camp one night. "The cops don't know what the eff they're doing, man," he'd told me conspiratorially, the sheer paint-blistering offensiveness of his whiskey breath making me wonder whether it might be prudent to be sitting farther away from open flame. "The sorts of things we're looking for, they don't follow lines or grids, you get me?"

I didn't. Luckily, Topher was too drunk, and too comfortable in his role as alpha-male to require – or even expect – a response.

"We gotta, like, listen to our *souls*, bro. They'll lead us true, you wait and see."

And as stupid as that sounded, it kinda sorta worked.

We'd been on the trail for hours. Lungs hoarse in the thin mountain air, Topher and Zadie snapping at each other all day in the benign way all couples do when their company runs brittle. They'd been pushing hard to find some scrap of fame-stretching evidence ever since the calls started drying up a few days after the discovery of the old woman, and they were both haggard, tired, and grumpy as all get-out. Not that I had a ton of sympathy for them. They had each other, after all, while I had no one, and on a pettier note, they got to walk all day with those ski-pole-looking thingys that helped with balance or whatever, while I was stuck pretending to be their cameraman. That meant hauling thirty pounds of camera around on one shoulder and maneuvering by viewfinder, which in turn meant I'd experienced several days of stumbles, backaches, and motion sickness. But I'd gotten my revenge, I guess. I was supposed to be editing and uplinking the footage of our mystical snipe-hunt every night from camp, but in fact, I'd been doing no such thing. Wouldn't even know how, to own the truth. Hell, there was a pretty good chance this camera I was carrying wasn't even *on*. Not like I could tell the difference either way. Best I could hope for was to remember to take the lens cap off.

But that goddamned camera was good for one thing, at least: it could see the fucking cabin. Which is more than I could say for the three of us. Though whether we couldn't, or just *wouldn't*, I'm not entirely sure; Lord knows how Brethren mojo works. The sensation was not unlike the one I'd experienced when I'd first arrived at the shuttered public bath house Magnusson had been using as his laboratory. But while that building simply resisted looking at, causing my eyes to slide right off it with nothing more than the scantest of impressions, the cabin flat-out would not show itself to my – or Topher's, or Zadie's – naked eye.

I'm getting ahead of myself. First I should tell you about the almost-murder.

We'd been trudging along for what seemed like forever, on jagged nerves and terrain to match. The afternoon was getting on, and the long shadows cast by the mountain ridge to our west bathed us in chill gray half-light like crushing depression, dulling colors, numbing limbs to sluggishness, and settling creaky into our every weary joint. My feet were blistered. My camera-shoulder ached. And my head was throbbing, on account of Topher and Zadie's bickering, which had begun as the occasional potshot a few miles back, only to escalate to a vicious barrage as the afternoon wore on.

Topher, early on, all brittle false-cheer: "C'mon – pick up the pace back there, woman! We got monsters to catch!"

"Quit hogging the water!" Zadie, later, whining.

"What're you, stupid? We're not going that way, it's too steep." Topher, evening the score a few paces later. And then they were off to the races.

"You're the one who marked the route, dumbass. Can't you fucking read a map?"

"Better than you can read a fucking sonar readout."

"Jesus, does it *always* have to come back to that bullshit in Loch Ness?"

"Bullshit?" Topher got up in Zadie's face, all pointy and indignant. "How can you stand there and call it bullshit? That sonar image was *definitive*."

"Definitively a piece of driftwood." As Topher got closer, Zadie made a face, squinching up her nose and eyes. "Holy hell," she said, "when's the last time you washed that shirt? It smells like gym socks soaked in Patchouli and bong water. I'm gonna lose my fucking lunch here."

"More like both our lunches, the way you've been packing it in."

"Excuse me?"

"I'm just saying, I thought I made it pretty clear I packed the ostrich jerky for *me*."

"Well then maybe you shouldn't have put it in *my* pack. Oh, wait! You needed room in your pack for that goddamned travel guitar, because God forbid I go one night without having to hear your horrible playing. You'd think in seven years, you would have learned *one* chord."

"You never complained *before*."

"You sure about that? Or is it that you couldn't hear me over the fucking racket you were making? Long as you insist on torturing me with that thing night in and night out, I'll finish the goddamn jerky if I goddamn well feel like it. And you're one to talk about putting on the pounds; your gut looks like fucking cookie dough pouring out over that stupid-ass belt buckle of yours."

"You sound just like your mother. And you told me you liked this belt buckle!"

"I swear to Christ, *Christopher*, if you tell me I sound just like my mother one more time, you'll be bunking with Nicky, you hear me? And believe you me, there's *plenty* of stuff I've said I liked that I'm mostly just enduring."

"You know I hate it when you call me Christopher! Christopher is my *dad's* name. And anyways, it's fucking rich, you teasing me about my name – your given name is *Susan*. You stole Zadie off the cover of a book, one you never even *finished*, for shit's sake."

At that last, Zadie looked directly into my camera, worried that she'd been outed to the world. (No chance: it wasn't recording, and anyway, I'd been zooming in on a cool-looking bird some twenty feet behind her.) Then, after one stricken moment of paralysis, she wheeled on Topher, and smacked him square across the jaw.

I was surprised. In my time with Topher and Zadie (Chris and Susan?), I'd seen 'em bicker plenty, but nothing ever came of it. They were peas in a pod, or whatever the hippie drum-circle equivalent would be. Macho and hembra bongos, I guess. (What? That's what they call the big bongo and the little one, respectively. Or maybe it's the little and the big. Okay, I may've been spending way too much time with these two.) Point is, I'd never gotten a whiff of violence repressed in their prior interactions. Which made the slap surprising, and what came next goddamn terrifying.

Topher looked at her a moment, shocked silent. Then he shrugged out of his pack in one quick motion and tackled her, his hands around her neck.

Zadie let out a squeal that became a gurgle as his thumbs pressed against her trachea. I belted out an involuntary "*Hey*!" and moved toward them to stop Topher from killing her. In my astonishment, I clung stupidly to the camera on my shoulder. It had become so much an extension of this meat-suit in my mind – so accustomed was Nicholas to carrying it – I simply never thought to drop it. It was a stupid move, because the weight of the equipment slowed me down, and could have cost Zadie her life, but in retrospect, my idiocy proved helpful. But not before we three tumbled down the embankment.

It happened like this. I leapt onto Topher's back, and tried to ride him to the ground. He would not relinquish his grip on Zadie, who was already off-balance from his attack. My weight plus the camera made him top-heavy. He tumbled forward onto her, me still on his back and then rolled into an awkward somersault, taking me along. His hands released her neck, too late to prevent her from tumbling after us. So the three of us rolled down the steep decline, maybe twenty feet all told, but the pitch was such it was more falling than rolling.

We hit bottom and scattered like jacks. I landed flat on my back with a hollow *whumph* and a plume of breath like a pair of bellows being squeezed. For an agonizing second, new breath just wouldn't come, and then finally my diaphragm listened to what my lungs were telling it and got back to work.

I found my feet and looked around, disoriented. Heard a shuffle of nylon ripstop, caught a glimpse of matching winter jackets through the trees, one following the other in hot pursuit. I had no idea what the hell had come over these two today, but I figured I ought to join in the parade. And so I did, the camera dangling behind me from its strap, its choking weight slowing me down enough I thought I might never catch up. But they weren't running for long.

Up ahead, I heard a scuffle, and then a sickening crack. Like a gunshot. Like broken bones. I worried it was Zadie's neck and put on whatever little speed I could with the camera pulling back on me like a yoke. In seconds, I spotted them, and breathed a sigh of relief. It wasn't Zadie's neck that snapped. It was her walking pole, which had apparently just broken in half. Unfortunately for Topher, said walking pole broke in half because she brought it down atop his head.

Topher, who'd been grappling – buck knife drawn – with Zadie when she cold-cocked him, wobbled a moment on his feet. His eyes rolled back, his face went slack, and his buck knife tipped slowly in his loosened grip, eventually falling to the forest floor point-down. Its handle wobbled back and forth as it stuck, in imitation of its owner, perhaps. Then Topher's knees buckled, and he went down.

I looked at Zadie, who was still holding the handled end of the walking pole like a baseball bat, its lacquered surface now terminating in a jagged metal O, and then at Topher's crumpled form. Zadie looked back at me, wild-eyed and panting. Then she threw the pole away from her in disgust, as if it had transformed into a writhing snake, and whatever malevolent urge had come over the two of them evaporated. She dropped to her knees beside her unconscious lover, and called to me, voice pleading: "Nicky! Nicky, get over here, and bring the camera. I can't tell if Topher's breathing!"

I did as she asked, struggling out of the camera strap as I approached. She snatched the camera from me like a desert wanderer might a canteen. Then she held the lens up to Topher's nose and mouth, her face splitting into a manic grin of relief as it plumed with rhythmic condensation.

"Oh, thank God," she said. "I thought I'd killed him. Hell, for a minute there, I thought *he* was gonna kill *me*." She chucked Nicholas-not-Nicky's camera aside without a thought. It bounced off a jutting shoulder of exposed mountain rock, and its oversized viewfinder swung open on its hinge. Somewhere deep inside his own psychic prison, Nicholas-not-Nicky let out a wail of sheer gearhead angst. But I wasn't paying him any mind. Nor, if I'm being honest, did I care much that Topher had regained a sort of swirly-eyeballed consciousness, thanks possibly to Zadie's gentle if insistent slapping of his cheeks.

But I *did* care about what he was pointing at with one unsteady hand as he blinked his eyes into focus, his face a mask of punch-drunk confusion. "Nicky!" he stage-whispered with awed incredulity. "Nicky, are you effing *seeing* this?"

And as I said some time ago, Nicky wasn't. But *I* was, and once Zadie followed the trail of Nicky's arm down past his pointing finger toward the camera, she was seeing it too.

The camera, propped crooked on the rock a few feet from us, aimed at a gentle, treeless patch of upslope, gray and barren as the moon, and as empty, too. The camera's viewfinder was open. And in it was that same patch of barren, empty upslope, though in the viewfinder it was neither barren nor empty.

On it sat a small log cabin, rough-hewn and lichen-scabbed. It sat a quarter-turn away from facing us, its front windows staring blankly into the middle distance from beneath their brow of covered porch as if indifferent to our presence. A thin wisp of oily smoke twisted skyward from its chimney. A patch of tilled earth arranged in furrows – a garden not yet growing – rested on its southeastern edge, now deep in sunset's shadow. The cabin was still and quiet beneath the waning light. No light shone from within. And though for our entire hike the forest had teemed with life, it had apparently abandoned us now, for all was silent and still as a crypt.

"The fuck *is* that?" Zadie muttered.

"That," I told them, "is proof."

"Of *what*?"

"That the world's a weirder place than even *you two* yahoos realize."

And then, before they knew what hit them, I attacked.

9.

"Ow! That pinches!"

"Does it?" I asked, giving the nylon line another tug. Topher wailed a little louder than was strictly necessary in response, if you ask me. But after the racket we made stumbling upon the cabin in the first place any attempt at a quiet approach was shot anyways, so I figured let him yell. "Good."

We were huddled in a cave some three hundred yards from where the cabin stood. More a depression in the rock than anything. Not quite deep enough for a bear to settle down in, but not so exposed to the wind and elements that these two would freeze to death if I didn't come back until morning. Probably. I mean, I'm not a nature guide or anything. But either way, I figured they stood a better chance of surviving hog-tied and tucked away somewhere than if I let them storm the cabin with me. I'd lost enough lives taking on the tunnel Brethren – three shit-bags and one innocent – to learn my lesson. The only hide I'd be risking today was Nicky's – er, *Nicholas's* – and even that was one more than I'd ideally prefer.

"What the fuck, Nicky!" This from Zadie, who, near as I could tell in the failing evening light, was giving me the scowling of a lifetime. "I thought you were our *friend*."

"If we're such good friends," I said, figuring I'd throw the consciousness who, when I left, would once more be driving this meat-suit a bone, "then you'd know I hate being called Nicky. And besides, this is for your own good."

"Yeah? How you figure?"

"Well, for one, believe me when I tell you, you want *nothing* to do with what's in that cabin. And for two, let's not forget whatever nasty juju they've enacted to keep folks from stumbling across it damn near made you two kill each other. But worry not, once I head in there and do my thing, you won't have either to contend with." *I hope*, I added mentally.

"Since when'd you go all Venkman on us?" asked Topher. "I thought you didn't even believe in this shit."

I rolled my eyes. "Venkman hunted ghosts," I told him, "and was a huckster besides. If you're gonna drop a reference, think I'd prefer Van Helsing."

"You mean that shitty movie by *The Mummy* guy where Wolverine wears that dumbass hat?"

"You know what?" I said. "Never mind."

"Nicky," Zadie said, only to shake her head and close her eyes by way of self-chastisement. "Nicholas," she corrected. "You don't have to do this."

"Do what?"

"Tie us up. Abandon us. Leave us out here to die."

"Zadie, believe me, you have no idea what you're talking about. Because, in order, yes I do; no, I hope I don't; and leaving you out here's the best way I can think to keep you breathing."

"If that were true," she said, "you'd leave us our packs, at least."

I eyed the backpacks lying at my feet – their zippers open, their contents strewn about. "You can keep your packs, and your food, and your clothes. All I need," I said, patting my stuffed jacket-pockets, "I got."

Topher glared at me. "Unless you're leaving us my buck knife, the whiskey, and our sat phone, consider yourself hella motherfucking fired."

At that, I smiled. Because I'd be lying if I said my plan didn't include his buck knife and his whiskey, if not his sat phone. And oh yeah, not just a little bit of fire.

It was full dark now, and the moon was new. This far out from any human source of light, the stars and my conscience were my only guides. And I hadn't heard much from the latter of late.

"Look," I told these two forlorn lovebirds, lashed back-to-back before me, "I won't be long. Unless they kill me, in which case I might be a little while. But either way, you have my word that I'll come back for you. I won't let you die tonight – not on my watch. Just stay inside this cave, you hear me? Nothing that means you any harm can breach it."

"Whadda you mean, either way?" This from Zadie.

"Never you mind," I said. "Now do me a favor and keep quiet. I've got a job to do."

They didn't listen. They just kept on screaming their fool heads off. But that was fine. I didn't really expect them to heed my request. If I had, I wouldn't have bothered scratching those protective runes into the rock at the entrance to the cave with Topher's buck knife; God knows the damn thing was more useful to me sharp than dull. But whatever, if the Brethren heard them carrying on, maybe they'd serve as a distraction, because if those same Brethren caught wind of what I had in store for them, they were bound to get a little pissy.

I trudged away from Topher and Zadie's hidey-hole and flicked open the camera's view finder and switched the image to infrared night vision. One of the perks of bumming around with cryptozoologists is they're accustomed to skulking around the forest at night. Meant Nicholas was pretty sure-footed in the dark. Meant his camera was built for it as well.

The night was cold and still and dark before me, but my viewfinder glowed with green-white light. It flared at the cabin's windows – the light unseen by my naked eye, the ground on which the cabin sat appearing wild and undisturbed – and at the chimney's outlet. I watched for the better part of two hours, hoping it would also give me some indication of how many creatures waited for me inside, but given that the source of the chimney's heat was not visible through the walls it was clear the camera was incapable of delivering such a penetrating image. The closest I could come to any kind of estimate were the brief flickers of movement at window's edge a time or two, as if whatever waited inside was pulling back the curtains to get a peek at me. But it, or they, were careful, and I never managed to catch a glimpse.

That was fine. I had no illusions of sneaking up on them even without my two idiot companions carrying on behind me, we'd made enough noise on our initial approach they couldn't help but have heard us. And anyways, I wasn't worried about going in to the cabin blind, because I wasn't going in at all.

They were coming out to me.

None of Topher's socks would fit and anyway, he didn't seem to have any clean ones left in his backpack, which is not to say that clean ones were required, only that they were preferable, since I wasn't dexterous enough in gloves to complete my task, necessitating bare-fingered handling. But Zadie's socks – particularly her wicking Rayon underlayer – were so just right, Goldilocks herself would've approved.

So I soaked one of them in Early Times and stuffed it into the bottle's neck to serve as a wick. Then I lit it with the Bic these three morons used predominantly to spark up bowls of weed, and I chucked it at the imaginary viewscreen cabin. It sailed in a lazy arc through the air, and I watched it bare-eyed as it flared against the velvet dark.

And then halted in midair, crashing into nothing.

Not nothing in the viewfinder, mind. On the viewfinder, the white-hot Molotov sun failed to complete its arching descent on account of the ghost-green cabin in its way.

I'll tell you what: I may not have been able to see the cabin with my – er, Nicholas's – naked eye, but when that bottle burst, I could damn sure see the flames. In that thin, dry air, that wood went up like so much paper, and suddenly, the house-shaped nothing blazed orange-white. The heat of it warmed my cheeks. The light forced me to squint. The sound as it caught was like a rush of water, a sudden wind. And yet still, the protective juju held, so that the something looked like nothing, even as it burned. It looked like a house made of fire itself. And I stood outside it, waiting, Topher's buck knife in my hand.

I had no idea how many of them lived here. How many were inside. Ada claimed that there was more than one, which represented the alpha and the omega of my intel. Could be two, or three, or five. Could be zero, I supposed. No saying they stuck around once Ada bailed. But I was guessing they hadn't. Looking back through a hundred years of local newspapers, the nearby municipalities had seen their share of missing children. I was betting the Brethren had stuck around.

What I hadn't counted on was them being as hard to see as the house that they called home.

I should've. Ada couldn't describe them, after all. But somehow, I hadn't considered the greater implications of that fact. Hadn't squared it with the cabin that wasn't there. Hadn't thought one lick about how it affected my approach, until the first of them was on me.

I didn't realize what I was looking at, at first. When I saw its flaming form burst through the crosshatched windowpane with a snap of wood and a tinkle of glass, I could see it fine, or so I thought. Then it hit the ground and rolled in the chill night air, extinguishing the fire that engulfed it, and before my eyes, it seemed to disappear. Only then did I realize my mistake.

I hadn't seen the beast itself; I'd seen the flames. Like the house I couldn't see beneath the flames I saw just fine. Problem was, the house wasn't capable of putting itself out, nor of going anywhere. The big scary whatever that just leapt out of it, on the other hand, was. Lord knew what kind of big and scary it was. I heard it huff and puff somewhere in the flame-split black as if catching its breath. It neither wailed in pain, nor cried in anger. Just breathed audibly, and rustled as it moved. And, if I'm not mistaken, stalked, circling my position as if attempting to discern its best angle of attack. On occasion I thought I caught a glint of starlit silver fur in my peripheral vision, which vanished whenever I wheeled toward it. I couldn't help but think that if the moon were high and full, by its light I'd see the creature fine. But I had no moonlight to rely on.

What I *did* have was the camera.

I held it like a talisman before me, swung it to and fro to no avail. There was simply nothing out there for me to see. My heart sank. My pulse raced. And then, as I gave up…

There it was, a lanky, matted, vulpine thing, naked or nearly so. It was half-hidden by the skeletal trunks of trees still bare from winter. Sucking wind as it sat on its haunches, waiting to strike. Unconcerned to see me facing it, because it was so very certain whatever enchantment kept it hidden from prying eyes remained undisturbed. Unaware it had been bested by technology.

I tightened my grip around Topher's buck knife and advanced upon it, all casual and halting, like it was sheer fucking coincidence I'd decided to strike out into the night straight toward it. I kept the greenish blob of it in the center of my viewfinder at all times, to ensure the fucker couldn't slink off while I played coy.

But it didn't slink off. It didn't even move. And why would it? I was playing right into its hands. I could damn near hear it smacking its lips as I approached, as if it couldn't believe its luck. I pictured the looks of sheer surprise on the faces of Magnusson and the border creature when I ripped their Godforsaken souls from their inhuman, undead chests, and thought to myself that this was just the first in a list of things this fucker was gonna have trouble believing.

That's when the second window exploded. Before I knew what hit me, another creature was atop me, and I was surrounded by the pop and smack of searing flesh and snapping jaws. My camera sailed into the night. My clothes singed as the flames that scorched the creature bald leapt from it to me.

But damn if I didn't hold onto that buck knife.

I rolled over beneath this second beast, the movement a struggle. Whiskey fumes bit at the soft tissues of my eyes and throat, harsh and sharp and explaining why this one still flamed, when its sibling so quickly doused. It grabbed my wrists, and my jacket ignited. A reek like curling irons and bacon filled the air. I screamed as Nicholas-not-Nicky's nylon shell melted, and his exposed skin blistered and peeled.

The creature was no better off than I – writhing in agony as it burned, but determined to take me out with it. The air between us seemed to waver like a mirage, like shimmering heat-lines rising off of desert blacktop, and through the distortion I caught a glimpse of amber eyeshine, of ropy limbs dusted with filthy gray-brown fur, curling black in advance of the orange sparks of flame that tore through it as the fire spread. Of a face once human warped by its feral ways into something snout-like, pointed at ear and nose and chin like some kind of devil dog – or perhaps a wolf.

The wolf-thing snapped at my throat with slavering jaws, and teeth three inches long. If they'd found their mark, poor Nicholas would've gone bye-bye. But they didn't, because in that moment, I kicked with all I had, and used the creature's momentum to backward somersault out from under its grasp. I tried to push my free hand into its chest to grasp its soul as I would a human mark. I'd not been close enough to the others to try, but it turns out, it was no use. The creature's body was strong, unyielding, and my attempt was unsuccessful.

Fine, then. Plan B. Which in this case meant that mid-roll, I drove Topher's buck knife into its chest.

Unlike Magnusson and Jain, when I plunged the blade in, nothing happened. No piteous wail, no big, dramatic death scene. Instead, I just wound up with a pissed-off wolf man who had my only weapon buried hilt-deep in its chest. Not too helpful, that.

That's when I realized my mistake. "Simple conductance", Lilith had said of the replica skim blade, gold-plated from tip to tail. "Nothing more". Apparently nothing less, either. Because the rebar – also metal from one end to the other – worked just fine. But Topher's carbon steel knife with a textured plastic grip was a no-go. And of *course* it was. The instrument was useless unless the soul presented itself to be destroyed, and for that, it needed to be coaxed out by a Collector.

Metal worked because it completed the circuit between the soul and, well, *me*.

The creature and I separated. It found its feet and spun to face me. The roll had doused its flames; my own, I patted out. But it was clear to see the creature'd taken damage. First off, I could see it. And second, most of its fur had burned away, revealing cracked red-black flesh at once dull in spots and glistening. One ear was a curl-edged nub, looking like the melted-candle counterpart of its intact mate. And one eyelid looked to have burned off completely, revealing a mad, bloodshot orb that rolled wildly by the light of the burning cabin.

The creature raised a hand to the knife handle that jutted from its chest, and with an audible growl, removed knife from flesh, tossing it to the dirt at its feet. The wound pulsed with blood as the blade exited. We faced off a moment, me eyeing him, him eyeing me. His flesh smoked. His outsized, muscular chest heaved in the bitter night air.

And then he pounced.

Not graceful like a cat, more the sheer brute force of an attack dog. Nails as thick as talons bit at the tender flesh of Nicholas' shoulders, and knocked me flat once more. But this time, I was ready. I jabbed my fingers directly into the seeping knife wound as far as they would go, and the creature howled in pain. The two of us seemed to vibrate all of a sudden, two tuning forks at odds synchronizing.

It bit my neck. Blood soaked warm into my collar. And then the creature's jaw went wide, my neck released. I held its dead dry soul inside my hand.

I squeezed.

It slackened.

The ground shook beneath my feet. The cabin this creature called home, weakened by flame, collapsed within itself just as its former inhabitant collapsed. A flurry of sparks spiraled skyward toward the star-speckled heavens from what now looked like no more than a goodly bonfire, as if the abode's soul were now somehow freed as well.

And then there was one.

The problem was, where?

I cast about for Nicky's – fuck, I mean Nicholas's – camera, finding it some twenty feet away, and in three pieces. I tried to reassemble it by the firelight, but it was no use. Cold-clumsy hands conspired against me, and it's not like it'd been carefully disassembled, the goddamn thing was broken, its viewfinder black and dead.

I cast the expensive hunk of useless trash aside, and wondered how the hell I was gonna find the second creature. Then I heard the screams – Topher and Zadie both – and the sickening wet pop of tendons and ligaments separating, like twisting off the turkey leg at Thanksgiving dinner. Zadie's screams became suddenly more desperate, Topher's thick and strangled.

Sounded like they'd gotten loose. Sounded like they hadn't listened when I told them they'd stay safe if they stayed put. To a one, protection spells are locational, not person-specific. If I could have carved the runes into their flesh and kept them from a horrid end, I would have. But as it stood, the best that I could do was bar entry to their cave by those who'd do them harm. I couldn't do shit for them if they decided to leave them damn selves.

But they could apparently still do something for me.

Because they'd just told me where the creature was.

I sprinted back toward their hidey-hole, stumbling on the uneven earth and slipping here and there on fallen leaves. This far from the cabin, the firelight dwindled, and the world was drawn in deep blues outlined on each object's eastern edge in orange. It was enough to keep me from bouncing off of trees, at least. And as it turned out it, was enough for me to see the horror of what had happened.

As I rounded the hillock whose far side afforded entrance to Topher and Zadie's narrow cave, I pulled up short. The beast stood plainly visible, just outside the protective barrier of the cave, back arched, and one hand held high above its head. In its hand was Topher's severed arm, dripping blood into the creature's open mouth. It hadn't seen me coming, it was too focused on the cowering girl inside the shallow cave. This creature was bigger than the last, and more wolven. Its back legs were articulated such that the joints appeared to hinge backward, not forward like a human knee; its broad chest was thick with muscle and dusted here and there with fur. Shriveled flaps of nippled flesh draped from each broad pectoral muscle; it took me a moment to realize that in its prior, human life, this creature was a woman. Its arms were massive, its left one reaching almost to the ground while its right held Topher's some ten feet in the air. Clawed hands the size of rowboat paddles dangled menacingly at the end of each thick wrist.

Topher's body lay at the creature's gnarled bare feet atop a forest floor slick black with blood. He'd been unzipped from crotch to sternum in one clean motion, no doubt by one swipe of razor-sharp claw. His viscera gleamed purple in the dim firelight.

As it drank from Topher's severed arm, the whole creature seemed to swell, a process accelerated when it cast his arm aside and twisted his head off of his lifeless body, raising it to its mouth and sucking blood and brain from it as if extracting marrow from a bone. Muscles strained its leathery skin to the point of splitting. Teeth pushed through grayish gums, crowding a snout that grew ever longer by the second. Clawed feet knuckled harder into the dirt as the beast struggled to keep its feet through a growth spurt that plainly seemed to pain it.

It rose to eight feet tall. Then ten. Then twelve.

Guess all those years of strict rationing while it fed in dribs and drabs off the life-force of small children left the pump primed for some serious binge-eating. Kinda wish the end result was diabetes and Rascal scooters like the rest of us, and not, you know, "Hulk smash!".

When it threw back its head and roared, I cowered like a frightened child.

But you know what they say: the bigger they are... the likelier they are to rip the head off your fucking meat-suit and drink lustily from its brainpan.

Then I thought of poor aged Ada, and the countless more like her loosed into the vast empty wilderness once they had nothing left to give, only to die of exposure or starvation because they were not so lucky as to be discovered and I thought, fuck it – let's kill this creepy hellhound.

But first I'd need a weapon.

Scratch that, I thought, as the creature cocked back one massive fist and punched the shelf of rock that formed the cave lip so hard it cracked directly atop one of my protective runes.

This thing wasn't as dumb as it looked. So my first order of business was to keep it from breaching my hasty defenses and snacking on yet another hapless innocent.

It punched the rock again, so hard its bones cracked, its metacarpals pushing bloodily through the hairy skin. The creature bellowed in pain and animal frustration. Zadie screamed and crab-walked as far back as she could go – a whopping three feet. A chunk of stone the size of a cantaloupe fell from the underside of the lip, right where Zadie's head had been. The rune was still intact, but damaged; it couldn't take another blow like that one. No time for me to formulate a plan, I had to do something on the quick. So, as the beast brought back its ruined hand for another devastating blow, I fell back on an old standard: snark and false bravado, with shit-all to back it up.

"Hey, bitch! How's about you try out a chew toy that might bite back?"

The creature turned toward me and cocked its head. Her head, I found myself thinking, because – warped though this creature was – the eyeshine reflecting off its retinas could not fully mask the humanity they contained, and her features had an inexplicably feminine cast to them at odds with her hulking physicality.

"That's right," I said to her. "Who's a good dog?"

A low rumble started in her throat and trembled her lips. "Who are you to speak to me this way?" she said.

"I'm the guy who's gonna end you," I told her. "Just like I ended your friend back at the cabin."

She chuffed in laughter. "Impossible," she said.

"Lot of that going around," I told her, making a show of looking her up and down. "But look at me – and at the runes that kept you from entering the lovely lady's cave – and tell me if I'm bluffing. Oh, and by the way, Jain and Magnusson send their best – or, rather, they would if they weren't dead as well."

Doubt crept into her eyes, her voice. "You lie!"

"You're right," I said. "I do. But not about this."

At that, she threw her arms wide, and let out a roar that shook the trees, and blew my hair back from my face.

And then she attacked.

She was smarter than her friend, didn't blindly pounce like he did. Instead, she first uprooted a full-grown tree with her uninjured left hand ,roots popping as Topher's shoulder had, and dry dirt sounding like rain as it pattered to the ground beneath, and hurled it at me with all her might, her own bulk following close behind. I dove aside, too late. The trunk drove hard into my shoulder blades, and I ate dirt. Honestly, that tumble probably saved this meat-suit's life. The dog-beast sailed clear over me, rolling on one shoulder and springing upright in one fluid motion, once more facing me. On all fours, she was the size of a goddamn Clydesdale. Only every bit of her, from snout to what appeared to be a gnarled, half-formed fleshy tail, appeared designed to kill.

I shook the cobwebs from my brain and found my feet. She approached me slowly now: threatening, unconcerned. I backed up to maintain the distance between us – twenty feet, maybe less – but it was no use. Her every step – powerful haunches flexing, hot blood-tinged breath pluming iron-scented in the night – brought her closer.

My eyes locked on her, my feet carrying me ever backward, I stumbled and went down hard. Like a goddamn amateur. Like some fucking horror-movie-teenaged-twenty-something-bottle-blond. That's when she leapt. I knew then I was screwed but good; no getting out of this one, Thornton. So I clenched shut my eyes, tensing for the killing blow, and thought of Guam.

I'll tell you, I don't know if it's all the hiking or what, but that Zadie chick has got some muscle on that tiny frame of hers. And she's damn quick, too. But then again, maybe I would have been as well, had I just watched my only shot in hell of leaving these woods alive just up and quit.

Tiny hands bunched the shoulders of my jacket within their grip, and yanked me backward. My eyes sprung open as I slid along the forest floor. A fraction of a second later, the dog-beast landed in the spot that I'd just vacated: too late, because Zadie'd dragged me back into the shallow cave.

"Are you all right?" she asked.

"Yeah," I said, incredulous, as if the news surprised me. "You?"

"Yes. You're not Nicky, are you?" she asked.

"He prefers Nicholas."

Her eyes glinted with good humor. "No offense," she said, "but so do I. Not so fond of being tied up."

"Nicky's got some audio files that argue otherwise," I told her. "You ever make it back to camp, you might want to see about destroying them." And though the light in the cave was dim, I could swear she colored at that last.

"So can you really kill this thing, or was that bullshit?"

"I can," I said. "I think. Hey, how's it feel to find a real, live monster?"

"Not great," she said. "This was always Topher's dream, not mine." She smiled, then, not with any real cheer, but with sadness and fond remembrance. "For what it's worth, I told him not to leave the cave. Once he got free from his restraints, I mean. But he wouldn't listen. He said he hadn't devoted his whole life to finding evidence of beasts like these only to go home empty-handed now. He said he'd rather die."

"At least he found what he was looking for," I offered weakly, as if the words would comfort her in the slightest.

"Yeah," she said, eyeing his cave-side remains. "And I lost what I was looking for."

"I'm sorry," I told her, and I meant it. After all, I thought, the image of Elizabeth rising unbidden in my mind, I knew exactly how she felt.

A huff of breath announced the creature's presence outside the cave. I looked up to find it hunkered down on its haunches, its eyes staring back at me in the near-dark. Even crouching as it was, the damn thing was taller than my meat-suit at full height. Curled up to fit inside the cave, I felt pretty damn insignificant by comparison.

"Fe, fi, fo, fum," I muttered. The creature snorted in what I realized was laughter.

"I smell more than blood," it told me. "I smell your fear. Your desperation. You'd given up, hadn't you? If your lady-friend hadn't saved you, you'd be dead right now."

"Nah," I told her. "Worst case, I'd be sipping Mai Tais on the beach. And she's not my lady-friend."

The creature sniffed the air. Her black canine lips parted in a smile. "Of course she's not; I can smell her scent all over this one. I suppose she and I have each taken something from the other now, then. The only difference is, I will soon get *you* back. Perhaps for her impertinence in stealing you away from me, I'll make her watch while I disembowel you."

Zadie scoffed. "For my impertinence, sure. What was your excuse for making me watch you kill my boyfriend?"

"His death was not my fault!" the creature bellowed. "For one thousand years, my brother and I have subsisted without killing a soul – taking only what we needed to sustain ourselves and no more. First from the animals of this vast continent, not so uninhabited as we'd hoped when we happened upon it in our self-styled exile from humanity, but absent enough of people we could, for the most part, avoid temptation. Then from those who settled here, tasting, sure, but never killing. The same can sadly not be said of Jain, nor of Ricou, both of whom we were forced to turn out centuries ago on account of their… unfortunate lack of willpower. But then *you* arrive," she said, jabbing a clawed finger in my direction, which bounced off the plane of the cave mouth as surely as if it had just met a sheet

of plexiglas, "and all we've worked toward goes to shit. Lukas is dead. My fast is broken. And I fear that after such delectable game as this," she said, licking clean her gore-strewn lips with her wet, black tongue, "weaning myself back off it may well prove troublesome."

"You could avoid the issue altogether," I told her, "and let me kill you here and now."

She mock-pondered my proposal for a moment, bobbing her monstrous head from side to side. "It's true," she said, "I could, provided you're capable, which I doubt. For if you were, why have you not yet struck?"

"Ask your brother," I goaded her.

"*Lukas,*" she enunciated carefully, as if speaking of him pained her, "was struck by your makeshift bomb when you attacked. He went up quick, and was no doubt quite weakened by the flames. Still, I hold out hope that, given time, he will recover; I shall bury him beneath the garden to allow him to knit himself in peace. For he and I have naught but time. As for the others, perhaps they are truly dead, or perhaps you're but a flim-flam man, lying to buy yourself time. But I assure you, I have plenty of it to spare; if I wished, I could just sit here and watch you two slowly die of cold and of starvation, and then go on my merry way. The idea does have its appeal. But I confess, my earlier meal has left me oddly peckish, and edgy, and eager for more... I'd forgotten how succulent the meat and brain of your kind can be. So I fear instead," she said, raising her ruined right hand to show the jutting bones, "I'll simply have to sacrifice my good hand, and hope that between the two of you, there's enough sustenance to make me whole once more."

The great beast rose. Zadie whimpered. I pressed her back against the far wall of the shallow cave, and stood before her like a shield. Fist met rock, and rock yielded. The creature howled in pain and celebration.

And as it crouched once more to strike, I snatched up the nearest kinda-sorta weapon – the handled end of Zadie's broken walking pole – and did the only thing I could think to do. I rushed the creature, put my hand smack in the center of its chest, and drove the jagged pole clean through both with all the strength I had.

10.

"Good morning, Collector. I see you're getting an early start."

I looked up from my drink – some strange carnivore's version of a Bloody Mary garnished not with a celery stalk but a single hot-smoked pork rib of all things – to see two blurry Liliths swimming in my meat-suit's vision, wearing wisp-thin matching silk slip dresses the color of black coffee. I confess, my choice of drink seemed a tad morbid and insensitive, given that I'd not nine hours ago seen poor Topher reduced to a disemboweled, blood-soaked corpse, but it was scarcely 10am in Colorado Springs, and my beverage choices were limited. Took me a good ten minutes' walk through the mostly residential, tree-lined streets surrounding the sprawling Penrose-St Francis hospital complex before I found anyplace that served booze, and even then, it was just a quaint little brunch joint whose drink menu consisted entirely of Bellinis, Mimosas, and Bloody Marys. You should have seen the looks I got when I ordered one of each to start, and then a round of three more Bloody Marys when I discovered I was none too fond of champagne cocktails. I'd waved off the wait staff's repeated – and increasingly desperate – attempts to solicit a food order from me, but now that I realized the room was spinning, and my vision was skipping about like a movie that's jumped its reel, I wondered if maybe I made the wrong call on that front. I made a mental note to ask for some steak and eggs if I hadn't yet scared the waitress off for good.

"Yeah, well." I slurred. "Rough night."

"So I gathered. Were you... successful in your mission?"

I snort-laughed at the politesse of her euphemism. "Yup. I succeeded the living shit outta them," I said. "And this time, I only killed one civvie doing it. I think my batting average is improving. Although my poor meat-suit probably won't be playing piano with that hand anytime soon."

Lilith looked around to see if anyone had overheard, but the waitstaff had long since started avoiding me, and in fact had taken to seating other patrons as far from me as possible about an hour ago, when they decided I was trouble. I think the only reason they'd yet to ask me to leave is because they were worried I'd make a scene. Even chance they weren't wrong.

You know the problem with going toe-to-toe with a pair of creepy, supernatural dog-beasts in the middle of the Colorado wilds? Once you're done getting knocked around six ways from Sunday and you kill the fuckers, you're still stuck out in the Colorado wilds.

At least the walking pole worked like a charm. Soon as I stabbed that evil bitch through Nicholas-not-Nicky's hand, she and I both started thrumming. My angle was awkward, though, and stabbing through bone both hand- and breast- meant I didn't drive the pole clean through like with Magnusson or Jain. So there was an awkward moment or two when Angry Dog Chick (it seems weird to me – sad, even – that I still don't know her name, but unlike human souls, the Brethren's do not speak to me when I touch them) was reeling backward trying to shake me, as I remained pinned to her dinner table-sized chest. Eventually, I rode her to the ground, and punched the pole through with all my might. The forest rattled and shook as she expired, the land she called home mourning her if no one else would.

Once the beast was felled, and the fog of battle lifted, the pain in Nicholas-not-Nicky's hand was excruciating. A tender, hesitant Zadie did her best to wrap it for me with a rag torn from her own shirt, flinching every time I winced. When she finished, I thanked her by name, and she corrected me. "Please, Nick, or Not-Nick, or whoever you are – call me Susan." I guess she was done pretending to be someone she was not – her hipster mask of cool remove discarded. Wish I could say the same, but my whole existence is pretending. Lying. Burying myself so deep I'm not sure I'll ever find the guy I was again.

Neither of us were in any shape to hike out in the dark. So instead, we called 911 on Topher's sat phone, and left the line open until they pinpointed our location. Then we huddled together beside the cooling embers of the cabin and waited for our saviors and the morning light to arrive.

Zadie – Susan, I mean – spent most of the night crying. I held her wordlessly and let her weep. What could I have said? There were no words to make her better. And I wouldn't have said them if there were, for what is mourning if not love's darker aspect? Seems to me, it's best never to quash love or push it away, regardless of its form, or of its cost. Sometimes, I think my last tattered shreds of love are all that keep me from becoming as monstrous as the Brethren themselves.

She loved Topher with all her heart, that much was clear. Enough to follow him on his insane quest for answers, for truth, for understanding. You ask me, we're not built for any of the three. We're wired for survival, nothing more. Topher's ruined form, which Susan insisted we drag nearer to the waning firelight so he would not be picked over by animals, stood as a sad monument to the fact that survival and truth were two ends often at odds with one another.

Christ. Listen to me. Leave it to booze to make even a denizen of hell all maudlin and philosophical.

Anyways, by the time the rescue crew arrived – by ATV, not helicopter as I'd envisioned – the embers of the cabin fire were cold and dead, and the two Brethren corpses had withered to dust. That left only Topher to explain. Poor Susan was too despondent to answer the men's inquiries, so I filled in the gaps where I could. Some kind of large animal. Hit too fast for us to see. Dragged Topher away from us so quickly, we gave chase without thinking, and wound up lost. By the time we caught up, this was all of him that was left. And this fire? Some kind of abandoned structure, we told them. Collapsed for decades, no doubt, before we ever stumbled across it. Without means to fell a tree, it was the only wood we had available to burn. And why not just pitch our tents? The body, I told them. She couldn't bear to leave it. And so we sat together in the bitter cold beneath the stars, and watched the fire die as we mourned our friend.

The men made some noises about bears and mountain lions, but it was clear by the looks they shared when they thought I wasn't looking that they had no idea what could have done this. But they didn't seem to think Susan or Nicholas did, so that was something, at least. They *did* ask whether we'd captured any footage of the attack, but I told them the camera wasn't rolling at the time, and anyway, it was damaged in the chase that ensued – beyond repair, as near as I could tell.

That last part was true enough. I spent twenty minutes bashing the camera with a rock before they found us on the off chance I'd inadvertently recorded anything.

I stuck with Susan until the hospital. Then I hopped a ride inside an orderly just before they put me under for hand-surgery. Felt the bile rise in his throat when I took over, but I sucked wind, and willed him not to puke. He didn't, his body acquiescing to my commands more easily than I would have expected. It'd been that way of late. Guess I was developing the knack. I wondered if maybe that means I'm a little less human that I used to be. I wondered why I didn't care much about that fact. Told myself it was because I had a job to do, but I didn't fully believe it. If you ask me, I didn't care much about my humanity slowly bleeding away because the part of me that would have was now in the minority.

Nicholas started ranting about monsters and possession just before I left the room in my new meat-suit. Freaked out and started thrashing on the gurney. They strapped him down – for his own safety, they kept telling him – and sedated him. His lids slammed shut like a set of blinds whose string'd been pulled, and the poor guy was finally, briefly, at peace. He'd probably start right back up with the freak-out when the drugs wore off. The scuttlebutt at the nurse's station afterward was that he'd experienced a mental break on account of all he'd seen. For what it's worth, they weren't far from wrong. Except for the part where they thought the insane nonsense he was spouting wasn't true.

Personally, I find that judicious application of alcohol helps stave off such mental breaks. Hell, some days it's all that keeps me from being Thorazined into oblivion and left to drool inside my very own padded cell. No lie, today was one of those days. Which is why – for strictly therapeutic purposes, you understand – I walked straight out of the hospital in my new meat-suit, not even bothering to ditch the scrubs in favor of street clothes, and found myself a drink or six.

"So that makes what?" asked Lilith, mock-sweet as Splenda, "Four Brethren down? Just think, you've only five to go."

"Yay," I said. "Can't hardly wait."

"I can tell. The enthusiasm's coming off of you in waves. No, wait," she amended, "those are vodka fumes."

"No worries. I'll ditch this skin-suit before the hangover hits."

"How lovely for him," she replied drolly. "Perhaps I could be of assistance in identifying your next vessel."

"I take that to mean you've got a new assignment for me?"

"That's right."

"Another feral Brethren?"

"Feral, no. Brethren, yes. Leads on the two remaining feral Brethren have been scant of late, I confess. For a time, I felt as though I might be closing in on one of them in rural Brazil. I've been following centuries of lore about a strange creature dragging villagers and livestock into the dark waters of the Amazon under cover of night. Rumors of new abductions came at a rate of one or two a week stretching as far back as there've been people there to spread them. But a few months back, they seem to have ceased."

"You think whatever's been, uh, eating all those people and chickens or whatever has gotten wise to what we're doing?"

"I think it's likelier than a sudden change in diet," she replied. "And regardless, I think you're unlikely to find the thing if it's not hunting."

I thought back to Jain's words in the tunnels, to the nameless dog-beast's in the forest just last night. "Ricou," I said.

Lilith's eyebrows shot up, and she flashed me a look of puzzled surprise. "Excuse me?"

"The thing you've been tracking," I said. "I think its name is Ricou."

"That's all well and good, Collector, but as I said, this Ricou of yours seems to've pulled up stakes, or at the very least, stopped hunting, which is one of two reasons why I think it's time to move on one of the three members of the Brethren who're still on hell's radar."

"Do I get to pick from off the menu, or do you have a particular one in mind?"

"As a matter of fact, I do. His name is Grigori."

"Okay," I said. "Why him?"

"His behavior's grown erratic of late. Ever since our ill-fated first attempt to eliminate he and his fellow Brethren, he's been moving vast quantities of money around – liquidating assets, reshuffling the deck on his portfolio of shell corporations, offshore accounts, and corporate holdings. Some of that went to the other two we'd been monitoring – known to us as Drustanus and Yseult – who've since vanished. And I think he's looking to do the same. The other two are far from feral, but they're both vicious and impulsive, operating strictly hand-to-mouth and leaving a bloody trail of bodies in their wake; without Grigori's aid, I've no doubt we could track them down in no time. But a man of his means, who's spent fifty lifetimes learning to live beneath the radar, can no doubt hide a good long time. If we allow him to vanish, it may take centuries to find him."

"'Ill-fated first attempt'," I parroted. "Funny way of saying this guy and his buddies slaughtered the last set of folks hell sent to kill them."

"I rather thought you wouldn't like to be reminded of that fact."

"Yeah, well, it ain't like I ever forgot. And you buried the lede just now, didn't you? The fact is, this guy ain't just my next target, he's the biggest and baddest of the bunch. Not only that, but he's helped the remaining Brethren on our list disappear, so for all intents and purposes that makes him our only play."

Lilith paused a good long while before answering. "You're not wrong," she said grudgingly.

"Okay, then, lemme ask you, if he's the guy who helped the other two fall off your radar, doesn't that mean the only reason he's number one on hell's Most Wanted list is because he fucking *volunteered*? Or, put another way, does this look at all to you like one seriously big-ass trap?"

"Possibly," she said, "but I'm afraid we've no other choice. These orders come down from on high."

"You've," I corrected.

"Excuse me?"

"What you meant was *you've* no other choice."

Lilith smiled as if she were a teenager caught sneaking a twenty from her pushover dad's wallet. "I suppose I did, at that."

"Fan-fucking-tastic. So where'm I headed?"

"That's the spirit," Lilith said, clapping me on the shoulder as if I'd responded with great brio and not resigned indifference. "And perhaps your task will prove less unpleasant than you suspect. After all, I understand the Carpathians are quite pleasant this time of year."

"The Carpathians." Me, incredulous.

"That's right."

"As in Transylvania."

"Mmm hmm."

"You're shitting me."

"I'll admit, it's a tad arch, but I assure you I am not," said Lilith

"You got an address?"

Lilith paused. "Not exactly."

"What do you mean, not exactly?"

She sighed. "When we last moved on him, he was at his summer home on the French Riviera, one of seven such homes we've routinely monitored over the years. Needless to say, he hasn't been back since. We've always suspected he keeps another abode – home base, perhaps, or safe house – but wherever it is, it's always been well hidden to our seers. He must have masked it with some kind of occlusion spell, the strongest of its kind I've ever seen, in point of fact."

My mind tracked back to Pemberton Baths, which seemed to go all Teflon beneath my eyeballs' gaze, and to the cabin of last night, which existed only in the viewfinder of Nicholas-not-Nicky's camera. "Seems the Brethren are quite fond of those," I said.

"Yes, well. Our seers had their third eyes on him after the Riviera debacle, tracking his movements eastward across the continent remotely, but then, suddenly, he vanished. Working with our best chronomancers, those seers were able to revisit the moment of his disappearance again and again in their minds, and have narrowed his position down to the twenty-square-mile patch of countryside surrounding Bucura Lake, which is nestled in the southeastern elbow of the Carpathian Mountains."

"Awesome," I said. "I can't tell you how psyched I am at the prospect of traipsing around a whole *new* batch of cold-ass mountains, looking for the biggest, scariest baddie left on the table."

"That's what I like to hear," she said, and then she left me to continue getting stinking drunk in peace.

11.

The sun was a pale yellow disc in the muted blue of the alpine sky when I piloted my rented Dacia hatchback into the quaint town center, which was really no more than a block-square patch of grass with squat, low-slung buildings huddled around. At one end of the square sat a modest but pretty wooden church, shingled and steep-pitched and obscured in part by scaffolding. A small inn faced it. Its roof was steeply pitched and shingled as well, but its walls were fieldstone, not timber. A couple of the other buildings that flanked the square looked to be businesses of some kind, what with their outsized storefront windows and hand-tooled signs hanging out over the narrow streets, but the signs were all in Romanian, their meaning lost to me.

All told, there couldn't have been more than two dozen buildings comprising this makeshift town, most on the center square, with some trailing off narrow side streets on either side. And honestly, I'm not sure they had room to build any more; the village was nestled into a depression in the hills so narrow you could scarcely even call it a valley. Sharp stone faces jutted upward, the trees growing ever thinner and more stunted on the upslopes until eventually there was nothing on them but bare rock, gouging free its territory from the sky.

At the very top of the highest peak in sight was a castle.

The ruins of a castle, to be more precise. No mere winter palace, this; everything about it – from its thick stone walls, stained with age and crumbling, to the narrow slit windows that graced its many parapets, to its very position atop the craggy, un-bum-rushable terrain, accessible only by a narrow dirt road that switched back time and again as it wound its way up the mountain – suggested this place was built to be defended, to withstand war.

Or to repel the advances of the angry, torch-and-pitchfork-wielding hordes.

I squinted up at it and wondered how it would fare against me.

If this village – or the castle looking down upon it – had a name, it was neither indicated by sign upon approach nor on any of the road maps that I carried. And these past two weeks, I'd accumulated plenty of them.

After the debacle that was Colorado, I'd decided my days of hitching rides in amateurs were over, at least until the Brethren were dead and gone. If I was going toe-to-toe with the biggest, baddest oogly boogly I'd yet seen, I was for damn sure gonna do it armed, preferably in someone battle-trained. And since I didn't know precisely where this hunt was gonna take me, I needed a meat-suit with a valid passport, the kind of vessel no one would question if they were to bounce erratically around the map Indiana-Jones style. That ruled out cops (too parochial) and military (who tend to raise hackles when they go AWOL.) Covert ops types are, by nature, hard to come by, and anyways, I hear tell both Langley and the NSA's headquarters in Fort Meade employ mystical countermeasures to keep out the likes of me. Which is how I settled on an air marshal.

Picked this one up in Chicago. Frank Malmon, according to his passport and the license in his wallet. No pics inside of pets or family, just the ID, two credit cards, and twenty bucks in ones and fives. And no wedding ring on his finger. That's why I chose him.

The Federal Air Marshals have an office in Chicago, makes them easier to spot than in the wild. Taken in ones and twos, they tend to blend in with their environment – by design, not accident. Their whole point is to look like just another airline customer until the shit goes down. Then you find out they've been trained to quick-draw their sidearm and pop a guy head and chest in a people-crammed tin can hurtling through the air thirty thousand feet above the ground at five hundred miles per hour without so much as grazing an innocent passenger or depressurizing the cabin. But in a crowd you know to be rife with them – say, the main concourse in O'Hare – a pattern begins to emerge. Early thirties. Compact build. Hair trimmed high and tight but not too, like a cop's, or maybe former military. Jeans, polos or button-downs, a windbreaker usually to hide their piece. No bright colors, no garish logos or bold graphics on their clothes. Polite but taciturn when addressed. Always watching, listening, assessing threats.

But never imagining the likes of me.

Grabbed this one when he ducked into the can. Not literally, mind. The orderly I'd ditched way back in Colorado. I'd cabbed it out to the airport from my liquid brunch half-smashed, and then body-hopped into an iPhone-noodling teenager who was in line with his parents to check in for their flight to Boston. Hood up, hat brim down, and headphones in, which meant I could – and did – make it all the way to the Windy City without his parents catching wise, or for that matter, speaking to another soul. When I body-hopped in, the kid's mouth flooded with saliva and his stomach fluttered, but I focused on calming both, conjuring an image of a dial marked "nausea" in my mind, and dialing it from eleven where it was pinned back down to zero. The kid's body's urge to purge itself of me abated.

My only gripe with the kid was the ten seconds of ear-splitting skronk I was treated to before I found the pause button on his smart phone's music thingy. I don't know what a Skrillex is – some kind of power tool for grinding metal by the sound of it – but whatever it is, it sounded like his was broken. It was all I could do not to yank the earbuds from my ears. But I figured that would blow my cover, so I left them in, and handled his phone like it was packed solid with nitroglycerin; I couldn't figure out how to shut the damn thing off, and I lived in mortal fear of triggering that aural assault anew at any time.

Anyways, I hopped the kid to Chicago, and used his layover to scope out my air-marshal options. Narrowed it down to two, when just my luck: my top choice decided to hit the restroom. I left the kid in one stall, walked out the other in a brand new Malmon-suit. His nausea dial was only set to six or so. Even if I hadn't concentrated on adjusting it downward as I did, I suspect he woulda been just fine. It was disturbing to me how easy this possession thing was getting.

The second I hopped into the Air Marshal, I knew I'd struck pay dirt. Didn't even have to check under my jacket to recognize the weight beneath for what it was – a big-ass handgun. But, thorough fellow that I am, I did anyways, and discovered it to be SIG Sauer P226 with two spare mags of fifteen .357 rounds each, meaning I had forty-five in total.

I walked Malmon straight out of the restroom and to the nearest ticket agent, flashed my badge, and said I needed to be on the next flight to Bucharest. The nice young man behind the counter didn't even bat an eye. I spent five minutes in line at security wondering why the TSAs were giving me the hairy eyeball before I realized they probably saw me twice a day. A couple pilots wheeled past the shuffling masses in their stocking feet with cheerful indifference, and slipped the black nylon barrier thing out of its track for long enough to duck behind it. As they refastened it, I ducked out of line and followed suit, and what do you know? No one stopped me.

I worried Romanian Customs would give me trouble over the piece, but it's amazing what the proper ID can get you. They kept me standing there a while after scanning my passport to make sure it came back clean, but once it did, they were all smiles, and I was on my way.

What I hadn't realized was that I was on my way to two weeks of fruitless poking around every tiny mountain hamlet for miles around the glacial waters of Bucura Lake without even a whiff of otherworldly foul play to show for it. I questioned villagers, visited small-town coroners by dead of night, trudged through crumbling ruins, inspected smoke-houses thick with the prickly spice-scent of curing sausage. I poked through rickety old barns and long-abandoned burned-out thatch huts and even, in the case of one creepy Lugosi-looking local whose odd demeanor set my Spidey sense erroneously a-tinglin', dug through a basement chest freezer. But I found no heads, nor blood, nor creepy monsters seeking same. Just normal folk leading normal lives.

Least the landscape was beautiful, I thought.

And boy howdy was it. Rolling hills rising high to peaks of green and gray, verdant valleys teaming with wildlife, shallow mountain streams running so cold and clean they seemed to be handed down by God himself to slake the thirst one developed hiking through the rarified, sun-warmed air. The days topped out near seventy. The nights were darn near cold enough to frost. And though everything, from the pitch of the roofs to the guarded cast to the faces of the locals, spoke of a culture used to hard winters and even harder rule, I found that by and large I was welcomed here, and I responded with rare good cheer.

I soon learned maps were useless here. Half these towns weren't on them, and the other half weren't where they were supposed to be. The one in which I currently stood was a bit of both. It, and the castle that once lorded over it, were referenced only once by a cartographer as far as I could tell from my extensive research, the valley labeled simply *"moarte"*, meaning death. The map itself was burned half to cinder when the library that housed it mysteriously caught fire some three hundred years back. And when I inquired around as to how I might find the town and the ruins of said castle today, the directions I got from the few historians and/or local mountain guides who would even deign to talk about it to me were at once so vague and contradictory, I got the impression that not only had they never seen the place of which I spoke, they clearly had no desire to do so. And those were the ones who didn't storm off or hang up on me when I broached the topic. Odd for a nation so reliant on tourism, and so proud of their nation's history and great natural beauty.

A whole country full of people avoiding the same village en masse? That sounded like Brethren mojo writ large to me. Which meant one way or another, I was gonna find the place.

The problem is, how do you find someplace that doesn't want to be found? And the answer I came upon was slow and painstaking, but ultimately worthwhile. I drove around the countryside for weeks, the car loaded up with bottled water, coarse Romanian jug wine, and cured meats, not to mention two cans of spare gas stashed in the trunk. Every time I came across an intersection, I flipped a coin, assigning one direction heads, the other tails (or, in the case of the Romanian ten-Bani coin I was using, the less satisfying crest and stamped number value, respectively). Whichever route won the toss, I skipped, opting to take the losing path instead.

I won't lie, I had my share of doubts that it would work, but the nature of the place I was looking for meant I couldn't trust my doubts, for they might not truly be my own. And no doubt, the strange aversion-mojo the Brethren seemed to so delight in employing was not the only tactic of dissuasion at play here, because even though I'd cooked up a method to thwart it, that damn coin led me down a whole lot of metaphorical blind alleys in the form of quaint little villages with nary a monster or set of creepy ruins in sight.

As I climbed out of my car beside the nameless town's square, though, I felt suddenly sure I had found the town at last. Because the second my foot touched the ground, an icy finger of anxiety dragged across my spine, and I was gripped with the sudden realization I'd left the iron on. Never mind I'd been living out of my rental car – which as far as I was aware did not boast an iron among its standard features – or that I hadn't found myself with cause to iron since I last counted myself among the living. Knowing that didn't prevent me from wanting to hop back in the car, hightail it out of here, and check the last five places I'd laid my head, just to make sure I hadn't inadvertently lit any of them on fire.

It's funny; the place didn't look like it'd exude such a village-of-the-damned vibe. It was clean and well-kempt, its buildings timeworn but charming. And it was veritably teeming with life for so small a town, folks no doubt driven outside by the beautiful spring day. A flock of small children ranging from maybe four to ten moved as one across the square – giggling, chattering, and shrieking in the way that children do when they're excited – with a soccer ball at the flock's center. An old man fed the birds between puffs on a corncob pipe from a bench beneath a willow tree. Younger men – some dressed like farmhands, others tidier as if more accustomed to life behind a counter or a desk – walked to and fro across the square, waving and smiling at one another as they passed, or ducking into one of the tidy little shops. Occasionally, one of them would reemerge with a paper sack of meats or cheese or bread, and head back the way they came, noshing on a little something for their troubles. Sure, they all cast the occasional sidelong glance at me, but who could blame them? I was an outsider, after all.

But then there was the small matter of the women. And of the windows.

Namely, I didn't see any of the former. A few pigtailed little girls mixed in among the little boys playing in the square, but none older than that, despite there being loads of men in sight from teenaged to elderly. And though the day was just as pretty as could be, all the windows that faced the square save for the storefronts were shuttered.

I suppose it could have been a fluke. Two flukes, I mean. The women were perhaps all off together having tea. The windows shuttered because no one occupied those upper floors. But two flukes seemed a little hard to swallow. Particularly in light of the twist of anxiety I felt the second I set foot here.

Well, I thought, guess it's time to poke the hive and see what comes buzzing out.

I strolled across the small town square in a diagonal, skirting the octagonal gazebo, map and guidebook in my hands, a smile on my face. All for show, of course. "Excuse me," I called to a young man headed past me in the opposite direction. He slowed a moment, eyes meeting mine, and I saw a flicker of understanding cross his face, as if he spoke enough English to've understood my interruption of his walk, at least. "I was wondering if you could help me," I continued, emboldened by his reaction. "I'd like to know about the castle." I pointed toward the ruins on the hill to underline my meaning. "It isn't on my map."

When I gestured toward the ruins, his eyes widened, and his pace quickened. "*Eu nu vorbesc limba engleză,*" he told me as he passed. I don't speak English. I'd heard the phrase plenty since landing in-country, often said apologetically, as if it was some failing of the speaker's and not my own ignorance of foreign tongues that was to blame for our linguistic impasse. But this guy was far from apologetic.

He was brusque.

Hostile.

Frightened.

I tried again with my inquiry, this time targeting a couple older gentlemen ensconced in genial conversation at park's edge. "Excuse me, sirs?" I called, trotting toward them. They looked up at me and frowned – language barrier or sun's glare, I wasn't sure. "Pardon," I amended (pronouncing it par-DOHN), making a show of consulting my guidebook as I did, as if I hadn't learned that word or asked the question that followed ten dozen times since landing in this country weeks ago. *"Vorbiți engleză?"* Do you speak English?

One of the old men shook his head, a little more emphatically than perhaps was called for. The other scowled and pointed at the church, metal scaffolding gleaming in the brilliant sunlight. I nodded, and massacred my way through *"Mulțumesc."* Thank you.

I headed toward the church. Up close, it was truly something to behold. Nestled in a copse of trees – that hid a small cemetery behind the church, which was framed in a low, decorative wrought iron fence scarcely two feet high, before giving way to the steep slope of the mountain – the church sat within the shadow of the ruins, and yet its quiet majesty seemed to hold the ruins' dark presence at bay. Romania is renowned the world over for its collection of ornate wooden churches – Romanian Orthodox, all – erected in the Middle Ages by master carpenters who'd dedicated their lives to the narrow specialty of constructing such places of worship. They carved these rural houses of God from the verdant forests that surrounded them, and their appearance – from the long curved taper of the bell tower's shingled roof, which terminated in a simple wooden cross, to the planed-smooth logs that joined in cross-hatches at the building's corners and into which narrow windows paned with leaded glass were cut – made them look as though they sprouted from the very ground itself, and suggested what lay beneath was not basement but fibrous roots. Many were lost to war or fire over the years, and most fell into disrepair during the brutal Communist rule of the last century. This one appeared to be among the latter.

As moss-laden and dry-rotted as portions of it appeared to be beneath the metal gridlines of the scaffolding, it looked to be a stunning specimen. A tower four stories high, a single, glossy slab of wood comprised its oversized front door – not new, but newly refinished. Framing it were broad planks of wood gone gray with age, into which was carved an elaborate bas relief depicting at its upper reaches a sky filled with cold, beatific angels each emitting radiant light, which gave way to an image of a village that was recognizably this one in the middle, and beneath that a fiery hell full of writhing, naked demons in various states of torment, or perhaps ecstasy.

I found the sculpture oddly captivating, and disturbing as well. Looking at its depiction of a carnal hell, I couldn't help but think I'd been privy to similar scenes a time or two before. In the basement of a Staten Island squat occupied by the demon Merihem and his human playthings. In an abandoned-sanitarium-turned-skim-joint in the wilds of New Mexico. I wondered if the artist had a similar first-hand inspiration for this piece.

"Quite something, isn't it?"

When I heard the voice beside me, I damn near jumped out of my shoes. My meat-suit was clearly not accustomed to being snuck up on. He was also pretty damn well-trained, I discovered in the fraction of a second it took me to gather my wits, muscle-memory had already kicked in, and my right hand was wrapped around the grip of my SIG Sauer beneath my jacket. Through force of will, I relaxed my grip, and let the hand fall to my side.

"I'm very sorry," said the man beside me. "I didn't mean to startle you."

I looked him up and down. Forty, maybe forty-five. Thick-stubbled, handsome, with dark brown hair lightened here and there by the sun and deep-set brown eyes flecked with amber. Good-humored, based on the crinkles at the corners of his eyes and the lines around his easy smile, but a forehead that showed the ghost of worry-creases suggested him a serious man as well. He wore the faded, dirt-ground jeans of a workman, and a tool belt stocked with tools. His shirt was a black button-down with a Roman collar, his shirtsleeves rolled up to reveal tanned forearms.

A priest.

I flushed at having been called out in my startlement. Covered with a change of subject. "You speak English," I said.

He looked mock-startled for a moment, and then quipped, "By God, you're right!"

"How'd you know *I* did?"

The man gestured at the guidebook in my hands. "You're carrying *The Know-Nothing's Guide to Historic Romania,*" he replied, his words scarcely accented, and his use of contractions rare among even the best Romanian English-speakers. "So I hope you'll forgive my impertinence, but it seemed like a fair bet."

"No forgiveness required," I replied, forcing myself to soften my stance and smile. "I confess, I'm happy to hear my mother tongue; it's been a while. And if you don't mind me saying, Father…"

"Yefi," he supplied, extending one calloused, working-man's hand.

"Father Yefi," I continued, taking his hand and shaking it, "your English is quite good. I'm Frank."

"An admirable quality," he joked. "And as for my English, I should hope it passes muster; otherwise, I'd think my years at Harvard Divinity ill-spent. And please, just Yefi – no Father required. I'm here to meditate and reflect, not minister, which is just as well. These people have little interest in whatever spiritual guidance I might offer them. Their faith lies… elsewhere." The priest's countenance darkened.

"Meaning what, exactly?"

The darkness lifted, replaced with false good cheer. "Meaning they're kind enough to leave me to my woodworking, is all. For which – most days, at least – I'm grateful."

I gestured toward his tool belt. "I always thought meditation was more sitting on a straw mat and less… whacking things with hammers."

"Yes, well, I prefer a more active approach. It's good for a man to have a project. There are very few burdens in life that can't be eased by a good sweat, by honest work. And idle hands are the devil's playthings, after all."

"I couldn't agree more. I'm here on a bit of a project myself."

He squinted appraisingly at me. "And what, pray tell, is that?"

I gestured up the hill toward the ruins – hard and sharp against the sky, like the spires of a wrought-iron fence viewed at an angle, so they crowd together in silhouette. "Exploration," I told him. "I'm trying to see as many of Europe's castles as I can."

"And your quest brought you here? I'm surprised. I would not have thought so humble and remote a town had made the guidebooks. Particularly since you're the first such tourist to happen by in my memory, and," he said, nodding toward the square, where the townspeople watched our conversation with naked, gawking interest, only to avert their gazes when we glanced their way, "a good deal longer, if their reaction's any indication."

His question came off all light and conversational, but I couldn't help thinking it was a test. Yefi knew damn well these ruins weren't in any guidebook, and further, that this town was hard to find. What's more, I couldn't help but feel there was a secret-handshake component to our entire conversation. He was feeling me out, but why? What did he know that he wasn't telling me?

Whatever it was, I thought it best to play along. I shook my head and feigned a sheepish smile. "To tell the truth," I said, "my trip so far's been pretty touristy. I only wound up here because I suck at reading road signs in Romanian. Pretty sure I took a dozen or so wrong turns since I left my hotel in Petrosani this morning. And in the interest of making a full confession, Father, I'm still not sure where the heck I've ended up, there was no sign I could see at the entrance to the town, and I can't make heads or tails of where I am on my map. But I figured hey, I'm hunting castles, and here's a castle, so maybe somebody upstairs is trying to tell me something."

"Well, I can help you in one capacity, at least. The town you're standing in is called Nevăzut. In Romanian, it means 'unseen' – a reference, no doubt, to its isolated nature, and the fact that it attracts so few visitors. I confess, I had some trouble finding the place myself when first I came, as if the roads themselves resisted bringing me. So perhaps there's something to your theory you've been brought here for a reason."

There was some steel behind that last sentence, as though he wished me to intuit some intent behind his words, but whatever it was, it was too subtle for me to understand. A threat? A warning? Some kind of coded cry for help?

I filed the thought away and soldiered on. "And does the castle have a name as well? Any chance you know somebody who could take me up there? A local guide, perhaps?"

At that, Yefi shook his head. "You're not likely to find anyone in this town who'll take you up there, nor even speak of it. I've lived in Nevăzut for years now, having leapt at so satisfying an assignment as restoring this church to its former glory, even if I'd not heard of the town in which it sat. But despite my own repeated inquiries on the subject, I've not so much as heard a local refer to the ruins at all, except obliquely. Even then, they speak in the hushed tones of the frightened, or the reverent. They refer to it variously as the Great Death, the Stone Protector, the Shadow Cast Upon the Valley. I confess, I don't even know the castle's true name, and after a few months here, I learned it best to cease inquiring on the subject. It was only once I abandoned my curiosity these people began to accept my presence here."

"You're telling me I should do the same? Abandon my curiosity, that is."

Yefi looked around once more, moving only his eyes, so the townspeople at their distance could not see.

"I'm telling you," he said, *sotto voce,* his face a mask of amiability despite the sudden weight his quiet words carried, "that this conversation is perhaps best continued inside." And then, loud enough for any person dropping eaves to hear: "I know you're just passing through, my friend, and eager to get back on the road, but my day's work has left me parched. Perhaps you'd indulge a lonely man of the cloth and come inside for a drink before you go?"

With that, he opened the front door to the church and stood aside to let me in. For a moment, I just stared at him, puzzled. Then, after casting another glance around the village's central green to see three dozen locals doing their damndest to pretend as if they weren't watching, I stepped into the hallowed darkness.

12.

"You wanna tell me what that was all about?" I asked the priest once we were both inside the church, and the heavy wooden door had clapped shut behind us. "The folks I've met since I arrived don't speak a lick of English. Can't imagine they'd have picked up much of our conversation. And anyways, I'm just a tourist passing through."

"Like hell you are," Yefi replied. "You, like they, understand a great deal more than you're letting on."

My hand crept once more to the gun in its concealment holster beneath my jacket. "I'm not sure I take your meaning, Padre."

"You take my meaning fine," he told me, "and I assure you, I intend you no harm. This is a place of worship, after all. Too long ignored, alas, both structurally and in intent, but a place of worship nonetheless."

I eyed him for a second, and saw no malice in his features, no threat implicit in his posture, so I relaxed. "What the hell is that supposed to mean? All the sudden, I get the feeling like you're here for something other than quiet meditation, or fixing up a dilapidated old church."

"To your first point, you're quite right. As for your second, though, you've missed the mark. I *am*, in fact, here to fix up this dilapidated old church, as you so callously called her; however, my reasons for doing so are far from contemplative. For you see, while Nevăzut – quite by design, though whose or what's exactly I could not say – does not appear on any maps, it's long been at the fore of my Church Patriarch's mind. The locals are not wrong to refer to the ruins that lord over them as a shadow, for a great darkness resides in Nevăzut, and taints every aspect of its inhabitants' lives. Yet for whatever reason, they welcome this darkness, into their homes, into their hearts. It fuels them. Guides them. Provides them strength and solace, when instead they should be seeking both in the love of one another, and in our Lord and Savior Jesus Christ. That is why I was sent here. To drive the wickedness from these Godless people, and turn them once more toward the light of God's grace. That is why I've dedicated myself to restoring His house; I consider it the first step toward restoring His flock. Or, at least, I did. Now I fear they're too far gone for my humble ministrations to save."

"Save the sermon, Padre, and skip ahead to the specifics."

"Certainly," he said, "although for that, I think perhaps we'll need a drink."

He retreated into the church's gloomy interior, sparking a camp lantern as he did. The interior of the building was suddenly awash in amber light, which reflected off the lacquered surfaces within and suffused the church with warmth and numinous beauty. What little watery light trickled through the tiny panes of leaded glass that graced the church's only windows had not done any justice to the stunning craftsmanship contained therein. Even in its work-in-progress state, it was really something to see. The steep pitch of the roof was two planes of honey-colored tongue-and-groove fading upward into darkness. Rough-hewn beams, each carved from a single tree trunk and affixed to one another with iron brackets and nails the size of railroad ties, propped the structure up. A few of these beams were splintered and met in a shallow V where they had weakened; replacements still golden-fresh were stacked along one wall, together with replicas of the original brackets and hardware to match. A roped-off spiral staircase missing half its steps led upward to the organist's balcony, and then up further to the bell tower. Pews of oak, some unfinished, others stained matte brown, still others stained and varnished both, rested above floorboards so old and age-desiccated their dishwater-gray surfaces bowed upward at the edges, showing black beneath, basement or earth I wasn't sure.

At the front of the room was an unfinished wooden altar scattered with tools. Larger items – a radial saw, a couple sawhorses, a stack of two-by-fours, another of plywood, and a couple dozen paint cans full of stain and polyurethane – were scattered haphazardly beside it. Above the mess hung a utility light, a bare bulb in a hook-hatted metal cage whose cord connected to an orange extension below, which in turn snaked away into the darkness to the rear of the church, beyond the altar. A faint engine thrum from outside suggested it was plugged into a generator.

I watched as Father Yefi set the lantern down atop the altar and clicked on the hanging light. Under its harsh glare, the magic in the room receded. Now it was just an old and dusty church once more.

It was then I realized this was more than just a church to Yefi, because behind the altar I saw a military cot upon which rested a tousle of blankets and a well-worn Bible; a mini-fridge; and a hot plate, beside which sat a stack of canned goods, a single saucepan, and a wooden spoon. "You *live* here?" I asked him.

"I do," he said. "It may sound foolish, but there are times I do not feel safe out there, among the villagers. Here, I am safe, if perhaps less comfortable."

"I didn't see a lock on the church door."

"The safety of which I speak is not merely corporeal," he replied, "although that which I fear is barred entry from this place just as surely as if it were locked."

"And what is it that you fear?" I asked him.

"Before I tell you that," he said, fetching two chipped, age-clouded juice glasses and a bottle of *Țuică* from beneath the altar and pouring us each a belt, "let me ask *you* something."

"Shoot."

"Why did you come to Nevăzut?"

I thought long and hard before I answered. Then I figured fuck it, thinking long and hard ain't what I do, so instead I dove right in. "You mentioned a great darkness resides here," I said. "If that's true, then I aim to kill it."

The priest laughed, full-throated and full of delight. It echoed through the dusty church, growing hollow as it rose, like a chorus of sycophants trying desperately to let the boss know they were in on the joke. Then he pressed a glass into my hand and clinked his to mine so hard both sloshed. "Well then, fair stranger, you and I are well-met, even if I fear you're as batty as this old girl's belfry."

He tossed back his glass. I did the same. The drink was hard and sharp, but with an undercurrent of fruit. Distilled from plums, if I recalled, *Țuică* was Romania's preferred form of moonshine, more rocket-fuel than wine. I set my glass down and wiped the sting of it off my lips with the back of one hand. Father Yefi poured a second for us both.

"So you wanna tell me what's *really* going on here?"

"When you arrived in town," he said, "did you notice anything peculiar?"

"You mean the no-women thing, or the business with the windows?"

He raised his glass in a toast of mock-salute. "Both, in fact, for the two are closely tied. Nice to see you do not miss a trick."

"Yeah," I said, tossing back my drink and feeling my eyeballs roll around loose in my sockets. This shit was *strong*. "Bully for me. So where'd they all go?"

"Oh, they're all *here*," he replied. "They're simply disinclined toward socializing in the daytime."

"Come again?"

"I confess, when I first arrived in town on this assignment, it took me a while to notice the women's absence. Blame a cloistered existence. A life spent among men and men alone. And at risk of committing the sin of pride, it took me longer still to inquire as to where they might be, for I was raised to be polite above all else. When I did, I was assured the women of the town had not fled en masse on my arrival. In fact, they were, and are, right here. It would seem the women of Nevăzut all suffer from a rare affliction – a blood disorder, to hear their husbands tell it – which leaves them pale and wan, and quite light sensitive as well. Some it seems are only mildly afflicted; others are wild, delusional, bed-ridden. Again, by day, you understand. At night they are as well as you or I. They dance, they drink, they cook, they sing. I'd not encountered them because I'd set my own internal clock to accord the day's light. My access to power is limited by my ability to keep my generator fueled, and my work here leaves me so exhausted at night, I've scarcely enough time to read a verse or two after dinner before sleep takes me. And my Lord, the dreams I've had."

"What kind of dreams?"

The priest took a long swallow of the spirit, like he was buying time, or maybe avoiding the question altogether. Given the color that rose in his cheeks as he did, I was betting on the latter. Then again, that coulda been the booze.

"Let me simply say they've been far from pious."

"You mean far from chaste."

"In part, yes. In fact, I'm ashamed to say there's not a woman in this town who hasn't featured in my subconscious' nocturnal meanderings, and never in fewer than groups of three or more. But there's another aspect to the dreams beyond merely addressing my own repressed desires of the flesh, for of course that's what I at first assumed them to be. Occupational hazard, you could say."

"Yeah? What's that?"

Another pause. Another shot. "They always end with me tearing the throats out of the women with whom I find myself entangled, and bathing in the hot, wet, sticky-sweet nectar that is their blood. The light of life guttering and dying in their eyes. Their last breath begging me to drink them dry. A request with which I'm always happy to comply. And invariably, they expire at the, ah, height of their enjoyment, if you take my meaning."

I downed my drink and wished hard I could unhear what he'd just told me. In life, I went to Sunday school, for God's sake. There's some shit you should never be forced to picture a member of the clergy do. "Trust me, Padre, your meaning's hard to miss."

"There is one fact that serves to blunt my shame, and cast doubt on the origins of those dreams."

"Yeah? What's that?"

"Many of the women who appeared in them I didn't meet until afterward. And by the glint in their eyes when they first saw me, I'm willing to wager they knew me just as well as I knew them."

"You mean to say–"

"That someone, or more likely some*thing*, filled my head with these vile, blasphemous fantasies? That the women of this Godforsaken town are in the thrall of that selfsame something? Now that I say it all aloud, I'm forced to admit it sounds ridiculous. And yet here you stand, the first stranger to arrive in town since I was sent here so very long ago, asking questions about the castle on the hill and claiming you're here to fell some ancient evil. So you tell me, is it ridiculous? Or am I right to make my bed beneath a symbol of Christ's sacrifice so that it, and He, may watch over me?"

I sighed and set down my glass, then poured myself another belt. "I don't know shit from Jesus, Padre, but I can tell you you ain't crazy to be scared."

"But *you're* not scared."

I laughed. I couldn't help it. "You kidding me? I'm nothing *but* scared. Been that way near as long as I can remember. But that don't change what I have to do."

He nodded, his face screwed up all drunk-serious. "Something's changed of late," he told me. "The dreams are more sporadic now, and less vivid than they used to be."

His words and tone didn't seem to synch. "That sounds like a *good* thing to me," I said, "only you're throwing off a vibe that says it's anything but. Why?"

"At first, I was pleased with the development as well," said Yefi. "I even told myself perhaps the light of my presence had dispelled the pall that hung over this poor, afflicted village. After all, I reasoned, I'd seen no overt sign of malignant intent from any of the women I'd encountered here in my conscious life, at least. Perhaps they were as much victims of these visions as was I, and once those visions abated entirely, everything here would return to normal. I even toyed with the idea of posting flyers advertising Sunday mass, the first such public Christian mass this village would have seen in centuries. But then I began to hear the night sounds, and shortly thereafter the children started disappearing. That's when I realized the evil in this town had not moved on after all. It had simply changed its tactics."

"What kind of night sounds? And what do you mean, the children started disappearing?"

"They're hard to describe," he told me. "Somewhere between a click and a low growl, and a sound like fine-grain sandpaper, or snake-scales dragging past dry leaves. Down by the river, mostly, and only ever at night. And as far as the children are concerned, I mean exactly what I say. Used to be, a day like this, we'd have fifteen, twenty children frolicking about the square. How many did we have today?"

I thought back. "Seven, maybe eight. But that hardly proves they're disappearing."

"Doesn't it? This village has no school. No daycare. Nothing whatsoever for the children to do but entertain themselves while their parents do as parents do to provide for them. So you tell me, where have the others gone?"

"You ask their parents?"

"Of course I asked their parents."

"And what did they say?"

"They told me to mind my own business. In fact, they veritably begged me to."

"And what did they say about where the missing children *went*?"

"That's just it," he told me. "They wouldn't admit there *were* any missing children."

"So their kids were all accounted for," I said.

"No," he said. "You misunderstand me. They didn't claim their missing children were safe and sound. What they claimed was that they'd never had those children to begin with."

We drank long into the night, the priest and I. Like drunks the world over, we spoke of heaven and hell, of good and evil, of life's plans sadly scuttled, of love lost or unrequited. We laughed and cried and sang tunelessly the only hymn I knew that was worth a damn the Stones' "Shine a Light," off of side four of Exile. And I'll be damned if this here man of the cloth didn't know every bloody word.

That song always brought a tear to my eye. Jagger originally penned it for Brian Jones, whose mood swings and struggles with substance abuse had, by '68, estranged him from the band. Never mind they were on account of the fact that Jones had hell breathing down his neck and damn well knew it. I felt like shit when Jones' deal came due, but by then, the band he'd sold his soul to found had already left him in the dust – all by the ripe old age of twenty-seven. Lord knows why that's when rock stars' deals always come due. Some say it has to do with the number of books in the New Testament, or some Kabbalah nonsense about the twenty-seven names of God. You ask me, that's just how long it takes for a working class kid with real talent to build himself a set of wings from feather and wax and then fly close enough to the sun to come tumbling back down. I left Jones' body face-down in his pool, but not before we two shared a drink. Figured what's the harm? I owed him that much. It seemed like he'd made peace with his fate. Guess it was fitting from the guy whose last recording with the band was "Sympathy for the Devil."

When I told that poor bastard it was nothing personal, you'd best believe I meant it.

Point is, me and the priest hit it off just fine. I never asked him what drove him to the cloth, and he never asked me just who – or what – I really am. But for one night by the suffuse, drunken glow of *Țuică* and golden lamplight reflected off of honey-lacquered walls, I remembered what it was like to be in Danny and Ana's company – to speak freely, without care.

To have a friend.

It wasn't until dawn broke I broached the topic of my attack.

We'd stopped drinking some hours before. As drunk slid inexorably toward hung over, we both fell silent for long stretches. Not sleeping, but no longer fully conscious, either. After one such stretch, I said to him, "I've got to go up there, you know."

His chin rested lightly on his breastbone. When I spoke, his head jerked upward, and his eyes opened. They swam a moment, as if bobbing atop a choppy surface of *Ţuică* and exhaustion, and then focused. "Go up where?"

"To the castle," I said.

He shook his head. "You can't."

"I have to. That's where I'll find the who or what that's causing all of this. I'm sure of it."

"You misunderstand," he said. "I don't disagree with you on that count. I simply mean you can't. The castle is… protected."

"Protected? Protected how?"

"It's difficult to describe," he said. "But as one approaches the castle – which none but me have dared since first came to town, so far as I'm aware – there's this point at which the forest changes. Well below the treeline, some three hundred meters from the castle, is a perimeter encircling the peak whose border is as sharp and well defined as a snow-globe's sphere. The barrier itself it tinted ever so slightly, as if what lies beyond is being viewed through a pane of dirty glass. The trees outside the sphere are hale and hearty, but those above are withered and gray, as if the sun scarcely reaches them. And yet the barrier itself is not solid. In fact, apart from the pervading sense of dread that envelops you when you approach the place, the unobservant could scarcely be blamed for wandering right through it, although I would hardly recommend it."

"Why's that?" I asked, but I was pretty sure I knew the answer. Least if this spell was anything like the barrier Magnusson had employed at Pemberton Baths.

"When first I stumbled upon it, my curiosity got the better of me," he said, "so I conducted an experiment of sorts. First, I threw a pebble at the barrier. It passed through without incident, neither slowing nor deflecting in the slightest. Then, a pinecone. The result was the same. I'd nearly screwed up the courage to step through myself when I heard a rustle in the underbrush some ten meters to my left. A rabbit, startled from its hiding place by some predator unseen, or, perhaps, by me.

It darted toward the barrier by sheer flight instinct, and in the instant before it passed through I swear I saw the animal tense, as if knowing better – as if suddenly realizing its mistake. And when it passed through..."

"Lemme guess, it turned to ash."

Father Yefi started in surprise. "It did," he said. "Ash as white as driven snow. And its eyes–"

"Were burned out of its head," I said, remembering the ill-fated crow outside of Magnusson's lair. "As if whatever lay inside the barrier didn't want anyone or anything outside to see what lay beyond."

"How could you *know* that? How could you, when I scarcely have the words to describe it myself? In the years that passed since that day, I've doubted countless times the veracity of my own memory – wondered if perhaps I had simply imagined it. I assumed I'd fallen victim to the ancient superstitions that plague the simple country folk of my blessed homeland, people too far removed from society to understand the monsters of lore hold no sway in the modern world. But deep down, I never stopped believing what I'd seen. And since that day, I've never returned to that Godforsaken place."

"I know, because I've seen magic of this kind before. I wish to hell I hadn't, but I have."

The priest grinned mirthlessly. "I'd prefer you direct your wishes toward a higher power than that, my newfound friend."

"Believe me, Padre, your higher power's got fuck all to do with what's up that mountain, and He sure as shit didn't send me."

"Don't be so sure," he said. "The Lord–"

"Works in mysterious ways?" I ventured.

"Has a plan for all of us, I was going to say."

"Not for me. Not anymore."

"So I'm to believe you're some servant of darkness, then? Because if I may be so bold, you come across as anything but."

I sighed. "You want the truth? Half the time I don't know what I am, or who I serve. I'd like to think I try to do what's right. But sometimes, what's right is hard to figure. Sometimes, I'm too damned tired to even think about it, so instead I do what's easy, and then convince myself it's right."

This time, the priest's smile was better humored. "Your words aside," he said, "you're not a man who gives an impression of ever doing what's easy."

"Maybe not," I said, "but it ain't for lack of trying. Turns out, I'm just not smart enough to figure out what easy looks like. Which I suppose is just as well, since if I plan on breaching the castle, it don't sound like there's much easy to be had. Last one of these barriers I saw I only passed through alive on account of I was invited; I got no goddamn idea how I'm gonna get through this one."

"Perhaps you put too little faith in the Lord," he said, eyes twinkling with sudden mischief, "or, at the very least, in His humble servants."

"Come again?"

"When I said you can't just walk up to the castle ruins, I meant it. But that doesn't mean we can't get you inside."

"I don't follow."

"Hold on," he said. "I'll show you." He retreated to the blond wood box that was the half-constructed altar and rooted around beneath a while. Apparently, the side facing away from the pews was open, and perhaps shelved as well. "Not much storage in an old church like this," said Yefi by way of explanation. "No basement, nor outbuilding, and the small rectory that once stood beside it burned down some hundred years ago. I've had to make do stuffing things wherever I can manage. Ah! Here it is."

He raised his hand in triumph. In it was a large leather-bound tome that I took at first to be a Bible, its cover dyed black and tooled into an elaborate filigree. A tattered ribbon bookmark dangled from the top of its spine and fluttered behind it like a train as he set the book down atop the altar. The spine crackled as he opened it, as if the book itself was protesting the intrusion on its sleep of ages. The pages were thick, yellowed, and stiff from years. From them emanated a scent like spiced rum. It reminded me of my time spent digging through the Vatican's archives. It was the smell of paper's sweet decay.

"I found this under the floorboards in the church's entryway, beneath the carved sigil of the carpenter who designed and built the place," he said. "A monk named Father Grigori."

My pulse quickened. The young priest now had my full attention. "What is it?" I asked.

"A sketch book," he replied. "It's been of no small use to me, as much of it is taken up by detailed plans of the very church in which we stand. His woodworking technique is unparalleled, and his diagrams have proved invaluable in duplicating it, even if I do fail to grasp the more esoteric aspects of what he was trying to accomplish."

"Such as?"

"His notes indicate he was very specific about the placement of this church, about the species of timber that should be used in its construction, about the patterns of the inlays, and even the very direction of the grain for every plank. There are notes that indicate he believed his design would result in a building outside the view of the Pretender to the Throne and the Adversary both. The Adversary, clearly, represents Lucifer, the Morning Star. The Pretender to the Throne, given the assumed date of construction of the church, I take to mean the conquering Ottomans, or perhaps the Habsburg monarchy, who also occupied these lands for quite some time."

Yefi wasn't wrong about the Adversary, but his interpretation of the Pretender was miles off. The Pretender to the Throne was the very God to which Yefi pledged his life and swore his fealty.

How'd I know? Easy. Charon told me.

"Your God is nothing more than a seditionist," he'd said. "A pretender to the throne. For eons before him I ruled, and my dominion was Chaos, the Great Nothing from which this filthy rock you call a home emerged."

Not that I was about to correct Yefi's fallacious interpretation. He was a man of faith, after all, and even faith misplaced is worth something. Far be it from me to disabuse him of it.

Or, for that matter, to inform him the very Grigori he held in such regard and the beast I'd come to slay were one and the same.

"This is all very interesting, Padre, but how's it gonna help me get into the castle?"

"Because church plans are not all Grigori sketched. He was quite the polymath, it seems. The book is filled with notes and sketches of local life – architecture, the annual harvest celebration, flora and fauna of the surrounding area, even a number of quite striking nudes of local townswomen, each annotated by name. The latter, I would have assumed, would have caused quite a stir, but perhaps the people of his time were more enlightened than we sometimes give them credit for. After all, he *had* taken a vow of celibacy, and all his nudes are religious in their iconography."

"And you think some antique nudie-pics are gonna somehow help me sneak in?"

"No," he said, jabbing a finger at the page to which he'd just turned, and spinning the book to face me. "I think *this* is."

I eyed the page in question. On it was a sketch of what appeared to be a heavy iron door set into a wall of natural rock. In the foreground were a pair of crosses maybe three feet high, rendered ghostly by the fact the artist had chosen to draw them transparent so as to not obscure the door beyond. Beside the sketch was a short block of precise script that spoke of years of practice with a quill.

"My grasp of Middle Ages Romanian is pretty nonexistent, Padre. What's this text say?"

"It says, in part, 'Hidden entrance to the castle keep.' Apparently, it was intended as a covert supply line should the castle ever find itself under siege, and an escape route from the keep down to the valley floor if necessary. His notes claim it accesses a cave system that leads directly to the main residence."

A smile bloomed across my face. "Does it now?"

Father Yefi responded in kind with a smile of his own. "It does, indeed."

"And do you know where this door is located?"

"I do," he said. "The door is located behind the church, in the town cemetery."

13.

We breached the door at midnight.

Me, I would've preferred to go in, guns blazing, by the light of day. But guns don't seem to be worth much against the Brethren, and anyways, Yefi insisted the cover of darkness was essential. The residents of Nevăzut are quite suspicious of outsiders, he reminded me, and swore fealty to the castle on the hill. As he explained, local folk wisdom dictated that the castle and its rumored occupant were not responsible for the sorry state of Nevăzut's women – *that* was due to a curse of nebulous origin and dubious design, passed down through the centuries – but were, in fact, all that kept them aboveground. The stories passed down by the elders suggested the effect of the castle's occupant was not life-*draining*, but life-*sustaining*, that without their unseen lord's influence upon them (and his rumored midnight ministrations) the women would have died long ago. And what's more, these people attributed every crop in this verdant valley, every child born, and every revolution this tiny hamlet managed to weather unnoticed, to that selfsame lord. So while the lot of them were frightened enough of their strange benefactor and his abode to steer well clear of the castle or its grounds, and none but the most fevered and delirious (and, coincidentally or not, the most beautiful) of the townswomen would even claim to've laid eyes (or lips, or other things) on its rumored inhabitant, they would no doubt take up arms against anyone who dared challenge him. And since the doorway stood at the rear of the small cemetery behind the church – within sight of the main square – that meant sneaking into the big, scary castle in pitch fucking darkness, or what would have been were it not for the moon hanging full and bright overhead, its face partly obscured by the towers and crenellations of the castle above: a bauble of beckoning silver; egging me on, daring me to scale the mountain, slay the dragon, and reap my knightly reward.

We armed ourselves as best we could for our endeavor. Yefi plucked a pry bar near as tall as he himself from the pile of tools and building supplies he'd amassed inside the church, and fashioned a torch from some old timber and rags stiff with polishing wax. Having learned my lesson that the Brethren were best felled with weapons made of metal tip-to-tail, I grabbed up one of the heavy iron stakes used to fix the beams that bore the church's weight in place, and the scarred wooden mallet Yefi used to drive them in. My choice of weapon elicited an eyebrow-raise from the good Father, at which point I shrugged and said, "Unless you got a bazooka tucked beneath the floorboards I don't know about, these'll have to do." He didn't know I carried a handgun by way of backup, and I didn't volunteer the information. For one, I wasn't sure he would approve. And for two, you can never be too careful.

Lord knows I never seem to be.

The graveyard was quiet, its tenants at rest. We walked on tiptoe down the narrow dirt path that sliced through it as if by unspoken consensus, our shadows long beneath the ghostly luminescence of the pie-plate moon. I told myself it was to avoid any undue attention from the townspeople. That would have been all-too easy to swallow by the light of day, but by moonlight, looking up at the castle that loomed before me, my lungs full of cold, crisp Transylvania air, it was hard to deny that some small part of me feared disturbing the dead's rest.

Funny, I know, coming from the only member of the unquiet dead around.

I didn't see the door at first. The path, of course, did not lead to it, instead veering to the left, and continuing on a little while before doing so again. Another left and you'd end up right back where we started – from church to graveyard and back again, an unbroken circle. Probably symbolized something. Everything these churchy types build or make or say or do seems to.The door was set into an outcrop of rock attached to a vicious upslope, more cliff than mountain. It was obscured by the same crowd of tress and scrub brush that blanketed every square foot of the valley floor not cleared by human hands, all alder and ash and ghost-white birch. The door itself was rusted matte brown and fuzzed here and there with moss, and looked of a piece with the rock that surrounded it. It wasn't until Yefi's closed fist bonged against it I realized it wasn't rock, and even still, it took him tracing the line of the circular doorframe with his torch for me to realize what it was I was looking at.

Before we pried it open, I leaned close, listening in the cemetery dark. The door was cold and damp and smelled of iron – of blood. Beyond, all was quiet and still, or else too muffled by the thick metal slab for me to hear. I traced my hand along its rough surface, my fingers catching on a raised crest of some kind. It took me a few moments of following its lines before I realized what it was.

It was an uppercase G. As in Grigori.

Yefi stuck his torch into the dew-damp grass, and wedged his pry bar into the narrow gap between iron and stone. Then the two of us put our full weight onto that fucker and made all manner of unpleasant grunting noises as we tried in vain to get it moving.

We adjusted the pry bar and redoubled our efforts, Yefi hanging from the bar's end while I climbed atop it and hopped awkwardly up and down. Still, it didn't move.

Then, at once, it did, and Yefi crumpled to the ground, me and the pry bar landing atop him in a heap.

The door hadn't moved far, just rolled a little to the right. Turns out, it wasn't hinged, but more a pocket door, intended to turn clockwise into a slot designed to house it. Rust and age and crumbling rock thwarted its no doubt elegant design, however, leaving us naught but a scant crescent aperture to shimmy through. It seemed we'd be crawling single-file into the still black beyond.

Before we dared, though, we lay frozen for a moment on the grass, panting and lead-limbed and thrumming with the nervy certainty that the clatter of our Keystone Cops approach to popping the door must've attracted some manner of attention; from the town, from the catacombs, or from both.

And after a fashion, I guess we had, for we heard a rustle building from somewhere deep beneath the castle, like a tsunami fast approaching. I lifted my head, and aimed saucer eyes at Yefi, only to find his fearful, wide-eyed gaze staring back at me, a silent shout declaring, "Yes I fact I *do* fucking hear that!" (I know what you're thinking. Servant of God that he is, he wasn't thinking *fucking*. And I get where you're coming from. I mean, I was raised a Christian, so I know damned well that sins of thought hold nearly as much sway as sins of deed. But if you were looking into his eyes at that moment, you'd have seen some cursing, too.)

The sound built and built, and with it came a high-pitched cacophony and a pressure against the skin of my face, which was raised to keep the aperture in sight. And as Yefi's flight response kicked in, causing him to try to gather himself up off the ground to make a run for it, I added up all the crazy signals I'd been given – rustlesquealwindcave – and realized exactly what was happening. I rolled onto my stomach and heaved myself at Yefi, tackling him to the ground behind the scant shelter of a nearby headstone and burying my face in the folds of his jacket just as the massive colony of bats reached the narrow entrance we'd created to their cave and poured out and up and around us, enveloping us in a living maelstrom of fur and fang and shrieking winds – all echolocatory squeals and leathery, rustling wings. For a full minute, we were caught in their barrage, and then, as quickly as they'd arrived, they were gone, swirling upward into the night sky in such numbers they dimmed the moon, and leaving nothing behind but two panicked men, frightened as little boys as they tried in vain to catch their breath between the tombstones.

The silence once the bats were gone was deafening. I watched them flutter across the face of the moon, swirling all around the castle keep, and wondered how long it would last. Whatever waited in the castle must have seen them, too, and wondered what exactly had disturbed them. And that's to say nothing of its minions in the village.

"The bats," I whispered. "They're unaffected by the barrier."

"They're also essentially blind," whispered Yefi in reply. "Perhaps whatever resides inside cares not to protect itself against that which cannot see."

The element of surprise was lost, I thought, but all that meant was tonight represented my last chance to catch Grigori somewhat unprepared.

If we were going, we were going now.

I went in first. Tossed my stake and mallet through the aperture, then wriggled through like one of those fish that live in rice paddies and are occasionally forced by dint of sun or human interference to make their way across short stretches of dry land to an adjacent pond. Once through, I gathered on my haunches and sat motionless, waiting for my eyes and ears to adjust. My ears did, finally, registering the quiet echoes of a thousand plops and plinks of water dripping in the darkness. My eyes remained as useless in this lightless world as my fingers would have proved at tasting things.

After a hundred count, I gave Yefi the signal – three sharp raps against the door – and he followed after. Torch first, handed through to me. Then pry bar. Then himself. As the flame passed through the narrow aperture, I recoiled, my pupils constricting like some subterranean animal's against the sudden onslaught of light. Once I'd adjusted, I found myself staring at the uneven rock walls of a natural cavern, glistening with moisture. The cold, damp air had a sharp, mineral tang, only slightly mediated by the breeze that swept in through the narrow entryway and set the torch flickering. The pry bar I leaned against one craggy wall. Then I grabbed Yefi's outstretched arms at the wrists – he grabbing mine in turn – and pulled him through. He slid in on his back, and quickly found his feet, brushing the accumulated filth off his black clerical shirt as he did. "Something about cleanliness and godliness comes to mind," he muttered awkwardly in explanation of his actions, a brittle attempt at levity that – accompanied by a single bark of laughter, which echoed through the darkness and announced our arrival to anyone or anything that might be listening – only served to heighten the tension of the moment.

I shushed him then, but I didn't have to. Even in the dim firelight, I could see the sound of his own voice reflecting back at him was enough to silence him, and ratchet up his own anxiety. The smile died on his face, replaced by worry lines as deep and well-worn as the crags of rock around us.

I plucked up my mallet and my stake. The priest collected his pry bar and his torch, and then we set out together down the narrow stone passage, headed toward the castle keep.

The ground beneath our feet was damp dirt, packed hard by centuries of travel. The walls, though natural rock, held brackets meant for torches, and at alternating intervals on either side were the rotted remains of some kind of wall hanging – a series of royal flags, perhaps, or tapestries meant to convey tales of heroic derring-do. Each was rendered in gold thread against a backdrop of crimson. Each was damaged to near inscrutability. From what little survived of them, I pieced together countless scenes of death and dismemberment, some depicting the castle surrounded by vanquished foes impaled on spikes, while others displayed the town below awash with blood, the bodies of men and children being feasted upon by fanged, ghoulish women in gowns beneath a gleaming moon.

"What can you tell me of this place?" I asked Yefi.

"Nothing I've not already," he replied. "It seems we're both off the edge of the map at this point."

"'Beyond here be dragons,'" I said.

"Let's hope not," he replied.

Inside the cave, the sound of water was all around. Countless drops and drips, falling from the stone spikes that hung above. Stalagmites or stalactites, whichever ones they are. What was that fucking mnemonic? Mites crawl up, tights fall down. Stalactites, dripping from the stalactites. But there was another water sound, as well. The low, cool rumble, felt as much as heard, of water falling from a height in volume. A waterfall.

Must be an underground stream, I thought, or else a spring, either way feeding into the shallow, rock-churned waters of the river on which Nevăzut was built.

What I didn't expect was a goddamn lake.

I so very didn't expect it, I damn near fell in.

We followed the passageway on a gently curving downslope, me in front, holding my hammer and mallet ready, and Father Yefi just behind, carrying the torch. The fact that we were headed downward made no sense to me. The castle was some unknown hundreds of feet above our heads, and by all accounts, this passageway was supposed to take us there. Which meant our trajectory did not compute.

Until I saw the lake. And the boat.

But I'm getting ahead of myself, because at first, I saw none of those things. See, I wound up a few paces ahead of Yefi as we stumbled through the distorted space of the flame-lit cavern, which meant that as the corridor jagged, my monstrous shadow seemed to consume the view in front of me whole, such that all that stood before me was a gaping blackness. My borrowed heart quickened as I realized I'd strayed beyond the fire's protective glare, and my mind cast itself unbidden back toward a time in which I'd experienced the choking, awful Nothingness that stretched both infinite and membrane-thin between the lands of the of the living and the dead, between heaven and hell, between Paradise and the Inferno. The In-Between. The Great Nothing over which Charon reigned.

The memory of my brief imprisonment in the Nothingness was enough to make my skin crawl, and left my mind a world away from where I stood, and so I didn't notice the shadows deepening, the echoed static of rushing water amplifying.

If Yefi hadn't grabbed a handful of my jacket, I might've fallen in.

He'd come around the corner in a hurried shuffle, realizing he'd lagged behind. The sudden light reflected bright across the black, still surface of a lake four football fields across. It was then I realized I stood with one foot poised to step clean off a narrow rock shelf that stretched like a dock out over the water.

In my startlement I flailed, trying in vain to regain my balance. My stake and mallet sailed into the darkness, arcing across the water in slow motion it seemed, as if taunting me, before they disappeared into the water with twin rippling plops. Yefi's grip twisted at the small of my back, bunching fabric and pulling me back from the stone precipice. Granted, the water was but three feet below where we stood, but Lord knew how deep it was, or how cold, or how sharp the rocks beneath might be.

That's really what went through my mind in the moment; deep and cold and rocks. Given what I now know about what those still, dark waters hid, such paltry fears seem to me a giant fucking failure of imagination.

At the far left corner of the massive chamber, a waterfall spouted iridescent in the firelight from a narrow hole some thirty feet above, its disruption of the lake's surface negligible at such a distance. To the far right was an arch that stood out by virtue of the fact that it had clearly been carved by human hands. It framed a narrow alcove – a second stone dock jutting from it like a tongue from a lolling mouth – and a hollow patch of deeper dark to one side of it suggested the presence of a passageway, or a staircase perhaps, leading upward from it to the castle. It was the only entry point to the enormous cavern I could see save for the cave through which we'd come.

As I regained my balance – my lead foot settling to the ground once more, my arms no longer pinwheeling – I heard a knock from just below and to the right. My gaze travelled automatically to the source of the noise. It was a rowboat tied to an iron cleat, its heavy figure-eighted rope frayed to a tangle of horsehair frizz at the dock end.

"Thanks, Padre, you saved my bacon. Or at least kept me from needing a good blow-dry."

"Don't thank me yet," Yefi replied.

"Why's that?" I asked, or tried.

But before the second word could clear my mouth, the motherfucker smacked me upside the head with the goddamn torch.

For a split second, my world was the painful, searing glare of hellfire, white-hot fading to orange around the edges, and haloed in sparks of falling ember.

Then my eyelids came crashing down, and it was bedtime for ol' Sam.

And as any kid'll tell you, bedtime is when the monsters come out to play.

Sometimes I can't believe we lie and tell them that there's no such thing.

14.

I woke in throbbing darkness. A subtle lessening as I opened my eyes, black shifting to orange-black. The effort hurt like you would not fucking believe. Like my lids had weights attached, and not with fucking glue, either. Barbed hooks, more like. Plus, the left side of my face felt like I took a sideways header into a fry-o-lator. I raised my hands to touch it. Meant to raise just one, but it turns out they were bound together with a leather strap. Hard to tell how many knots there were in the dark. But what I can say is my attempts to untie it with my teeth resulted in one fewer knot, and no greater mobility. The rest of the knots – two or three or ten, for all I knew – were pulled too tight to make any headway.

When I flexed my legs to make sure they were still working, I noticed they were bound as well.

I prodded at my meat-suit's cheek and temple, wincing as I did. The skin was cracked and blistered and stung like a motherfucker. Plus it smelled like burned hair and under-seasoned pork. The realization of the latter made me queasy.

Then again, maybe that was the fact the world was rocking.

I closed my eyes, drank deep of the cool, subterranean air. Took stock of my situation.

It wasn't the world that was rocking, I realized, just the boat.

I was lying face-up in the rowboat. The goddamn motherfucking no-good bitch-ass rowboat.

And as annoying as I found that fact, Yefi seemed to think it was hilarious. I could hear his laughter echoing off the walls and ceiling of the cavern, the sound my only indication said walls and ceiling were out there, for they were lost in the deep shadows of the flickering orange-black all around.

Guess my face failed to snuff out Yefi's torch. Yefi'd better hope my bare, bound hands had as bad of luck when I wrapped them around his neck.

Or should I call him Grigori?

I sat up. Heavy-headed. Awkward. Not gonna lie, with my hands tied together, and a mental fog I'm guessing was borne of a concussion, it took a couple tries. And once I finally succeeded, the damn boat rocked so hard I thought I'd puke or fall out or both.

By force of will or maybe just dumb luck, I didn't do any combination thereof. I wondered if maybe that meant my luck was on the mend. The very notion made me laugh. Laughing made my head hurt so bad, I damn near passed out. That sounded more like my kinda luck.

Now that I was sitting up, I realized I was bobbing in the center of the underground lake, water dark and still as glass all around. Yefi's torch was a pinprick of orange against the black, its glow scarcely reaching me, but illuminating him well enough to see. At his feet, I saw a pair of oars, no doubt taken from this very boat. Looked like if I was getting out of here, I was gonna hafta swim.

"You've an odd sense of humor, Frank," called Yefi. "I understand why *I* am laughing – I have bettered my opponent, and played him for the fool. You, on the other hand, don't seem to have much cause."

"Sam," I called back. The volume of my own voice hurt my ears.

"Excuse me?"

"My name ain't Frank, it's Sam. Figured you oughta know."

"I confess, I fail to see why that's important at this juncture in our relationship."

"Seems to me a fella oughta know the name of the guy who's gonna end him."

Not gonna lie, I said that partly cause it sounded badass. Also a little cause I meant it. But mostly I said it because I had to keep that fucker talking while I worked at the knot that tied my feet together.

"Really? Then by all means, do call me Grigori. Tell me, Sam, how do you propose you're going to – as you so charmingly put it – end me? There are a few hundred tons of stone and earth between you and the nearest viable vessel, which might make locating it a bit difficult. And at present, you're lying bound and adrift atop an underwater lake, while here I am, lounging comfortably on dry land."

"For now."

"Now is all that matters," he replied airily. "Now is all I need."

"What the hell is that supposed to mean?"

"Oh, come now, Sam. You don't really think *this* was my master plan, did you? To leave you tied up in this place forever? Of course it's not. I've had other plans in motion for quite some time, plans which will soon come to fruition. The fact is, I never expected you to find this little village of mine; its protections are not insubstantial. Your arrival forced me to improvise. To neutralize you for a time while my siblings held up their end of our bargain."

"You mean Drustanus, Yseult, and Ricou."

"How adorable," he replied. "You're using their names to demonstrate to me you've done your homework. Of course, if your homework was worth a damn, you'd know Ricou hasn't been in any state to make or keep bargains for quite some time."

"Meaning?"

"Meaning my dear brother is, to put it mildly, no longer home. He was the first of my kind to be driven mad by the cost of what we'd done; the lives lost to the Great Flood, and by the cold, dark reality of our eternal hunger. You see, my kind has a constant need for living sustenance. Blood, brain, or flesh will do, to varying degrees. Its life-force invigorates us and fuels our magicks, as well as our transformations. I'm sure you've noted in your hunting – for I hear you've been a busy boy indeed – that we Brethren have, shall we say, drifted from the norm of human appearance."

I thought back to the freaky, patchwork hand-beast that was Magnusson; the spindly stick-bug beneath the desert floor, known as Jain; the half-glimpsed wolf-creatures of the Colorado wilds. "Yeah," I said. "You could say I spotted that particular trend."

"Do you know why?"

I sighed theatrically, as if annoyed to be playing along with his Bond-villain monologuing. In truth, I was through two knots on the leather straps around my feet, and my tweezing fingernails – cracked and bleeding – had just found purchase on a vulnerable loop of the third and last. "I suspect you're gonna tell me," I said.

"In fact I am. My old friend Charles-Louis Montesquieu once observed that if triangles had a God, they would give him three sides. A lovely sentiment, don't you think?"

"Sure," I said. "Pure poetry. The hell's it got to do with your little pack of weirdoes?"

"Everything, my poor, dear Samuel. *Everything.*" His words had turned now. Where once was maniacal good cheer, now there was only naked menace. "You see, on that fateful day we Nine gathered to cast off our bonds of slavery to hell, we accomplished more than we dared imagine. We did not simply free ourselves, we made ourselves anew. We began that day as

Collectors. We ended it as newborn Gods. No longer were we shackled by the confines of our Maker's design. We were free to become something better. Something stronger. Something of our *own* design."

"Must be why you're all so pretty," I said.

He shook his head. "I confess, not all of my siblings were strong enough to handle the gift that they'd been given. To control it, as I can. For with me, as with demonkind, you see only what I wish you to." His form rippled, shifted, flickering for a moment past a twisted mass of naked flame-scarred flesh before settling once more. Now he appeared a gaunt, berobed man with high cheekbones, deep-set eyes, long black hair pulled back from his face, and a long scraggly beard to match. Another flicker past the nightmare beast beneath, and he was suddenly a squat, towheaded child, no more than ten years old. Yet another, and my own meat-suit stared back at me. And after one last, brief glimpse of monster, the man before me was young, handsome Yefi once more.

"Neat trick," I said.

"And handy, too," he replied, ignoring my biting tone. "Although it does have its limitations. Unlike demonkind, my power lies not in altering my own appearance, merely your *perception* of it. For that reason, reflective surfaces are to be avoided, for they reveal to the onlooker my true visage. And the ability to project the appearance of one's choosing requires discipline, commitment – two traits some of my siblings seem to lack. In fact, their varied countenances have proved in many ways a window to their souls. Simon, who feared senescence, wound up a withered, aged husk of a man. Jain, Lukas, and Apollonia feared giving into their hunger, and became little more than animals. All but Drustanus and Yseult – and, one hopes, Thomed, though no one's seen him in so long, it's hard to say – ended up a slave to their urges, and those urges in turn shaped the beings they've become, Ricou most of all.

As another great thinker once chastened, 'We are what we pretend to be, so we must be careful about what we pretend to be.'"

"Huh," I said. "Wouldn't have pegged you for a Vonnegut fan."

"One benefit of eternal life is that it affords one no small amount of reading time," Grigori replied. "It's a shame your meddling in Brethren affairs will rob you of the pleasure of finding out."

"I didn't meddle in your goddamn affairs," I said, "you all meddled in *mine*. I was minding my own fucking business when your brother Simon kidnapped me and tried to shelve my ass by drugging my meat-suit into oblivion."

"Ah, Simon, you damned fool," he said, voice tinged with wistful exasperation. "Don't get me wrong, I loved the man, but we never did see eye-to-eye. He was infatuated with modernity, whereas I prefer the old ways: magic, not medicine; influence, not outright power. Hell, I haven't even *seen* Simon since that glorious summer we spent together in Geneva, feeding, dancing, laughing. 1816, this was, before the world caught wind of our kind. It was Simon's idea to burnish our legend by filling our fellow revelers' heads with such wild dreams of our exploits. I rather hoped one of the poets with whom we whiled away our days – Byron or Shelley – would write of me, but instead my tale was told by that damn-fool doctor Polidori. Simon, for what it's worth, fared better. Who knew Percy's wife would prove such a writer? And anyways, that Stoker fellow embellished upon the idiot doctor's mangled version of my story quite nicely some years hence. Still, I've always regretted giving in to Simon's insistence that our stories should be told. It's proved more trouble than it was worth, and more embarrassment, as well. If you ask me, the modern iteration of my own myth is downright shameful. I mean, look at me. Do I appear as though I sparkle to you?"

"Only your personality," I replied.

"Funny," he said. "But really, the thought I'd go all moony over some mopey teenager, when to me humans are nothing more than cattle to be slaughtered. For years now, I've suspected Simon of inciting that preposterous tale of vampiric emasculation just to goad me. It would be just like him."

"Yeah, that guy was a total douche," I said.

"You'd be wise to watch your tongue, Collector. Simon was still my brother, and I loved him as such. His death was devastating to me. I mourned his passing for weeks after I heard the news. I merely told you what I did so that you'd understand I'm not surprised to hear he brought this down upon us all. And to hear that he intended to drug you to induce a coma is the icing on the disappointment cake. I haven't the faintest idea why he doggedly insisted on solving all of life's problems with science when he had magic at his disposal. It's like trying to tie a bow with one's feet."

"Yeah, the fact he tried to dope me up instead of abracadabra-ing my ass was the source of my objection, too."

"So now what?" he asked. "My dear brother tries to shelve you, and now you're hellbent on revenge? Because I assure you, whatever else my other siblings have done, they've had no quarrel with you – not until you gave them cause. You have no one to blame for your current predicament but yourself."

"This ain't a revenge trip for me, pal – it's an *assignment*. Once the truce between heaven and hell crumbled, you and your kind were no longer protected. And when they found out thanks to your brother's botched attempt to shelve me you could be killed, they decided it was open season on the Brethren. Hence the raid at your Riviera place."

Grigori smiled. "And how very well that went for hell. I would have thought that my message of displeasure at having been targeted would have been well and truly understood. After all these centuries, to target me and my kind now seems arbitrary and ridiculous, and as I demonstrated, foolhardy at best. Still, it's a shame I had to give up the house in Nice; it had such stunning views. And believe me when I tell you, Frenchwomen are delicious. One assumes it's all the wine and clement weather."

"Bummer."

"You mock."

"Just seems kinda bourgeois for a guy with his own damn castle – his own damn *town* – to bitch about how hard he's got it."

"And it seems a tad presumptuous for one's captive to taunt one's captor," he said, "but I digress. The fact is, Nevăzut has long been my option of last resort, for my existence here is both lonely and tenuous. Yes, the townspeople hold their master on the hill in fearful reverence, but he is a folktale to them, nothing more – glimpsed only in dreams, or in the case of those whose blood I taste, in the thrall of my most powerful obfuscatory enchantments. To allow them any greater access to my physical person would only serve to deflate the myth, and provide a target for any potential rebellion should human nature's more violent tendencies one day insist on asserting themselves. Which is why I only ever pass among them in the guise of Yefi, a man of God they both tolerate and largely ignore. For their master on the hill is the only God they know or care to."

"If that's true – if these people are so thoroughly in the tank for you – then why worry about rebellion?"

"Because humankind is locked in an unending cycle of subservience and rebellion. Given long enough, even the happiest of subjects will rebel eventually. They always do. They did at my castle in Wallachia some centuries ago, when I lived as Wladislaus Dragwlya – Vlad Dracula, to your vulgar American ears. Such glorious times, with heads on pikes and blood running freely betwixt the courtyard paving stones, at least until they came for me, and I was forced to flee into the forest with naught but the armor on my back. It was then I decided a more subtle form of influence might prove expedient. And that policy proved wise indeed, at least until St Petersburg, 1916, when it was decided I had perhaps more influence over Tsar Nicholas – and his lovely, not to mention delicious, wife Alexandra – than any peasant should. I was living then under my given name once more, but in keeping with my newfound dedication to anonymity, I'd adopted the common Russian surname of Rasputin. You're no doubt aware how spectacularly I failed at maintaining the low profile I so desired. Those so-called nobles stabbed and poisoned and shot and beat and drowned me into unconsciousness. I woke to the crackling sounds of my own funeral pyre lighting. I understand I frightened no shortage of onlookers when I sat up amidst the flames, which thankfully soon engulfed me so thoroughly I was able to escape unnoticed as they scattered."

"Why tell me all this?" I asked to cover the sudden knock of my left leg against the boat's side as I finally released it from its leather binding. The boat rocked precariously for a moment and then settled. "Why not just kill me or leave me or whatever it is you plan to do?"

"Because I'm lonely," he answered. "Because I'm tired of all this fighting. Because I think that if you could only understand where I'm coming from, you'd realize we two have more similarities than differences." He paused and smiled. "That is the sort of thing you wish to hear, is it not? Alas, I fear the truth's far more mundane."

"Oh, yeah? What is it, then?"

"I was simply killing time until my brother woke. You see, it won't do to have you following me as I leave this place for what may well prove the last time. And while I spared no expense to capture and transport my poor, feral brother Ricou here from the dank South American lagoon he called home in an attempt to keep him from your grasp, I find I now have no better method for neutralizing you than to offer you up to him, much as I've offered up so many of the village's children these past few weeks. You see, Ricou, though no longer human, is not quite animal, either. He seems to take sadistic pleasure in playing with his food. Apparently, fear is quite the seasoning. My guess is he'll keep you alive for days before he finally kills you and evicts you from your current vessel. One poor girl lasted the better part of two weeks, although she was quite mad by the time he finally ripped her in two. Once he's finished with you, Dru and Izzie and I shall no doubt be prepared to take you on in earnest as we'd initially planned. So you see, it wouldn't do to let you escape before he had his crack at you. And yes, I know you must have slipped your bonds by now, so I elected to keep you company until he rose from his slumber. Unless my ears deceive me, he now has."

I listened hard, and heard a strange noise in the darkness, somewhere between a click and a low growl. Then a rasp like fine grain sandpaper on a two-by-four, or scales sliding across cold rock. Then a splash, as whatever we'd roused from slumber in the darkness dove into the water and disappeared beneath its surface. My stomach dropped. My mouth went dry. Adrenaline prickled on my tongue, and my heartbeat began to speed.

"Until we meet again, Samuel," he called, and then he tossed the torch into the water, where it extinguished with a hiss.

His footfalls echoed through the cavern as he retreated back toward the cemetery door. Minutes later, I heard the grind of stone on stone as it slid shut. I knew that even if I could get back there, there was no way I could open it on my own.

I mouthed a silent prayer, hoped to God that I'd get the Frank meat-suit out of here alive. That he wouldn't wind up Ricou's next meal. Thought to myself: This is why you don't take living meat-suits, fuckball. One of 'em kicks, and it's on your conscience forever.

But I didn't upbraid myself for long.

I didn't have the luxury.

For in the darkness, beneath the surface of the water, Ricou approached.

15.

For a feral beast who knew nothing but all-consuming hunger and the unmatched bliss of sating same, he announced himself politely enough: with a soft knock against the underside of my vessel. Manners or no, that knock scared the ever-loving shit out of me. For one, the cave was so damned dark, phantom colors swam before my eyes, my meat-suit's synapses misfiring in the absence of stimuli. Bobbing hands-bound in the water with neither any means of navigation nor landmarks by which to guide my way, I could do nothing but wait – and listen, and dread – so that first knock only served to ratchet up the tension in nerves already frayed to breaking. And for two, the knock was my first indication of Ricou's apparent size, because although he seemed to barely brush against the boat's wooden hull, connecting with neither speed nor malice but instead a kind of awful patience, the rowboat responded by lifting a good six inches upward in the water, settling back down as he glided silently away.

Five full minutes passed before Ricou struck again. Five minutes of straining to hear some indication of where he was past the sound of my own shallow, panicked breaths and the low, static roar of the distant waterfall. They may as well have been five days.

It wasn't until the faint germ of hope that he'd lost interest had begun to blossom in my mind that he struck again.

The second time, he hit harder. A bone-jarring thud, accompanied by the whine of dry wood taxed halfway to cracking. He must have hit the front half of the boat – nearest where my feet lay – because suddenly the whole shebang was canted wildly, my ankles above my head. By instinct, I tried to shoot my hands out to either side to brace myself, but they were still bound, and I thrashed in vain.

This time he was gone in a flash, leaving empty space between the bow and the surface of the lake. The bow crashed down so fast the old boat took on water like a log flume at a fair. I sputtered and gasped as it filled my mouth and nose, aspirating some into my lungs despite my best efforts to the contrary and damn near choking on it.

That cold splash, and the coughing fit that followed as the boat's wild bobbing slowly settled, spurred me to action.

Then again, maybe what spurred me to action was the fact that slamming back onto the water's surface caused a sharp, angular pain to blossom just beneath my right kidney, like I'd just landed on my keys. Only I hadn't just landed on my keys. I'd landed on Frank's gun.

Sure it wasn't gonna be enough to kill ol' Ricou here. But that doesn't mean it wouldn't slow him down.

I rolled onto my side and doubled over, curling fetal and pulling at my wrist restraints with all I had. Searing pain at each wrist, an inch or so of give at most. Not enough to slip my hands out, but enough to wrap my elbows around the outside of both knees. For an endless, awkward moment, I writhed like a fresh-caught bass at the bottom of the boat, my shifting weight chopping the still water of the lake around the tiny vessel, but then I managed to pull through first one foot, and then the other.

Ricou struck a third time, then, clipping the ass end of the boat and setting it skittering across the water's surface like a child's skipping rock. I rattled around inside, my face smacking against the bench seat hard enough to split my forehead open and set it bleeding, my hands helpless behind me. A decade back, I snatched a soul mid-ride on Space Mountain. Got bounced around something fierce barreling around in the dark with no hint as to when the next turn was gonna come. But that couldn't hold an unlit candle to the bat-blind ass-whupping I was receiving at the hands – or fins, or who-knows-what – of Ricou.

The boat hit a wall, and settled. I forced myself into a sitting position and leaned forward, ass aimed toward said wall, so I could reach out with my hands. I was hoping for a ledge, or railing, or passageway or whatever, but all I got was a craggy arc of cold damp stone, leaning slightly toward me as it stretched upward into the darkness. Unclimbable and useless to me, even if my hands were free.

Back to Plan A, I thought, and started scrabbling for my gun.

The gun was in a concealment holster inside my jeans, cheating slightly right of middle so Frank's dominant hand could more easily reach it. So goes the theory, anyway.

Here's an exercise. Put your hands behind your back. Lace your fingers together, and clasp them tight. Now try to stick that double fist in your back right pocket. Not so easy, huh? Now try doing it in a rocking boat, knocked silly and scared half to Guam, with your eyes closed.

Which is to say, I dropped the fucking thing.

Luckily, I dropped it into the bottom of the boat. Which, sure, had taken on some water, but it was drier than the lake, at least.

When I heard it hit, I sat down on it right quick, pinning it where it lay lest the unseen Ricou knock us for another loop and send it flying. Then I began the awkward shimmy of shuffling my hands up under my butt, past my knees, and one by one around my feet. When I finally got them up in front of me once more, now clasping Frank's SIG Sauer, I felt a rush of savage delight, and the unmistakable urge to express it by talking shit to the near-immortal feral lifeforce-eater I was trapped inside the cave with.

Sam Thornton may be many things, but thoughtful and level-headed he ain't.

"Hey, Ricou! Guess what? I've got a gun now, fucko. Which means you're in a world of trouble. Whaddya think of *that*?"

Not much, as it turns out. Because he decided at that moment to smack the boat once more, this time glancing off the left side and rearing up out of the water on his way to eat the tender, delectable morsel that was me. I know, because I reacted by falling backward onto the right-hand wall of the boat, which dipped below the surface and caused the tiny vessel to flood, while squeezing off five rounds in the direction of the disturbance, bringing to bear every ounce of speed and accuracy Frank here's muscle-memory could muster.

Blam blam blam blam blam! Five shots fired faster than you could say the words. Five camera-flashes that seared a zoetrope of Ricou's approach into my retinas. The only glimpses of the beast before me I'd ever see, for scant moments thereafter, he upturned the boat, and plunged me into the chill, mineral water.

And what a beast he was.

Thick, muscled limbs, armored heavily with green scales. His hands and feet were thin webbing stretched across elongated bones, with translucent spines jutting out at the end of every phalanx – more fins than human appendages. A glistening, striated chest – fish-belly white – that faded to muted green as the fine scales of its underside gave way to thicker plates of armored flesh. A head near as wide as his torso, with mucus-slick flesh the color of bile tapering slightly to a gaping mouth two feet across, ringed all around with needle-sharp teeth of the same transparent substance as comprised the spines. Gill-flaps pulsing rhythmically on the thick, muscled trunk that passed for his neck. And on either side of his bullet-shaped head, dead black eyes like a shark's – soulless, lifeless, unblinking.

He sailed toward me in stop-motion, every muzzle-flash bringing him closer, until he was upon me. Bullets chunked off bits of flesh, off-white amidst the black spray of blood. Spines gouged at my own flesh as he slapped away my gun – severing the leather strap around my wrists – and drove one finned hand into my throat. Breath whistled through my punctured trachea as I tipped backward, flailing. His jaw snapped shut again and again scant inches from the tender flesh of my face, his breath reeking of bait and rotting meat. It's a good thing I was too scared to think of what that stench represented. Even money he hadn't flossed since the last child he ate. I stiff-armed him, my fingers finding purchase between teeth three inches long as I tried desperately to keep Frank's face intact. But he just kept on coming, and so we tipped backward. Suddenly, said boat was upside-down, and me and the fish-monster were a tangled, writhing mass of limbs in the water.

Ricou rolled me once, then twice, like a croc might a water buffalo. The water churned around us, my nose and mouth filling with water that tasted of my blood and his blood and mountain rock, all alkaline and bitter. I was certain I was going to drown. Hell, I halfway prayed for it. Least it'd mean I'd be out of Nevăzut on the quick. But just as my lungs insisted they couldn't go another moment without inhaling – water or air, they cared not which – Ricou released me, and glided off into the untold depths.

I don't know how long he left me for. Minutes, I guess. Twenty, maybe more. It felt like a lifetime. The echoes of our struggle died down to nothing in the vast still hollow of the cavern, leaving no sound to fill the space but the ragged hitching of my frantic breaths, and the waterfall's constant background roar. The water was achingly cold, and too deep for me to touch bottom. For a time, I splashed madly about; half to frighten him away, and half because I was sure the cave wall or the rowboat must be nearby, but it was clear soon enough Ricou had dragged me toward the middle when he rolled me, because no matter how much I flailed in the stifling dark, I encountered no landmark, no assistance. Eventually, I ceased my thrashing, instead electing to tread water as efficiently as I could manage, because my arms and legs already throbbed in protest, and I had no idea how long I might be stuck out here, waiting for him to come kill me.

When I heard the knock of wood on stone, I could scarcely contain my excitement. It was the upturned boat, bumping against the cavern wall.

It knocked again. I paddled toward it. Cautious, quiet, with neither hands nor feet breaking the plane of the water's surface, for fear of summoning the Kraken. Or, at least, its feral Brethren fish-monster stand-in.

I needn't have worried, because in this case, the Kraken was summoning me.

As I approached the boat, the knocking increased – not in periodicity, but in intensity. What at first sounded tentative, as if the water's gentle lapping had incited it, became purposeful slams, like Neptune himself dashing the vessel against the rocks. And as soon as I realized there was some manner of intelligence behind the knocking, I began to reverse course, but too late. My feet kicked against soft, muscled fish-flesh just as the boat made its final voyage, slamming into the rock wall so hard it shattered.

Ricou had destroyed the boat.

That managed, he turned his attentions once more to me.

I broke into a full-bore freestyle away from him. No destination in mind but away. I made it five strokes before he grabbed my ankle and pulled me under.

The weight of the water pressed against my temples, my eyeballs, my ear canals. My punctured trachea was clotted, but not enough. Water seeped in and made me cough, which in turn caused me to take on more.

Still we descended.

How deep the cave was, I'll never know. Because as I thrashed against Ricou's grasp – he gliding with speed and purpose under the power of the three limbs not holding me – I somehow managed to break free. I clawed my way to the surface like a man possessed – which, it occurs to me, is precisely what I was – and upon breaking it, filled my lungs with blessed air.

Until Ricou pulled me under once more.

We plunged again. Again I struggled. And again, I managed to break free.

The third time we played our little game of down-and-back-again, I realized something, I hadn't managed shit. That fucker kept letting me go, just to get my hopes up so he could dash them all over again, as surely as he'd dashed my boat against the rocks.

Well, fuck him. I was done playing his game.

Time to play one of my own.

The next time he pulled me under and let go, I shuddered and went limp.

And listened.

And waited.

My lungs burned. My limbs ached from cold and lack of oxygen. All I wanted was to kick my way up to the surface. But with a little help from Air Marshal Malmon's peak physical condition and strict mental discipline I didn't. I just floated, neutral-buoyant and lifeless. Like a drowned rat.

Like bait.

But Ricou was the cautious sort. I guess it's how he'd spent so many centuries haunting the Amazon without winding up on the angler's hook, the hunter's blade. He didn't come at me head-on. Not at first. Instead, from nowhere it seemed, he bumped me hard, at speed, and then disappeared once more into the cold black water.

The blow startled me. Knocked from my chest what little wind I had. I chewed at my cheeks and clenched my eyes and begged Frank's body to hold onto consciousness for a little while longer, promising I'd reward such cooperation with getting it out of here alive. I didn't know if I could keep that promise, but I knew for sure I'd try.

As with the boat, the second blow was harder. This time, he hit me full-on in the chest. I heard ribs snap. Felt sickly heat bloom at each break.

When he hit me again, I was ready. I'd studied up. I'd listened to his first two approaches, and I thought I could gauge the vector of his approach by his fin-strokes. Direction and velocity, enough for me. Vision dancing with phantom spots as my brain screamed out for oxygen, I struck, punching the cold nothing in front of me.

And feeling teeth.

Then cold, wet guts.

Ricou was built for power. Built for speed. And he was coming at me all lickety-split like, thinking he'd bust me up but good. Mouth open, chompers ready. Unfortunately for him, it wound up he swam mouth-open right onto my fist, plunging it so deep down his own throat that when he snapped his jaw shut on me, it left a semi-circular dotted line across one pectoral muscle, and another on my back. Which hurt like all get-out, but if his thrashing was any indication, not near as much as me clawing my way through his esophagus and into the soft-and-squishy that surrounded it.

We danced like that a while. He thrashing, me neck-deep in nasty fish guts and yanking away like a magician looking for the end of my rainbow handkerchief, both bleeding like crazy in an environment too lightless for us to see the water go all Kool-Aid. And then I found it, a small sphere, about the size of an acorn, the only thing chalk-dry in his whole mucusy body. I got a hold of it and squeezed.

It crumbled.

Ricou stilled, teeth still buried in my back and chest.

And as one, we sunk together into the depths.

Then

Despite the vents at regular intervals through which faint, dilute wisps of spring cool sluiced downward, the air inside the bunker hall was warm and dry and still. It smelled of tobacco, pipe and cigarette, as well as people too long confined. Many of the doors that graced the hallway on either side were closed, and all were unmarked. Those that were open revealed a strange hodge-podge of seemingly unrelated rooms, as if they opened into different buildings altogether. To the right, a bare-concrete-walled war room, where dour, jackbooted men pushed what looked like children's toy tanks and airplanes across a table at the center of the space, wholly occupied by a map of Europe, while headphoned others manned radios, reading codes to others still who clacked away on the odd, typewriter-y cipher devices of which the Nazis seemed so fond. Across from that to my left, posh living quarters hung with large gilt-framed Carravagios and three-quarters filled by a mahogany four-poster bed, which stood, draped with rich linens and multiply bepillowed, atop a plush Oriental rug of tan and green and red. Past that, a room piled high with rations, guns, and ornate trinkets – candelabras, tea services, jewelry – in gold and silver. And yet further down, there was a dark room bare but for ten cots, on top of two of which slept fitfully a pair of fully clothed soldiers.

I trod the busy hallway in mute slow-motion like a specter, flinching reflexively whenever anyone got too near, as if contact might break whatever spell allowed me to pass among them unnoticed. Despite the heat, I'd left my overcoat on, and even buttoned it, but I could still detect the faint, acrid scent of bile emanating from my shirt. My hands shook. My eyes darted fitfully from face to face, certain I'd be fingered at any moment as an interloper – a spy.

But no one seemed to pay me any mind.

"Lilith!" I hissed, once the general who hurried past me with a wordless head-nod greeting had disappeared up the stairs, leaving me momentarily alone. "Damn it, Lily, what the hell am I supposed to do now?"

And though I could not see her, and the hallway was plainly empty but for me, Lilith replied as low and clear as if she'd breathed the words into my ear. "For starters," she said, "you'd best never call me Lily again, or you'll find out what fresh hell it is to wind up on my bad side. Understood?"

Given the lusty pin-up image Lilith's throaty purr conjured in my mind, I had trouble picturing her *having* a bad side, though I confess I wouldn't have minded spending a couple hours looking for it. Still, I was clueless in the belly of the beast and desperately needed her help, so in the interest of appeasing her I said, "Understood. Now – what happens next?"

"You see that door up on your right? The windowed one with light shining through?"

"Yeah, I see it."

"That's Hitler's office."

"He in there?"

"There, or the adjoining living quarters," she said. "He's been holed up inside for weeks. It's almost as if he knows you're coming..." she chided.

"Sure. Nothing at all to do with the fact that damn near every army on the planet wants him dead, or that the Ruskies have been doing their best to bomb Berlin clean off the map. So what do I do?"

"Your job," she breathed.

"How?"

"That, Collector, is for you to figure out. I'm afraid whatever happens next, I cannot intervene."

"So this is like some kind of Collector rite of passage, then? A 'see if the new guy passes muster' sort of thing?"

"Don't be silly," she said. "You'll almost certainly fail horribly, and likely get your vessel killed in the process. In fact, I'm betting on it." Visible or not, she sensed my sudden panic. "Fear not, Collector. If your vessel dies, your soul will simply be evicted, and reseeded somewhere else at random. No one ever knows quite where. I've selected Angola in the office pool, which is why I'm forbidden from influencing you from here on out."

"Shit," I said.

"Yes, I know it's a long shot, but what was I to do? I drew a crap number in the lottery, so all the populous nations were already taken by the time I was allowed to choose."

"I *meant*, 'Shit, I'm fucked.'"

"Oh. Yes. Most probably. But, you know, good luck regardless and all that."

"Thanks," I said, my tone biting, but it didn't matter. If my gut was to be trusted, Lilith was gone.

As I approached the door to Hitler's office, it swung open, and I was buffeted by what sounded like heated conversation. My heart fluttered in sudden fear, so certain was I I'd been discovered. But then a man – older, birdlike, with a faint dusting of close-cropped hair across his liver-spotted pate – burst forth from the door, dressed in doctor's whites and clutching a full-grown German Shepherd to his chest. The dog, I saw as he shouldered past me, was dead, eyes bulging, tongue lolling, pink-tinged foam dripping from the corners of its mouth. The man I recognized from many a newsreel, always standing beside Hitler or close behind. His name was Werner Haase. He was Hitler's personal physician.

Haase muttered a few words to me as I passed, the only one of which I understood was *Adolf*. But his tone was concerned. Tender, even. It was clear he was worried for his friend, as, he assumed, would I – would *Goebbels* – be.

I nodded tersely and continued to the office, stopping short in shock as I laid eyes upon the man himself. Partly because he always seemed more an abstract concept to me – a black-and-white capital-letters Bad Guy writ large across the silver screen, while here he was full-color flesh and blood. And partly because that full-color flesh-and-blood Hitler looked small and wan and frail behind his broad oak desk, which was scattered with maps and papers all weighted down by a Walther PPK. His hair, normally slicked back, dangled oily and lank down over his forehead; his trademark mustache was unkempt, as if it'd been too long since his last trim, his face was sallow; his eyes were red-rimmed, wet, and swollen. In one hand, he held a brown glass bottle filled with pills. In another, a kerchief, damp with the Führer's tears. And as I stood in the doorway, greeted by the stares of Hitler's inner circle looking stricken to a one – though Hitler himself had scarcely noticed my approach in his despondency – I detected the faint note of bitter almonds in the air.

It took me a moment to piece together what had happened. The pills inside the bottle were suicide pills – cyanide, unless Goebbels' nose was much mistaken. And the dog – one of Hitler's own – was their first victim. A test subject to ensure they'd work.

Which meant this human monster, this man who had the deaths of millions on his hands, was crying because he'd lost his dog. A dog *he'd* ordered killed. And all because he wanted to ensure his exit plan would prove successful when the time came.

For a brief second, I wondered if that meant I was off the hook. If Hitler was considering suicide, why bother going to all the trouble of killing him? But in my heart, I knew the truth. This man could not be allowed to decide his own fate, to dictate the terms of his own exit.

And I realized something else, as well. I *wanted* to be the one to end him. Wanted the last thought that passed through his mind to be a fearful one.

I looked forward to collecting him.

Hitler dabbed his tears and tossed his kerchief onto the desk. Then he waved his hands in dismissal at the dozen-odd people scattered around the office and barked a few quick words in German. The room cleared, all its occupants save three shuffling past me. Two of those who remained were clearly guards – uniformed, armed with rifles and sidearms both (the former held across their chests, the latter holstered at their hips), and standing at attention on either side of Hitler's desk. Both struggled to remain stoic, pretending with all their might they hadn't seen their Führer just break down.

The other occupant of the room was Eva Braun.

I knew nothing of her at the time, of course. Her relationship with Hitler remained secret until the war ended. Seems he thought he'd have more sway with the women of the Third Reich if they thought him a bachelor. Which, technically, he *was*, at least until two nights before I found myself standing in his presence; as I'd soon discover, the two had recently and, of course secretly, married.

But as I said, I knew none of that. In fact, the notion that Hitler might have a lady friend seemed so preposterous – like a shark keeping a housecat – it had honestly never, until that very moment, crossed my mind. And if it ever had, I suppose

I might've pictured him secretly cavorting with some severe Aryan bombshell complete with skintight uniform and matching riding crop, not the vapid, mousy creature who stood before me.

Her face was round and unlined. Kind, even. Her clothes were neat, if plain. Her hair was done up all nice in mouse-brown curls; her eyes were vacant, and tinged with concern. As I stood watching, she placed a hand on Hitler's shoulder, and cooed a German platitude I could not understand.

The gesture made me sick. It was more than he deserved. I turned away, only to have him call to me. Seems he mistook my anger for politeness. As if I were allowing them their quiet moment of affection, rather than seething at them for it.

"Joseph," he said, *"Kommen Sie, bitte*!" I looked up at him once more to suss out the meaning behind his words, and found him beckoning for me to enter. Hesitant and trembling, I acquiesced.

"Joseph, was ist los?" he asked. I blinked in response. I had no idea what to say to him. Turns out, I didn't have to say anything. I was saved the trouble when the small device at the corner of his desk began to move.

It was a strange looking device, two crossed sticks atop a spindle such that they sat parallel to the desk's surface, with cups at each stick's end to catch the wind and spin the crossed bits clockwise. Only there was no air current in the room to speak of, and anyway, the device wasn't spinning clockwise, it was spinning counterclockwise – ever faster as I approached.

I had no idea what it meant, but evidently, Hitler did. He slid back from his desk so fast, his chair toppled, and with a barked order, had both his guards train their rifles at me.

"Mein Gott," he muttered to himself, *"war Mengele richtig*!" And then, to me, *"Das Passwort."*

I said nothing, instead putting my hands up like some busted movie bank-robber. The strange wind machine – an anemometer, my brain uselessly supplied – continued to pick up speed, spinning so fast its cups blurred, and riffled the papers on his desk.

"Das Passwort, Joseph – jetzt!"

I shook my head. Couldn't figure a way out. The anemometer spun so fast it began to shake.

"Jetzt!"

The anemometer toppled. When its spinning rotor hit the desk, it flew apart in a crazed scatter of debris.

"I don't know your fucking password!" I shouted, clenching shut my eyes in anticipation of the shots to come. But the shots did not come. Hitler stilled them with a hand on each barrel, lowering them away from me.

"Aaah," he said. "American." The word was heavily accented, but nonetheless in English. No small feat, for a man not thought to speak it. "Tell me," he said, his words halting and heavily accented, "is Joseph still in there?" "Yeah," I answered, over Goebbels' insistent cries in the back of his own mind. "He's still here."

"Good," he said. It sounded more like *goot*. "Mengele said that someone like you would come. That is why he constructed for me this machine." *Vat eesss vye he contructed for me zees machink*. "Und insisted on using passwords. I thought him a fool. It would seem that he is not."

With a smirk, he gave the guards an order in rapid-fire German. From what little I could glean, it seemed the plan was to knock my ass out and keep me in the brig until I could talk German again.

The guards approached me. I closed my eyes and swallowed hard. A rifle-butt to Goebbels' temple, and he went down like a sack of potatoes. Then the two guards slung their rifles over their shoulders and each grabbed one of Goebbels' arms, dragging him from the room.

It mattered not to me. In fact, I was kinda glad they knocked him out. If they hadn't, he mighta ratted on me.

But, unconscious as he was, he couldn't. Nor could this Mengele's magic anemometer, now in pieces on the floor. So, Goebbels and the guards gone, I crossed the room and closed the door, wearing the flesh of Hitler's new bride, Eva Braun.

16.

"Collector!"

Lips like summer peaches against my own, warm and sweet. Fingers caressing my bare chest. My eyes opened to slits, eyelashes crosshatching the scene before me as I struggled to raise my head. Lustrous curls of fire-red hair that smelled of vanilla and musk cascaded down across my field of vision. Through the gorgeous locks, which tickled as they dragged across my naked skin, I caught a glimpse of wine-colored nails leaving half-moon imprints on my pectoral muscles. Felt the pressure of the palm attached to them against my breastbone, a steady rhythm.

A fella could get used to this, I thought.

Then my chest seized and I doubled over, expelling a chum-bucket's worth of murky, bilious water from my lungs and stomach both. That part was somewhat less erotic.

My lungs' contents purged, consciousness began to return in dribs and drabs as blessed oxygen suffused my cells with its glorious, life-sustaining whateverness. (Seriously, I sometimes feel like I shoulda paid more attention in biology – if for no other reason than the stranger aspects of it seem to play a very real, and very squicky, role in my everyday existence.) Much to my surprise, I was not in Guam, but in the cave beneath

Grigori's castle keep, a cave in which I'd been certain I was going to expire.

I racked my brain, remembered crushing Ricou's soul with my bare hand, remembered his bear-trap jaw not letting go even in death. Remembered too his weight pulling me down down down into the cold, black depths.

Then a taste like summer peaches. And then right back to the here and now.

I looked around, slick hair splashing water to and fro as I did. My clothes were sodden, my shirt undone. Buttons scattered on the rock ledge all around me; the stone was splotched dark where I lay, and dusty brown everywhere else. Not the one nearest my point of entry through the cemetery, but the other; the one framed out by the pointed arch. Though as I looked across the chunky fish-stew water of the underground lake, its surface pocked with sickly bits of bobbing gore and pale white flesh, I realized the dock onto which the cemetery tunnel opened was likewise framed. How I could see so far with no obvious source of illumination, I had no idea.

Then, as I cast my gaze about, I saw Lilith's silhouette – framed in a corona of light of her own making, which rendered her as obscure as an eclipse – and I realized it was she who saved me, and it was she who lit my way.

"What… why…"

"That thing you killed," she said, looking fresh and dry despite the fact she'd not only just pulled me from the murky water, but resuscitated me as well, "was somehow tied to Grigori's occlusion spell. It was not Grigori, was it?"

"No," I said, my voice hoarse, my punctured trachea aching from the strain of speaking, "that wasn't Grigori. It was Ricou."

Lilith smiled in triumph, and a hint of something else as well. I don't know why, but it looked to me like relief. "Ricou," she said. "Of *course*. That's why he was funneling money into

Chile, Bolivia, Guyana, Colombia, Brazil, and Peru. He was looking for his brother. He was trying to keep us from getting to him first."

"Guess we showed him," I said, wincing as I ran my hand across the crescent of bite-marks that curved from my right clavicle down to my armpit.

"Indeed," she said, arching an eyebrow at the mess that was me.

"So the occlusion spell..." I prompted.

"...lifted once you killed Ricou," she said.

"Why? Why wouldn't Grigori keep this place hidden?"

Lilith frowned a frown that coulda won awards. "Perhaps he did not anticipate Ricou would be so easilydispatched. Or perhaps he simply did not intend to return, and needed a physical anchor onto which to transfer the spell. Who am I to speculate as to the peculiarities of his magicks?"

I shook my head. Doing so hurt. "Dunno. Seems fishy. Doesn't track."

"I think that's you you're smelling," she said, her perfect nose crinkling. "Tell me, Collector, did you kill Ricou by crawling inside him and then burrowing your way back out?"

"Near enough," I said. "But that business with the occlusion spell, it doesn't explain what prompted you to come, or to pull me from the drink."

Until that moment, I don't think I'd ever seen Lilith look sheepish before. "I thought you may have needed help, is all. Turns out, I was right."

"You know you saved this meat-suit's life."

"Yes, well, *this* one – unlike the corpses you've historically favored – happens to contain a living, breathing mortal man, and I know how you hate to have deaths not assigned to you weighing upon your conscience."

"Why Lily, that may just be the sweetest thing you've ever said to me."

Lilith bristled. "You misunderstand me, Collector. I merely meant to suggest your subsequent moping at the sacrifice of this man would stand in the way of doing the job at hand. And time, I'm told, is of the essence."

"You know what, Lil? I think I understood you fine."

In the distance, I heard a scrape of metal on stone. It was the door to the cave through which Yefi – or rather Grigori – and I had entered, grinding open once more. Lilith glanced toward the noise, her brow furrowing in worry.

"What is it?" I asked her.

She answered with a question of her own. "Can you walk, or must I carry you?"

I flexed my legs each in turn. Climbed unsteadily to my feet, while a strange, scrabbling sound drew ever closer on the far side of the underground lake. Found to my great surprise that I could support my own weight. Said, "I'm good to walk – why? What's out there, Lily? What's headed our way?"

Lilith put a hand to the small of my back and pushed me into the narrow aperture at the back of the small stone platform. It led to a spiral staircase, carved into the natural rock. "Grigori's little hamlet may be once more visible to me and those like me– "

As if there were anyone who fit *that* bill, I thought.

"–but that does not mean he's left it unprotected."

"Meaning what?"

"Meaning by the time that I arrived, every man and child in town was dead, bled dry by the townswomen – or, rather, the beasts that they've become. The blood gives them strength, and stokes their hunger. And," she said, closing her eyes as we ascended, the glow she emanated dimming slightly as she allowed her attentions to wander beyond this narrow staircase to the town beyond, "it seems that they can sense their master's absence, because to a one, they're on their way here. And they're not happy."

"Jesus," I said, feeling Lilith's glare of disapproval on the back of my head as I ascended in front of her, "he wanted to keep this place safe, he couldn't just use ADT?"

From below us, snarling. Lilith's hand on my back, urging me onward. "The fuck is going on down there?" I asked.

"Don't worry. They can't cross water. They'll have to find a way around to reach us –scale the walls, perhaps – which should slow them down a little, at least."

"Okay, a) I think you haven't the faintest idea what the words 'don't worry' mean if scaling the walls is only gonna slow them down a *little*, and b) how the fuck could you possibly *know* that?"

"I've seen their kind a time or two before. This isn't the first time Grigori's employed them as a smokescreen to mask his flight."

"Nor the first time hell's gone after him, apparently," I observed drily, which might have been tough for her to discern on account of my rising panic and stair-induced huff-and-puffing.

"You forget, Collector, that I'm a good deal older than the Great Truce, and so are the Brethren."

"Here's hoping his hell-bitch version 2.0 didn't get the aqua-upgrade."

"Honestly, do you hear yourself sometimes? What you people have done to the language of Shakespeare seems far more blasphemous than anything Lucifer or I have ever done."

"See?" I said, smiling. "You *can* act your age. All you're missing is an impassioned 'get off my lawn'."

A strange slavering kicked up behind us. The townswomen had reached the base of the stairs, their animal utterances echoing up the spiral staircase like ocean-sounds through a conch shell. As I glanced worriedly over my shoulder, I caught a glimmer of amusement in Lilith's eye. "I could think of nothing more fitting to punctuate my point than those being the last words this poor vessel of yours has the ignominy of uttering."

"Yeah, well, I've never had much use for punctuation."

We reached the top of the stairs. Hit the wooden door – arched to match the stairwell, and the platform below – at a run. Pushed it open so hard I damn near toppled out.

Good thing, too. If I hadn't stumbled when I went through the door, the crazy undead townie chick woulda taken my head off with her goddamn battle-axe.

The lady wasn't looking so hot. Too thin and wiry by half, all bone and gristle and harsh angles. Skin so pale it appeared translucent, and hypoxic blue as well. Red-rimmed eyes shot through with blood, and retinas blood-red to match. Nails grown unnaturally long and sharp, thick and yellowed and splitting – from her fingers *and* her bare feet. Face smeared red around a wide gash of mouth too wide for her face, as if Grigori's infection had warped her very physiognomy, inside which gleamed elongated canines glazed pink. I wondered if that was her husband's blood all over her face, or her child's. It was spattered elbow-high across both arms, as well, and her simple cotton housedress was stiff from it – an apron of gore. But given her crazed, lustful stare – inhuman eyes rolling, her pupils pinpricks on account of the castle's ample lamplight – I'd say whoever's blood that was, it had only served to whet her appetite.

She'd been swinging for my head. Which, thanks to my stumble, was a good head lower than it usually was. The axe-blade whistled past so close, she parted my meat-suit's hair. I stumbled forward, Frank's muscle-memory carrying me through a tuck-and-roll before I so much as realized what was going on. I came out of the somersault on one knee, pivoting and reaching for a gun that wasn't there.

Turns out, it didn't matter. Lilith was just fine on her own.

The woman's swing continued full-bore past me toward Lilith. Lilith laughed and caught the blade midair with both hands – grabbing the sharpened edges as if they were rubber-gripped handles – and used the momentum of the woman's (ah, to hell with it – I may as well just say *vampire's*) swing to lift her off her feet and slam her into the stone wall. She hit hard enough to loosen mortar, and then stuck there, nails dug in as she peered with rage and hatred down at us over one shoulder. She scurried up the wall, then, like a spider – faster than I would have thought possible, had I not seen Simon Magnusson perform a similar trick – and then hurled herself downward toward Lilith.

Doubtless she was going for a killing blow. Unfortunately for her, when it came, she was on the receiving end of it.

As she plummeted toward Lilith, claws and teeth bared like a jungle cat's, Lilith spun, swinging the axe in a loping uppercut with such force that she split the vampire in two from head to crotch. Each side hit the stone floor with a wet *FWACK*, bouncing from the force of impact. Brain matter and entrails spewed across the floor and walls, but still, the woman's left side and right flailed madly about, eyes moving independently as what was left of her human consciousness tried and failed to grapple with the confusing barrage of nonsensical stimuli its body was supplying. Luckily, it didn't have to grapple long. Lilith brought down the axe blade in two quick chops, lopping the split remains of the woman's head. Then Lilith ground the mangled beast's stilled heart to pulp beneath one bare heel. "Head and heart," she said. "Only way to be sure."

"Words to live by," I said, wide-eyed, horrified, and trying not to puke.

Lilith shook viscera off her hands with nonchalant grace and stepped lightly toward the arrow slit to the right of the door we'd just exited. Three feet high, but a scant six inches wide, it looked out over the craggy mountain slope, the village of Nevăzut, and the switchback dirt road that connected the two. "Come on," she said, "we'd best get moving."

"Why's that?"

"Because the rest will be here soon."

I trotted over to the window and looked out. The mountainside was crawling with them, hundreds, maybe more. Ten times the number I would have guessed the town contained. Some, as haggard as the one Lilith just felled, charging up the dirt path at a sprint; some even farther gone scrabbling on all fours straight up the steep mountain slope. A few of the more human specimens carried torches, which pushed back the night and their fellow creatures both, who shrank from the illumination as would any nocturnal beast. All but the most animal of them had weapons – pitchforks, scythes, axes, and the like. And they were all headed this way. In fact, even though I peered out from a narrow slit in a slab of rock meters deep, I couldn't shake the feeling that, to a one, they were looking at me.

It occurred to me then where they'd all come from. These weren't simply the *current* female occupants of Nevăzut. This was all the women who'd ever lived here. Ten generations. Twenty. Robbed of the release of death by a dark master intent on amassing an army on the off chance they'd prove necessary.

Looking at 'em all, I wasn't too psyched to be that half-chance.

"You know what?" I said. "You're right, let's get moving. Where to?"

Lilith gestured down the broad, drafty hall, toward a vast open space with ornate staircases on either side. "Up," she said, "to Grigori's study. Our best bet to find out where he's gone."

We ran in silence down the hall and up the stairs. The hall was pale stone, studded everywhere with heads of large game: bear, deer, elk, ram, musk ox. The modern era's decorative equivalent of Grigori's favored heads-on-pikes motif, I guessed. As the hall widened into the great room that housed the twin staircases, I saw he had complete specimen trophies as well:

elephants and lions and gazelles, all staring at us with lifeless eyes of glass as we sprinted past.

I took the stairs two at a time, my hand trailing along the wooden banister for balance, each footfall sinking into the heavy pile of a runner the color of blood. One floor. Two. Heavy wooden doors, fixed with hinges and cross-braces of iron, blurred by on either side. Lilith moved so fast ahead of me I could barely see her.

Somewhere, in the distance, I heard the brittle-bone-snap of old wood splitting. Pictured a door much like these only larger giving in and vampires pouring through like ants out of a mound.

They were inside.

We reached the main landing, onto the left- and right-hand side of which the two sets of stairs on either side of the great room connected. I turned and looked behind me, then wished I hadn't. They'd reached the great room, scrabbling along the floor and walls. I watched, frozen in horror, as they approached. And then I felt Lilith's iron grip on my elbow, pulling me backward, toward the landing's largest door, which was centered on the back wall of the room.

She threw it open, tossed me inside. And then she stepped inside herself, slamming shut the heavy door and dropping into place what sounded in the darkness like a heavy wooden beam, barring entry to anyone or anything outside.

A lantern flared, bathing the room in amber light.

An office. Large, drafty, and high-ceilinged, with two slit windows like down below, no glass in either, and a cold, ash-filled fireplace expansive enough for me and five friends to stand inside, provided I actually *had* five friends, and we all agreed to stoop a little. I worried its chimney was large enough to afford some enterprising vampire entry to the room, and apparently, so did Lilith, because she yanked at a lever to one side of the mantle, and – with a grinding protest of long-immobile iron – closed the flue, for all the good it'd likely do.

Above the fireplace was an oil painting, four feet by seven or thereabouts. It depicted a smiling Grigori in the foreground. Behind him was the castle in which we stood – blood running from its windows, and heads on pikes all around. Two tapestries hung floor to ceiling in the room, one between the narrow windows, and another on the wall that contained neither door nor fireplace. The former depicted a great war between angels and demons, with nine observers to one side looking on. The latter depicted a great flood.

In the center of the room was a desk. It was the size of your average aircraft carrier, piled high with books and scrolls and, to my surprise, a sleek desktop computer, the kind that's all flat-screen and wireless and stuff, with a keyboard and a mouse that aren't attached. But the computer was tipped over and all smashed up, a small pry bar atop the ruined tech. I guess he didn't want us checking out his search history or me Googling to find a prospective new vessel. Behind the desk was a tall, ornate chair that looked as if it had been originally intended for a place of worship; it had a tapered back some seven feet high with a peak like a church steeple, and a wooden cross atop it.

I guess irony wasn't dead after all.

I took in the scene, huffing and puffing from my recent sprint up the stairs. My Ricou-bitten shoulder was throbbing like toothache. My scabbed-over trachea had begun oozing blood anew. As I sucked wind, I caught a harsh, boozy note in the chill office air, and noted that the papers on one side of the desk were stained yellow and warped into an undulating, crinkly mess, as if wetted and then dried. Glass shards glinted dully among them, as well as an intact, corked bottle neck, and as I approached to look, I caught a glimpse of something else, on the floor behind the desk; something disgusting. A shriveled, glistening green-brown mess of strange organic matter about the size of a high-end sleeping bag – the kind that looks like a mummy's wrap, or a cocoon – gone downy white in patches from some sort of fungal infection, its mucoid secretions seeping into the stonework beneath and running weak-tea-brown in the cracks between the flagstones. Beside it was a stack of folded clothes I recognized as Grigori's. Some feet away there was a small wooden crate, its lid pried open and leaning against one side of it, a mass of straw visible within.

"Grigori, you naughty man," said Lilith, and I thought I caught a note of admiration in her voice. "Ricou wasn't all you brought back here from the Americas, was he?"

"Come again?"

"I know where he's gone – or, rather, I've I good idea how he *got* there. And more importantly, how you can follow."

There was a thud at the door. Two hundred pounds of wood and iron rattled like cheap particleboard. Strong though it was, that door wouldn't keep them out forever.

"You mean how *we* can follow."

"No, I don't. This mode of transportation is inaccessible to those of us who no longer inhabit organic vessels – to the Chosen, to the Fallen, and to me. I suspect that's why Grigori went to the trouble of procuring it, despite its rarity, expense, and unpleasantness."

Another smack against the door, more forceful this time. I heard a groan as the bolts that affixed the metal brackets holding the beam lock in place began to loosen. "Okay," I said, "you wanna tell me what, exactly, we're talking about here?"

"Sure," she said, plucking an unlabeled, clear glass bottle full of slightly cloudy yellow liquid, in which floated something thumb-sized, curled, and white, from the shipping crate. She held it up for me to see, "you're going through a wormhole."

"You mean like science fiction?"

Lilith laughed. "No, I fear this is far messier and more magical than that. You've heard of the alchemical practice of astral projection, have you not? Remote viewing?"

"Of course, but I was under the impression the people who were doing it were just tripping their faces off on whatever wacky shit they ingested to induce the state."

"Well, you're half-right. The compounds employed to induce the state are potent, indeed – some of the harshest toxins of the plant and animal world both – and the practice itself has largely become a joke as the old ways died off, only to be halfheartedly revived by latter generations of dilettantes and pretenders with no notion how to harness and focus the incredible power of the tools they yield."

"So what *is* that stuff, then?"

"This *stuff*, as you so glibly refer to it, is a staggering work of alchemical art, crafted some four hundred years ago by one of the finest practical magicians this world has ever known. A witch doctor, you might have called him, by the name of Shaddam, who made his home in the swamps of what is now south Florida, and who was burned at the stake by the Spanish during their Inquisition for his crimes against God and nature both."

"All very impressive," I said, impatiently. Then, with worry, as I saw the white something inside the bottle wriggle, "Uh, is that a live worm?"

"Don't be ridiculous," said Lilith. "It's only half of one. And a damn rare half of one at that. I thought this species long since banished from your plane."

"Right. Because it being *whole* is the implausible part. Not the four-hundred-years-old-and-still-alive bit." I looked at the shards of glass atop the desk. The papers stained from the liquid within. And no sign of any worm, half or otherwise. "Wait – don't tell me I've gotta *eat* that thing."

"Of course not," she said. "You're going to drink it. The whole bottle, in fact. Every drop."

My stomach fluttered at the very thought of that worm thing sliding down my throat.

I nodded toward the desk. "Grigori didn't drink the bottle down."

"Grigori's body courses with centuries of dark magic, and he's long strengthened himself by feeding on the blood of others. He is no longer entirely human, even if his body is, or near enough. He has no need of the medicinal properties of the tincture in which the worm resides. It is a potent mélange of wormwood and peyote, psilocybin and belladonna, all steeped in pure grain alcohol. Believe me when I tell you, you're going to want to be drunk for what happens next."

"And what happens next?"

"As I said, this bottle contains but half a worm. The mouth-bearing half, to be precise. The, uh, bottom half is somewhere else. Once you consume it, it will, well, cause you to generate a sac of sorts, much like the one you see at your feet. Its other half will do the same. Within the cocoon, the worm will feed on you, causing your vessel to be digested. Fear not, it derives no sustenance from your meat; what it gleans its energy from is the molecular resonance which anchors you to this particular plane of existence. The creature itself exists across many planes at once, which is why it can be split in two without injury. Once it's done with you, you will pass, reassembled, like so much refuse from its system. This worm was long used whole to facilitate astral projection, for in its normal feeding cycle, the victim would simply experience wild hallucinations only to awaken precisely where they were they began. But a few dark mages realized its potential for physical transport as well."

She handed the bottle to me. I eyed it dubiously. "So I drink this, and then get eaten, and then get shit out someplace else?"

"The same someplace else as Grigori, one imagines. The bottle, you see, is unlabeled, and if the crate is any indication, one of six – though two more, it seems, are missing, given I'd assume to Drustanus and Yseult – so it's doubtful they lead to different locations."

"What if he – or they – are waiting for me on the other side?"

"A possibility," she said. "In which case, I recommend you kill them before they kill you – as is your intent in chasing them anyway. But I doubt they will be."

"Yeah? Why's that?"

She nodded to the mass of organic matter on the floor, which was decaying before our very eyes, and in so doing, releasing a gag-inducing stink that didn't serve to calm my already mutinous stomach. "Because *that*," she said. "And this, remember, is just the mouth-end."

"Jesus," I said.

"Mind your tongue, Collector. The point is, they're not likely to stick around at the other end of their makeshift sidereal conduit, not when it could potentially be used to follow them. And anyways, Grigori's got several hours' head-start on you, so there's a chance he and his fellow Brethren's trail will prove long cold by the time that you arrive."

"This plan of yours sounds better by the minute," I said. "I get eaten by a worm and then maybe ambushed or maybe find the place deserted."

"I fear you haven't any other options at this point, Collector. But take heart, this mode of transport *does* have its benefits."

"Yeah? Like what?"

"It's the only way that poor meat-suit of yours gets out of here alive."

"And what about you?"

"Oh, I can take my leave of this place any time I want," she said, striking a dramatic pose and vanishing, only to reappear a moment later across the room. "But somebody's got to stay and clean up Grigori's mess before it spreads beyond this little hamlet to the world at large. These poor women are too far gone to save, but not yet too powerful to kill."

"So you get to go all Buffy, and I wind up worm food?"

Lilith smiled. "My dear Collector, you wound up worm food long ago. Now drink up. You've a bad guy to kill."

I uncorked the bottle. Watched the grub-looking worm thingy wriggle toward the surface, its front end opening into a four-pointed star of a mouth, exposing a pink interior ringed all around with tiny teeth. Got dizzy from the sight, and from the tincture's noxious fumes.

And then, eyes closed, I drank.

17.

I downed the contents of the bottle in five quick gulps, draining dry a liter's worth of booze in seconds, save for the stray rivulets that escaped my lips to run down my chin and neck.

For a moment, nothing happened.

Then the bite came, a white-hot stabbing pain inside my stomach.

Then the office door caved in.

Then my pores began secreting a resinous brown goo that hardened as it hit the air.

The vampire women poured inside. Lilith tore them limb from limb with her bare hands – her back to me, ensuring none got to me before I was safely encased.

I fell to my knees, my head swimming from the booze and God knows what else, my body wracked with jolts of excruciating pain. I tried to scream, but my mouth and nose were filled with resin, so instead my diaphragm spasmed in useless panic. Then my eyes were covered brown, and my world went dark. Suddenly, a vast bluish plane unfolded all around me, dotted with a billion billion points of light. Souls, I realized or was told or always knew: all that are, or were, or ever will be. The whole of human existence, laid out across a thin skein of light. I zoomed backward from it – weightless, bodiless – and that wisp-thin plane became but one whorl in the vast fingerprint of all existence, a single undulating tree-ring in the cross-section of the universe. The other planes were red and green and purple and black and a thousand other colors not yet imagined, or perhaps impossible for our own eyes to discern. And between those planes swam flew floated massive beasts like whales like sharks like snakes like oh my God like giant worms and I was *in* one I *was* one I *am* one I will forever *be* one and then, as quick as it began, I felt a pain in my stomach that reminded me I had a stomach I felt a tingle in my limbs that reminded me I had limbs I felt an awful burning in my sinuses that reminded me how godawful that rotting worm sac smelled and then I was tumbling twisting falling naked in a slick of amniotic fluid toward a filthy flop-house mattress a massive ruptured cocoon hanging above me and it was cold and damp and dark a basement I thought or a storeroom or a warehouse empty and abandoned and still I fell as if forever but not forever merely seconds and somewhere nearby or faraway both trumpet-loud and whisper-soft a phone was ringing ringing ringing in the dark.

Dazed and knocked windless, I lay on the mattress spattered with afterworm for seconds or minutes or hours, sanity returning by degrees. I looked around, and realized I was, in fact, in a basement – the wired-glass-windowed, pipe-laden basement of a commercial building, to be more precise. Six mattresses were scattered across the floor, all bare and cheap and worn from use, three others caked brown with fallen gore and sprinkled all around with glinting shards of shattered glass. Above mine and those ones hung cocoons – mine fresh, glistening, and steaming slightly like sweat rising from a body on a cold day, the others downy-white and desiccated to varying degrees. Above the other unused mattresses hung bottles like the one from which I had drunk, rough twine knotted at bottleneck and then around the building's heavy piping, pale worm-halves swimming around inside.

So this was their rendezvous point, I thought. Their fallback position, should I get too close to any one of them. Meant I had 'em on the run, I thought. It didn't occur to me, but should have, that there's nothing more desperate – more dangerous – than a cornered animal. Unless, of course, it was a trio of cornered sociopaths with near-unlimited means and access to some for-seriously dark magicks.

Beside my mattress, I found a coarse blanket and a stack of clothes: jeans, sweatshirt, socks, shoes. All cheap, tacky, and off-brand. I used the blanket to towel off, and then dressed hastily. The shoes were too big, the pants an inch too long. But they'd do to get me out of here, at least.

And still, from somewhere, a phone rang.

I staggered to my feet. Touched a finger to my meat-suit's throat, only to find it healed. Rotated his right arm in its socket, and no longer felt the pull of Ricou's bite-marks. Looked like the worm-thing did me one better than just getting Malmon out alive, it patched him up some, too. Put him right, physically, at least. I kinda hope he was too overwhelmed by the experience of what we'd just gone through to even try to process it. Better he thought it nothing more than a bad dream – or, more accurately, a bad trip.

By the pale gray light trickling in through the windows, I saw a tray table in the distance, on which sat two items: one a rectangle of black with a green dot of light at the center of its upper edge, the other a cordless phone standing upright on its base, a red light on it blinking in time with every trill of its ringer.

I walked cautiously toward them, certain they must be some kind of trap.

Which they were, but not in the way that I'd imagined.

I reached the table without incident, nerves jangling. The rectangle of black, I realized, was an open laptop computer. And unless I was much mistaken, the green light I'd seen from across the room indicated that its built-in camera was activated. The table it and the phone were sitting on reminded me of the type folks used to eat their TV dinners off, pressed tin and collapsible, its surface painted beige with brown trim, an ugly orange floral still-life at its center.

Still the cordless rang. I picked it up. Heard Father Yefi's cheerful voice on the other end of the line. "Samuel," he said, "so good to see you!"

"Wish I could say the same," I replied.

"In due time," he told me. "I trust my brother didn't give you too much trouble?" His tone was playful, jovial.

"You aren't pissed I killed him?"

"The Ricou you killed was an animal, nothing more. I mourned his loss a long time ago."

"Then why'd you go to all the trouble of bringing him to Nevăzut?"

"I felt I owed him that much, at least. A chance to live, in whatever stunted way he could. But your untimely arrival rendered my gesture moot. And so his final act was one of sacrifice for the greater good. As, I suspect, will yours be."

"The greater good? I think you mean your own continued well-being."

"Yes. Mine, and Drustanus', and Yseult's," he said, without a hint in his voice that my reprimand had stung him any. "I assure you, were he in any position to've chosen such a path, he would have done so. He was once a decent man."

"Sure he was," I said. "But then again, weren't we all? Speaking of Drustanus and Yseult, I'm looking forward to meeting them. What say we arrange a little get-together? You, me, them, an iron stake or three..."

"Funny you bring it up, Samuel. arranging a little get-together's precisely why I'm calling."

"Is it, now."

"That's right. It's high time, don't you think? In fact, we're overdue, but it took my siblings longer than expected to make the arrangements I'd requested. I wanted it to be quite the to-do, you see."

"You're a regular Gatsby, Grigori. And you remember how well that ended for him."

"Be that as it may," he said, "the time has come to extend to you a formal invitation. It's why I allowed the occlusion spell protecting Nevăzut to expire, after all, and left your handler the breadcrumbs necessary to lead you here. I trust your journey was a pleasant one?"

"Peachy," I said. "Where and when?"

"How's now for you?"

"Good as any time, I guess."

"Excellent. Do me a favor, and press the touch pad on the computer to your left."

"A computer? Really? Seems disappointingly non-magic-y for you, Grigori. Simon might consider that a victory, were he not, you know, all dead and stuff."

"My apologies," said Grigori drolly. "I do so hate to disappoint. But don't worry, I think you'll be suitably impressed by what we have in store for you. Now, the computer, please. She hasn't much time. My siblings bore easily when prevented from toying with the living, and our new pets are growing hungrier by the minute. I cannot ensure her safety for much longer."

She? She *who*? With growing dread, I did as Grigori asked. As the touch pad clicked beneath my finger, the computer's screen awoke. On it was a webcam feed of a man, bound to a plain wooden chair in the center of what appeared to be one of those all-day breakfast chains, Denny's or Cracker Barrel or whatever. The kind of place with pictures on the menu and a stupid name for every dish. The guy was paunchy, middle-aged, with a long beard streaked gray and nicotine-stained around the mouth. A trucker-cap on his head, a tan Carhartt jacket over flannel, tucked into well-worn jeans. Split lip, black eye, blood running from one ear. The eye not swollen half-shut was wide with fright. The dining room around him had been cleared of all its furniture. Tables and chairs were tossed into the booths on either side, probably to make room for the elaborate concentric circles of runes around the fellow's chair, all rendered in drying blood.

Grigori and his compatriots hadn't, however, cleared the room of all the bodies.

They lay sprawled across the floor amidst the broken plates and clots of drying egg in damn near every pose imaginable: face up, face down, curled fetal, arms akimbo. Necks torn out, but little blood around them. Some women, sure, and little girls as well, but none in danger, on account of they were dead already.

"Uh, Grigori? Maybe you've been outta the game a while, but that's a dude I'm looking at."

"Oh," he said through the phone to me as he picked up the computer on his end and turned it to face his own smiling face, "I wasn't talking about *him*. He's to be your new vessel. And I hope you like him, because you're going to spend quite some time inside him. You see, my brother Simon was not wrong about you; you're a threat that needs neutralizing. But he was a fool to lean on science when magic is so much more utile in this situation. A coma would only bind you until death. The proper ritual will seal you in stasis indefinitely, a shelving to last until the stars burn out."

"Good plan," I said. "A couple notes, though. Note the first: for it to work, you'd need me to hop into that-there meat-suit of my own accord, which I sure as shit ain't gonna do. And note the second, you put me on ice, and hell's just going to send another like me to finish the job."

Grigori laughed. "To your second point, I have this to say, if you believe that, you're far more clueless than I've given you credit for. I assure you, once you're neutralized, the threat to me and mine will be as well. And to your first point," he said, swinging his laptop around once more, "I've arranged what I think you'll agree is appropriate enticement."

On the screen was a young woman in a waitress' uniform, tied to a chair like the man was, and gagged as well. She was flanked by a couple who looked no more than twenty, both bright-eyed and beautiful, with smiling, arrogant expressions that spoke of casual, even gleeful malice. The male had a single streak of blood trailing away from the corner of his mouth. The female held a kitchen knife to the bound girl's left eye. Around them, crouched and feral, were red-eyed, blood-streaked restaurant patrons – five or so at least – whose necks still bled from where the Brethren fed from them, and whose features were warped and animal, like those of the undead women of Nevăzut. Some tried in vain to drink from the lifeless corpses of those patrons the Brethren hadn't turned, or gnawed eyeballs from unblinking sockets, while others eyed the girl in the chair with unfettered hunger, eager to partake of her blood, her tender flesh.

It couldn't be, I told myself. It wasn't possible.

But it could be, and it *was,* though how they found her, I didn't know.

The girl in the chair was Kate MacNeil. The one I'd saved in New York two years back, when she'd been marked for collection by a rogue angel intent on sparking the End of Days by tricking hell into laying claim to a pure soul. I was told that she'd been hidden. Given a new face, a new name, a new life far removed from the horrors of her last.

Clearly, the powers that be hadn't hidden her well enough. She was a little leaner, sure, and more angular, with high sharp cheekbones and a determined cast to her features at odds with the bright-eyed girl that I'd once known. Her once-creamy complexion was now sun-kissed bronze, and her once-auburn hair was streaked through with blond – not the result of cosmetics, but of honest-to-God physiological changes to her coloration. She was a few inches taller, her frame coiled tight with lean muscle. But all those changes added up to nothing: I would have recognized her at a hundred paces. You think whoever hid her woulda done a better job, but maybe some things about ourselves, no one can really change.

The image spun around again. Once more I was looking into Grigori's eyes. "As I was saying, Samuel, Dru and Izzie are tiring of babysitting, and I suspect once their patience wears from thin to nonexistent, the transition will not be a pleasant one for the MacNeil girl – or Smith, I should say, since that's what her nametag reads. They may simply take an eye, or an ear, or a finger. Or they may decide to throw her to our new pets, who – as you can see – grow hungrier by the minute, and unfortunately, this entire restaurant full of food appeals to them no longer."

I heard a struggle in the background. A chair rattling, and some kind of sudden scuffle. Then Kate's voice shouting, *"Don't come for me Sam Thornton, I'm–"*

And then a vicious slap. And then silence once more.

"You son of a bitch," I said to Grigori. "That girl's an innocent. You let her go."

"You have my word I will, provided you're here in the next, say, three minutes?" He swung the camera once more toward the bound man in the chair. "You'll find us at the Pancake Palace in Bellevue Washington. I trust that's enough information for you to reach out and find us?"

Bellevue, Washington. Whoever hid Kate had a sense of humor, I'd give 'em that. Bellevue *Hospital* in Manhattan is where Kate and I first met. Where I'd shown up to collect her, only to abscond with her instead when I touched her soul and found her to be an innocent.

And sixty-five years before *that,* Bellevue Hospital was where my Elizabeth was cured of tuberculosis – right before she told me we were through. That she couldn't stand the man that I'd become. What she hadn't realized is that I'd become that man living up to my end of the devil's bargain that saved her. What I hadn't realized was she would have rather died than see me lose my way.

"It is," I said.

"Good. Understand the building is protected. No one will be allowed in or out lest they suffer the same fate as the rabbit in the woods of which we spoke. Do you recall?"

I did, and said so. Burned alive from the inside, starting with the eyes, same as the crow at Simon's place.

"Excellent. You should also know no one else remains alive here but for Kate and the fat man. Should you elect to possess her instead, my siblings and I will use the full force of our combined magicks to prevent you, and likely kill her for your impudence. I'm afraid you have no play here but to relent to our demands."

I thought of Magnusson's gun thug, Gareth, and my battle against Magnusson to control him, which I lost. I didn't relish the thought of trying to slip into Kate's mind while it was guarded by three others as powerful as Magnusson had proved to be.

"The clock is ticking," said Grigori, his words dripping with the superiority of one who's won the day. "And I do look forward to seeing you again. Even in this flabby meat-suit, you'll make a fine addition to my trophy collection, my first living exhibit. *The Collector who nearly felled the mighty Brethren.* Perhaps I'll have a plaque made."

"Something to look forward to," I said. "I'm on my way." I slapped shut the computer. Hung up the phone. And extended my consciousness toward Washington.

But not before I made a phone call first.

18.

You wanna know the worst part about a pack of sociopathic immortal nutjobs getting the drop on you? It's not the torture, though there was plenty of that, from the second I hopped into the scruffy, chair-bound trucker they had waiting for me, Dru and Izzie took turns cutting on me some, Kate screaming at them to stop the whole while, leastways until they gagged her. They dug cone-shaped pits out of the tender flesh of my cheeks with the rounded tip of a potato peeler, jabbed toothpicks underneath my fingernails, Dru even lopped off my left ear before a furious Grigori castigated him for doing damage to his new trophy that would not heal itself with time and did his best to mystically reattach it, all crooked and wrong.

It's not the humiliation at being bested, either, though there was that as well; blunted somewhat by the fact that these deranged motherfuckers had hunted unseen in humanity's midst for centuries, but stinging nonetheless.

It's not even the growing certainty you'll wind up frozen in a cheesy action pose in some evil fucker's living room for all eternity right beside his startled-looking stuffed gnu, his mountain lion poised to strike, and his tacky bearskin rug.

No, more than anything, it's the monologuing. The nonstop, mustache-twirling gabfest that you're forced to endure before they just do the deed already. And the worry that it won't stop once they lock you inside this body forever. That Grigori is gonna while away his lonely centuries nattering at my magic-stilled ass, and there won't be a goddamn thing I can do to shut him up.

"I confess, Collector," he said, "I misjudged you some when first we met. I didn't think you'd best fair Ricou so easily, which is why you and I are forced to kill time now. The sigils inscribed in blood beneath you must be fully dry before the ritual can begin. Three hours at minimum is recommended. Five, if one has the time to spare. But it does, at least, mean Dru and Izzie get some time with you. They take such delight in pain, you see – nearly as much as they take in one another. Touching, is it not, to see such devotion across the vast expanse of time? Theirs is truly a love story for the ages."

"Yeah, real heartwarming," I said, spitting blood and tonguing the spot where the glistening molar in Izzie's hand had recently resided. Izzie smiled prettily at me and held out her prize for Dru to see. Then she popped it in her mouth and swallowed it, while Dru looked upon the scene with the dopy infatuation of a teenager's crush. In the hour and change the two of them had been cutting on me, I hadn't heard them say a word. "Plus, they don't seem to talk much, which I'm kinda fond of. Maybe *you* should try it."

"Oh, the Lovers haven't spoken in centuries," Grigori told me. "They've no need to. The only bond they truly care to foster is between each other, and said bond is far deeper than mere human utterances could hope to express. Which is why they choose to express it in *suffering*."

Dru, who'd waited patiently on deck while his blushing bride removed my molar, stepped up to the plate to take his swing. In his hand was a paring knife from the kitchen, dull orange-ish and glistening. As he approached, I wondered almost idly, thanks to shock's kind remove, what he'd coated it with. Then, in the instant before he jabbed it handle-deep into my thigh, I caught a whiff and knew.

The fucker'd drenched the blade in Tabasco sauce.

I thrashed in agony, beet-red and screaming. Kate, gagged and wide-eyed, mirrored my movements, in her case a futile protest.

Dru removed the blade and licked it clean. Izzie clapped, coquettish, as if he'd just performed the most *delightful* party trick.

"Understand I derive no pleasure in your suffering," Grigori said. "But I feel I owe them a little leisure time, having yanked them so abruptly from their home. Much as I was forced to back in Whitechapel, 1891, when their playful dismantling of several lowly streetwalkers attracted a hair too much attention from Scotland Yard. For the longest time, London was their playground, but then Simon's precious modern science made such play far riskier as the livestock began collecting evidence and doing proper detecting rather than simply hanging whatever pauper they could get their hands on. The Ripper killings were too high-profile, I told them, and continued feasting on the delicious, fear-drenched viscera of London's whores too risky if they both wished to evade capture. From then on, I endeavored to settle them in less civilized locales, where their avant-garde expressions of their besottedness might raise fewer hackles. Luckily, the twentieth century proved quite the extended honeymoon for them. The Armenian genocide of the First World War. The wholesale massacre of Kurds in Dersim in '37. Poland, Russia, Croatia, and Yugoslavia during World War Two. After that, unfortunately, the whole of Europe got disappointingly civilized, but a series of bogus humanitarian aid posts on the Dark Continent made possible by my purchase of a number of respected charities allowed them to continue indulging their outré predilections without fear of reprisal – for a time, at least. Recently, they've spent their days feasting on the tender flesh of the young women of Juarez, Mexico, some two hundred dead and mutilated, yet no one seems to care. It's the ideal arrangement, really. All these two have ever wanted was to be left alone to kill."

"How can you sit there and say that like it doesn't bother you?" I asked. "You and your so-called siblings were human once. How can you stomach having become such fucking monsters?"

"Let me answer that with a question of my own. Which is worse, that monsters lurk in the dark corners of Man's existence, or that Man is such a brutal, vicious creature in his own right that he's scarcely even noticed?"

"I'm pretty sure the answer to that is, 'Fuck you and the giant tidal wave of evil you rode in on.'"

"Samuel, that stings. But not, I fear, as much as this ritual is going to. For you see, the sigil's dry. It's time to begin."

Outside, I heard the traffic's din build, a diesel engine revving somewhere outside the wobbly translucence of Grigori's protective bubble – weaker, it seemed, than the one erected around his castle, but present nonetheless. It seemed strange to me, this showdown, this potential end to my life's story, taking place inside a dime-a-dozen chain restaurant situated in a strip-mall parking lot in a bland commercial district beside a highway. It could have been anywhere in America. It felt like nowhere at all. Time was, they'd've had the decency to make a trophy outta my sorry undead ass inside a nice little mom-and-pop place, at least.

I glanced toward the broad expanse of tinted glass that faced the road. Saw the dim reflection of my own unfamiliar body, and across the room, Kate's as well, while between us stood three ancient, twisted, repugnant creatures nothing like the physical forms they each projected, but somehow instantly recognizable nonetheless. I guess they could not hide their true selves from us entirely.

Beyond the glass, and the reflections, I saw the yellowy stare of headlights looking in.

"Kate," I shouted, "avert your eyes."

"That's sweet," said Grigori. "You not wanting her to see your final defeat."

"It's not that," I said.

"Then what?"

"It's just, my ride's here."

Grigori tilted his head and regarded me with confusion. Kate's eyes widened, and then clenched shut. She knew me well enough to listen first and ask questions later when I start spouting the crazy.

And then the big rig plowed into the restaurant in an explosion of crumbling drywall, rent metal, and shattered glass, collapsing half the fucking building, scattering the Lovers and the newborn vamps – two of whom were crushed to pulp beneath the eighteen-wheeler's many tires – and pinning Grigori to the far wall before grinding to a hissing, ticking stop.

When Grigori slammed into the wall, his face contorted in agony and sudden fury, and his human aspect faded to nothing, revealing the knotted, ancient mass of scar tissue that was his true self. Likewise, without his efforts to maintain it, his protection spell flickered and blinked out. The driver's side truck door opened, and out stepped a lithe, muscular black woman damn near seven feet tall – eight, if you counted her afro – a sawed-off shotgun in her hands. One of the young vamps bum-rushed her, and she unloaded, turning its head to so much pulp. Her sightless eyes blinked rheumy white against the sudden spray of blood and brain, and she called out, "Hey, Sam Thornton, are you in here?"

I laughed despite myself. "Sorry, Theresa," I called, "no one here by that name. Guess you took out the wrong damn Pancake Palace."

"That's what you get, letting the blind chick drive."

"Hey fuckers!" called a gruff voice from the street. "That eyeball-cooking mojo down yet, or is my fat ass stuck outside while you get to have fun knocking baddies' heads together without me?"

"Sam?" Theresa, deferring to me.

"It's down, Gio!" I shouted. "Welcome to the party, pal!"

Gio ran, screaming bloody murder, through the hole the truck left in the side of the restaurant, brandishing in one hand a makeshift cross of pencils stuck together with a wad of gum, and using the other to shield his eyes. I started to open my mouth to tell him how goddamned ridiculous he looked, his cross all droopy and lopsided, his face buried in the crook of his elbow, but at that moment, a wild-eyed newborn vamp in the unholy-hunger-warped body of a middle-aged woman pushed free of the rubble at his feet and launched itself at his throat.

I croaked a warning. Theresa swung the sawed-off toward the sound of the impending vampire strike, but she hesitated, unsure in her blindness whether the man she loved was in the shot or not.

Luckily, Kate – who'd freed herself of her bonds during the attack – was not similarly paralyzed. She rocketed out from beneath the semi's trailer with such speed and grace I could scarcely believe my eyes, sailing over the lunging vampire and wrapping the length of rope that had until recently affixed her to her chair around its neck. She tucked as she landed, and rolled such that she wound up once more on her feet. The force of her roll yanked the young vamp off-course, and flipped it hard into the far wall. Kate didn't hesitate. Dropping her rope in favor of a nearby steak knife, she pounced on the vamp, yanked back its head with a handful of gray-brown hair, and drew the knife hard across its neck. Blood gouted as flesh parted in vulgar parody of a smile, but the creature did not die, instead bucking like a bronco trying to toss a stubborn rider. Kate wouldn't be shaken, though, she just kept sawing and sawing, gore spewing across the room like the devil's own sprinkler, until finally, the body she rode slumped to the floor, and she rose, her smile a gleam of white amidst the spattered red, holding the woman's fanged head up by the hair as an angler might a large-mouth bass.

I said nothing for a long second. Just stood and stared. As, for that matter, did Gio who, as the scuffle erupted inches from him, seemed to've abandoned both his useless pencil cross and all pretense of protecting his eyes from going melty. As our gazes met, he said, "Jesus fuck, Sam, who's the skirt?"

"Gio..." said Theresa, like a teacher chastising a recalcitrant student.

"I mean, uh, who's your lady-friend," he awkwardly corrected.

"Gio, Ter," I said, "meet Kate. Kate, meet Gio and Theresa."

"Pleased to meetcha," said Kate, and then. "Hey blood-breath, head's up!" She winged the head she was holding at a vamp who'd been slinking toward the gaping hole in the restaurant wall; it caught the head, and gave the dripping severed neck a sniff before recoiling in revulsion – dead vamp blood apparently proving useless to fellow vamps. Theresa followed the sound of the head's landing, and let loose a quick blast of her sawed-off, blowing a hole through the young vamp's chest and leaving it, slumped and lifeless, against the wall.

"Sweetheart," said Theresa to Kate, "You and me are gonna get along just fine."

"Where the fuck'd you learn how to do that?" I said to Kate. "Kill vamps, I mean. The White Hats juice you up with some warrior mojo?"

She looked at me like I had two heads. Funny, since she briefly had herself, if you count the one she'd just wung across the room. "Warrior mojo? Not hardly. Fact is, when the forces of evil try to condemn your innocent ass to hell, you start to take a vested interest in your own personal safety. And as for *that*," she says, nodding toward the headless mess that was, until recently, a vampire, "head or heart, Sam – that's the rule. Vampires or zombies or whatever, it's all the same. I swear, it's like you've never seen a movie in your life."

"You shoulda seen his face when I tried to get him to use Google," Gio said to her.

"Great," I replied, smiling. "The three people in the whole world I can fucking stand, and they've decided to gang up against me."

"Hey, I didn't ask to get dragged into this one," said Kate. "These creepshows found *me*."

"Us neither," said Theresa. "In fact, this place was hard as shit to find. It's got a freaky vibe about it, or at least it *did*. Even when Gio pointed me and the truck right at it and told me to just hit the gas, it was all I could do not to turn away, like it didn't want me getting too near, you know?"

"Yeah," I said, "it rings a bell."

"Sam Thornton," Theresa said with a grin, "why can't you ever take us someplace *nice*?"

"The day a Collector agrees to meet you someplace nice is a day you oughta worry," I said.

"Uh, dude?" Gio, looking around. "Where'd your friends go?"

I looked around as well. Grigori, Drustanus, and Yseult were nowhere to be seen. The latter two, I'd lost track of in the course of Gio and Theresa's Big Damn Rescue, but last I'd seen, Grigori had been pinned to the wall by Theresa's semi. Now the truck sat a good foot from the wall, and Grigori was gone.

"Son of a *bitch*!" I said. "We cannot let those three outta here alive. If they disappear–"

"They won't," said Kate, peering out the gaping hole in the restaurant and into the street. "I've got a bead on 'em. If we get moving, we can maybe catch them before they get to where they're headed."

I followed Kate's gaze. Saw the three Brethren, no longer projecting their human guises, bounding across the four-lane blacktop on all fours. Well, all *threes* in Drustanus' case, since it seemed his left arm had been severed in Theresa's attack; his stump left spatters of fresh blood bright red in a trail that snaked across the street after him. I followed the trail back inside to its source with my eyes, and saw his missing hand jutting out from beneath one set of the semis' double-wheels, fingers curled inward like the legs of a dead spider. Wondered what was behind the worry in Kate's tone. Then I saw the sign beside the entrance to the half-empty parking lot they were traversing, leaping parked-car to parked-car, and I feared I knew.

"Kate," I asked, "what's over there?"

"A school," she answered, wiping her knife off on her pants and starting after them. "Across the street's the middle school."

19.

It was Saturday, at least, which wasn't nothing. Meant there'd be fewer kids. Fewer, but not none. The cars in the parking lot spoke to that fact, and the lights burning in every third window or so.

Clubs, I thought, inasmuch as I thought anything at all. Chess. Math. Anime, for all I knew. Heard once on the news that was a thing. Kids getting together to watch overdubbed cartoons or some shit. I remember thinking at the time, aren't *all* cartoons overdubbed?

Lights showed too in the windows of the gymnasium, all placed high up so you'd have to work to knock one out with an errant ball. Meant I couldn't see inside from the pancake place. Could be it was full. Could be just a janitor, waxing the hardwood floor. What did middle schoolers play come spring – basketball? Floor hockey? I had no idea. The fields outside the school were empty, which was both a blessing and a curse. A blessing because it meant three injured, weakened Brethren looking to recharge their batteries with a fresh helping of life's blood couldn't swing by the drive-through and nosh to their blackened hearts' content, they were gonna hafta go inside. Bad because that meant we had to follow after, and find them before they made with the snackin'.

"Let's move," I said, heading toward the school at a trot. Kate didn't need telling, she was already across the parking lot and out into the street – horns blaring as traffic swerved to avoid her, because she didn't so much as break stride. Me, I was ready to follow, and Gio, round fellow though he was, looked keen to as well, but Theresa was just standing there, mucking with her sawed-off.

"Ter…" said Gio, egging her along.

"Just a sec," she said, and then I realized what she was doing. She was breaking down her weapon. She unscrewed the barrel cap. Dumped the spring and her spare shells. Then she removed the barrel, hefted it in one hand like a club. The rest, she chucked to the ground. "You think I'm bringing a gun into a goddamn school, you're fucking nuts," she said, "but that don't mean I'm leaving it here where folks might do ill with it, neither. Now let's go save some kids, shall we?"

We sprinted across the street after Kate, following the jagged line of Drustanus' blood. Me lumbering out front in my sturdy new trucker meat-suit, Gio and Ter trailing behind. It was awkward the way they were forced to run. She was damn near twice his height and athletic to boot, while the body he was stuck in was as squat as it was short, but her blindness forced her to rein in her natural grace and shuffle alongside him, her hand gripping his upper arm. But like everything about those two, as odd and clumsy as it seemed, it worked – albeit slowly, in this case.

Sirens wailed in the distance, fast approaching. They'd be too late to save those kids, though, and so would we, if we didn't hurry.

I scaled the front steps to the building two at a time, this big guy's knees protesting against the strain. Gio and Ter fell behind – horns honking, tires squealing, the two of them cursing as they navigated as best they could across the street. The double-doors at the front entrance had been kicked in.

Their small, square panes of glass had shattered, but were held in place by diamond-patterned wire. A foot-sized dent was in the middle of each, the doors buckled all around. The left one still rocked slightly where it lay just inside the entryway. Meant they weren't far ahead.

"Sam!"

Kate's voice, hoarse with panic, from the direction the blood drips veered. Away from the sign declaring open auditions for Guys and Dolls, thank God. I woulda thought that too sumptuous a meal for the likes of the Brethren to pass up.

I followed down the darkened, locker-lined hall, my only accompaniment the echoes of my footfalls. As I rounded the corner, slipping on the buffed-shiny vinyl tiles, I spotted Kate crouched and tense, her back to me. She was a good twenty yards away. Twenty more past her hunkered down a muscled beast, pocked with a crosshatch of thick, pink scars and random, bone-threaded piercings – across his face, his shoulders, his naked haunches, his dangling, mutilated member... and his sole remaining arm. Drustanus. By the angle and the regularity of the scars, they mostly looked self-inflicted. The piercings, of which there were dozens, were amateur and thick-scarred all around as well, through cheeks, through muscle, a couple even looking as though they'd been forced or drilled through bone. Each one looked to've been more excruciating than the last.

In his hand, he clenched with bleeding fingers a long, jagged shard of window glass. He must've run the whole way over from the restaurant with it in his grasp. But why?

He answered as if I'd asked the question aloud. "My brother tells me metal implements put you at an advantage," he rasped, his words baring a crowded jumble of jagged yellow-brown teeth, and a tongue forked, black, and glistening. "Which is why I've chosen to gut you and your pretty little human here with something less conductive."

"Good thinking," I said. "Of course, you should have enlisted your missus to help you out. I don't plan on going easily, after all, and it looks like you could use the hand."

Drustanus looked down at his bleeding stump – which had begun to knit itself back together, but still pattered globs of red-black clotted blood onto the floor – and then back at me. I was hoping to prod him into anger, maybe prompt a careless, ill-considered attack, but instead Drustanus laughed.

"I suppose I should be honored to hear the dulcet tones of your sultry, sultry voice," I said. "I hear tell you ain't been much for talking these past few hundred years. But then maybe that crazy bint of yours just ain't worth talking *to*."

"Your jibes," he said, "sting not, for Yseult knows full well the depth of my love for her. Every bit of suffering I inflict, and every bit that I endure, serve to demonstrate my devotion to my own dear, sweet Yseult. She is the sole goddess to whom I sacrifice, and I am the sole god to whom she does the same."

"Cool. I'll tell you what, when I kill your ass – and believe you me, I'm gonna – I'll be sure to dedicate your dying breath to her. It's just a shame she won't be here to see you off. I'd hate to rob you of such a touching moment."

"Fear not," he croaked, "you haven't."

A door shut just behind me. I hadn't even heard it open. I wheeled to find behind us the mottled flesh of the no-longer human-looking Yseult, slinking toward us from a once-more shuttered classroom.

Her frame was still small and feminine – almost childlike. Her arched back, small breasts, and duck feet suggested dancer. Her ratty accidental-dreadlock hair and oozing open sores suggested meth-head. The fact those sores crawled with maggots, and that her mottled purple livor mortis skin was sloughing off in chunks – exposing muscle here, yellow adipose there, a gleaming white glimpse of bone at knee, and of tooth through gaping cheek – suggested that this dancer meth-head had taken a long walk off a short pier into cold water and didn't wash up for a week or two, once the crabs and lobsters had their fill.

It took me a sec to realize the sores that polka-dotted her dead flesh weren't sores at all. They were too round, too regular, a Venn diagram of overlapping circles, some knotted old scars, others seeping lymph and pus, still others raised with fresh blisters.

They were burns: from cigarettes, from cigars, from orange-glowing coils of old-fashioned automobile lighters. Self-inflicted, no doubt, to demonstrate how much she burned for *him*.

It'd be sweet if it weren't so goddamned disgusting.

When I saw a shard of glass in her blue-tinged, black-nailed hand as well, I realized too late what had happened. The words fell from my lips as soon as they occurred to me.

"This is a trap," I said. "Grigori told you to lay a trap for me, didn't he?"

The question was, by default, directed at Yseult, since she was the closer of the two, and therefore the one that I was facing. But it was Drustanus who answered. "She won't tell you anything," he said. "She can't."

"Aw, c'mon," I chided, trying to buy some time, "cat got her tongue?"

"Actually," he said, a note of affection evident in his tone, "it was a hyena she fed it to, once she bit it off to prove her love to me." She opened her mouth and stuck out as best she could a ruined stump of blackened meat that was once a tongue. "She always has been better at expressing her devotion than I."

"He set you up, you know," I said. "Grigori, I mean."

"He didn't." Drustanus' rusty voice was full of defiance and false bluster, doubt shading both.

"He did," I insisted. "Just like he did to Ricou. What was it he told me? That Ricou was a sacrifice to the greater good. How's it feel to be tied down atop the altar right behind him?"

Kate leaned in close and muttered, "Uh, Sam? You think when we find ourselves stuck between Zombie Bonnie and

Clyde is the right time to practice your taunting skills?"

I ignored her. And the voices in my head saying pretty much the same damn thing – one mine, the other the trucker's.

"You're mistaken," said Drustanus.

"Yeah? Then answer this, whose idea was it you should lead me away from him while *he* went and found someone to eat?"

Drustanus' hideous features darkened. "It was only logical," he said. "My injury left a trail, after all, and Grigori knew we two would not assent to being separated. If we wished to confront you in numbers, it had to be Yseult and I."

"You sound just like him. He wound you up with all his pretty talk and let you go, didn't he? That must be why he waited until the bitter end to make a punk bitch out of you, no one likes to have to put down their favorite lapdog."

Drustanus roared. Charged. Blood dripping from his stump, and from his one remaining hand, which still gripped the makeshift blade of glass. And then, in that slow/fast/out-of-sequence/all-at-once way times of blood and valor seem to unfold, the scene shifted. Yseult coiling to pounce in support of her one true love, a low growl escaping her lips. Kate, beside me, assuming a defensive stance – knees bent; weight on the balls of her feet a shoulder-width apart; hands open, not balled into fists; arms up and ready. Me, looking back and forth between the two threats, handicapping the odds of each reaching us before the other. A rush of footfalls. Drustanus, distracted, looking past me and away. Me following his gaze. Yseult turning, twisting, and then with a metallic *thunk* and a crack like shattered bone, she's going down, jaw shattered, head half caved in. Gio, behind her a little ways, doubled over, panting, one hand against a nearby locker for support. And Theresa following through with her swing of the steel pipe that was her dismantled shotgun's barrel as if she were Hammerin' Hank himself, knocking a ball into the stands.

Drustanus still coming. Eyes wide and wet and not on Kate or me, instead locked on Yseult's dazed, flopping form; her eyes rolled back, her limbs rigid, mangled mouth foaming pink at the corners.

"Ter," I yelled, "the pipe!"

Ter's a good soldier. A fighter through and through. She didn't question, didn't hesitate, and – despite her blindness – didn't miss. She chucked the barrel to me, and I lunged toward the speeding freight train that was Drustanus, jabbing it forward with all I had.

It struck his ruined flesh, his fragile bone, underfed and undernourished in the face of all the energy he'd been expending – and, thrumming with sudden electricity – punched straight through.

He slumped to his knees. Blinked in confusion. Dropped his shard of glass onto the floor. It shattered. He tipped forward. And as I plucked the yellow, chalky remains of his soul from the end of the gun barrel, grinding them to dust between my fingers, his last pained, reverent word was, "Yseult."

His body caved in before our eyes. Shook the building from foundation to rafters. While behind us, unnoticed at first, Yseult struggled to her knees, and plucked her own glass shard up off the floor.

It was her strangled pleading I noticed first. A wet, guttural sound, like an animal not known for the ability trying to mimic human speech. When I turned away from her fallen lover, I saw her, head dented like a rotten Jack O'Lantern, moving her shattered jaw, her face all twisted up, not with anger, nor malice, but simply grim determination.

When my gaze trailed downward to what her hands were doing, I realized what she was trying to say, what she was trying to ask of me.

She'd used the shard of glass to slice open the flesh of her chest; gouged deep furrows into the yellowed breastbone beneath, and cut muscle and connective tissue away from between her two exposed ribs. Pushed her tiny fingers through the gap – probing, searching, to no avail. What she wanted could not be found without assistance, without the touch of one of my kind to make it present itself.

She was trying to gouge out her own soul.

To follow her beloved to the grave.

As Drustanus had said, she always was better at expressing her devotion than was he.

I approached her, hand extended – equal parts a calming gesture, and a promise of death's reprieve. "Sammy, the fuck you think you're doing?" asked Gio with alarm. "You just killed that freaky bitch's boyfriend. Now you're gonna make all nice?"

He took a step toward me, intending to intervene, but I waved him off with my free hand.

"It's okay, Gio. Yseult's not going to hurt me. If she did, if she evicted me from this meat-suit, it would only delay her in following Drustanus. Isn't that right, Yseult?"

Tears shone in her eyes. She nodded almost imperceptibly.

I couldn't help but feel some kinship with her. My eternal damnation, after all, was nothing more or less than an extended demonstration of my love for my dear, sweet Elizabeth. As my hand found her shoulder, and her body shuddered from the sudden current of my touch, I told her, "I'm sorry, it's nothing personal."

Her hand dug deep into her own chest once more, and then her eyes went wide. With her last ounce of strength, she pulled it free, and then slackened.

Her withered soul fell from her grasp, cracking as it hit the floor.

I let go of her. She slumped to the vinyl tiles. Then I ground her soul to dust beneath my boot. Her body followed suit, desiccating before our eyes.

"Now," I said, "let's go find Grigori."

20.

"That was some messed-up shit back there, dude," said Gio, huffing and puffing while we sprinted for the auditorium, but somehow still finding breath to speak.

"In case you hadn't caught on, Dead Guy I Stuck Into a Different Dead Guy's Body, messed-up shit is sorta my specialty."

"Yeah," he said, "but even for you, man, this is fucking bugnuts."

"Ugh," said Theresa. "Don't mention bugs."

Kate looked at Theresa, and then back to me. "Bugs? What'd I miss?"

"Nothing worth mentioning," Theresa said, "if you ever wanna sleep again at night."

We sprinted past the busted down front doors, continued onward down the hall. No sign of Grigori. No signs of life at all, I thought.

Then a door opened to our right, yellow light spilling into the dim hall. Two girls deep in joking conversation shuffled, smiling, out. Their expressions faded to worry when they caught sight of us, and shot on past toward fear; an enormous afroed black woman arm-in-arm with a short, squat Pesci-in-Goodfellas-looking mofo; a bruised and battered waitress, her uniform spattered with blood; and a beefy, bearded, gore-streaked trucker with a crooked ear and a bevy of seeping wounds who was carrying a pipe caked with bits of rotting lung and heart and brain.

"Get back inside," I said, jabbing my finger toward the classroom they'd just vacated. "Are there more of you in there?" One of them nodded. The other elbowed her.

"It's all right," I said, "we're not gonna hurt you. Just get back in there. Lock the door if the door locks. Barricade it either way. And don't come out until the cops come get you. You understand?"

This time, they both nodded. Then retreated. The bar of light that shone underneath the door went out, and I heard the slide of something heavy being moved.

And we continued down the hall once more.

"You know, Sam," said Kate some twenty silent paces later, "that shit back there with Drustanus and Yseult? Kinda sorta personal for *me*. I mean, those evil bastards upturned my life. Wrecked my place of business. Turned a table of my best tippers into the blood-drinking undead. Cheesy catchphrase aside, if that ain't personal, then what the hell do *you* call it?"

"An average Tuesday?" Theresa ventured.

Kate laughed.

Despite myself – and these godawful circumstances – I couldn't help but think I'd missed these three.

Up ahead, a child of twelve or so was slumped against the wall, two holes puncturing his neck, blood oozing down it and soaking into the collar of his shirt. "Grigori, you monster," I muttered, and forced my new XL meat-suit to put on a burst of speed. Kate – not carrying fifty extra pounds of beer-and-chicken-fried-steak weight – still reached the kid first.

"He's got a pulse," she said, two fingers to his neck on the side opposite the wound, "but weak. He's going to need a doctor, and soon."

The sirens outside brayed loud enough to make my meat-suit's ears pop. Lights, red and blue, splashed through the hashmarked windows facing the ruined Pancake Palace and projected strobing diamond patterns across the far wall of the hall. "He'll get one," I said. "Won't be long before they wind up over here. Let's try and keep their workload light, shall we?"

"Sam – up here!" Gio and Ter stood before a set of double doors a little ways down the darkened hall – the entrance to the auditorium. As they opened the doors wider, I heard the sound of children singing – "Luck Be a Lady," unless my good ear deceived me.

And then a commotion.

And then screaming.

By the time I reached the auditorium door, Grigori had climbed onto the stage, which though bare of set-dressings was dotted with tweens in street clothes, their singing halted, many of them now cowering stage-right against the curtained wall. If he'd come at them from the other aisle, they would have had a shot at making the exit, which was stage-left, but Grigori was too clever for that, shepherding the whole flock toward the slaughter so he could regain his strength and make his escape. For the child in the hallway had not come close to slaking his thirst, healing his injuries, or restoring his human visage. In fact, looking at him, it almost made his appearance all the worse. His features were now half-human, half-ruined. His body, crushed from the ribcage down by the truck's front grille, was reassembling itself unpleasantly before our eyes, muscle stretching, pulsing, splitting off as it coated exposed bone, vasculature spreading like some kind of malignant vine. As I watched, he reached into his gaping chest cavity and snapped a rib that had knit together crooked, wincing as he did. It came off in his hand, and then he reattached it once more, this time correctly.

He stepped toward the children, jaw as wide as an anaconda's, outsized canines catching the footlights and gleaming sickly yellow. They cowered. Shrieked in terror. Wept at their fate.

Well, their almost-fate. Because that's when I had me an idea.

Credit Kate and Ter and Gio for showing me I was not alone. That I was better with friends by my side.

No, I thought. Not friends. Family. Because we'd been to war together. We'd bonded in a way that couldn't be broken. Found a strength together we lacked apart.

As could these kids.

As *would* these kids.

Grigori closed the gap between himself and the frightened children. I sprinted toward them, an old Chesterton quote ringing in my ears. "Fairy tales are more than true," he'd said. "Not because they tell us that dragons exist, but because they tell us that dragons can be beaten." These kids knew damn well the world was full of horrors; the news reminded them of that fact on the daily. It was time someone showed them they could *do* something about it.

As I belly-flopped onto the stage and scrabbled awkwardly to my feet, Grigori grabbed a child by the wrist, and pulled him close. Then he turned to face me, holding the boy between us like a shield.

"Any closer, and this boy dies."

I stopped, and put my hands up. "You aim to kill him anyway," I said. "You aim to kill them all."

The kids behind him gasped, and cried, and wailed. Kate, Gio, and Theresa stood frozen in the aisles of the empty auditorium, the only people in the room not on the stage.

Grigori shrugged. "It's true," he said. "But perhaps, if you're willing to let me leave, I'll feed on only half of them. Or feed on each just half to death."

"I've got a better idea."

His one human eyebrow arched. Then the mental projection of the human face he struggled to put forth flickered, and the eyebrow disappeared.

"You do?" he asked, amused. "What's that?"

"Your gaping chest contains a soul," I said, my gaze leaving Grigori's face for a moment and locking briefly with that of the trembling boy in his grasp. "Withered. Vestigial. Dead.

Inaccessible to most, but attaining physical form the second I lay hands on you. Once it's crushed, you'll be no more, and you'll no longer be able to hurt these kids, or anyone else."

"I know this," said Grigori impatiently, tightening his grip on the boy in his arms. "Why do you think I choose to use this child as a shield? You cannot reach into my chest through him."

"True enough," I said, raising my voice and hoping the kids behind would take the hint, "but that's the thing."

"*What's* the thing?"

"*I* don't have to be the one to crush it."

His eyes widened.

I leapt at him, and grabbed his wrist, pulling it away from the young boy's throat.

The boy, newly brave, twisted to face Grigori and drove his tiny hand into the monster's chest, while as one, the children who'd been cowering behind Grigori pounced, coming to their fellow student's aid.

And when the dust settled, Grigori was no more.

"Hell of a goddamn gamble, Sam." This from Kate. "Turning these kids into monster-killers."

"I encouraged them to protect themselves," I said. "You of all people should get that."

"I do," she admitted. "But still. After today, they're gonna have some serious shit to work out."

"And their whole entire lives in which to do it."

"Uh, guys?" Gio, trotting back into the auditorium from the front hall, which faced out toward the Pancake Palace crime scene. "I hate to break up this little philosophical discussion, but those of us stuck in their bodies for the long haul gotta motor. Them cops outside are headed this way."

"You two got an escape plan?"

"Always, brother. We stashed our ride a couple blocks away before we boosted the truck. Clean papers, clean tags – both fake, of course, duped from an identical ride three states away, but they'll hold up if someone runs 'em, and we got IDs to match."

"The authorities are gonna be closing in fast. I hope your ride is speedy enough to get you outta here before the whole town gets locked down."

Gio gave me a who-the-hell-you-think-you're-talking-to look. "The beauty we boosted's a 1970 Torino fastback with three hundred seventy-five horses under the hood. Only thing she can't pass is a gas station."

"Good. Take Kate with you. Keep her safe."

Kate: "Hey!"

Gio: "We'll *take* her, but we can't promise she'll be *safe*."

"What the hell does *that* mean?"

It was Theresa who answered. "You think we been hiding out this whole last year? Well fuck you very much, Sam Thornton, cause we ain't been running, we been *fighting*. In case you somehow failed to notice, shit's gotten rough out in the world of late. Angels and demons and everything in between so intent on bashing in each others' skulls, they no longer seem to care who gets caught up in the middle. I'm talking ordinary people caught up in shit they shouldn't be – in a covert war that ain't theirs to fight. So we been out there helping 'em, wherever and however we can. Kate wants in on that, she's welcome, but she for *damn* sure won't be safe. Wouldn't blame her for saying no."

"Actually," she said, "count me in."

"Yeah?" I asked.

"Yeah?" asked Gio.

"Yeah," said Kate. "You can see how far hiding got me. Mayhap it's time for me to fight."

Booted feet like hoof-beats as the cops stormed the front door. Not SWAT, I thought – not yet – just uniforms. The three's window for escape was closing. Mine had closed already. Someone was gonna hafta delay the police, after all.

"This place got a back entrance?" I asked the kids.

One nodded, and pointed toward backstage. "Out the door and down the hall," he said.

"Thanks." Then, to my friends: "Go."

"But Sam–"

"There isn't time," I said, biting back tears. "Just go."

Kate hugged me, sobbing into my neck. Gio put a beefy hand onto my shoulder. And then the three of them took off, leaving as the cops came in.

The story I told the cops made no goddamn sense. I'd been eating breakfast at the pancake place. Three crazy people – all freaky and messed-up looking, like out of a horror movie – crashed a goddamn semi into the dining room, and made ground beef of half the patrons. They fled across the street to the school. Me and a couple other patrons followed them, trying to stop 'em before they could hurt the kids. Two we did. One we didn't. But the kids were braver and tougher than the last one musta thought, because they defended themselves, and – thank God – came out on top. And I had no idea what happened to my fellow Good Samaritans.

They held my meat-suit for a week. He never once after I abandoned him contradicted my story. Nor did the children. And the sad state of the Brethren bodies aside, the physical evidence didn't, either. Security cameras caught some of what transpired, and eyewitnesses supplied the rest. Eventually, they let him go a hero. I saw him on Barbara Walters a few months back. He said you never know in those moments how you're gonna react. Said the whole thing was a blur. True enough for him, I guess.

Some shit I seen, I wish like hell it were true for me as well.

Then

The sun rose over the battleships to the east of me, dull patches of pale gray amidst a sea that blazed with the full spectrum of the sun's rays, scattered to rainbows by the undulating waves. Gun battlements flanked me by some fifty yards on either side, two points in a dotted line that studded the white-sand beach as far as the eye could see, guarding against surprise attacks from Japanese fighter planes eager to steal this hunk of rock back from Uncle Sam a second time. A little nothing of an island in the tropics by the name of Guam – two hundred square miles of beach and rock and jungle on which many men on both sides had lost their lives. I hadn't heard of it before this morning, although I hear tell the US has occupied it since the 1890s; Lord knows why the Empire took it from us in the first place back in '41. But in the wake of Pearl Harbor, them taking it was enough to make us want to take it back. So take it back we did – ten months ago, this was, in '44 – landing Marines at beaches north and south and pushing back the Japanese until they ran out of ground to hold.

Strategy or vengeance, I wasn't sure. But it sure was a pretty place to watch the sun rise, so long as you don't mind the warships mucking up the view, or the B-29s juddering overhead as the runway spit them northward toward Japan.

Word around the mess hall was a few hostiles had taken refuge in the jungle, living wild and popping out every now and again to slash Jeep tires or trash supply sheds. Consensus was they wouldn't last out there for long, though history would prove that consensus wrong. The last holdout would not surrender until '72, nearly three decades after we reclaimed the island, and even then, the fella came in under duress. Turned out he'd been living in a jungle cave the whole time, certain there was a war still on, and that the Americans who'd by then put their conflict with his nation in the rearview were still the enemy.

Amazing the conditions folks can live through. The fear. The loneliness. The constant struggle to survive in hostile territory. I guess any situation becomes your normal if you live it long enough. Though I couldn't help but wonder how relieved he felt when, instead of a trip to the brig, he got loaded onto a commercial airliner bound for home. Maybe not back to the world he left behind, but one that wasn't trying to kill him at every turn, at least, or turn him into something less than human.

The sand was cool as night beneath my well-worn military fatigue pants as I sat, tank top-bared arms hugging knees, shivering beneath the waxing light as it chased the stars westward. But it wasn't on account of the sand's chill my new vessel – a Marine named Seamus Scanlon, according to his dogtags – was goosebumped and trembling.

No, that was on account of Hitler.

When I closed the door to his bunker office wearing the flesh of his betrothed, I knew I didn't have long to make my move. The anemometer supplied to him by his apparently quite mystically inclined science advisor Mengele may have shaken itself apart, but there was still the pesky matter of me not speaking a goddamn word of German. Not to mention the fact I was inhabiting the body of the most evil man in all of history's new bride; if that icky motherfucker got all randy on me, there'd be no stopping the barf-fest that ensued.

Actually, come to think of it, I thought as I clicked shut the door behind the guards ushering an unconscious Goebbels to the brig… and then I puked all down the front of my housedress.

Son of a whore. Lilith warned me that'd happen every time, but even after Goebbels and the Hitler Youth getting all ralphy on me, I still didn't see it coming.

When I threw up, Hitler was by my side in a flash. At first, I thought the jig was up once more. Maybe Mengele had warned him this was a side-effect of possession, and he was planning to attack me, or summon a fresh batch of guards. But instead, he wrapped his arms around me and pulled me close asking, "*Bist du in Ordnung, meine Liebe*?"

And though the nuance of his words was lost on me, I got the gist. This human garbage was worried about me, and hoped I was okay. Hard to say what specifically he thought had gotten to me. Maybe the poisoning of the dog he'd made me watch, maybe the cold-cocking of a dear friend. But one thing was clear, this fucking stain on our whole species, this monster who'd rounded up Jews and dissidents and slaughtered them en masse and who'd caused bloodshed the world over, was deeply concerned about his new wife's tender tummy.

As he enveloped me in his embrace, a burning rage fell over me. It thrummed through me like an electric current. He cooed his unintelligible German platitudes at me, my anger growing inside me like a living thing, so naturally, I assumed that the vibration I was feeling was my building fury, nothing more.

It was only when he drew me tight to his chest that I realized the vibration was coming from him, not me, and that despite the fact it threatened to shake the fillings from this idiot woman's teeth, the Führer here didn't seem to notice.

That's when I remembered my last moments on this earth.

Seeing my Elizabeth on the busy city street, child-plump and beautiful.

Calling her name despite myself, even though I knew it wouldn't matter, that she'd made her choice.

The mad-eyed man in his pageboy cap and woolen overcoat, his smile manic, his mischief-glinting eyes locking on mine and never deviating.

His hand reaching for my chest.

Plunging inside.

Grasping tight my soul.

It wasn't until the Führer screamed that I snapped back to reality, as unreal as that reality seemed. My hand was buried deep inside his chest, straight through his clothes though his body offered up no resistance, and there was no wound. His eyes were wide, his mouth an "O" of shock. My long, feminine, enameled nails grazed against something warm and round and alive, and instinctively, I grasped it. And just like that, the bunker office dropped away, as did the planet, and my own thoughts and memories to boot.

It was then that I discovered what hell truly was.

Touching that man's blackened soul, atrophied from disuse, experiencing every moment that led him to my grasp. The choices he'd made. The lives he'd sacrificed. The delight he'd taken in the suffering of others.

Lilith never told me it would be like this. That I'd see what he'd seen. Do what he'd done. *Feel* what he'd *felt*.

She never warned me.

Never said.

She must have known I'd never do it if she had.

You know the worst of it, of watching in mute horror as this madman's blasphemous existence unfurled before me? It was experiencing the sense of smug self-satisfaction he felt. The entitlement. The bitter, petulant insistence even now that this fate which had befallen me (*him* protested the part of me that held on tight to who I was, *him not me but him*) was Not My Fault, Not My Doing, Not The Life of Greatness I Deserved.

These feelings weren't my own, you understand, but *his*, overlaid atop my own revulsion at his every thought and deed.

That's what I told myself. What I tell myself still, about that and every collection since.

But the fact is, in that moment, experiencing the sum total of your mark's life's arc, there's scarcely a job where you don't – if only for a single, horrible, illusory second – get the secondhand sense of certitude at your (their/our) incontrovertible *rightness*. And it's that moment of every job that steals a little bit of who you are. Because our actions *can't* all be justified, and Lord knows those of the folks I take sometimes fail to come within a country mile. But still, to a one, they're all so goddamned *certain*. Something about that reaches cold hands into the core of you, into that tight-tied hidden bundle of convictions and true things that make you *you*, and that you've kept so secret and well-protected all these years, and shakes it, hard.

In that moment, you don't know anything. You *can't* know. You can't believe. Because you know you're just as likely to be misguided as were they.

After all, why the fuck else would you wind up with a gig as a Collector in the first place?

That head-trip's a lot to take in on *any* job. And Adolf Hitler was far from any job. It didn't leave me rattled, it left me shattered.

Annihilated.

When I finally tore free his soul, it was by accident. I'd simply crumpled to the floor with my hand still wrapped around it, and yanked it out as I fell. The swirling morass and piercing discord that was his soul's corrupted light and song vanished like someone had flipped a switch.

I shook as if with seizure, so wracked with guilt was I when I was once more myself (or something like it, I thought, draped as I was in a strange woman's flesh) it felt like a physical affliction. Snot and tears poured uncontrollably from me, from his lover's face. My mouth was open in silent imitation of a scream; I think I would have wailed aloud had the horrors I'd just experienced not ripped the breath from my lungs.

For a time, I was outside myself – my new self, I corrected, my meat-self, my borrowed self – hovering above my fleshly vessel it seemed, driven half-mad by all I'd seen. I drifted in and out of consciousness for what felt like days, but by the clock must have been minutes. When I finally came around, I found myself guilt-stricken sobbing with my head on the floor, staring across its concrete sheen at the lifeless body of the man I'd been sent to kill.

I found my feet, shambled over to him and kicked him hard across the face. It didn't help, so I kicked again, harder. That didn't make me feel any better, either.

From somewhere a thousand miles away, I heard a voice like bourbon layered over honey. "Collector," it said. "You've done well. Now we must bundle up his soul and go."

Lilith. I ignored her, dropped to my knees and pummeled the lifeless body before me with my fists. They were delicate and ineffectual, and soon swelled with every blow, hurting me far more than it could ever hurt him.

He was gone. Dead. There was nothing more that I could take from him.

But then I heard his wife crying in the back of her own mind, forced to watch as I'd felled her beloved, and shrieking ever louder with each blow I (she/we) landed on his corpse, and I realized that wasn't true.

I lurched toward the desk. Found the bottle with its amber pills. Dumped a handful into my hand, and tossed them into my mouth, Lilith shouting behind me all the while.

I bit down hard, chewing until my mouth was full of deadly paste that stank of bitter almonds. Then I swallowed it all down.

A stabbing pain in my gut doubled me over. I collapsed onto the surface of the desk, atop its mess of papers. Atop Hitler's own gun.

By force of will, I made my meat-suit stand. Her vision swam. Her limbs trembled as the poison kicked in, made picking up the Walther hard, ade standing harder still. I fell to my knees, straddling the Third Reich's dead Führer. Then, Lilith shrieking, I stuffed the barrel of his gun into his mouth and pulled the trigger.

"Guess I'll see you both in hell," I said.

Then I woke up, wracked with the pain of my first death experienced without the gauzy veil of blissfully numbing shock, in a barracks bunk in Guam.

"You mind a little company?"

The sun was full up by the time Lilith arrived. The sand was sun-warmed all around me, and my skin a darkening brown, but still my shivering had not abated. Just like at the flat in Berlin, I hadn't heard her approach.

She didn't wait for an answer, which is for the best, because there wasn't any answer coming. Instead, she plopped down on the sand beside me in a white bikini made, it seemed, from spider-silk and happy thoughts. We sat in silence for a good long while – an hour, maybe more – our shoulders close enough to touch. Her skin was warm against my own. A small kindness, a simple comfort. In that hour, my shaking finally abated.

"Took you long enough to find me," I said, not tearing my eyes from the horizon.

"No," she replied, "it didn't. As your handler, I can locate you at a moment's notice. I simply thought it might be best to give you a little space."

"You didn't tell me. What it would be like. How it would feel."

"You're right, I didn't."

"Why?"

"I suppose I didn't see the point."

"You didn't see the *point*?" Hurt; incredulous.

"No, Collector, I did not. The job was yours to do whether you knew what you were in for or not, which means I would have accomplished nothing by warning you but making your task more difficult. I completed your collection, by the way, wrapped the soul and interred it as required. I've been assured by my superiors that the Deliverants who take responsibility for the soul once it is buried have deemed my actions acceptable – this time, at least. I suspect they'll not prove so lenient again, which means next time the task shall fall to you and you alone."

I considered what she'd said about warning me, considered the ramifications of knowing and not knowing. Decided reluctantly she wasn't wrong.

"Sam," I told her.

"What?"

"If we're to work together, you should really call me Sam."

"No," she said, "I shouldn't. Do you know why? Because I am not your friend. I am not your ally. And I am certainly not your confidante. I am your jailor. Your tormentor. I am one of many architects responsible for constructing your own personal hell, and you would do well to remember it. That is why I choose to call you by your title. To remind us both precisely where we stand. Because I assure you, if you give me half an opportunity, I will use you. Hurt you. Betray your trust. Deceive you. I'm sorry, it's nothing personal. It's simply that I cannot help it. It's in my nature. It's who I am. It's what I have become."

I shook my head. "I refuse to believe that."

Lilith smiled then, sad and wan. "You'll come around."

"But not today," I said, my hand finding hers, our fingers intertwining. It wasn't a romantic gesture, but one of basic human kindness, for in that moment – and perhaps only in that moment – her beauty held no sway over me.

She flinched as if stung, but she did not take her hand away. "What exactly do you think you're doing?"

"Look. You've done your civic duty. Warned me how big and scary you are. How you plan to chew me up and spit me out if given half a chance. But not today, right? Because today, for me, was a giant fucking shit sandwich. Today, I've had about all that I can take. So if you want to use me and abuse me, you'll have to wait your turn, because today I'm already used up. Which is why it seems to me we may as well enjoy our time in the sun. Unless, of course, I'm wrong, and you plan on getting started ruining me today."

She looked at me a long while as if I were insane. But she never removed her hand. "No," she said finally, resting her head upon my shoulder, "not today."

And so we two damned souls sat for hours beneath the blazing sun in silence, and watched its rays glint off the water, bright and pretty as God's grace.

21.

It was dusk when I arrived at the temple.

Temple was too strong a word, really, for the tangled heap of stone and jungle life I saw before me or, given said heap's strange elemental majesty, too weak. In reality, the ravaged remains of the building didn't look like a human structure in the slightest. The weathered sandstone spires seemed to rise out of the jungle as if not built but grown. The bas relief ornamentation – some Hindu, some Buddhist, and some animist – had been all but obliterated by the centuries, once telling tales of gods and men, but now nothing more than mossy crenellations on a wall. And in the thousand years since the site had been built – the nearly seven hundred since this site in particular had been abandoned – the jungle had done its level best to swallow the structure whole. Strangler figs pressed woody limbs through every hint of a crack. Massive thitpok trees draped surfaces with their fluid root structures which seemed to slither down across the rock face like the tentacles of a giant beast. Garlands of ropy vine strung themselves across every peak and column – always pulling, tugging, taking until the stone itself was forced to tender its crumbling surrender.

Believe me, I knew how it felt.

I'd been hiking for seven days, following Lilith's vague directions – scrawled on a napkin from an ex-pat Irish bar in Phnom Penh – through the dense, forbidding wilds of Cambodia. The legends claim that Lilith has dominion over the warm Southern wind, and as the hot salt breath of the Gulf of Thailand blew ever northward with me, I couldn't help but feel like she was with me – guiding, goading, or maybe just gloating it wasn't her who had to carry the goddamn backpack.

Honestly, the whole country was so hot and sticky, I'd soak clean through my shirt by the time I shrugged the damn thing on. The fifteen miles or so a day I'd manage on foot – twenty, if a fisherman took pity on me and ferried me up the Mekong in one of the ubiquitous low-slung fishing vessels that sprinkle the river like so much flotsam – would leave me looking as though I'd taken a dip in the briniest of ocean waters, and smelling like the locker room to boot. And the one day I managed to hitch a ride – thirty-five miles in the back of a rusted pickup with a pair of orange-robed monks, whose sandals were made from tire-rubber and whose rice bowls (for all the Buddhist monks I encountered on my journey carried rice bowls, which locals delighted in filling with food from their own tables, and which the monks were quite willing to share with a poor, starving stranger) were, sadly, empty – the plumes of dirt kicked up off the unpaved road left my eyes and hair gritty, and my benefactor's insistence upon driving over every fucking pothole left my tailbone so bruised I could scarcely sit the whole next day.

I was wearing the flesh of a middle-aged, middle-management Seattleite named McCluskey, who'd scheduled a layover in Phnom Penh on his way to inspect his company's new call-center in Bangalore with the intention of exploring Cambodia's ruins. I caught up with him when I overheard he and his wife Skyping in a Greenwood Avenue coffee house, not too long after the nightmare showdown in Bellevue. Thanks to me, he missed his bus to Angkor Wat, but I didn't figure he'd mind. He'd shed a good five pounds of paunch on this little trek of mine, and anyways, I was showing him a *real* set of ruins – as in, the kind no one had laid eyes on since Columbus sailed the ocean blue.

No one but the last remaining Brethren, that is; the one that Lilith called Thomed.

After Bellevue, I confess I didn't relish the notion of going toe-to-toe with another one of Lilith's oogly booglies, particularly given this one went bamboo so long ago, having disappeared into the jungle not long after the beastly Ricou split from the group. God only knew what I was walking into. And when, as best as I could tell, I reached the end of Lilith's map midday today and there'd been no temple to be found, just a modest fishing village comprising a few ramshackle stilted huts clustered around a muddy tributary too small to have a proper name, I'd half-hoped I wouldn't have to, that perhaps Thomed simply wasn't here. But when, with the help of McCluskey's travel dictionary, I inquired in broken Khmer (which sounded close enough to Sanskrit to my ears to make me worry I might wind up inadvertently summoning a Rakshasa demon) as to whether there were any ruins nearby, their dogged insistence that they could not understand me, coupled with their refusal to meet my eye or stand in my presence for ten seconds before gruffly shouldering past, indicated that I was in the right place after all. And given all I'd learned about the Brethren these past few months, locating Thomed's little hidey-hole from that point was a breeze. I just forced myself to walk in the direction my instincts screamed I shouldn't, and within hours, I was there.

The question was, was Thomed?

I stepped gingerly through the remains, the ground an uneven hodgepodge of roots, fallen trees, and long-eroded manmade blocks. My eyes peeled and wary, my ears straining to pick out any sign of life, or failing that, of prior occupation. But aside of the teeming wildlife of the jungle – a living vine that proved to be a tree-bound python, the rustle in the bushes of a chocolate-brown wild boar, a monitor lizard basking on the crumbling stone face of a long-toppled god – I caught no sign of him. And so, against my better instincts, I squeezed past the cascade of thick, fibrous roots that hung like organic draperies in front of the ancient temple's sole remaining entrance as if the very land itself wished to bar my entry, and stepped into the stifling dark.

Once my eyes adjusted, I realized the darkness of the temple's interior was far from absolute. Shafts of golden light pierced the roof at regular intervals, the cracks through which it passed framed by encroaching plant life. And inside, too, the plants had taken hold, draping nearly every surface with roots and vines and, nearest the stagnant, black-watered puddles that graced the stone floor here and there beneath the roof-gaps overhead, fresh shoots sprouted up from the crumbling rock, leaves stretched skyward toward their Maker's light.

The room was pillared, but unfurnished, and otherwise unadorned. Many of the pillars had toppled long ago, and in some places the ceiling had followed suit. I crept slowly deeper into the temple's murk, mindful at every turn of any sense of motion that might signal Thomed's attack.

At the head of the narrow, ruined room, I discovered a lone statue, moss-dusted and vine-bound. Not of a god, it seemed, but of a worshipper, cross-legged and eyes closed, its stone hands clasped in prayer or meditation. I had the strange sensation of embarrassment at interrupting its long penitence, for clearly it had sat in that same place so long that the temple had crumbled around it. The statue sat on a patch of jungle earth just large enough to accommodate it, from which sprouted countless vine-like growths that stretched upward toward the scant light leaking through the ceiling cracks above, winding like braided rope around the stone figure as they climbed. The effect was such that it appeared this praying figure had sprouted from the ground itself. I couldn't tell if the growth had pushed up through the temple's stone floor, or if the temple's architects simply left this square of jungle bare. Though I had no idea why they might've elected to, the latter seemed the likelier option, since everywhere else plant life pushed through, it left cracks and stone debris in its wake, whereas here the borders were crisp and clear, a perfect square unmarred by broken rock.

I didn't realize until its eyes opened that this statue was not a statue at all.

A sudden glimpse of yellowed whites amidst the cracked gray flesh I took for stone, surrounding irises and pupils rheumy with age. Yellow again as lips split to reveal the not-statue's teeth. The simple acts of eyes and lips opening shook free a thick layer of dust from the being's face, which drifted like ash onto its vine-strewn lap.

It took me a moment to realize this statue, this man, this *whatever*, was smiling.

"Oh good," he said, with a voice like snakeskin dragging across dead leaves, "you're here." "Thomed?" I ventured. He nodded, loosing yet more dust from his face, his hair, his head. As it fell away, I realized beneath the inch of collected filth he was wizened and emaciated, a living skeleton wrapped tight with age-cracked flesh. It, and his hair, was near as gray as the dirt that coated it. It was clear he'd been sitting there for a long while; centuries, perhaps. "You've been *expecting* me?"

"I've been expecting *someone* for quite some time," he said. "Though not you specifically..." He tilted his head by way of polite inquisition. It took a second for me to realize he was asking my name.

"Sam," I told him. "My name is Sam."

"Sam," he repeated. "Well met."

"That remains to be seen," I told him.

"True enough," he replied.

His voice was accented, but only slightly. How that could be, I didn't know. If he'd been sitting here half as long as it appeared he had, he couldn't possibly have the grasp on modern language to understand me.

I said as much. He smiled wider and replied, "It is surprising what one might learn if one simply takes the time to listen."

"To what?" I asked.

"To everything. To nothing at all. To the soul-song of the universe."

I took a careful step toward him, my right hand inside my pants pocket, gripping tight the timeworn bowie knife I'd traded a fisherman McCluskey's watch for two days back. Thomed didn't move a whit. Bound tight with vines as he was, I wondered if he could. But I remembered the deceptive strength of his fellow Brethren, and decided I'd err on the side of caution.

"Do you know why I'm here?" I asked.

"I do," he replied. "Just as I know about the knife you carry, and as yet wish to conceal. You've come to end my life."

I thought about protesting the fact. I didn't see the point. "Forgive me for saying so, but you don't seem too broken up about that."

"If it is my Maker's will that I should cease to be, then I shall cease to be. If it is not, then She will spare me. I am prepared for either eventuality."

"That's awful accepting of you."

"Yes, well, I've had some time to think upon the matter, and to come to terms with either outcome."

I cast my gaze around the ruins, warm and silent in the waning afternoon. "Exactly how long have you *been* here?"

Thomed fell silent for a full five minutes then, his face screwed up in thought. I began to wonder if he'd ever answer.

But eventually, his eyes opened once more, and he said, "One thousand seven hundred sixty-seven years, three months, two weeks, and four days."

I snorted in surprise and disbelief. "What, no hours?"

He flashed age-dulled teeth once more, a brief, kindly smile. "I fear the time is hard to tell when one cannot see the sun."

"I hate to be the one to tell you this, but I think your math's off. It puts you here a good eight hundred years before the culture that built this place."

"Your assumption is fallacious," he replied.

"Yeah? How's that?"

"You assume I came to this temple to worship, when in fact this temple came to me."

"So *you* built this place?"

"No. I seek neither the comfort of shelter nor the vanity of monument. Simply peace."

"You mean to say whoever built this place built it *around* you?"

"I do."

"Why? You, like, some kinda god to them?"

Thomed laughed. "Actually, and to my great surprise, the temple builders hardly seemed to notice my presence here, save for the fact they seemed compelled to not disturb me. My suspicion is that they were drawn to this place for much the same reason I was."

"Which is what, exactly?"

"I assume you noted the strange silence that fell over the jungle as you approached this place?"

I did, and said as much.

"That's because this is a special place, one of beauty, of reverence, of reflection. It has been since long before I happened by. Since long before humankind discovered it and sought to honor it with their temples. The trees know it. The animals know it. *I* know it. In the centuries that followed my kind's abhorrent ritual, I found myself lost, despondent, rudderless. I had not foreseen our ritual resulting in such senseless devastation; I blamed myself and my fellow Brethren for the resultant loss of life, and felt truly crushed beneath the weight of it. And so, ashamed of what we'd done – what we'd become – I struck out on my own into the wilderness. Perhaps it was an act of self-flagellation on account of the terrible, consuming hunger I experienced, or the destruction we Nine caused. Perhaps a cowardly flight from all that reminded me of what we'd done. Whatever it was, it somehow – across my decades of ceaseless wandering – led me here. I was so taken with this spot, so certain it was where I was supposed to be, I never left. And now I expend no small amount of effort to protect it, to dissuade those who might wish to desecrate it, to ensure it remains unspoiled."

"That's why it's so difficult to find?" I asked.

"Yes," he said.

"What makes this place so special?"

"Cambodia is a nation of fertile spiritual soil, soil in which many religions took root, and, oddly, intertwined, flourished together as one rather than waging war against each another. Here native animism blends seamlessly with Hinduism and Buddhism, despite their many differences, creating something at once new, and very, very old. Whether this syncretic nature is some aspect of the land imprinting its character upon its people or the other way around, I do not know. But regardless of the cause, the cultures that have sprung up here have an astonishing ability to reconcile the irreconcilable, to hold two contradictory beliefs at once and to find solace in their inherent contradictions. For life itself is contradiction and compromise. Life is reconciling the irreconcilable. As, I've spent some time discovering, is death. So this seemed the perfect place for me to try to reconcile with myself and my God what I'd done."

"Sounds like you've been at it a while. A very *specific* while, to hear you tell it."

"I count my days of waiting as best I can. It seems important that someone should."

"Days of waiting. Waiting for what? For me?"

He shook his head, slow, sorrowful. "Waiting for acknowledgement. For absolution."

"From whom – God?"

His expression showed surprise. "Who else?"

"Look, I hate to tell you pal, but before you and your Brethren buddies staged your little breakout, you were condemned to hell. Seems like when it comes to God's forgiveness, that ship has sailed."

"That is but your opinion."

"Yeah? What's another?"

Thomed looked me up and down. "One of the many apparent contradictions on which I've ruminated is the notion that a loving Maker would condemn Her children to an eternity outside the light of Her good grace for the sins of their infancy. If our souls are, in fact, immortal, why would our Maker confine Her judgment to the first twenty or fifty or one hundred years of life? Put another way, why would a loving parent punish their child for any longer than it took for that child to learn its lesson? And my conclusion, long coming, is that She would not. That absolution lies not beyond our reach, no matter how far gone we seem – at least, so long as we stretch forever toward it."

"That presumes our Maker is a loving parent," I said. "Which, I've gotta tell you, some days is pretty fucking hard to swallow."

"True indeed, my friend. But what you describe is the very essence of faith. I have faith in the inherent decency of my Maker. I only hope my Maker has the same faith in me."

"I'm not your friend, Thomed, I'm your executioner. I've been sent by hell to kill you."

"As I said, Sam, this is a land of contradictions. Here, it is possible that you are both. But I understand your point. You claim my time is nigh, and for your sake I do not wish to belabor the point. As I recall, a certain measure of remove is necessary to retain one's personhood while functioning as hell's emissary. So, please, do what you came to do. I will not stop you. Whatever happens is the Maker's will."

He closed his eyes and raised his face up to the heavens. His expression was one of peace, not fear. I stepped toward him with purpose, and rested my left hand upon his shoulder. "I'm sorry," I told him. "It's nothing personal." And then I plunged my hand into his chest, or tried.

Because that's when Thomed and the temple disappeared.

22.

I found myself in a field of heather. The sun hung bright above, warm against my skin, but not so much so as to make me sweat, and a gentle breeze rustled the trees that dotted the rolling landscape. Wildflowers dusted the distant hilltops with party-bright confetti, sprinkled in among the heather's soft purple, and filled the air with their sweet perfume. And there was not a soul, nor sign of human habitation, in sight.

I spun around in confusion, a spindle at the center of this swirling, idyllic landscape. Where was I? What was I doing here? What in hell had happened to the temple? To Thomed?

"So many questions," came a voice from behind me, inhumanly low and rumbling, "and for each an answer, if only you care to listen." I nearly jumped out of my shoes. Instead, I turned to face the source of the voice.

What I found in a space I knew for sure was empty just moments before were two beings. One was a hulking beast some fifteen feet tall, with an eagle's head and wings to match, and eyes of flames. Thick-muscled arms, each as large as my own meat-suit and velveted with close-cropped silver gray – fur or feathers, I knew not which – terminated in taloned hands. Haunches as big and powerful as a plow-steed's stretched from broad torso, feathered black. Its feet were lost to me beneath a sea of undulating heather. Its skin seemed to crackle with electricity, blue-white arcs rippling across its surface and charging the air around us with the ozone scent of a felled power line or recent lightning strike. And as I looked upon it, its face changed, shifting as if in response to my gaze. Now a lion. Now an ox. Now an eagle once more.

The other figure was a child. What kind of child, I had no idea. It seemed at once a boy and a girl; blond-haired, and brown-, and black-; fair-complexioned and dark as fertile soil; a child of four, of eight, of ten, dressed in robes, in jeans and ringer-T, in country tweeds. But unlike the massive beast, whose visage shifted, the child's appearance didn't seem to. Instead, it suggested the impression of a thousand children, a million, an entire human history of them, all beautiful, all smiling eerily with unnerving, unnatural knowing, and all occupying the same space.

"My name is Legion, for we are many," I muttered.

The enormous bird-beast laughed – a bass-filled chuffing that shook the trees and set my meat-suit cowering. "Is *that* what you think of me?" it asked.

"I was talking about your friend," I said.

"My friend," it said, "is who you're speaking to. This creature is but a trusted servant, which lends its voice to one whose voice you cannot hear."

"So you're mute, then, is that it?"

"Not mute," said the creature. "Merely beyond your capacity to hear."

"Like a dog-whistle," I snarked. Blame the nerves.

"If that helps you," said the beast, now lion-faced once more, the child smirking mischievously beside it. "A dog-whistle that could liquefy your insides."

"So he's what, your spokesman?"

The child nodded. "Though perhaps a better term is *conduit,*" said the beast, its now-ox-mouth awkward around the words, "or, best yet, *attenuator*."

"Not much of a looker," I said. "But on the other hand, he has a lovely singing voice."

"Your use of humor in the face of fear is peculiar. Reverence is by far the commoner response."

"Yeah, well, I guess that means I'm no commoner," I said, "and anyway, it seems to me there's two likely options as to who you are. One of 'em's in charge of hell, and the other's responsible for the platypus. The former deserves no reverence from me, and the latter's *gotta* have a sense of humor. Now, you wanna tell me what I'm doing here?"

"A better question would be what it was you were doing in Cambodia."

"My fucking *job,* that's what."

"Were you, now?"

"You're damned right I was."

"But why?"

"I go where they point me. That's the gig. That's my forever. You don't know that, then what the hell are we all doing here?"

"Ah. I see. So you were simply following orders, then."

"That's right."

"It amazes me that your kind was given the greatest gift in all of Creation – free will – and yet you're all so willing to forsake it at the slightest provocation."

"The slightest provocation?" I repeated. "Is that what you call being damned to hell for all eternity? Because it ain't been exactly a basket fulla kittens."

"No, I suppose it wouldn't have been. Still, Samuel, I'm surprised that you, in particular, would succumb to such weakness of character. I would have thought that with all you've experienced, particularly given the target of your maiden collection, you'd be reluctant to rely upon that old chestnut. Many a war criminal has pled the same, to no satisfactory result."

"That's not a fair comparison," I said.

"Isn't it?"

"My orders don't leave a lot of wiggle room."

"Don't they? What of New York? Of young Katherine MacNeil?"

"The order to collect her was based on false pretenses. She was an innocent. Neither can be said of the order to kill the Brethren."

"Really? What of Thomed, then?"

"Whatever peace he's come to now, it can't change who he is or what he's done. And let's not forget, the body he's been fused to since he and his buddies' little ritual had to belong to someone."

"Are you certain about that?" the creature asked.

"As certain as I am of anything," I replied.

"On that, at least," it said, "we do not disagree."

The child-thing raised its hands, first finger of each raised, and made a rotating motion with the two of them as if setting an invisible plate spinning. The world seemed to twist beneath my feet, and my vision swam. I took a knee and closed my eyes, my equilibrium lost, my stomach threatening mutiny. When the world steadied, I opened my eyes once more, and found that day had turned to night and that the child, its mouthpiece, and I were not alone.

A bonfire was burning some twenty yards away from where we stood, pushing back the dark. Its flames reached high into the sky, struggling against a cold wind to lash at the crescent moon. Beside – but not around it – stood a group of people huddled in twos and threes. I counted nine – no, ten – all but one of them in simple cloth, undyed and rough, robes and tunics and the like. Some affixed with bits of rope, some wrapped such that they affixed themselves. Feet bare, or sandaled. The lot of them looked as though they'd stepped straight out of the history books.

And not one of them noticed our presence.

"They cannot see us," rumbled the child's pet beast, the child once more unnerving me by responding to my unsaid thoughts, "because we are not here." The child gestured like a maître d' showing me to my table, and I took his hint, wandering puzzled into the strange gathering.

Beneath my feet, I noticed the heather had been burned back – scorched black plant matter forming a circle maybe twenty feet around. Inside the circle was drawn a pentagram so large its five points touched the outer edge of the burn zone, white ash against the black. Though I shuffled, puzzled, through it, my feet did not disturb the delicate ash line. As I reached the interior of the pentagram to find another, smaller one rendered inverted inside it, realization dawned. I'd seen something like this once before, during Ana's failed attempt to recreate the Brethren's freeing ritual.

A ritual that I was about to witness.

I scanned the faces in the crowd, all frightened, expectant, their worry-lines etched deep by the long shadows of the firelight. A blond-haired boy of twenty hugging tight a fresh-faced girl with chestnut hair and a smattering of freckles across her nose, cooing, reassuring. Drustanus and Yseult, I guessed. A brash, muscular young olive-skinned man pacing back and forth on thick, powerful legs as fast and smooth as a shark through water, his face a brittle mask of arrogance. Ricou, I suspected. A pack of three conversing in nervous whispers, one an Indian boy of not more than fourteen, the other two wild Roman-era Scots, or Vikings maybe – a male unkempt and hirsute; a female small and quick, her hair a simple plait. Jain and Lukas and Apollonia. A broad-faced Asian man in monk's robes sitting cross-legged in meditation was the furthest from the firelight, young Thomed's knitted brow indicating his thoughts were far from peaceful. And at the center of the double-pentagram, over a small stone altar, stood two men: one young, handsome, dark-haired, dark-eyed, at ease; the other older, bird-thin, sharp-angled, and feverishly intense, hands worrying at a small jute bundle in his hands. Grigori and Simon, respectively.

I reminded myself that these physical forms were meat-suits, nothing more. That the entities inside were older, harder, crueler than they appeared. But still, I could not shake the notion that they were but children, goading one another to go and ring the doorbell of the creepy house at the end of the street.

Forgive them, Father, for they know not what they do.

Then the tenth of them stepped into the light, draped despite the chill in a slip dress of parchment-colored silk, and carrying in her delicate hands an ornate, glinting gold skim blade. My borrowed heart damn near stopped. My breath caught in my chest.

The tenth was Lilith.

"Did you bring it?" she asked the older of the two standing at the center of the circle: the one I knew as Simon Magnusson – although her word-sounds did not synch up with the movements of her mouth. But when I thought upon that fact, I realized it was not exactly true. What I'd *heard* had matched her lips' movement just fine, but what I *understood* her to say did not. It seemed my child-companion had done me the courtesy of translating.

"I did," said Simon, his word-sounds and meanings also decoupled in my mind. He unwrapped the tiny bundle in his hands to reveal a small, dark orb, projecting rays of black across the field that seemed to dim the fire, and proved darker still than night itself: a corrupted human soul.

"Good," she said, and then glanced up at the sky. "The heavens are aligned, which means it's time." She handed the handsome dark-eyed man – Grigori – the skim blade, and then with one open palm caressed his face. He leaned into her touch and smiled, one more in a long line of victims to her otherworldly wiles, I thought. "I trust you understand what must be done?"

"I do," Grigori replied.

"Then do it, and be free."

I watched the rest in numb horror, knowing all too well how it was going to play out. They took their places around the altar, Grigori and Simon at the center, the soul in the very middle, their hands raised up above their heads, both of them clasping the skim blade well above it. As one they chanted, and the firelight extinguished. A bitter wind ripped across the meadow, stinging against my skin.

The blade came down.

The soul was shattered.

A shockwave of pure, unfettered evil rippled outward from the circle's center. The Brethren were each buffeted by it, but stood fast, as if anchored by the ash-lines on which they stood. The world around them was not so lucky. The black shockwave expanded exponentially, gaining speed as it blew past me and disappearing beyond the horizon in all directions. The very earth beneath my feet shuddered violently as if with sudden fright. It left nothing of the landscape standing – leveling trees, withering heather to dead husks, felling small game to burst half-rotten in mere seconds.

I fell to my knees, weeping at the sight. Those inside the circle looked stricken – panicked.

From somewhere distant I heard a roar, like every radio ever built was tuned to static and turned up as far as it would go. A salt wind buffeted my cheeks and tousled my meat-suit's hair. The distant horizon seemed to rise up before me in the starlight, faintly luminescent.

And grew.

And grew taller still.

In the moment before it reached me, I finally realized what I was looking at: a wall of water five hundred feet high, hurtling toward me like God's own vengeance.

As it bore down upon me, I closed my eyes. Placed my hands over my head. And prayed.

The water hit. I felt its impossible weight slam me to the ground, and crush my bones to dust.

Then the world shifted.

The wall of water was gone.

I stood once more in a vast field of heather, the child-thing and its mouthpiece at my side.

23.

"So now, you see," the child-thing's mouthpiece said.

"See what?" I asked, my voice shaky and hoarse with fear. "Why would you *show* me that? What the hell's it got to do with *me*?"

The massive creature sighed. It sounded like two boulders rubbed together. "It is ever a fault of your kind that you each assume yourselves to be the hero of your own tale. Perhaps it is my fault, for creating you with so narrow a point of view. Thanks to your limited perspective, you see yourself in every scene, and therefore conclude that you're the star. I showed you this because you need to understand you've been nothing but a pawn for all this time, a pet Collector for Lilith to do with as she saw fit."

"Meaning what?"

"Meaning the hierarchy of the Depths did not order you to move against the Brethren. They were protected by the Great Truce, and despite recent skirmishes, remain protected by it still. Given that fact, hell alone cannot order their termination; such an order must be unanimously decided by all parties. Charon, for his part, might have assented, for he's long seen the Nine as an affront to his authority. Lucifer would only act against the Brethren if it proved in some way expedient to him, and he assures me at this fragile time, he considers any violation of the Truce to be quite the opposite. And *I* certainly did not consent. Which means your orders to eliminate them came from Lilith and Lilith alone."

"That's not true. It can't be."

"I'm afraid it is."

"But what of the demonic raid on Grigori's place on the Riviera? On Drustanus and Yseult?"

"They were conducted by Lilith's partisans. She has a great deal of support among the foot-soldiers of hell, as one might imagine of a woman of her wiles. It seems she's no shortage of blunt instruments to manipulate." That last was pointed, and aimed at me.

"That's not fair," I said.

"Isn't it? You can't deny you've acted recklessly of late. That your heart has hardened."

"I can't be blamed for that. After all I've been through. After all I've lost."

"I won't deny your path has been one of great suffering, that you've taken your fair share of wounds along the way. But wounds are a funny thing. If ill-tended, they scar over, grow numb, deaden he who carries them to the sensations of the world around him. Collect enough of them, and so too shall you be. But if treated properly, they reveal new skin beneath. Sensitive, certainly, painfully so, but more capable of feeling than what came before."

"You're saying I've let go of too much of me. That I've become something less than what I was."

"I'm saying the healing process is both long and painful, but ultimately it's up to you how well it goes – and how you deal with the challenges it poses along the way. Even flesh twisted by consuming fire can be taught to feel again with time."

"Save the fortune-cookie bullshit for someone who might give a damn," I said.

The creature and boy both shook their heads in time. "I think you care more than you dare let on."

"So okay, I've been played – or allowed myself to be. Why? What's Lilith's angle?"

The child shrugged. Its monster said, "Perhaps upon discovering your ability to end the Brethren, she saw the chaos created by the recent unrest as her opportunity to clean up a mess made long ago, one that very nearly came back to haunt her when Ana Jovic and Daniel Young attempted to recreate the ceremony she herself devised. She, unlike the Brethren, is not protected by the Great Truce, and therefore can still be punished for her actions should they come to light. Or perhaps her reasons are somewhat more obscure. Whatever they are, they're known to her and her alone. But if you're curious, you could ask her when you catch up with her."

"It's usually Lilith who catches up with *me*," I said. "She's not really one to come when called. She prefers to make an entrance – usually of the appearing-when-I-least-expect-it variety. Come to think of it, you and her should hold a contest."

"I fear her days of wielding such power are behind her," he said.

"Meaning what?"

"Meaning I've taken the liberty of stripping Lilith of her powers. She is human once more. And Lilith's fate is in your hands: for as ye sow, so shall ye reap."

"You're telling me I have to collect her."

"I'm telling you it falls to you to do what must be done."

"There has to be another way," I said.

"There always is, but I beseech you not to seek it, for it will not end well for you."

"What if I just refuse?"

"Then someone else will be chosen for the task. But I suspect you might prove more humane. It is up to you. Only you can decide what's right."

"I wouldn't even know where to find her," I said.

"On that count, I can provide some measure of guidance, for you see, your journey with Lilith is a closed loop. It will end where it began."

"You mean–"

But I never bothered to finish my question. The child-thing and its mouthpiece-beast were gone.

24.

Berlin had changed so much since I'd first laid eyes on it in the last flagging days of the Third Reich. Then, it seemed an apocalyptic wasteland, ground zero for the worst evil the modern world had ever known. The decent people who'd lived there did so in quiet and in fear, scarcely glimpsed because they were as afraid of their own fascist regime as they were of the Allies intent on leveling the once-great city they called home. Now, the city was great once more. A bustling modern metropolis – vibrant, colorful, and lively. A shining example of what humankind can accomplish, a center of art and commerce, of science, of community.

It seemed the child and his grotesque conduit were right about one thing – given time and tending, even the deepest of wounds can heal.

It was amazing to me the building in which I first awoke as a Collector was still standing. It had been redone tackily sometime in the decades hence – a sad, Sixties-modern façade slapped up over the original brick face – but it seemed Berliners found the new façade as much of an affront as I, because it was halfway through the process of being removed. Scaffolding climbed up one side of the building, and on the rooftop sat an idle crane; yellow construction refuse tubes led from upper windows to dumpsters below. For a moment, I wondered where the workers were – it was scarcely twilight, after all – but then I realized it was Saturday, the city awash with the spark of possibility that only ever seemed to fully ignite come weekend.

I wore the body of a young man who'd expired ten hours prior, the result of a congenital heart defect. Dropped over on the soccer pitch, bleeding out inside but not yet dead. Docs patched him up enough for my purposes, and filled him with fresh blood besides, but couldn't spark his heart back into rhythm. Made the online version of Berliner *Morgenpost*, which the web-browser in the Edinburgh internet café I used to access it translated well enough for me to glean the salient points.

I hadn't taken many dead vessels of late. I'd told myself they weren't worth the bother. Sacrificed my ideals for expediency, and told myself that I deserved the break for all I'd done. Saved the world twice over by my count. Started thinking of myself as a caps-implied "Good Person". Problem with that is, Good Person is a moving target. And this past year, I found that target moving on without me. Maybe my run-in with the creepy child-thing had gotten to me. Maybe it was the sting of Lilith's betrayal. Whatever it was, I realized I couldn't just keep on keeping on – that the path on which I'd stood led nowhere worth going.

The construction site around the building was paddocked with chain link six feet high – new and shiny, just like the city itself, untarnished by the corruption of the ages. The gate was fitted with a keyhole lock. Easier, even, to pick than a padlock, but hardly worth it when I could duck into the quiet, empty alley, and be up and over the fence in seconds.

Which is what I did.

The front door was unlocked. Too many subcontractors coming and going to bother, I suppose. Once inside, I considered searching the place from the bottom up, but something tugged at my gut like swallowed fishing line, pulling me inexorably upstairs.

"It will end where it began," the child-thing had told me.

I found the stairwell by memory, felt the eerie sensation of decades dropping away. The stairs had been restored to their prewar state, though construction-dusty and unlit as they were, they reminded me of my first visit here, bomb-shaken and powerless. Not sure if those last adjectives were intended to describe the building then, or me, or both.

There were no apartments left intact upstairs. They'd been gutted. All that was left of them was framed-out walls run through with ductwork and electrical wiring, black against the twilight blue that spilled in from the windows on all sides. I strolled through them like a ghost in my own life, passing through the walls and years both, and not stopping until I stood atop the dusty floorboards facing a familiar window, glass broken in my mind, but here so new its gleaming white frame and double panes were still affixed with stickers emblazoned with the manufacturer's logo.

Bare footprints, woman-petite, disturbed the pale dust at my feet.

I followed them with my gaze. They led toward a large jetted tub.

Delicate fingers looped around the edges of the tub – their owner crouched and still, hiding, hoping I couldn't see.

"Lilith," I said.

Her reply was shaky, frightened. "Sam?"

She rose, then, her jerky unsure movements a far cry from her trademark otherworldly grace. She was naked. Cold. Shivering. Her eyes wide, furtive, and dark-rimmed.

When she saw the grim expression on my face, she frowned.

"So this is how it's to be, then. I'm made human once more so that I can have the privilege of being killed, collected by my very own."

"You set me up, Lilith. You used me."

She smiled, but there was no humor in it, only sadness. "All those years ago, back on the beach, did I not tell you that I would? It's what I do. It's who I am. So let's not overly prolong this little reunion, shall we? Just do what you came to do and get it over with."

"I think I deserve some answers first."

"You do, do you?"

"I do."

"And what makes you think I have any to give?"

"I need to know why. Why after all these years – after all that we've been through – you still think so little of me. First using me to wage your little war on God so you could pay him back for damning you, expecting me to collect Kate MacNeil and jumpstart the apocalypse. Now using me as your fall-guy to clean up all evidence of what you did in helping the Brethren escape the bonds of hell and bringing forth the Great Flood."

Her face looked pained. "That's what you think you were in this? A scapegoat? A patsy?"

"What *else* am I supposed to think?"

"It doesn't matter," she said. "What's done is done."

"It matters to *me*," I said. "The *why* is every bit as important as the *what*."

"Look around, Sam. Did *you* take the fall for what I did? No, you didn't, *I* did. I wasn't setting you up, I was *insulating* you. Protecting you from the retribution I was certain was to come. I won't deny helping the Nine was the greatest mistake in my long and storied existence, but I didn't task you with killing them in order to erase the evidence. In fact, I knew killing them would likely bring said evidence to light."

"Then why?"

"Because for the longest time, I thought that they could not be killed. Because your encounter with Simon taught me otherwise. And because a very long time ago, I made a promise to a friend."

I laughed, a shrill, humorless bark that echoed through the skeletal dark. "I thought you didn't *have* any friends."

"I don't. Not anymore. Do you know why I've held you at arm's length all these years? Why I went out of my way to convince myself that you meant nothing to me?"

"I always assumed it was out of the unkindness of your heart."

Lilith lowered her head. "I deserve that. But you should know, as Collectors go, you weren't my first."

"Yeah, you might've mentioned it a time or two," I said, bitterly. "I've heard no shortage of bitching through the years about the burden and the insult that was you being saddled with the likes of me. I'm sure I'm just the latest in a string of hundreds."

"No," she said softly, "you were my tenth."

It took a moment for her words to sink in. "You mean…"

"…that the Nine were all assigned to me? I do. And what I did, I did only to save them. Nothing like it had ever been attempted before. I swear, I had no idea that the Flood would come. Or that they'd become such monsters. If I had, I never would have gone through with it. You want to know why I wanted so badly to punish your precious God? It wasn't for damning me. It was because he allowed my greatest act of kindness – the best, most selfless thing I'd ever done – to result in the greatest genocide this world has ever known. And once the floodwaters receded, all I was left with for my trouble were the corrupted shadows of my former wards, my only friends. They were decent people once. Flawed, yes, but brave and kind as well, not unlike you. Did you know they each of them selected deceased vessels for the ritual? Not *one* of them was willing to displace a human soul in return for their own freedom. And they waited a century for the proper celestial alignment to perform the ritual. Not because that's how long it took to come around, but because it was the first time the alignment occurred in a place uninhabited by the living. We knew, you see, the force of the soul's destruction – a savage warlord whose forces had raped and slaughtered hundreds, by the way – would shake the very ground around us, but we had no idea just how severe the effect of releasing such heinous evil would be. To the world, and to those within the ritual circle. It hardened them. Tainted them. Made them into something darker than they were. But then, I shouldn't need to tell you that, your own experience in Los Angeles was but a hint of what they experienced, Daniel's soul being far less tainted than the one they used, and look at the effect it's had on *you*."

"I'm sorry," I said, and meant it. "But that doesn't change what has to happen next."

She stepped toward me then. Out of the tub and across the narrow expanse of floor, her scuffing heels leaving streaks in the ghost-white dust. Her strange, mystical guile was no more. The woman before me was awkward, coltish, fragile, determined.

A strange thought struck me then. In all the time I'd known her, she'd never looked more beautiful.

"I know that," she said. "And I don't blame you. In fact, I welcome it. It's time I paid for all I've done. I just wanted you to understand." She stood on tiptoes, and kissed me on the cheek. Then took my hand, and placed it against her bare chest. I felt the warmth of her skin, the rapid beating of her heart. "Goodbye, Sam Thornton. Be well."

"Goodbye," I told her. And then I reached my hand inside her chest, and wrapped tight her soul.

It was like nothing I'd ever experienced before. Her soul was at once ancient, and brand new. Wisp thin and blown-glass fragile in my hand. No gray-black swirling, nor blinding white, it was instead all the colors of the rainbow, and none at all. The most vibrant, beautiful light I'd ever seen. And her entire life, spread out before me. Her coming to in Paradise, all full of hope and possibility. Her subsequent fall – she so confused at what she'd done. The Brethren a beacon of redemption in her mind. The pain of finding out how wrong on that count she truly was.

And amidst it all, the briefest moment of hope and joy – of love – a blinding bright pinprick of happiness before a long descent into bitterness and despair: Lilith, standing in a field of heather, the heat of a nearby bonfire on her cheek. A young, intense, dark-eyed man, his arms around her, their foreheads touching. Grigori, I realized.

"It's almost time," she said, in a language I did not speak, but through her ears, her mind, her experience I understood. "Soon, you'll all be free."

"But not you, my love." He held her tight. Kissed her. Kissed me. Tender, sweet. "I can scarcely bear the thought of leaving you to this existence."

"Knowing you're free is enough for me," she said – I said – caressing his stubbled cheek. "Knowing you're free will give me the strength to endure anything that hell dare inflict upon me."

"Promise me something," he said.

"Anything."

"If this goes wrong–"

"It won't."

"If this goes wrong," he repeated, "and we emerge as… something less… then you owe it to us all to end us."

"That won't happen," she said. "I know the mages warned against it, but we've taken every precaution."

"Every precaution but one: your promise to kill us should it come to that."

"But I couldn't."

"You *must*. We've all decided. We beg it of you. None of us wish to end up monsters, to be as enslaved by our own darkest impulses as we now are to our demonic masters. Without your promise, there will be no ritual – not tonight. Not ever."

She smiled then, tears rolling down her cheeks. "Then I promise."

Grigori's face crinkled into a smile as well, and he kissed Lilith once more. "Thank you, my love." Then he looked to the sky and said, "It's time."

Then the ritual. Then the flood. And untold anguish at what she'd done.

I released Lilith's soul, gasping. We were huddled together on our knees in the half-built flat. Outside, twilight had given way to starry black. I wrapped my arms around her shivering, naked form, and we sat like that a while; shattered, sobbing, too broken to do anything else.

As we held each other in the darkness, the child-thing's mouthpiece rang in my ears.

"The healing process is both long and painful", it'd said, "but ultimately it's up to you how well it goes – and how you deal with the challenges it poses along the way. Even flesh twisted by consuming fire can be taught to feel again with time."

and

"Lilith's fate is in your hands: for as ye sow, so shall ye reap."

and

"It falls to you to do what must be done."

"There has to be another way," I'd pleaded then. To which he told me:

"There always is... Only you can decide what's right."

So, weeping in the darkness, that's exactly what I did, I decided what was right, and did what must be done.

I took off my coat and button-down, stolen from the morgue from which this meat-suit came, and wrapped first the latter and then the former around Lilith's shoulders. She eyed me a moment in confusion, and then buttoned the shirt with clumsy fingers.

Her shivering abated.

That done, I kissed her on the forehead, my eyes still wet with tears, or perhaps wetted anew.

Then I rose without a word and left her in the darkened building.

Broken.

Human.

Free.

25.

It's not often one has occasion to meet the Devil.

Mine came some hours after I'd left Lilith at the apartment, as I stood upon the well-trodden apartment courtyard, grass patchy and shiny from bikes and balls and countless feet, that sat above the spot Hitler's Führerbunker once occupied.

I'd been there a while. Pondering right and wrong, punishment and absolution, trying to get my head right regarding all I'd seen and done.

The voice of the child-God's conduit had guided me back at the flat, I thought – guided me in a direction I'd not considered until that moment, though in retrospect seemed the only thing I ever could have done. I suppose as an implement of judgment, I was well chosen, if double-edged, for if I could forgive Lilith her trespasses against me, it was a reflection on us both. Now, though, as I stood upon this once unhallowed ground that had somehow given way to normalcy, it was Thomed's voice that rang in my ears.

"If our souls are, in fact, immortal, why would our Maker confine Her judgment to the first twenty or fifty or one hundred years of life? Why would a loving parent punish their child for any longer than it took for that child to learn their lesson? My conclusion, long coming, is that She would not. That absolution lies not beyond our reach, no matter how far gone we seem – at least, so long as we stretch forever toward it."

"That presumes our Maker is a loving parent," came a voice from behind me, echoing the very words that I'd used when I replied to Thomed.

I turned to find beside me a handsome, blond-haired man of maybe seventeen, with sharp-angled, almost pretty features, blue eyes, and smile-bared teeth of gleaming white. He wore an age-creased leather jacket open over a vintage Judas Priest T-shirt, and a pair of whiskered blue jeans. Well-worn black Chuck Taylors graced his feet.

"How did you –" I began to ask, but he waved me off with a laugh.

"Your mind – and, hell, your very soul – are an open book to me, Sam Thornton. I own the latter, after all. Although at the moment, you're wondering if perhaps I'm only leasing it. After all, if Lilith can get a reprieve, then why not *you*?"

I didn't argue the point. I couldn't. He was right; I was.

"The question you need to ask yourself is, a reprieve from *what*? A wise man who lived and died not far from here once said the only thing that burns in hell is the part of you that won't let go of your life – your memories, your attachments. That by burning them away, hell is not punishing you, it's freeing your soul. So perhaps, Sam, all you need to do for your reprieve is to let go."

"That's a nice speech," I told him, "but I think I'll take my chances with the high road."

"You *could*," he said lightly. "You surely could. But think on this: Lilith was the first woman in all Creation, the first of your precious Maker's pets to fall from grace. If it took Him this long to get around to redeeming her, how long do you figure it'll be before you get your turn?"

"I'm okay with waiting," I replied.

"Really?" he asked, smiling brightly. "I've never thought of patience as one of your strongest suits. Nor do I consider it a virtue. If you ask me, patience is a sign of weakness, an unwillingness to pursue that which you desire."

"Maybe," I said, "or maybe that which I desire is best obtained by not pursuing it."

The boy rolled his eyes. "Fuck – five minutes with that damn-fool monk Thomed, and already you're spouting nonsense Zen koans. You know he's crazier than a shithouse rat, don't you?" I opened my mouth to object, but he placated me with raised palms. "Okay, okay, say for the sake of argument you're right. That your Maker has a plan for you after all. Maybe what you should ask yourself is why should you assume His plan is worth a damn?"

"Come again?"

"Think about it. If all you've experienced to this point has been your Maker's preposterous Rube Goldberg plan to redeem His very first lost soul, doesn't that make you nothing more than a patsy? A bit player? A hapless pawn in a rigged game that placed heaven and hell at odds with one another and resulted in no shortage of suffering for you and those you love? If your Maker has a plan, then every awful aspect of your life was ordained before you were even born, dictated by the petty whims of a power-mad deity bent on forever pushing the limits of his poor, pathetic subjects just to see what makes them break – like some fucking hard-hearted toddler standing above an anthill with a magnifying glass. If your Maker has a plan, then it was His plan, and not simply those strikebreakers, who shattered your knee and rendered you unemployable. It was His plan, not random chance, that caused your beloved Elizabeth to contract tuberculosis. It was His plan that you take Dumas's deal and give your soul over to the likes of me. His plan that drove your wife from you, and resulted in her granddaughter and her family getting slaughtered at the hands of a rogue angel. Hell, that resulted in the Flood that so pissed off Lilith in the first place. And if your Maker truly *is* both omniscient and omnipotent, how do you square the horrors that brought you to this very patch of ground so many years ago? Why would a loving God allow Hitler to live at all? Allow millions to suffer and die at his hands?"

"Seems to me free will's to blame for most of the horrors in this world. Free will, and maybe you."

"Sam, that hurts, particularly because you show such promise, such verve. I don't deign to visit *all* my charges, you know – just the ones in whose future I see great things. I'd hate to see you squander such potential sitting around, waiting for the phone to ring. Perhaps your Maker will finally get around to redeeming you a million years from now; perhaps not. But what I offer you is concrete. It's here-and-now. And it's there for you whenever you decide."

"What exactly are you offering me?"

"I'm offering you a seat at the table. A chance to make a difference – to serve as trusted council for yours truly, and as a guide to those like you who've suffered the misfortune of somehow offending their mercurial Maker. Perhaps under your tutelage, they need not find their path so rocky."

"And if I say no – what then?"

The boy smiled. "You mean how will you be punished? You misunderstand my offer, Sam. If you say no, I'll simply ask again. And again. And again. A million years is a long time to keep on asking, and affords countless chances for you to tell me yes."

Just then, a woman's voice called from a balcony above. *"Sven? Sven, wo bist du?"*

The boy's smile faded, replaced by sudden confusion. He shook his head in puzzlement, and muttered something that sounded like a sneeze, which I assumed was German for "excuse me". Then he turned and trotted across the square toward the building from which he called, the boy a boy once more, the Devil inside him gone.

I was alone.

Acknowledgments

You'll note that as this series goes on, these acknowledgments ain't getting any shorter. If you people don't cut it out with all your love and support, I'm gonna end up way too cheery to write these things. So if book four finds Sam eating his way through Tuscany and relearning how to love, remember: it's on you.

Thanks to Marc Gascoigne, Lee Harris, and the whole Angry Robot crew for making my Collector novels the best versions of themselves. Thanks as well to Martin Stiff and Amazing15 Design for turning Marc's brilliant cover concept into the best pulp covers in the business.

The following folks are but a few who've lent me a hand along the way: John Anealio, Josh Atkins, Jedidiah Ayres, Patrick Shawn Bagley, Frank Bill, Nigel Bird, Stephen Blackmoore, Jerry Bloomfield, Judy Bobalik, Paul D. Brazill, Drew Broussard, R. Thomas Brown, Kristin Centorcelli, Joelle Charbonneau, Sean Chercover, Adam Christopher, David Cranmer, the Cressey clan, my fellow *Criminal Minds* bloggers, Sean Cummings, Laura K. Curtis, Paul and Sarah Damaske, Hilary Davidson, Vanessa Delamare, Neliza Drew, Jacques Filippi, Sarah Fischer, Renee Fountain, Cullen Gallagher, Victor Gischler (who, it should be noted, supplied the name for Admiral Fuzzybutt),

Kent Gowran, Guy Haley, Rob W. Hart, Janet Hutchings, Julie Hyzy, Abhinav Jain, Sally Janin, Jon and Ruth Jordan, John Kenyon, Larry Killian, Owen Laukkanen, Jennifer Lawrence, Benoit Lelievre, Ben LeRoy, Sophie Littlefield, Jeremy Lynch, Jennifer MacRostie, Sarajean Malpica, Dan and Kate Malmon, Erin Mitchell, Scott Montgomery, Micah Morris, Joe Myers, Stuart Neville, Lauren O'Brien, Sabrina Ogden, Dan O'Shea, Miranda Parker, Brad Parks, Todd Robinson, Linda Rodriguez, Ian Rogers, Melanie Sanderson, Ryan Sayles, Brandon Sears, Kieran Shea, Julia Spencer-Fleming (and her husband Ross), Josh Stallings, David Swinson, Brian Vander Ark, Meineke van der Salm, Steve Weddle, Chuck Wendig, Elizabeth A. White, and Shaun Young.

I'd be remiss if I didn't thank my family – Holm, Burns, and Niidas – for their unflagging enthusiasm and support; anyone within earshot of them knows they peddle my books with impunity.

And last, but never least, my deepest gratitude to my wife Katrina. These books simply would not exist without her. Nor, in any version I'd recognize, would I.

About the Author

Chris F. Holm was born in Syracuse, New York, the grandson of a cop with a penchant for crime fiction. He wrote his first story at the age of six. It got him sent to the principal's office. Since then, his work has fared better, appearing in such publications as *Ellery Queen's Mystery Magazine, Alfred Hitchcock's Mystery Magazine, Needle Magazine, Beat to a Pulp*, and *Thuglit*.

He's been a Derringer Award finalist and a Spinetingler Award winner, and he's also written a novel or two. He lives on the coast of Maine with his lovely wife and a noisy, noisy cat.

chrisfholm.com

ANGRY
ROBOT

THE FIRST MACHINE DYNASTY
VN
Madeline
Ashby

THE SECOND MACHINE DYNASTY
iD
Madeline
Ashby

WINTER SONG
COLIN HARVEY

DAMAGE TIME
COLIN HARVEY

ADAM CHRISTOPHER
SEVEN
WONDERS

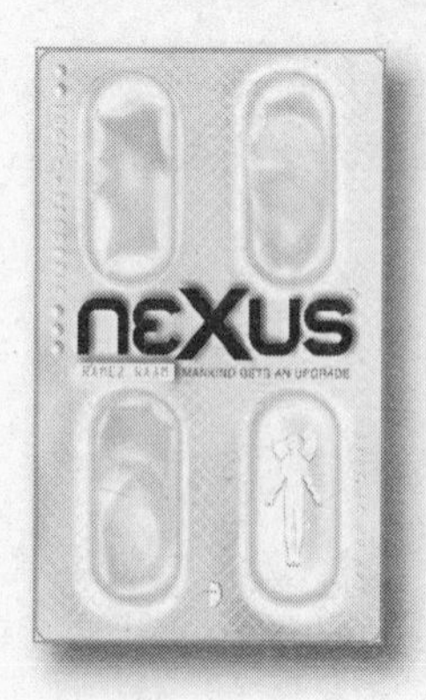
nexus
RAMEZ NAAM
MANKIND GETS AN UPGRADE

GUY HALEY REALITY 36
A RICHARDS & KLEIN INVESTIGATION

GUY HALEY OMEGA POINT
A RICHARDS & KLEIN INVESTIGATION

The complete *Courts of the Feyre* saga.
Urban Fantasy at its best.